DARK SOULS
MASQUE OF VINDICATION

MICHAEL A. STACKPOLE

Illustration: Jun Suemi

DARK SOULS: MASQUE OF VINDICATION
Copyright© 2022 by Michael A. Stackpole
© 2022 KADOKAWA CORPORATION
Dark Souls™& ©Bandai Namco Entertainment Inc. / ©FromSoftware, Inc.
First published in Japan in 2022 by KADOKAWA CORPORATION, Tokyo.
This edition published by arrangement with the author c/o Howard Mohaim Literary Agency Inc., Brooklyn, through Tuttle-Mori Agency, Inc., Tokyo.

© 2022 by Yen Press, LLC

Yen On
150 West 30th Street, 19th Floor
New York, NY 10001

Visit us at yenpress.com
facebook.com/yenpress
twitter.com/yenpress
yenpress.tumblr.com
instagram.com/yenpress

First Yen On Edition: October 2022
Edited by Yen On Editorial: Jordan Blanco
Designed by Yen Press Design: Wendy Chan

Yen On is an imprint of Yen Press, LLC.
The Yen On name and logo are trademarks of Yen Press, LLC.

Library of Congress Cataloging-in-Publication Data
Names: Stackpole, Michael A., 1957- author.
Title: Dark souls : masque of vindication / Michael Austin Stackpole.
Description: First Yen On edition. | New York : Yen On, 2022.
Identifiers: LCCN 2022030867 | ISBN 9781975360887 (hardcover)
Subjects: LCGFT: Fantasy fiction.
Classification: LCC PS3569.T137 D37 2022 | DDC 813/.54—dc23/eng/20220718
LC record available at https://lccn.loc.gov/2022030867

ISBNs: 978-1-9753-6088-7 (hardcover)
978-1-9753-6089-4 (ebook)

1 2022

LSC-C

Printed in the United States of America

DARK SOU

MASQUE OF VINDICATIO

MICHAEL A.
STACKPOLE

NEW YORK

*To Chantelle Aimeé Osman, who saw me through
the pandemic and lockdown with impeccable style and grace*

DARK SOULS
MASQUE of VINDICATION

CHAPTER 1

I felt again. For the first time in perhaps a long time, I *felt*. I felt because I *chose* to feel. Indifference to feeling, apathy about everything, is the soul of being dead. And not because of an incapacity to feel, but simply because of the lack of necessity.

Death, as a life state, encompasses all. You are, simply by not being in any way. Nonexistence defines you, and for countless people, this lack of existence is an improvement over what they have known before. Those who have wallowed in pain and sorrow, regret and mortification, betrayal and cold disregard—for them, the cessation of being is the cessation of all that was negative. Their eternal reward is the escape from the perdition of life.

To feel again is to risk. It might seem ridiculous that the dead have anything to risk, but we do. We have our pride. We hope we are remembered. We can revel in the anger of those who hated us, the nightmares of those who feared us, and even the carefree laughter of those who destroyed us. Those traces, harbored in the memories of the living, are people sinking roots deeply into time itself. They are the means by which we gain immortality.

But the apathy of the grave smothers the fear of risk. Most find apathy a warm blanket for a cold grave. They never venture forth again. Some cower within its folds, shrinking as memories of them shrink. When they are no longer remembered, they surrender to apathy simply because this is the easiest option.

Easy options bore me, for they are also the safe options. They are devoid of risk, and without risk, there is scant chance of reward. To court risk, to assess it properly, to plan around it requires curiosity—which is boredom's hated foe. I remembered being curious before I knew who I was, and now could define myself as curious once again.

I chose to feel. I lifted a finger. It moved. Not strongly, not well, but it moved. My skin felt taut and desiccated. I shifted carefully lest my flesh tear or my sinew snap.

I tested more fingers, straightening them, then letting them curl in toward my palm, as if I were strumming a lute. A simple motion, hesitant at first, but more fluid as I did it a second time.

From there, my wrist and then my elbow. On my right side. My left arm refused to move. But as my right arm came up, then straightened, my hand touched a worn stone surface. Something skittered away as my hand flattened. Grit scraped beneath my palm. Sand, clearly, dusted over the stone.

I pushed against the stone. My shoulder ground, seemingly packed with sand itself. But it held. It worked. I pushed harder, then hardest. For a moment—two or three heartbeats, had my heart been beating—I felt incredibly light, as if I were floating.

Then my back smashed into the stone. My legs tangled, but my left arm came free. It had been trapped beneath me—I had lain on my left side. For how long, I could not hazard a guess.

I chose to feel with my left arm, and those fingers moved, too. Not as well as the right's, mind, but well enough. I extended my arms on both sides. The left plowed into a layer of sand and then brushed over the flat stone upon which I lay.

My right hand collided with a perpendicular bit of stone that rose to at least three feet in height, and likely went higher. My fingers traced cuts in the stone, but whether decorative or the result of vandalism, I could not tell by feel.

Which is when I chose to remember being able to see.

And to hear.

That I had not thought of those senses first did not surprise me, as I'd always found touch to be more immediate—that much I recalled. Indeed, the sensations explored by touch, the intimacy of them, delivered in textures as easily varied as a rainbow of colors or as cacophonous as the symphony of a storm at sea, had always pleased me the most.

I opened my eyes. It took me a moment to remember how to see, but it returned quickly enough. The scant light available reduced everything to soft shadows and moldy glows, but it defined the small room in which I found myself. The light came through a jagged hole punched through the roof, barely large enough to admit a man. Sand drifted down through it in a dry fog, and the wind that drove it hissed. A legion of scorpions that had fallen in or found some other access clung to the walls, curved tails ready to strike.

I sat up, pleased that my spine did not snap. I looked to the stone my right hand had encountered, but the wan starlight could not penetrate the shadows. Still, I understood what it might have said, for the stone itself had been a bier, upon which my mortal remains had lain until a thief shattered the box containing me. Perhaps in frustration, perhaps hoping my body lay atop a hidden treasure, he had cast my body to the crypt's cold floor.

Once my arms worked to satisfaction, I unplaited my legs and returned them to functionality. That accomplished, and defiant of the wind's mocking sibilance, I stood. Slowly, of course, and reliant upon the bier to haul myself up. Hunched, I rested against the stone, my forearms supporting me on the surface where I had once rested.

This allowed me to see the other desiccated corpse half-buried by sand beneath the hole.

"Was it you who disturbed me?"

He chose not to answer. Content to be bored or simply determined not to feel, I could not say. Definitely rude, however. Unless, of course, I had been wrong and this was not my tomb. Had he and I robbed this place and found the former resident reluctant to cooperate?

Unlikely, that. The starlight revealed a tomb as stark in aspect as it was compact. The bier lay opposite what I took to be a doorway, but it had been sealed with a massive stone. Builders had not bothered to plaster the walls. No artisans had been invited to paint murals to glorify my life. I had to accept that my dead companion's confederate might have made away with the entirety of the grave goods interred with me, but I found that doubtful. Still, aside from the sand, scorpions, and shards of the stone box in which I'd lain, the tomb was empty.

I hoped someone had the presence of mind to curse the thieves who'd disturbed my rest.

My sarcophagus, as with my tomb, had nothing about it of interest. Nothing indicated my station in life—excepting its very existence, which marked me as something more than a pauper. The plain nature of its construction suggested no one would have taken note of it, yet the tomb itself and the slab sealing it indicated people had gone to great pains to secure my remains.

I turned my attention to the black basalt slab trapping me in these tight confines. The stone's color provided sharp relief with the lighter stones surrounding it, yet as I scraped a thumbnail across the color divide, I couldn't detect even the hint of a seam. In fitting the wall's stones together, the masons had done an outstanding job, but I could feel the hems between the blocks. Some other agency had sealed the doorway, and my brain would have had to rot to dust for me to think it was by means other than sorcery.

"Whoever you were, you did your work well." My voice had a harsh quality to it, dry and clipped, since my jaw had not loosened.

Though he had chosen to ignore my first question, the dead thief took umbrage with this pronouncement. He stirred, as if a man waking, half-drunk, from beneath a blanket of sand. He rocked side to side, then sat up. He brushed sand from himself, then reached around to his back and plucked free a long poniard, which apparently had last been used to murder him.

He rose to his feet unsteadily, shifting his grip on the knife and raising his fist for an overhand blow. He roared inarticulately, confusion and rage mixing easily. He lunged forward, pushing off his right foot, planting his left.

This was his undoing.

Unaware that the drop through the hole above had fractured his left ankle, likely because it had happened postmortem, he put weight on his left foot. Bones crumbled, and a few popped free. His foot tumbled into loose bones and stringy flesh. His right hand came down, the blade missing me by inches.

Being dead, the thief could not comprehend why he failed, and had no idea what strategies he could use to recover.

Nor did I. Yet from ancient memories, those burned into leathery muscles and dry bones, I acted. My right hand shot out, catching him by the throat. I lunged at him, using my body to bash him against the far wall. As he struggled, I pressed my left hand to the side of his head, tight against his skull, right above the withered blossom of his ear.

A silvery-white light built in my palm, then blasted out. It pierced the thief's skull, pulverizing bone. It reduced the creature's brain to a purple grey paste, then into a geyser that painted the wall as the energy blew out the other side of his head. The corpse's roar sank into a weak mewing, and the body collapsed into the pile of detritus it should have already long been.

In the flicker of an eyelid, I began to tingle. Something of the thief flashed over and through me. I caught a sense of who he had been, of his outrage at being stabbed. I saw through his eyes the stars that watched him die.

The sense of his life faded swiftly, but his recollections kindled something else in me. Before I'd struck, I had no hint that I knew any sorcery at all. What I had taken from him, the essence of his being, kindled memories in me. My sense of who I had been glowed like an ember beneath a gentle gust of breath. My knowledge of sorcery seemed proper and fitting. I had been acknowledged as skilled in that art. Moreover, sorcery felt natural. It was to me as breathing is to the living.

I sank to a knee and swept the sand away from the floor's perimeter, scattering scorpions. There, in a strip three fingers wide, an inscription had been worked by delicate hand, etched into the stone itself. As I traced a necrotic finger over it, I caught a dim sense of recognition, but the meanings remained frightfully opaque. Even though my mind functioned slowly, the intent seemed obvious. This writing had been meant to keep me from ever escaping my crypt.

I dug into the sand beneath the hole, appropriating the thief's knife to speed the process. There, at the base, sigils had been chipped, and the line circumscribing the floor had been broken. The thief, or his confederate, had tossed down something that scored the rock. Thus, they had destroyed the integrity of my prison.

Likely illiterate, they had no clue as to what they had done.

And being grave robbers, they hadn't the scruples to care.

I searched for anything else of use, but the knife proved to be the only treasure buried with me. I laughed at the thought—taken aback less by the croaking quality of my laugh than the strangeness of hearing it again. "You were the poorest thief in the world, my friend, for you left more than you took."

Those who had buried me had taken precautions against my return, and had shown their contempt by burying me in such mean circumstances. Yet it was their lack of generosity that permitted my escape. Had they built the mausoleum with a higher ceiling, I should have remained imprisoned forever.

I clambered onto the stone bier, turned toward the hole, and leaped with arms outstretched. At least, they were outstretched on the third or fourth attempt. On the previous tries, I bashed myself into the wall and slid down on the sand. It took me a few moments to recover, then I leaped again.

And again.

By the fifth time, or the fifty-fifth time—time fades in importance for the dead—I managed to coordinate my arms, legs, and hands such that I flew high enough to catch hold of the hole's edge. I drew myself up, resting halfway out before slithering free and onto the sand. I lay there, facing the night sky. I had gained my freedom, yet remained trapped.

"This is not good."

I recalled the constellations from the thief's last mortal moment, but they did not match the positions of the stars above. Things had shifted by a dozen-dozen degrees, and some stars no longer appeared. Of those things I had known to be planets, the red one had disappeared, and a new and brighter gold one replaced it. I felt a sense of foreboding, and yet found that shifting into curiosity.

The night sky, as alien as it was, proved a tonic against boredom.

I returned to the hole and noticed two things. The wind had cleared the sand from the structure, revealing it, and just as quickly would bury it again. But there, where the thieves had shattered and removed red tiles, they'd also obliterated writing similar to that which had been traced on the floor below. So my captors had not been wholly foolish, which salved my ego, since I'd believed they'd thought so little of me to take proper precautions.

Caught beneath a tile, trapped beneath a layer of tar, lay a leaf. Apparently, I knew more of astronomy and astrology than I did botany, for I could glean little more from it than that it was, in fact, a leaf. I had seen such leaves before and had a sense of lush tropical surroundings.

Yet now I found myself at the heart of a dune sea.

The world is no longer that which I knew.

I came around and down the dune to the front of the mausoleum. The wind had excavated the upper-left corner of the black slab. I set myself to removing more of the sand, wishing the wind would hasten my work. It did not, nor did it oppose me, but simply swirled and scolded as I worked.

A third of the way down, I stopped. The tops of letters emerged, big letters, yet without chisel marks. They'd been formed as the slab had been, *when* the slab had been. Sorcerers wielding fearsome magicks had melted stone into a black slurry that masons shoveled and smoothed to seal the tomb. Then the sorcerers, the chief among them to be certain, used yet more of the arcane arts to write upon that slab.

I stared at the occulted word. I searched for fear but merely found uncertainty. Had they laid a trap for me, believing that if I escaped, my vanity would make me look at their handiwork? Would revealing it draw me back inside and repair all damage, snaring me until this place became a jungle again or more planets died?

I smiled carefully, not wishing to tear lips or cheek. No, those who had trapped me here had been drunk with their conquest. They demonstrated no respect in creating the tomb, for had I been making it, the inscriptions designed to hold me would have been writ large and gilded. I would desire the tomb's resident to know who had trapped him. Those who had created this tomb had done so quietly, victorious but somehow refusing to anger the person they had laid low.

Taking great double-handfuls of sand, I dug my way down. I disinterred the word. It appeared unfamiliar at first. I traced a finger over the deep-set letters, unimpressed with their height and even the script chosen for their display. This word was not meant to inspire awe or fear. It felt informational, as would a street sign, and clearly meaningless to any who would look upon it.

Save for me.

I nodded slowly. *Ferranos.* I took this to be my name. The name of a man meant to be forgotten.

It was time, I decided, that memories should be stirred.

DARK SOULS
MASQUE OF VINDICATION

CHAPTER 2

Though the half-moon painted the desert's shifting sands in silver, darkness swallowed the world at the edges. I would have used the stars for dead reckoning in the past, but their misplacement made that a dubious proposition, and my mind seemed incapable of performing the proper calculations regardless. Instead, I traveled more by instinct, as a moth is compelled to find a flame, yet I did not go without all reason.

The weight of the dagger in my hand focused me on the dangers of the world. I saw no immediate threats, but I wondered if that was because of my dead eyes. All colors appeared bleached, as if the sun had burned them dull. The moon's silver light shined brightly enough from the sands that I shielded my eyes. If such harshness were the hallmark of the world after death, it would not surprise me that so many of the dead willingly lurked in dark tombs and deepest shadow.

I shambled in a direction I chose to believe was east—a decision prompted by the moon's slow transit through the sky. Walking toward the rising sun would grant me the earliest warning of its appearance and afford me time to find a place to *rest*. I knew not if, in my state, I actually needed to rest, but the idea of finding a place to *hide* repelled me. Even dead, even clearly having failed to outrun at least one enemy, I hated the idea of being considered prey.

As the barest trace of fire nibbled at the horizon, it silhouetted a square structure perhaps thirty feet tall and half as wide. I made for it as quickly as I could. It appeared to be an old watchtower at the corner of a fortress the desert had swallowed. I slid down the side of the wind-scoured bowl and crept in through a window toward the fort's interior.

I stood on a small landing, with stairways screwing down deeper and higher. I chose to descend into the depths, attracted by a soft glow. I moved as silently as I could and felt certain I'd approach unnoticed, but I gathered my ears had not yet become sharp enough to hear my own footfalls.

"Come, my friend, come." A man in the same condition as me sat cross-legged on the other side of a small fire. It provided a weak light, and even less by way of heat. He'd built it in what had been the ground floor of the tower, and tiny piles of sand lay at the base of the door, where the weight of dunes had cracked some of the door's boards.

I stood at the bottom of the stairs, the dagger clutched firmly and easily visible.

"It has been a while since you have had a conversation, hasn't it?" The man shrugged. "So it is for me. Few are the guests I entertain. Few are the guests articulate enough to be entertained."

I sat across from him. "Thank you for sharing the fire."

"You'll find it a comfort. Perhaps so much so that, like me, you decide leaving is unnecessary."

As he spoke, he shifted and reached out. He grasped something I could not see and placed it into the fire. The fire did not react, neither growing nor diminishing. I had a sense that he was not acting consciously, but out of fear. The fire gave him comfort, and fires needed to be fed, hence he would feed it regardless of lacking sticks or any other fuel.

His movement also shifted his robes, affording me a view of his legs. The flesh had long since become dried and cracked. Gaping wounds exposed ivory bone, and where his shins crossed, the robust bones had long ago fused. He could not have moved had he wanted to.

Content with the strength of his fire, my new friend smiled. "I take it, by the knife, you have met a Hollow and gotten the better of him."

"A Hollow?"

"Like us, but not like us. Mindless creatures really, bent on consuming the vitality that drives us. They can do nothing with it, just hoard it, but that desire is the reason they have not faded into nothingness. They share the curse with us, of course, but lack the will or capacity to function intelligently within it."

"I killed…" I hesitated and cocked my head. "Did I kill that which is already dead?"

"As good a word as any, though I prefer to think of it as freeing them." He leaned in. "You felt it, didn't you? When the last vestiges of its essence seeped into you. You saw something. Or heard something. I remember once catching the scent of a rare flower."

Had I not experienced the thief's death, I would have thought my companion completely mad. "It is different each time, then?"

"In its own way, yes."

"And his essence, it sparked something within me."

"Yes." He spread his hands wide. "Imagine your life, when you had one, as a mural painted in the brightest colors. Everything you did and saw, ate and loved, everything you experienced depicted on it. And then when you… A great wind came, a scouring wind, blowing all this sand to scrape away all you were. But you are cursed. So with each bit of essence you draw into yourself, you splash color onto that mural, you restore it in little bits, here and there."

"Can you get it all back? Can you…"

"Return to life? The wind whispers that seductive tale every night, and the oceans sing it with every wave's soft retreat." He shook his head. "I do not know the truth of it. Some believe you can return as a god, and those who have regained life or have become gods, well, they've not deigned to report back to me."

I nodded toward his legs. "You have been here a long time."

"Oh yes, and content to stay. I have my fire. I have my visitors." He smiled. "You're welcome to share it as much as you desire."

I did find the fire something of a comfort, but I felt that this was as it was for him, the hint of a memory gilding a common experience. "To know what you know, you must have traveled much."

He shrugged. "When I came to this place, the desert had only begun to spread to it. I found many Hollows here and dealt with them."

"Are there more?"

"There are always more, my friend. There are many things here, buried deep." He pointed toward a small doorway beneath the stairs. "It goes farther down, deep down. You could go—many do. They always return."

"No danger, then?"

"More than most are willing to accept. More than I am willing to accept." He rested his hands on petrified knees. "You will see. Go on. It won't hurt much, or for long."

* * *

I took my leave and entered the darkness beyond the little hole in the wall. The staircase did not spiral down as it had in the tower above, but descended at a steep angle and turned ninety degrees at small platforms in the corners of a square shaft. I almost tripped a half dozen times, as the risers on these steps were taller than the others. And the stones that made the walls had been joined oddly, with curved joints fitting them together as if pieces of a puzzle.

The room with the fire had not been the tower's ground floor. That tower and fortress were themselves built on something deeper and older— something ancient that had not been shaped by the hand of man. I looked to my right and tried to peer down the center of the shaft, but I heard nothing and saw nothing. I didn't shout, less for fear of alerting something to my presence than having no desire to hear my voice vanish without even an echo.

Six twists down, or eight, it didn't matter, but far enough down that I saw not even the tiniest hint of light from the fire above, a corridor extended off to the left. Its ceiling arched overhead just beyond the reach of my fingers.

That knowledge, coupled with the height of the stair risers, made me think the place had been built for giants. This did not please me, but I headed down the corridor, the fingers of my right hand holding the dagger tightly and those of my left brushing over the stone.

My touching the stone started something. A pale green light glowed in three lines to the passage of my fingers. When I stopped, the light raced ahead, then the three lines diverged and split. They rose and spiraled, carried across the ceiling vault, and curled down over the far wall. The arabesque designs displayed symmetry but did not duplicate themselves, nor did they depict any language I knew. It occurred to me that the display was laughter, laughter made of light.

Farther down, another twenty feet or so, the lights split and ran left and right through crosscut passages while also continuing as the main corridor curved to the left. Pleased at the choices, I started forward, then stopped as something grunted or groaned.

It came around the corner from the cross-passage, a mushroom-fleshed creature, hunched over and bristling with sharp spines. Short legs and a narrow waist gave way to broad shoulders, a well-muscled chest, and long arms ending in claws. The misshapen head projected forward. The creature rolled from side to side as it walked, and it fixed me with the glare from one bulbous eye.

I stared. Then, too late, I began to back away.

Making good use of the high ceiling, the creature rushed at me, leaped up, and pounced. It slammed me into the floor and landed full on my chest. Ribs cracked. It raked its short feet back, disemboweling me. Its mouth gaped open. Fetid breath washed over me, then the thing bit off my face.

* * *

I stood at the edge of the firelight, staring down at the man whose legs had fused. He reached out, gathered invisible twigs, and fed them into the undying fire. "Welcome back."

I looked down, expecting to see jagged ends of ribs protruding from my chest and a ropy string of guts dangling between my legs, but there was nothing. It was as if what I recalled had only been a vivid dream, from which I'd wakened not soon enough. I could still feel the pain of shattered ribs and claws rending my flesh, yet even those sensations faded.

I shivered. "How is it I am here?"

"You always ask that."

"Given the circumstances, I think I should have remembered asking that question before."

He sighed. "This is the first time *you* have asked, but the others... We've had some grand conversations about it. The most popular explanation is that the gods, or demons, or some thrice-damned sorcerer who is the cause of our affliction, wished us to relive our mortification and failure. You fail, you return, and you eventually despair at ever going farther. The gods drink our frustration. Demons mock our determination in the face of futility."

"You are telling me no one knows the truth."

"But many have vowed that when they become gods, they will change it." He chuckled indulgently, as a parent might at a joke offered by a child. "At some point, those who come to my fire decide that the descent here is not the way forward. They wander off to other climes."

I sat. "How far did you get?"

He frowned for a moment. "Deep, fair deep, but there are things there that hate us, hate those foolish enough not to know they are dead. Worse, there are things beyond them that terrify the things that hate us."

"But you got farther than I did." I arched an eyebrow. "Now, the first creature, the hunched hulk in the tall corridor, how did you get past that...?"

* * *

I sank to a knee beside the fire, reaching up to secure my head as the pain of my decapitation faded. "You did not tell me of the warriors wandering down there. Past the corridors of lights, down through the channels, they swarm. I could not destroy them all, and then one, the tallest, swung an ax and took my head."

My friend raised his hands. "A thousand pardons. I had forgotten them. I never fought them. I caught glimpses once or twice, but I hid, and they missed me. They wander. I call them the Lost Patrol. You might never see them, and then they could surround you."

I grunted, fairly certain my head was going to remain in place. "I am not going to give up. There will be a time when I do not return because I am through."

"Your determination is fearsome, my friend, but everyone wears down."

"I do not. Ferranos does not surrender."

My friend blinked. "You remember your name?"

"I know it, yes."

"I don't know mine. Perhaps that is why I am content to sit here. Who I was matters not. Now I just keep the fire."

I bowed my head. "That is not for me. There is something drawing me on. When I am down there, with each step I take, I sense it is a little bit closer. I cannot tell you what or where, just that it is not here. I am not meant to remain here. So I will win my way through. I will."

The keeper of the fire stared at me, focused enough to forget tending his fire. "When you're a god, Ferranos, will you change things?"

"For some, I imagine. For you, yes."

He nodded, then fished in a pouch on his belt. He withdrew a flask and passed it to me. "This contains an elixir that will help you heal. It availed me little, but it will help you."

"You could have given me this before."

"You got far without it. Farther than I ever did. I hoped, perhaps…"

"That I would tell you enough that you could escape, too?" I pointed to his legs. "Could it heal them?"

"I am certain, *if* I had the will to have them healed." He fed the fire with invisible kindling. "When you're a god, you'll bring it back to me, yes?"

I caught his gift in my left hand. "My first task. Thank you."

"Not yet." He smiled. "I'm sure we'll talk a time or three or three dozen more. *Then* thank me."

I nodded. "Done, but I say this happily: I hope not to see you again for a very long time."

DARK SOULS

MASQUE OF VINDICATION

CHAPTER 3

I sat beneath an iron sky on the pile of flesh and bones that had once been the Lost Patrol. I stared into their captain's dead eyes as his head sat in my left palm. "Finally, I have finished you." I took a swallow from the flask and felt the horrid rents in my flesh sealing themselves.

Perching myself atop the bodies of my enemies might have seemed heinously ghoulish, but I *was* dead. More important, in slaying the lot of them, I'd absorbed their essences. Though each Hollow contributed almost nothing, the aggregate overwhelmed me. My body tingled as if I'd been scourged with thorned lashes and put to the torch. Unsteady, I sat. When feeling returned to my arms and I lifted the captain's severed head, I felt stronger than before.

I'd met them on a bridge over a turgid black river. What flowed between the banks bubbled and churned in thick swirls. Occasionally, things bobbed to the surface—usually a rodent, or part thereof, slowly being dissolved in the torpid current. Mostly, the dark fluid trickled on, noxious and uninviting even to the Hollows.

The keeper of the fire had not been wrong, for I had returned to his fire many times since he gave me the flask. The Lost Patrol had become a true problem. He'd only caught glimpses of them because he'd never made it near the bridge. The bridge they believed they had been commanded to hold.

And hold they did, with a valiant effort that, had bards been there to bear witness, would have been fodder for songs by the dozen. I'd have been the villain in all of them save the last. With each battle previous, I had lost, yes, but had also grown better with my magicks. In the tomb, I'd touched the thief to kill him. With each encounter at the bridge, I'd learned how far away I could hit something and how hard. Somewhere along the line, I'd found a discarded stick, which now served as a makeshift staff, allowing me to focus my magicks.

Finally, when I had the Lost Patrol crowded on the bridge, I laid waste to them. I found it no simple feat, but one requiring concentration. Magick worked best when the sorcerer had time to think. Having a slavering horde clambering over one another to tear you limb from limb, therefore, was hardly ideal; but after countless repetitions of the battle, I struck more by instinct and intuition than deliberation.

And having gotten this far, I felt the pull more strongly than ever before. Something out there compelled me to continue. I couldn't identify it with any certainty, nor could I deny it existed. It felt as if I were staring at the rising sun and seeing a dark splotch on the horizon. I had no doubt it was there, but I had to get closer before I would see it in any detail.

The bridge lay quite deep beneath the sands and farther east than I'd ever been before. An iron dome capped a round room that served no easily discernible purpose. Three streams flowed in from the west, joining to make the black river, and it passed under the bridge and continued out through three stonework openings. East of the bridge lay another corridor.

I tossed the captain's head into the river, then sorted through the bodies for anything useful. I found scant little, save another dagger and a better pair of boots than I currently wore. I poured dark fluid from the boots and, while I would have preferred to give them time to dry, pulled them on. The boots ran a bit big, but I expected they would shrink as they dried.

Having no desire to enter the river and explore the dark holes into which it poured, I headed east. The boots squished with each step. This meant I had to pause every half dozen steps, giving myself a chance to listen for pursuers or any ambush that might lay ahead. The corridor continued east for a short distance, then south, and once more turning to the east. At each new intersection, I explored a bit, choosing whichever route got me to an easterly run most quickly.

Unmolested, and fully assuming that with the next step I'd die and reappear back at the fire, I caught hint of a bright light around the next corner. I paused at the edge and looked, ducking back quickly. Then again, raising a hand to shield my eyes. The corridor ended nearly twenty feet farther, opening into sunlight.

I knew I should be joyful, but I held myself back from rushing into the light. I had been cautious too long to act foolishly and return to the fire. I turned the corner and crept along carefully. Within ten feet a cool breeze reached me. The scent of flowers came with it, replacing the musty stench of the underground.

Gravel crunched beneath my boots as I stepped into the sunlight. A short path ran uphill to the left, still visible despite being half overgrown. It cut through sparse golden grasses, which rustled as I passed and tore at my clothes with saw-edged blades. A dozen paces on, I reached a high point. To my right, the land fell away into a dark valley. On the left, the arid hillside rose steeply. Beige clouds rippled at the top. I'd come out from beneath the desert's edge, and the breeze rising from the valley teased sand from the arid plateau above.

The trail curled down to the left, away from the precipice, and passed beside a small clearing with a circle of fire-blackened stones at its heart. I gathered some grasses and some scattered twigs, building from them a fire. Lacking a tinderbox, I dropped to a knee, thinking to ignite it with a spell.

But even as I thought of igniting the tinder, the fire sprang up as if of its own volition. I pulled back, not wanting the fire to spread to me, then noticed that a gust of wind ignored it. The flames burned brightly, but gave off no discernible heat. This unnatural blaze reminded me of the fire my friend kept in the far distant tower.

Moreover, I felt safe in its presence, which I should not have.

I made myself abandon the fire and continued along the trail. The golden grasses grew everywhere, partially obscuring white chalk cliffsides and chunks of stone. Then the path broadened, leading down into a bowl, at the heart of which lay an arena of sorts. Worn and pitted white stone columns arched together at the top and upheld marble crossbeams. Brush, stone, and the contours of the land hid the arena's floor from me, so I turned away and explored some of the village ruins nearby.

The stench of death rose from the well at the heart of the small square around which the village had been constructed. Someone had dumped a goat or two down the shaft. Dead or alive when they went in really didn't matter. The bloated and decaying bodies had blackened the water, poisoning it.

I looked around for other signs of wanton vandalism and found plenty. Broken arrows and bits of bone had been scattered about. Through the open doorway of one building, shattered furniture was easy to pick out. I climbed the steps to the doorway and peeked into a small rectangular space strewn with debris, the only comprehensible bits being things I also recognized as being broken. The roof had long since caved in, and the sun had faded the walls' bright murals—those bits that had not long ago chipped and flaked away—to weakly tinted shadows.

A low growl alerted me, and I spun, my makeshift staff coming up. An emaciated figure with a bulbous skull, flesh tinged with necrosis and long, stringy hair waving about the breeze, shambled from the shadows of the next building over. The thing lifted its head, sniffing—empty eye sockets made that necessary. Arms outstretched and fingers clawed, it came for me.

I focused for a moment. Harsh blue light coalesced around the head of the staff. With the flick of my wrist, I launched the sorcerous bolt. It slammed into the creature's chest. The ball exploded into searing tendrils that burned their way through its flesh. A second bolt hit just above the first, dissolving the creature's neck. The head bounced backward as the body staggered on for another step, then collapsed into the dust.

I absorbed its essence, which amounted to little more than an acute sensation of hunger. That thing, whatever it had been when alive, had surrendered all but the barest sense of animal existence. It triggered nothing in me, save for a moment's relief that I wasn't its lunch.

Cautiously, then, I searched the buildings. I killed two more ghouls, each the equal of the first in all ways. I found a few old coins, which I kept, not certain of their value in the world through which I moved.

One in particular intrigued me because the weight in my hand felt familiar. Unlike the other copper and silver bits, this one had been minted of gold. The face on the coin had been disfigured on purpose. Someone had gouged out the eye and punched a hole through the ear deep enough that it left a pinprick opening on the other side. Whether the vandal expected that would afflict the figure with blindness and deafness, I could not tell. Perhaps he feared that otherwise the figure could see and hear him via some sorceries worked through the coin.

I made out the lettering on the edge of the coin. It read *Parnyr*, which did not feel alien in my mouth. I'd said it before and said it often. I had no memory of how I'd said it—if it had been shouted in anger, I'd have thought my throat might hurt. My comfort with the word and the antiquity of the coin confirmed the fact that I'd lain in the tomb for a very long time.

I headed back to the path and discovered it ran down into the arena. I paused and searched for another route, a way around, but it appeared my only choices were to return to the complex from which I'd escaped or press on forward through the arena. Trepidatiously, I walked up the slight rise to the arena's highest lip and peered down in.

My fear had not been baseless.

The massive figure of a man stood center on the arena floor. He could have been carved from granite, given his size and coloring—at least the coloring of his armor. Half as tall as me and easily three times as broad, he wore heavy plate armor, with mail showing at the joints. The armor bore scars of combat, but no obvious breaches. A full helm hid his face, and his hands rested on the butt end of a huge stone mace. The rock appeared to be the size of my torso, massed considerably more and, I had no doubt, would more easily pulverize me even with a glancing blow.

I dropped to a crouch so he would not see me. On the edge of a stone seat near me, written in brown blood, was the legend, "Here you will die."

"But apparently, not instantly." I rose again and began my descent into the arena. I studied the steps before me for any signs of impact from the man's mace. As he remained still as death while I approached, I hoped to gauge when he might notice me and react. Would he warn me?

The answer: No.

I also learned that the person who had written the warning had been quite spry. The first blow had only pulverized his legs. Thus broken, he'd managed to drag himself to that spot and inscribed his prediction for others.

Of course, I reached this conclusion during my fourth trip into the arena. And confirmed it well before my last.

As I had before, I found myself standing before the fire on the hillside. Agony coursed down my left arm and through my ribs, as if they remained crushed. I dared not put weight on my left leg, lest my hip collapse. I balanced there, waiting for the pain to fade like the echoes of thunder. Which it did slowly, the flames mocking me with their lively dance.

Once I could balance again on two feet, I took a moment to collect my thoughts and prepare myself to again engage the creature. What I had gleaned so far was that I could cast magick from near the top of the arena and hurt him. He was slow enough that I could cast two or three more bolts before he would reach me. If I kept moving, I could continue the sorcerous assault, but as yet, I had no clear sense of how badly my spells hurt him.

And if ever I missed with a bolt, I found myself back at the fire in an eyeblink, pain fading, bones knitting.

The key, I realized, lay in avoiding injury while I hurt him. Simple and elemental in the abstract. In practice, however, difficult. While dodging through the arena seating might slow him down, chances for me to twist an ankle or trip over a bench abounded. Even that one time I'd lured him out of the arena had left me hopeful because of how slowly he moved up the stairs. I found him decidedly quicker in the village, and he splashed me from well to outhouse and back. The only thing for it, I understood clearly, would be to face him in the arena. I could still move, and that helmet narrowed his vision. *Perhaps my bolts will be more powerful at shorter range, as well.* I had no evidence to support that idea, but I deceived myself into believing it might be true.

I strode down the steps and leaped onto the arena's floor. My opponent had never moved before I attacked him and showed me that courtesy even as I invaded his territory. I brought up my staff, cast a spell, and began to move.

The sorcerous bolt hit him squarely in the stomach. Lightning tendrils played up and over his chest, then down to his hips. They left no mark on his armor, elicited no response other than the fluid motion with which he brought up the mace and pivoted toward me.

I'd begun to circle to my right. I veered in toward him, then danced back as the mace arced down through the space where I'd been. I ducked, dropping to a knee, as the stone head returned in a backhanded blow. It whistled above me, having missed my skull by a fingerbreadth.

I stabbed the staff at him and cast. This bolt slammed into his left flank, right up into his armpit. The lightning set every ring in the mail glowing. Then I dove forward in a roll as the giant's club pounded the arena sand flat behind me. Wheeling, I triggered another bolt, which caught him over the left hip, then I dodged farther right, hoping the damage would slow him.

It did.

It didn't slow the mace.

He swung heavily, letting the momentum help him turn. The weapon's edge clipped me in the left shoulder, splintering bone into pain. I whirled away, leaving my feet, and bounced down hard. I rolled to the arena wall and gathered my feet beneath me.

Which is when I found myself between a rock and a very hard place.

* * *

I collapsed by the fire, all my limbs, every bone fragment, rattling around inside me. A wave of pain lifted me and dashed me against the ground with the fury of an ocean assaulting a foundering ship. I'm certain I moaned.

A none-too-gentle booted foot toed me over onto my back, and the tip of a sword rested at my throat.

I stared up at an armored figure.

CHAPTER 4

I peered up the length of the blade, over the words etched into it, and past the crest worked into the cross guard. "I fear, in this place, beside this fire, a threat to my life lacks the gravity it might warrant another time."

"You're a talker." He straightened up, and the blade slid out of line with my throat. "At least it means you're not one of them."

"Of the Hollows."

The armored man grunted. "Fitting name."

I levered myself up on my elbows. "Your blade, the sigils. You are one of the Knights of Virtue."

He nodded and sheathed his weapon. "I am. Was. I am not certain." He reached up and unfastened his helm. He removed it, setting it beside his kite shield on the ground. I found him to be a handsome man with thick blond hair and a tight, curly beard to match. His eyes had the hue of a deep ocean, a blue so close to black as to suggest they had no color at all. "My name is Krotha. You have a name, yes?"

"Ferranos." I sat fully up, folding my legs beneath me. "Please join me at my fire. Or this fire. I should not claim ownership. How came you to be here?"

Krotha jerked a thumb over his shoulder at the sea. "I thought I could swim in this armor."

"I thought I could outrun a stone club." I fished into a pouch on my belt and tossed him the gold coin. "Do you recognize this?"

"It is from Alkindor, but…" He squinted, then rubbed his thumb over the mutilated face. "I should know more. I can feel that."

"Allow me. That is Parnyr. His name sticks with me, but I had forgotten Alkindor. And most about the Knights."

He tossed the coin back to me. "The Knights of Virtue. We pledged our lives in service to Alkindor, to the king. Likely to your Parnyr. I was—am—the Knight of Truth. I cannot lie, nor can I abide lies."

"Then I shall always be truthful with you, save when I cannot remember." I wished the fire would pop and crackle sufficiently to fill the silence. "How are you here? Not at the fire, but here? It seems fruitless to deny that you and I have lain in tombs for eons."

"If you slept, you were luckier than I." He sat on a rock opposite me. "All I recall is fighting, endless battle. And then something befell me. My body burned, not a real fire, but something that made me think I was on fire. In my blood. And then, after darkness, I found myself in a small cave, sealed inside it, with a fire much like this burning there. I stared into its depths for how long I cannot say. Then at once, I felt an urge to leave. I picked up a rock and began pounding on a wall. When that rock had been battered into dust, I chose another and continued. I measured time in inches. Thirty-three feet later, I walked free."

I arched an eyebrow. "A smaller tunnel would have been finished sooner."

"A Knight of Virtue does not crawl." The stern expression on his face softened just a bit. "I have slain creatures and revenants, remains of men and ghosts and ghouls. I returned to my cave several times and always walked free again. Now I am here."

I pointed off in the direction of the arena. "The urge, it draws you, yes, that way?"

"You know it, too?" He hunched forward, forearms across his thighs. "There is an urgency, and yet regret. I…" He pressed a hand over his heart. "I know I must go, and I believe I should know why. But to remember…"

"But you have felt memory return as you kill Hollows, yes? Their essence invigorates you."

"Is that what you feel?" He sighed. "For me it is a raindrop and I am parched soil. It is something, but not nearly enough. I see things from them, hear it, know it, but so little connects to me. Though I did slay a Hollow who had been a mason. From him I learned my tunnel was not nearly so crude as I imagined."

"I avoid more than I slay, but some are inescapable." I took up my staff and drew the arena in the dirt. "The path from here leads to an arena in which a giant warrior—I shan't insult you by considering him to be a knight, though he is as formidable as one—bars our passage."

"Our passage?"

"I presume, forgive me, that our paths now lie together."

Krotha raised a hand. "Fear not, friend. I am not insulted. It is that I have been alone for all I can remember. Your use of *our* sparked something. A sense. From long ago when the Knights protected the kingdom. Protected its people. People like you. You do not presume in any way, save in believing I would honor the oaths I made when I became a Knight of Virtue."

"You do not feel released from them by death?"

"My oaths are eternal. Perhaps that is why I am here." He smiled. "What oath did you swear?"

I shrugged. "I remember no oath, though likely I spoke in haste at some time, invoking spirits and fates that have trapped me thus. You are bound by your will, and I by senselessness."

"It matters not. We are here now, together." He nodded. "And yes, my sense lies beyond your arena. I am called in that direction. We shall be companions for as long as the fates pull us in the same direction, shall we, Ferranos?"

"It would be an honor, Sir Krotha Truthteller." I got to my feet. "Come, see what it is we are facing."

* * *

"A giant of Druutheim." Krotha's eyes narrowed. "There is a memory I did not need returned."

"He has killed me more times than I can count."

"Not a surprise. Raiders from the north, from Druutheim, used to attack settlements on the coast of...of...on the coast. And on each of their boats, they'd have one of these things. Men said the Druu stole them as children from the giants and raised them to fight." He half smiled. "That you fought against this at all tells me much about you, my friend."

"It tells you I have no sense." I glanced over at the village. "It was raided. Perhaps the Druu left him here."

"Possible." Krotha settled his helmet onto his head and tightened the chin strap. "He bars our way."

"Have you slain one before?"

"Only as often as you have." He laid a gauntleted hand on my shoulder. "Confidence, friend. I am a better fighter than I am a mason."

He bounded down the stairs, armor clattering, and leaped into the arena. He bashed his blade's pommel against the surface of his triangular shield. "I am Krotha Truthteller. It is the last name you will be given cause to remember."

The giant turned toward him and swept his crude mace skyward. The knight just stood there, shield raised, sword down by his right thigh. As the mace descended, Krotha crouched, then sprang to the side. The stone mace's head sank into the earth all the way to the haft.

Krotha darted forward. His blade, bright in the harsh sunlight, flashed. The sword cut the giant's left knee, front and back, not severing it, but sending black blood cascading. Even before the first droplet hit the sand, Krotha passed beyond the creature and spun to face it again.

The giant tugged the club free with surprising ease. It pivoted, but on its right foot. The club whirled around in a backhanded blow. Krotha ducked beneath it, then smashed his shield against the giant's knuckles. Black blood stained the steel, and Krotha staggered back a step or two.

Favoring that left leg, the giant lunged forward on its right. It cut off

Krotha's ability to move to his own left, forcing him to cross in front of the giant. And the club came up and around, curving into a smooth arc low enough that Krotha couldn't duck it, yet high enough that he couldn't leap above it.

I cast quickly, though better than ever before. The bolt sizzled down into the arena and barely missed the giant's right fist. The arcane ball exploded against the mace's haft, shattering it. The stone head whirled off, slamming into the arena floor just behind Krotha, then bouncing off the arena wall. It flew up into the air, spinning lazily.

The giant, both hands extended and grasping, grabbed at it.

Krotha, true knight and killer, ignored the stone. He wheeled around and drove at the giant. He stabbed it deep in the groin, sliding his blade in to the hilt. The tip burst free of the giant's flesh over its right hip, then vanished again as Krotha ripped the blade free and slashed up at the giant's belly.

The creature stumbled backward, hands now covering its stomach. Midnight blood oozed between its blunt fingers, but poured in a torrent from the hole in its groin. It gushed with each heartbeat, each splash a bit weaker. The giant wavered, then dropped to a knee and finally pitched over onto its back. Its great chest heaved once or twice more, then a shudder ran through the creature, and it lay still.

Krotha gave the thing a wide berth and shook his blade to rid it of the black blood. "Thank you. But for your spell, it would be me on the sand."

"You give me too much credit." I nodded toward the body. "I saw you bruise its hand. I saw your strategy and thought I might be able to help. As it was, however, I missed."

"And yet your failure served a greater purpose than your success would have."

"Would you have me fail often, then?"

"Only when it serves our purpose, Ferranos." Krotha washed the blade with sand, then wiped it clean with the giant's hair.

It was at that moment when the giant truly died and its essence flowed free. Krotha stiffened, limbs outstretched, head back, mouth open. I staggered, going to a knee with my hands wrapped round my midsection. Splinters of the giant's life stabbed my brain. Its world had become the arena. It knew fear, never taking elation from its victories, just letting the fear subside for a moment. I caught sadness from when the Druu had abandoned it, for slave though it had been, it had never been alone. And then it spent an eternity alone, save when someone wanted to kill it.

Krotha reached up and placed a hand on its brow. "Had I but known…"

I nodded as he turned toward me. "I saw. I felt."

He sighed. "When your only tool is a sword, all problems end in death."

"That holds true for more than swords, Sir Krotha, but most often the means of death are less clean, less honorable than this." I rose to my feet and extended a hand to the east. "The way is clear."

"And the urge redoubled." Krotha slid his blade home in his scabbard. "It may be miles before we find another fire."

"Agreed." I fell into step with him. "And may it be many miles before we need one."

DARK SOULS
MASQUE OF VINDICATION

CHAPTER 5

Krotha and I traveled toward the sunrise, drawn on by a sense of order and satisfaction. To turn away, even to deviate from that easterly course to avoid an obstacle, was to be haunted by the feeling that we'd made an error—an error that grew graver with each step. And then, when we could amend our course, we could not help but smile, for all that had been wrong with the world suddenly vanished. Our path rewarded us with an intangible aura of victory, and we could not help but be pleased.

The journey could not be measured in days, for to the dead, such time-keeping made no sense. Nor did distance, in that there were times when yawning gulfs passed in an eyeblink, as if we were giants striding across the world. Other times it felt as if we waded through eternities of waist-high snowdrifts.

Combats could have measured our steps, but only to make the journey seem longer, as we lost many before we won the few. Fires might be another marker, for we found a number and welcomed them. They rewarded us for a victory and succored us in defeat. A few we kindled ourselves, but others we found burning. Still, at these latter ones, we never discovered any other necromantic travelers such as ourselves.

Here and there, we found living people, but only in scattered settlements—most often reclaimed ruins—or residing on their own, far from others. Many of the living fled from us, our dark pallor making it clear what we were. I felt no inclination to kill them, and Krotha likely would have stopped me if I had.

A few hearty souls traded with us. An armorer pounded out dents in Krotha's shield and metal carapace. I obtained knowledge of spells, which expanded my repertoire, though in my current state, I had difficulty focusing on more than one spell at a time. We also found Krotha the same sort of flask I'd been given.

What we really wanted was information, and the few bits we obtained about our course came tinged with dread. East lay a land known to many as the Sunken Place, or the Swamp of the Lost. Tales about how it had earned its name varied, but all included licentious sinfulness, blasphemy, and a great deal of blood. Most people warned, "To go there is to die...," their voices trailing off as they understood what they had said.

We kindled a fire on a wide ledge overlooking the Sunken Place. Twenty feet above, at the edge of the cliff we'd descended, the sun had warmed us, and low clouds had hidden the swamp. Beneath that thin layer, darkness fell, and a rotting scent thickened the air. Golds and reds of sand, sun, and rock became dusky blue and fog grey, with the black specters of trees barely discernible, awash in dark brackish water.

"Should we spend the night here, friend Ferranos, or continue immediately?"

"A difficult choice." I shrugged. "If we remain, how will we know morning has come?"

"If we descend in haste, I am certain we'll be back here straight away regardless." He set down his shield and doffed his helmet. "The desire to push on has grown more intense, yes?"

"With each step on this path down, yes." I smiled. "All the more reason to resist, I think, lest we betray ourselves with haste."

"I do not feel it is a trap seducing us. The sensation is genuine. My duty calls me."

"And the urgency frightens you." I rolled my shoulders. "I feel as if I am being driven toward something out there. I just wish I knew where this place was or what it was, back in a time when that might have been important."

"Yes, it is as if coming across a great hall with the remains of a banquet still on the tables but all the people gone. You can still eat, and some might say you've partaken of the feast, but in truth, you are but a scavenger and an outcast."

I raised an eyebrow. "A comment on our journey *and* upon our current state of being. Certainly the living consider us scavengers, though their circumstances are hardly preferable to ours."

"True, my friend, but I have the sense that even in life you and I were set apart. Were that not so, we'd likely not be here now." He pointed toward the swamp. "That which set us apart is clearly calling us forward."

"Then there is no reason to delay our advance." I brandished my staff and started down into the thickening fog. We passed through layers of it, each time the air becoming thicker and cooler. At the cliff's bottom, thick mud greeted us, and luminescent eyes glowed in the distance.

"I should go first and choose a path. We don't need you sinking in this morass." I carefully probed with my staff and picked my way toward the east. It made for slow going, especially with me memorizing our path to make short work of it on our return journey. Amphibians croaked and other things hissed to protest our passing, but the angriest of the swamp's denizens were the bloodsucking bugs, which found in us nothing to their liking.

We passed deeply into the swamp and found a small island with a ruined tower on the northern edge. Had it been possible, we'd have kindled a fire there. We took some time to explore the place, and I imagined, like the first tower I'd seen, this one extended deeply beneath the island, but silt and flood debris had long since filled it. I did, however, notice graffiti carved into the stone lintel above a window. Mildew all but obscured it, but I cleaned it off with the swipe of a hand.

"'No sun sets as beautiful as in Trafaram.'" I closed my eyes as something echoed deep within my thoughts. "Carved by a soldier homesick for his nation?"

"I think not, my friend." Krotha's gauntleted finger scraped over the words. "Trafaram was never a nation. It is Alkindor's prime province, a jewel. To be stuck here and away from it would cause heartache."

I opened my eyes again. "I do not remember Trafaram, though I have a sense of haughty arrogance."

"Then you recall the Trafaramites quite clearly. Their troops functioned well for a show—no force paraded as well as they did, and as honor guards they excelled." He looked around. "For a troop of them to be stationed here, however, the mission must have been of the utmost importance."

"And conducted with the utmost of secrecy?"

"Yes, there would be that, too." He patted his hand over his breastplate. "Perhaps dispatched after my time."

"Likely dispatched because the Knights of Virtue were unavailable."

My companion fell silent for a moment or three. "If that is true, then dire must have been the circumstances. Which means they might yet be dire. We should press on, Ferranos, with haste."

I would lie if I suggested that our greater haste came at his urging alone. Our sense of duty had continued to grow until it gathered like a thunderhead in my chest. Had my heart yet beat, it would have been pounding loudly and fast. I felt less pushed than drawn, like iron to a lodestone. I tested our path as before, but did not seek the best route, simply the most expedient, and Krotha either did not notice or did not care to complain.

We had doubled the depth of our penetration into the dismal swamp when hidden enemies attacked. Hollows, of empty eyes and clawed hands, wearing the flesh of crocodiles, surged up out of the water and engaged us. The first caught me with a tackle around the waist, knocking me from the narrow causeway, and carried me into the water. His fingers dug into my back, and he went to tear out my throat with his teeth.

I jammed the head of my staff into his mouth, blocking that attempt, then cast. Bright blue light built in his mouth, radiating out through his throat and eyes. A moment later his head exploded, bone and brains battering my face. Blinded, I twisted and kicked, breaking his death grip around my waist. His body began to slip away, and I struck for the surface. Then something clamped heavy and hard onto my ankle. It jerked once, then rolled, spinning me. I clung to my staff as I floated downward. The pressure eased for a moment, then tightened mid-thigh. Peg teeth sank into my flesh, then the crocodile spun again, yanking my hip out of the joint. Pain exploded up through my spine and into my skull.

I fought panic, forcing pain and anxiety away. Panic would send me back to the fire, back to safety, but I refused to surrender. To give in would be the first step on the road that meant I would sit by that fire until my legs fused, and I would not do that.

I had promises to keep.

I thrust down with my staff, driving the tip along my leg and into the creature's mouth. I raked it along the crocodile's soft palate and thrust it into the throat. The staff hadn't enough of a point to pierce its flesh, and I didn't have enough strength to impale the beast. I just wanted the stick lodged deeply enough that it would remain even if I let go.

Wrapping both hands around the staff's head, I cast my spell. Blocked from traveling out of the head, the energy coruscated down the shaft and into the crocodile. It burned my leg as it passed, but that pain added little to what I already felt. Then a shock wave ran through the water. Blue light flashed below me, and the crocodile shuddered.

But its jaws remained tight on my leg, and the dead weight of its body dragged me farther down. I levered the staff up and down, but I couldn't force the jaw to release. So I pulled back on the staff, then pushed the head away before casting again.

And again.

The fifth time, I succeeded in blowing apart the crocodile's jaw. What was left of my right foot and ankle went with it. As the reptile's bulk continued to sink, I floated toward the surface. Pain washed over me in waves. My missing foot felt as if it were on fire. Because of how I lost it, I actually looked down to see if the lower part of my leg was burning. It was not, and I reached the surface a half dozen feet from the causeway, the body of the soldier who had attacked me bobbing beside me.

Krotha, standing tall on the causeway, lashed out with his shield, crushing a skull and spinning the Hollow into the swamp. He blocked a slash from a Hollow wielding a sword, then took off the sword arm at the elbow. He smashed his fist into the last Hollow's face, then swept its head off with a quick slash.

The essence of the Hollow I'd killed trickled into me, followed by that of the crocodile. The Hollow's experience came muted and dark. Despair defined what it remembered. So far from home and certain he would never see his loved ones, he had been dead long before life abandoned him. The reptile, on the other hand, had been as powerful as it had been simple. Hunger and anger drove it. It had attacked me as much for my entering its domain as it did any desire for a meal.

Better, even to the point of death, it had been utterly unaware of how lost it was.

The Knight of Virtue stabbed his sword into the moist soil, then crouched and hauled me from the swamp. "Can you run?"

"Will an earnest limp do?"

"Not for the pace we need to set." He leaned down, threw me over his shoulder, recovered his sword, and sped deeper into the swamp. I had no idea where he was going, and I was certain I was not alone in that, save that the sense we'd been following built as we raced along the causeway.

Behind us, the soldiers armored in reptile flesh gathered in pursuit.

A hundred yards on, the causeway broadened and inclined upward. Paving stones covered it, and Krotha took each of two small staircases at a leap. A tall building rose in the darkness at the far edge of a courtyard, defining a small island. He passed to the courtyard's heart and set me down.

"I can defend the stairs. Can you…?"

"Grab my right leg at the knee. Pull hard."

He cast sword and shield aside and did as I asked. Lightning struck in my hip as the femur slipped back into place. I screamed—likely I had underwater, too—and lay back, shaking.

An inarticulate cry spun Krotha around. He snatched up his sword, but his shield remained on the ground. One of the soldiers crested the stairs, sword in hand. It tried hard to grin, and dislocated its jaw in the effort, making the expression all the more horrid.

Which, I presume, is why Krotha's first blow took off its jaw.

He kicked the soldier square in the chest, pitching it back into more of its fellows coming to the attack. Krotha laughed, bold and strong, cleaving one skull in half, then sweeping the legs from another of the attackers. His pommel crushed the skull of a third.

I pulled myself toward the building, hands seeking any purchase they could get on the paving stones. I reached for another handhold, and the stone felt distinctly cool to the touch. I brushed away leafy debris and dragged myself back. Whereas most of the stones were dark and rough, this one felt smooth and lighter. In fact, at my touch, the stones appeared to glow.

"Krotha, quickly, come back here."

"I can't fight them there."

"If I am right, you won't have to."

"Ha! And if you are wrong, we shall have to again win every step."

I hauled myself past the lighter stone, noting it was but one in a line of several. I brought my staff around and pointed it at the stairs. "Now, Krotha, now!"

The Alkindoran knight leaped away, and I cast. My blue bolt blasted through the chest of one soldier and melted the head of one following. The others recoiled for a moment, then cleared the stairs, but by then, Krotha had reached my side and tugged me farther from the stairs.

The stones began to pulse with light, and the crocodile soldiers shrank back again. They snarled and snapped at us, but none took so much as a single step in our direction.

Krotha sank to a knee beside me. "How did you...?"

"I didn't." I fished my flask from my sodden belt pouch and drank. The pain eased immediately, and a tingling sensation flooded my leg. It lingered in my hip, then drained down into my ankle. The only benefit of my boot being in the belly of a dead crocodile was that I could see green tendrils of light playing around the jagged ruin of my leg, knitting bone and flesh back together.

"The stones, Krotha Truthteller, are old, older than even we are perhaps, and meant to keep this place safe."

"From what?"

"Hollows? Things with evil intent?"

He doffed his helmet and scratched at his beard. "Discerning magick, if it discriminates between those things and us."

I spun around on my butt and pointed toward the dark building. "There, at the base, a glimmer of gold light. Can you see it?"

"Barely." His eyes narrowed. "You think this is why we were drawn here?"

"Do you doubt it? Do you doubt our duty is why we have crossed this barrier while the Hollows cannot?" I extended him a hand and shifted my staff to support myself. "Help me up. We are here for a reason, and I hope it is a good one."

DARK SOULS
MASQUE of VINDICATION

CHAPTER 6

Hanging heavily from Krotha's shoulder, I made my way with him into the dark building's doorway. A descending narrow stairway immediately presented itself. Krotha left me leaning against the wall as he advanced. Halfway down, he stopped, and, fully illuminated by a golden glow from beneath, he looked up at me. "I do not know what to make of this."

"Stay there." I continued leaning on the wall, but with my good leg and the staff, I managed to work my way down the stairs. The golden light hit my ruined foot first and redoubled the tingling in it. I glanced at it as toes sprouted. The light warmed my flesh in a way it had not been warmed since, I supposed, I entered the grave.

Despite the sensation being welcome, I was not wholly comfortable with it.

Krotha continued his descent a step or two, and I rested my left hand on his shoulder. "I share your truth, Krotha, for I am uncertain what I am seeing here."

We had entered a square chamber with a ceiling roughly a third high as the room was wide or deep. I had to assume the stones were the same grey as those in the structure above, but I couldn't be certain because the golden light painted them all in the same shade. It honestly seemed as if the light had penetrated the stone and the walls and ceiling radiated the golden color themselves.

A low, round dais dominated the room's center. A bier rested on it, and on that lay a sarcophagus. It was the source of the light, which shimmered like sunlight passing through the ocean. Thus, it appeared that the sarcophagus itself might not be the source of the light, but something inside it. Moreover, the sarcophagus's translucent amber walls provided a shadowed glimpse of a body lying on its back, suggesting he might be the light bringer.

My hand tightened on Krotha's pauldron, preventing him from stepping onto the chamber's floor. "I think the chamber will be as hostile to us as the stones above were to the Hollows. The magick here is more than decorative."

"Beautiful and deadly, then."

The light, as it played over the stone walls, was as if a lantern lit in darkest night, bringing into brilliant, colorful relief scenes from the life of a clean-limbed youth with abundant golden hair. He walked with a noble bearing, head high, a pleasing grin on strong, elegant features. He dressed as a peasant, and some scenes showed him herding wooldron. He appeared as docile as his charges, save in one scene where, staff in hand, he beat back a half dozen wolves, then wept over the rent body of a lamb he had not been able to save.

"Do you recognize him, Krotha?"

The knight shook his head. "He is familiar, but I cannot put a name to him. But that there, the land he lives in, that is Trafaram. And I would know, since that was the land of my birth."

"You are a Trafaramite? Then what I said before, if I insulted you, my apologies."

Krotha laughed, and I found it a welcome sound. "Until I saw this, my friend, I did not know that was my home—rather, I had not remembered. And now that I do, your description of haughty arrogance feels true. We are a vain people, and yet I am apart from them. Truthtelling and vanity seldom blend well. I chose Truth over my own people, and I do not find in me any regret."

I looked back up the stairs. "The Hollows who chased us here, am I wrong in thinking they could be Trafaramites as well?"

He nodded. "One of them might even have scratched that message into the lintel. In fact… Come, back to the courtyard."

Krotha helped me return up the stairs, but simply because squeezing past me would have been more inconvenient than otherwise. My foot had largely grown back, and while it ached to bear weight, it didn't restrict my movement that much. I slid to the side as we emerged, and he walked straight to the line of glowing stones.

Hollows lurked at the courtyard's edge, snarling and moaning, but ignoring their motionless companions.

I leaned against the building. "What are you looking for?"

"I wonder at this place and their connection to it. We know they were sent here, to whatever this place was, whenever it was, to watch and wait. And these stones hold them back, but would they not serve that purpose in the absence of guards? And is this not a rather obvious structure, and an important structure? If one wanted to hide someone, why so grand a place?"

I thrust aside unbidden images of my own occulted tomb, and my eyes narrowed. "You think this place was meant to safeguard someone or something, and perhaps the guards were placed here to apprehend any visitor thwarted by the line that stopped the Hollows?"

"Yes, but how would it have worked, and why stop the Hollows who were once allies in the mission?"

I chuckled slowly. "I think we go back to your haughty arrogance, my friend, and the heartsickness of the graffiti. Those soldiers were given a sacred duty, one they were proud to undertake, and yet, while years ground on, their sentiments soured as they received no recognition. They grew to resent and hate that which they were to guard because it trapped them away from home."

He glanced back at me. "And these stones here kept out anyone harboring resentment or hatred?"

"So it would seem."

"Which would mean that what lies trapped below was not meant to be trapped forever." The Knight of Virtue's eyes widened. "Could he still be alive, Ferranos? Are the bits of story playing over the walls his dreams? Could what has been forever for us have been but a good night's sleep for him?"

I shrugged. "All things are possible, my friend. It must be possible to work such magicks, since we have seen the end result. But to do so would require high magicks, serious magicks, and they would not be employed unless the subject has great value."

"Can you break those magicks?"

"Truth be told, I do not know." I levered myself off the wall. "But I am willing to try."

With my leg almost completely functional again, I descended and sat near the base of the stairs. Large blocks made up the floor in an eighteen-by-eighteen grid. As light streamed out of the sarcophagus and displayed scenes on the walls, the images moved up and down and across. When they struck the floor, they tended to play along one row or column, and many died when they reached another wall. The speed of progression seemed to match the nature of the vision. Pleasant, pastoral scenes moved languidly. Harsh scenes, as was the wolf attack, moved more quickly and less fluidly, as if the dreamer wanted to look away and shift to more enjoyable sights. The myriad of other dreams, some of mundane activities, some from infancy, and others featuring a woman of unparalleled beauty—despite a scar marring her forehead—unfolded at a more leisurely pace.

"I think you had the right of it, Krotha; these are dreams. I do not know if that means he is alive or not, but I recall no dreams while in my tomb, so we can hope." I pointed toward the amber box. "You see there, around the lid, the sigils worked half on the sides, half on the lid's edge? They would go all the way around and, when recited in the proper order, would unseal the sarcophagus."

"But to see them all, you will need to get to the dais."

"I fear that task is beyond me."

"How can this be so?"

"He would reject me." I ran a hand over my jaw. "This is not a simple puzzle. There are no levers to push, no knobs to twist, no wheels to turn because the dreamer is directing his own defense. The stones above recognize resentment and hatred. They punish it harshly enough for the Hollows to have learned to dread it. Here the dreamer must recognize the one who approaches. Perhaps, when this was built, it was assumed a lover or parent or child would come when the time was right. The dreamer would recognize his rescuer and allow her to approach. The dreamer will not recognize me."

"So we must seek another."

I smiled. "No, my friend, I think you'll do."

"I said he was familiar to me, but I doubt the reverse will be true." Krotha shook his head. "I would think we should now be compelled to seek the other, but I do feel myself yet drawn here."

"I feel the same, and this is why I believe you can reach the dais." I pointed toward a vision of the youth walking through a field of summer grasses, smiling, wholly at ease. "You are a Trafaramite. You know the place he walks, or one like it. You certainly know how it feels to wear that smile. What do you see there on his face?"

The knight frowned. "Happiness. Pride, certainly, with us always pride. And freedom, perhaps. It could be many things, but those, certainly."

"Good, yes. I think, were you to match your feelings to his, he would recognize in you a kinsman. He would see you are no threat and allow you to get closer. You will walk an emotional maze, matching your feelings to the dreams as your feet step on the stones where the dream unfolds itself."

Consternation darkened his expression. "But look, there, a dream dies where the wolves begin."

"Yes, but there, a row away, another dream, a similar dream, traces its way across the floor." I opened my arms. "You leap from one to the next."

"I am not a gazelle, Ferranos. And leaping past a line strikes me as a hostile act. I should no more carve a new path through a garden maze than I would not take every step he desires."

I tapped a finger against my chin. "You likely have a point there. So you must hope for a fortuitous run of dreams, or shift your emotions to match his in an eyeblink."

"The testing will become harder the closer I get."

"Likely."

Krotha shook his head. "I should be more pleased to do this were we able to kindle a fire above."

"I will help as I can. Call out what I see."

"Ha! You'll wait here until I fight my way back to this place."

"That as well."

Krotha sat on the stairs. "I should study the dreams. Learn them."

"Find memories of your own that match them."

"That as well."

One benefit of being dead was that trivial things like a need for food or sleep no longer existed for us. I have no way of knowing how long we sat and studied the dreams, but we did so intently. A couple of times we discussed the possibility of going out to harvest Hollows to see if their splinters of memory could help. We decided we'd undertake such a course only if a series of failures made it seem a necessity.

Krotha approached the unlocking of the dais as a tactician would a battle. He studied the dreams and chose the ones that resonated the most closely within him. He watched as they played along the walls and sought any pattern to their frequency. While neither of us could identify anything of the sort, dreams of a similar emotional nature did tend to follow one after the other.

Finally, he turned to me. "I think I understand. You believe this is what we are meant to do?"

I pointed back to the stones outside. "The magicks let us get this far. It senses no ill intent in us. I trust you can do this."

"Thank you, my friend." He smiled. "If I fail, I shall fight my way back here, and we will try again."

The Knight of Virtue left his sword and shield on the stairs beside me and quickly walked along with the youth's walking across a field. As that vision vanished against the far wall, he moved to a quiet summer night tending his flock. A breeze teased the shepherd's hair. As the youth reached up to brush a strand from his face, Krotha did the same thing. That dream took him a row closer and around the corner to the side.

"Quickly, Krotha. The wolves, they come."

The wolf dream arrived unexpectedly, born of the night. It moved faster and cut at him, bisecting his path. Krotha stopped abruptly, as if he'd run into a wall, then recoiled a step or two, clutching his ribs. Ragged scraps of his tabard floated to the ground and burst into flame as they struck the floor.

The wolf dream came down and around, angling in for another slash. Krotha glanced toward it, then straightened up and pulled his shoulders back. He stared at the vision, contempt curling his lip, then crisply side-stepped into a winter dream, in a tiny home, watching stew boiling in a black pot over the fire in the hearth. The wolf dream passed closely by, but evaporated in the fire's warmth.

Krotha let himself linger in the winter dream, for it lasted longer than most, as befitting a winter's long night. Then he let an autumn dream slide past and instead followed a springtime journey bringing the wooldron to the summer fields. That dream took a lazy course, and Krotha followed it serenely, even happily.

I, too, smiled. *He has it.* The knight had figured out that the youth was a lock, and he a key cut by emotion to fit. Likewise, his very presence, his drawing closer to the dais, shifted the youth's emotional state. By moving from winter to spring, by bravely facing down the wolves, Krotha proceeded in a natural and virtuous manner. His actions denied his threat. As he acted as the youth would have acted, the youth accepted him.

The knight moved from spring to summer to later summer, drawing ever closer to the dais. The wolves made another run, but Krotha ignored them. He waited for another dream of the lees of summer, passed quickly to harvest, and followed a dream about leading the lambs down from summer pastures to the dais itself.

With his first step onto the dais, the dreams died.

Krotha, on the far side of the sarcophagus from me, reached a hand toward the amber capsule. "It's clear, Ferranos. I can see him. He's no older than in his dreams, and modest in his dreams as well. What do I do now?"

"I am not certain. I need to study the sigils."

Krotha's eyes widened. "You'd best hurry, then. The boy, he's turning blue."

CHAPTER 7

Throwing caution to the wind, I crossed directly to the dais.

Krotha had been correct: The dream image of the youth was by no means as handsome as the reality, even as the color of his flesh changed. The young man had a strength to his unblemished features that gave me little doubt that the wolf dream had been remembered accurately. This was the face of a man who would be steadfast and brave no matter the situation he faced.

I started at the head and traced a finger along the sigils as I walked around the amber box. I had apparently recovered enough vitality from the Trafaramites we'd slain above to read what had been written. The same sigils had graced my bier, though I could not remember them well enough to reconstruct their message now. These were plain enough and yet frustratingly obtuse. "'In the Lair of Air, the Fair Heir Is There.'"

"What does it mean?"

"I do not know, and it just repeats. Six times." My hands balled into fists. "It is no incantation I recognize, and I do not believe that is simply because I have no memory of it. And what order for the words? They are nonsense."

Krotha leaned on the amber lid, staring down at the young man trapped beneath it. "It has to be something. Is he the key, as he was with the dreams? He *is* fair. He could be an heir. What is the Lair of Air? Did you see anything in the dreams that might apply?"

I gritted my teeth. "The Lair of Air... Is that not a mythical place from tales to entertain children? And *Air* and *Heir* are written differently but sound the same."

"And *hair* sounds alike, too." He pointed toward his own head. "Would hair as fair as mine be needed to open this?"

"I don't know!" I spun on my heel and paced back to the stairs. It was incomprehensible. We'd had time to figure out how to get past the dreams, but now, with the youth clearly breathing his last in the box, we had no time to unravel the puzzle, and yet urgency weighed down on me.

"Think, damn you, Ferranos. We cannot have come this far to fail when this close to success! We cannot let him die."

"I'm thinking, I'm thinking." I scrubbed my hands over my face. The verse made no sense. Nor did the youth's death. Someone had taken great pains to keep him safe. Why would they arrange things so someone they wished to protect would die when his rescuers arrived? It made no more sense than the verse.

Then it struck me. "It makes no more sense than the verse."

I scooped up Krotha's sword and lofted it to him. "The pommel. Smash the amber. Free him as you freed yourself!"

The Knight of Virtue caught the sword and stared at me for a moment as if I'd gone mad, but then raised the sword and smashed the hilt onto the amber. The lid cracked, and sharp amber shards flew. Krotha spat one out and struck again and again. He screamed as he did, then yelled, then grunted. Each blow chipped the amber as if it were ice. The divot grew. Cracks spread. And finally, with one mighty blow, he fractured the lid, and a quarter of it slid off to shatter on the dais.

The knight flung away the rest of the lid and reached down, but I grabbed his wrist. "A moment, Krotha."

The golden glow from the walls softened the shadows over the youth's face, but there was no doubt he'd been the man in the dreams. He lay there, naked save for amber dust and an amber disk on his forehead, his body unnamed, unscarred, and seemingly as vital as the day he'd lain down in the amber shell. I had the sense that he'd done so willingly and that the promises of those who had entombed him still rang in his ears.

Krotha slipped his wrist from my grasp easily, but did not reach into the box. "You fear more magick."

"Anticipate instead of fear." I bent down and studied him, especially the disk on his forehead. "The disk, if you look closely, the dreams run through it. I fear, were we to remove or upset it, it might take his mind with it."

"We are to waken him, aren't we?"

"We were drawn here for a purpose, and I do not yet feel any relief from that burden. Do you?"

He shook his head.

I scratched at the back of my neck. "I think, perhaps, we are standing in the Lair of Air. That in opening the box, we have brought him into it."

"You said the verse was nonsense."

"It was. For opening the box." I smiled slowly. "I believe whoever worked the magick to have the dreams guard him anticipated someone like you cleverly piercing the mystery of getting past them. It seems to me that they then laid a trap, which spoke to the vanity of that person."

"Who likely was going to be a vain Trafaramite."

"Indeed. The vain person would seek a solution as clever as outwitting the dreams, and no one would think that brute strength alone would solve that puzzle." I snorted. "In fact, few who could be that clever would be strong enough to shatter the lid as you did."

"Their contempt could have killed him."

"Or they might have presumed that the method for opening the sarcophagus would be known to his rescuers." I shrugged. "That is immaterial at the moment. My sense is that with new air, the youth will sleep normally and then waken as gently as he would otherwise. But this means we have work to do."

The knight frowned. "Such as?"

"It is all well and good, my friend, that you and I do not worry about food or drink, but the young man likely will wake very hungry. And perhaps he would like to clothe his nakedness."

"We might want to take care of that." Krotha crossed to the stairs and grabbed his shield. "Do you think the stones will still work to keep the Hollows away?"

"That is a very good question." I followed him to the surface. The stones still gave off their soft light, and Hollows lurked in the shadows, clearly quite wary of the magick. "I cannot tell how long the magick will continue to work."

The knight smiled. "I suppose, then, we should get the young man some clothing." He stepped up to the line and banged his sword on his shield a few times. The Hollows hissed and snarled in reply. Then he stepped forward and set himself.

I am not certain I ever really understood how special the Knights of Virtue were. Paragons, absolutely, and meant to inspire people, without a doubt; but how many got to see them in action? Not many, I suspected. They mostly saw the Knights on parade and at court, not as I saw Krotha now.

The Hollows came as quickly as they could, a shambling mass of stringy flesh, leathery skin, and yellowed bones, all wrapped in crocodile skins and whatever tattered cloth they could find in the swamp. A few carried weapons—old, rusted, and pitted things—but most came with fingers clawed and jaws agape. They intended to rip him limb from limb.

Krotha wanted no part of that. With the calculated ease of a farmer bringing in a harvest, he swept his sword low, splintering legs. He danced back as his falling kinsmen dashed their skulls to pieces on the paving stones. Swinging his shield wide, he battered one of the skeletons past, propelling it toward the line of stones. The Hollow slammed into it and then carried on through, reduced to bone dust, as if ground between unseen millstones.

Brushing dust from my sleeves, I leveled my staff and cast. My blue bolt sizzled through the crowd pressing Krotha, melting ribs and vaporizing spines. As those skeletons tumbled into a jumble of bones, what little vitality they gave up flowed into me. As with the others, it barely registered, though I did catch faint, faded glimpses of a golden land far away. Krotha harvested heads and pruned limbs. I blasted through bone. Had the Hollows carried any sense of who or what they had been, they might have fled, but they lacked even the basic sense of self that would have prompted them to desire continued existence.

Then again, oblivion had to be preferable to being a Hollow.

Krotha crushed the last skull with his sword's pommel, and the Hollows were no more. The bones crumbled into tiny grains, which the wind would carry off or a rain would wash into the swamp. The knight toed some of the cloth scraps, then poked makeshift crocodile armor. "Not really fitting for the youth."

"It will have to do until we find better. But they were really a distraction. We need to find food and water."

"I think we'll find food *in* the water, my friend." Krotha trotted over to where I'd lost my foot and dropped to a knee on the causeway. "There is a crocodile floating here with half its jaw missing."

He tugged it from the water, and I helped him drag the monster into the courtyard, despite my hip aching again. The knight cut it open and plucked something from the reptile's gullet. "Might need to patch it."

I caught my old boot, then tipped it over to pour out dark water. I removed my old foot and tossed it far into the swamp. It splashed, then a couple other things splashed. I found it easy and yet unsettling to imagine creatures fighting over that tidbit, which had once been part of me. Then again, the young man would be eating one of them, so I imagined it somehow made a sort of sense.

Krotha peeled the skin off the back and tail, then cut meat from both sides running all the way down the spine to the tip of the tail. "Do you think we can make a fire?"

"I doubt there is enough dry wood in this swamp to do that, but…" I squatted near the beast's head. "It looks as if the jaw muscles here are cooked."

"You mean *charred*."

"I never claimed to be a chef in my previous life. Now, if I might borrow your blade."

He handed me the short knife he'd been using to do the butchering. I sliced off a hunk of meat roughly the size of my fist, then stabbed through it with the blade. I slid the holed meat onto the tip of my staff, then moved away and grabbed the shaft in both hands. I began to cast my combat spell, but slowly and with great restraint. The staff glowed blue, and tiny tendrils of lightning played over the surface. They ran down and over the meat, causing it to lightly char and steam.

The scent wasn't that unpleasant, but I didn't find it particularly appetizing. Then again, not needing to eat apparently killed whatever part of me felt hungry. "I think this should do."

Krotha nodded and took back his knife. He scraped down the skin, then sighed. "We haven't the time to tan and dry this skin."

"You've done that before?"

"Crocodile, no. But once with a dragon. We dragged it back to Parnyr, and he had it made into armor." He smiled. "Mind, I can remember it being done, but I've not recovered the *how* of doing it."

"Well, let us hope we kill Hollows who were once poachers, and you recover that memory."

"Or a grand sorcerer for you."

"Better a chef."

"Or that." He deposited the skin near the entryway, then grabbed the carcass by the tail and started dragging it back toward the swamp. "No need to encourage others of its kind to come up here."

"Good idea." His efforts left a bloody smear in the courtyard, and the blood sank between the stones quickly. *Too quickly.* "Krotha, do you see this?"

"What?"

I dropped to a knee where the crocodile's body weight had scraped away a carpet of leaves and silt. The blood filled sigils carved deep into the stones.

Etched in the same style as the lettering on my tomb. "Is this…? I think it reads 'Balarion'?"

The Knight of Virtue abandoned his bloody burden and stood over me. "Yes, that is 'Balarion.' But…"

"What? What do you recall?"

"The name is familiar, as was his face. I don't believe I knew him, but knew *of* him. Whispers." He sighed. "I am the Knight of Truth. As such, I tended to avoid rumors and gossip. It would…"

"Gossip is a poison. It denies you clarity of mind." I rose to my feet. "I have a sense of it, too, a dark sense that does not seem to match the youth below, nor his dreams. A sense of foreboding. That you recall him from rumors suggests this might be justified."

Krotha shook his head, then descended into the lower chamber. I gathered the meat and the skin, then followed him. I set my cargo beside the stairs. Krotha stood next to the sarcophagus and stared down at the sleeping young man.

"He looks too innocent to be a threat, Ferranos."

"The innocent are the most threatening of all."

Krotha glanced up at me. "That's more cynical than I expected of you."

"To those who are inclined to see threats and conspiracies, people who appear innocent and uninvolved are simply people who have not exposed themselves yet." I opened my hands. "Think on it, Krotha. Someone hid this boy away here, and set snares for those who would resent and hate him. Does that not suggest that someone thought he was a threat?"

"You have a point. And clearly someone wanted him protected." The knight frowned. "And I have to think my compulsion to find this place is also to protect him."

"There is something else that concerns you, isn't there?"

"A sense, but no clear memory. The Knights of Virtue, we served King Parnyr and Alkindor. It was said, however, that he had another agent against which we were balanced. Could that agent be the one who hid the youth here? If that is true, why would I want to protect him?"

"I do not know, nor do I know why I am here and feel the same way you do." I shook my head. "I do not understand why anyone would consider my presence beneficial."

Krotha laughed. "If not for you, Ferranos, I'd be sitting on those stairs for an eternity wondering what I should do."

"But now we have to wonder what we are supposed to do for Balarion."

The moment I spoke the youth's name, his body jerked. His back arched, and he sucked in a huge, wheezing breath. Then he coughed and rolled over on his side. The stone fell from his forehead, and Krotha reached down and grabbed his shoulder.

The youth shuddered again, then looked up. His hand covered that of the knight. "By the gods…" Another racking cough. "Krotha, it is you, yes? Tell me it is."

"I am Krotha, yes…"

"Do you not remember me?" The youth twisted around and sat up. "You must remember."

The knight shook his head. "Truthfully, I do not."

"'Truthfully'… Well, it *is* you, then." The young man smiled happily. "I am Balarion. You served Alkindor at behest of my father."

"Your father?"

"Yes, King Parnyr." The youth nodded solemnly. "I am the bastard son of your lord and master."

CHAPTER 8

The disarming and even joyful smile on the youth's face as he proclaimed himself a bastard caught me off guard. I failed to recall the term ever having been used with pride. Moreover, his reference to "lord and master" meant he was claiming kinship with King Parnyr of Alkindor. The king had three children—two sons and a daughter—and if this Balarion was his bastard, his existence would have been a highly protected state secret.

Worry crinkled Krotha's brow. "You speak as though you know me."

"I do." The young man hesitated. "I mean, I know you as all of Alkindor does, and as all of Trafaram rejoices. I have seen you. You rode through my village once. We did not meet then, but I am honored now."

The knight nodded distractedly as his eyes narrowed. "And you claim to be Parnyr's child?"

The young man's smile drained away. "It is only what I have been told, and I scarce believe it myself, but those who brought me here told me the story, told me why it was necessary for me to be hidden. But now it must be safe, yes? And this is why you have come for me."

I stepped up onto the dais. "Perhaps, Balarion, we should explore this from back to front. Who brought you here?"

Balarion turned to face me, and I read no recognition in his eyes. "Two others of the Knights of Virtue, Zyritha of Shadows and Dhorrax of Haste. They told me that powerful interests had evil intent on my life. I am a flock warden. No one wished me ill, and this I protested to them. But they insisted and spirited me away in the night. From there, they passed me to small groups of people. I'd travel with them for a night or a week, only to be passed off to someone else. No one knew where I would be going, and some of the short jaunts seemed to backtrack—never directly, but we also never went in a straight line forward."

Krotha scratched his forehead. "Small groups, unconnected, unknowing about the larger plan, certainly makes sense for a journey conducted in secret."

"All knowledge hidden from everyone save the person providing the orders. And his recital addresses your earlier concern, Krotha." I looked at the young man. "Continue."

"We journeyed for a long time, I think. Zyritha had given me a powder to take with meals that dulled my senses. She said it was so those who might capture my essence would be confused as to my passage. After a time, we came here, to this chamber. I was given a last draught and bidden to lay down in this box, to sleep until it was safe for my return." He glanced from Krotha to me and back again. "This is why you are here, is it not? My father has sent for me?"

"Your father did not send for you." Krotha sighed and rested a hand on the boy's shoulder. "The world has changed."

"Your touch is so cold, Sir Krotha. Are you well?"

The Knight of Virtue looked over at me.

I softened my voice. "Balarion, Krotha and I were compelled by magick to come here and find you. To release you. We know not why, and at least for me, since the moment you stirred, the sensation that drove me has diminished. What had been a roaring fire is now the gentle heat from dying coals."

Krotha nodded. "For me as well."

I opened my arms. "As for us, well, much time has passed since you made your journey. Krotha and I have made a journey, too. Not just to get here.

We have stepped beyond the veil of life. This is why his touch is cold, and neither of us would be as you remember us exactly."

The knight slid his hand from the youth's shoulder. "And neither of us remembers all of what we once did, either. However, it seems apparent to both of us that much time has passed. Your father, Alkindor, they are long dead."

Balarion sat back, drawing his knees up against his chest and holding on to them tightly. "It is all gone? That cannot be."

"Perhaps, Balarion, you would share with Krotha what you recall of this, your resting place?"

"Of course, for I only arrived last night. Or it seemed like last night. We came at dusk into a valley with steep sides, forested. A stream ran through it, and built right there, at its heart, lay a stepped pyramid. I'd never seen anything so tall—man-made, that is. I'd seen mountains, and this must have quarried one down to a plain. We climbed up the sides to a flat court-yard and then down those stairs to this chamber." He frowned mightily. "You tell me much time has passed, but how much? For me, no time has passed—perhaps a month or two since I left my home. Maybe a season. But here, I have only lain for a night."

Krotha started to speak, but I held up a hand. "If you would, Balarion, come with us."

The youth, unconcerned and unembarrassed with his nakedness, climbed out of the amber box. Krotha steadied him as the stiffness of his limbs took time to drain. I lingered behind, reaching for the amber disk, which had rested upon his brow. I was uncertain as to its true nature or what magicks had been worked into it to keep him asleep, but I hoped I would someday be able to figure that out.

Thus, I lagged behind as they reached the top of the stairs. Balarion cried out, then his legs collapsed. Krotha caught him under his arms, then eased him to the courtyard floor. The young man knelt, then doubled over. Sobs racked his body.

I slid the stone into my pouch and stood opposite Krotha by the youth's side. The two of us stared out into the persistent gloom, openly hoping something would approach, attracted by the young man's grief. I definitely would have relished killing something, and I gathered from Krotha's expression that he shared my desire but was thinking in terms of dozens.

Balarion sat up, wiping away tears with his fingers. "This is... I never wanted to believe what they said."

I dropped to a knee. "What did they say? You refer to the Knights of Virtue, yes?"

He nodded. "Zyritha never said much. She just lurked."

Krotha grunted.

"But Dhorrax, he explained. He said that *forces* opposed my father. That his children, the princes and princess, were working against my father. They wished to overthrow him. Each was afraid the others would inherit, that Father would choose a favorite and bestow the throne of Alkindor to that chosen heir. The three of them would split the kingdom among them rather than risk having nothing at all. My father feared that they would use me, my very existence, against him. So I had to go away."

Krotha lifted his chin. "I never got on with his children, largely because they avoided truth as night terrors avoid sunlight."

Balarion hugged his arms around his belly. "The last night, the night I lay down to sleep, a messenger came and said the children were moving against my father. I protested, but the messenger said only if I was safe here could my father prevail against them. He said it would take time, but he could not have meant this much."

"And yet, my lord"—I added the honorific because it could hurt nothing—"much time has passed. Those you knew are but dust."

"Or like Ferranos and me."

Balarion shook his head. "I am not like you. They could have survived as I did."

I pointed to the night sky. "The stars do not lie. You know that. Centuries, even tens of centuries have passed since you slept. Your father is gone." "But he isn't, Ferranos." Balarion laid a hand on Krotha's armored thigh. "He yet lives. I can feel it. I know he is out there. He needs me. He awoke as I did, and without me, he cannot be saved."

"Is that possible, Ferranos?" The knight turned back toward the stairs and chamber below. "Could there have been a link between Balarion and Parnyr? Could it have lasted all this time?"

I held up my hands. "Too many facts that are unknown and unknowable, Krotha. If Balarion *is* or *was* Parnyr's child, the blood they share would make for an easier link. That concept of *contagion* is common in all magicks. But this would have been higher magicks, requiring skill and training I have no way of understanding."

"That you remember, my friend."

"True, but unless we're going to find a Hollow of some high master of magicks for me to kill and absorb, the likelihood of my learning that is nil. It is also immaterial." I tapped a finger against my chin. "Balarion, you feel this connection even now?"

The youth nodded and pointed past the building, toward the east. "I have a sense I want to go that way."

"I will go with you." Krotha offered Balarion a hand. "The Knights of Virtue were sworn to serve the king and court of Alkindor. I was led here by old oaths. I am yours to command."

Balarion stood and then looked at me. "And you, Ferranos? Did old oaths lead you here as well?"

"I don't honestly know, my lord. And I don't know that they command me to follow you, but curiosity begs it of me."

"How so?"

"You know who you are. You remember the world. I do not." I smiled slightly. "I believe our journey just might make me whole again. That quest is one well worth pursuing."

* * *

We made preparations for travel, which included Krotha surrendering his tabard, and I my boots, to our young charge. I didn't mind, as they'd not proved terribly useful to me, and if my feet became torn up, the flask solved that problem. With the tabard wrapped around him, Balarion looked less the herder than perhaps a squire.

Balarion wolfed down the crocodile meat with nary a complaint, which boded well for the journey. He set the pace as we traveled, clearly in a hurry but not incautiously so. Krotha warned him about Hollows and suggested he hang back. Balarion countered by selecting a passably stout piece of wood to defend himself, and I had no doubt he would further arm himself as opportunities arose.

We set off to the east through the swamp, and even it appeared to welcome Balarion's passage. The fog drained off and with it the sour stench of rotting plants. The herder found small pools of clear water—none of which I'd noticed before, but then again, I had not been looking for them.

Balarion regaled us with stories of his life, which made up for their lack of drama by including incredibly trivial details of village life. The wolf dream reflected the most dangerous experience the youth had ever had, and the wolves had appeared so big and so ferocious because Balarion fought them before he'd reached puberty.

The only aspect of his life that did not fit was that his village, rather fortuitously, played host to a succession of scholars and wise men who tarried there for a week or a month, teaching the village's children. No one had appeared to single out Balarion for special treatment, but he'd been a keen student. He'd shown a great deal of curiosity about the wider world and yet offered no evidence of wanting to explore it.

This struck me as utterly incongruous, so I asked him about it.

"I had responsibilities, Ferranos, to my family—I guess those I believed to be my family—and to the village. People needed the wooldron fur and flesh, and someone had to keep the wolves at bay."

"But didn't you even think about going away?"

The youth scratched his head. "I was never one given to daydreaming. I asked my uncle, I remember that. He promised that one year we'd go to a big town for market day. The idea of going to Vataria, the crown jewel of Trafaram... It would have taken too long. I had my duty."

"Yes, to the village and to the people." I raised an eyebrow. "Out of curiosity, what was the farthest you traveled from home? In miles. Excepting the trip that brought you here."

"No more than ten?" The youth's eyes tightened. "What are you thinking?"

"I am thinking that if you are not Parnyr's child from the wrong side of the sheets, it was intended you would be taken as such. The scholars teaching you. Krotha, have you heard of that happening in any other village in Alkindor?"

"A town, perhaps, on a river, where travelers would stay for a time and earn their bread while they waited for a caravan or a flatboat?" The knight shrugged. "Uncommon, but not unique."

"And your lack of wanderlust, my lord." I nodded toward Balarion and farther east. "You have taken to this trek as a seasoned traveler might, with none of the hesitation one might expect from a person who has never traveled before. And, no, the journey here would not count, since you said you were drugged for most of it. I daresay you remember little more about it than you have told us."

"If I recall anything else of use, I shall let you know."

Krotha looked over his shoulder. "So you think he *is* Parnyr's get?"

"Most likely. A small chance he was made to appear that way to protect someone who truly was." I smiled. "You were at court. Did the king have mistresses?"

"I was not always by the king's side, my friend, and when I was, I refrained from listening to gossip, as I said before." The knight shrugged with a clank. "Some of my absences were long enough that someone could have borne the king a child and I would have known nothing of it."

Balarion frowned. "But he entrusted to you the most important things, Sir Krotha, to you and the other Knights of Virtue."

"The king did not rely on us alone, Balarion. He had his armies. He had other agents who fulfilled his will, as I mentioned. We were just the most visible, to give the people hope and heart. To suggest it was otherwise would be to deny the truth."

"Sir Krotha has the right of it, Balarion. The fact that your journey began with Knights of Virtue and continued with others underscores the truth." I nodded slowly. "And it tells me that your story is true. You are the last of the line of Parnyr, and if what you know of the king is true, you are duty bound to rescue him. Now, let us make all haste in aiding you to save your father."

CHAPTER 9

Balarion quickly became the leader of our trek. Neither Krotha nor I remembered the world from before—not in any useful way, in any event—but the young man did. This provided him a focus. Combined with his sense of urgency, he drew us onward, pushing himself hard. He would have gone harder, but Krotha and I could both read in him the weariness that neither of us felt, and we contrived to stop at any of the fire circles where we could kindle flames, which provided us some sanctuary.

To his credit, the young man did not surrender to the despair that almost anyone else would have. Part of that clearly came from the calling he felt within. I saw that in the way he would look wistfully toward the east in unguarded moments. He reminded himself that he wasn't where he needed to be and resolved to close the distance.

Yet, for him, travel was not the only thing he thought about. The very first evening away from the pyramid, he turned to Krotha, his eyes tight. "I shall require of you a service, sir knight."

"How ever may I help you?"

"I need you to teach me to fight."

Krotha unburdened himself of an armful of firewood—for the fires that warmed the undead proved dreadfully inadequate for cooking the food required by the living. "I am proud to act as your sword arm, my lord."

"If I cannot fight, I am a burden, not a help, to my father." The youth smiled. "I will do my best to quickly learn the ways of killing so we can both save my father."

I arched an eyebrow. "Perhaps he should first learn the ways to avoid dying."

"Yes, that too, Ferranos." Balarion hefted his cudgel. "Perhaps teach me a little now, while we have the last of the sun."

Krotha made to protest, but I held up a hand. "I will gladly set about building the fire and seeing if there is something suitable for food to fill Balarion's belly."

The Knight of Virtue frowned. "I would not reduce you to a servant, Ferranos."

"I have offered, friend, so it is not a place you have assigned me. Besides, he needs your mentoring. We have no idea what we shall face when we find Alkindor."

The warrior sighed. "Yes, a quick lesson, then."

I gathered firewood and built a material fire within the same pit I'd ignited previously for Krotha and myself. I felt that hiding the flames that nurtured us within those that would sustain Balarion was for the best. The youth had accepted our condition easily enough, but I did not trust that all the living would feel the same way.

I left Krotha teaching Balarion about balance and energy as I stepped out into the night. I relished the darkness. I could see well enough in starlight to travel, yet the cold light robbed the world of color, so the dull pallor of my flesh didn't remind me every moment that I was dead.

And I might have said "every heartbeat," save that I didn't have one. I would have suspected that such knowledge would have frightened or saddened me, but I found it to be an incontrovertible fact of my condition. Worry or grief would not change it and thus seemed a waste.

The other curious thing that came to mind was the lack of umbrage I felt at being reduced to the role of a servant. Given the nature of our group, the role would logically fall to me. Balarion, being of royal blood and having his sense of our mission, naturally rose to the position of leader. Krotha's strong arm would keep us safe; and now he had the additional role of teaching Balarion how to defend himself. Krotha accepted that as easily as he had orders from the king.

I, it seemed clear, had also been a servant of some sort. That can be said of any person, for we all have those whose station is above ours and whose orders we must follow. Even the king is governed by the whim of his people—or should be, if it is his desire to remain securely on the throne. So it struck me that in accepting my new role, I simply acknowledged what had been the truth of my previous life. That I felt nothing in doing it seemed to verify the justice of it.

As I ruminated, I also traveled through sparse grasses. Since we'd emerged from the swamp and moved upland, things had dried out considerably. Trees gathered in small stands—we sheltered near one of these. Other tree stands had been reduced to stumps by axes, though the silvered wood seemed well-aged and I had little concern over any contact with the living.

Twenty yards off, something moved, then froze. A springheel. I lifted my staff and snapped off a spell. The coruscating ball of azure lightning struck the creature full in the flank and exploded. The long-eared creature gave a shrill shriek, and I ran toward it.

Or what was left of it. In this case, most of the skull—defleshed—a front paw, and scraps of bloody fur. The magick that could eventually burn through a Hollow did its work far too well on so tiny a target. And while the bits of flesh I located had been well-cooked, they'd be hard-pressed to amount to a mouthful, much less a meal.

Fortunately, the local springheels had bred with great gusto and apparently feared little in the way of predation. I found another, shifted my aim to a foot in front of it, and let fly. The sizzling blue ball hit the ground and sank halfway into it before exploding. The beast flew another dozen feet, landed hard, and bounced all loose-limbed. I found it hidden behind a tuft of grass, fur singed but otherwise little worse for wear. In fact, the spell had only stunned it, so I grabbed the hind feet and dashed its brains against a rock. Two of its fellows joined it, and triumphant, I returned to the fire.

In my absence, which had been largely unnoticed, Krotha and Balarion had gone from simple instruction on stance and balance to actually sparring. Krotha, in his armor, stood no chance of being injured by Balarion's club, but *only* because of the armor. Balarion, his sweat-soaked body glowing in the firelight, moved fast and with such agility that Krotha's attempts to block his blows might deflect them, but not fully. I caught no sense that the Knight of Truth was holding back or humoring his charge. Nor did I get the sense that his lack of life hindered him, for he fought Balarion with all strength and vigor he'd exhibited against the Hollows.

I dumped the springheels next to the fire. "It appears, my lord, you learn very quickly."

Krotha held up a hand to forestall another attack. "You do not mark it a sign of how good an instructor I am?"

"In truth, Krotha, your tutelage would be the source of all the skill he exhibits." I sat on a rock, plucked up the first carcass, gutted it, and cut the skin off with my knife. "Woe be unto any wolf hungry for wooldron flesh."

Balarion dropped to a knee, sweat dripping from his face. "Wolves, or the human equivalent."

"Or Hollow." Krotha sheathed his sword and came over to the fire. "When we find more of them, we should be able to take their weapons and properly outfit you."

"Yes, the world is in a sad state." The youth wiped his brow with the back of his hand. "I did not expect I should ever see it."

I skewered the first bits of meat on a sharpened stick and set it above the fire. "You sound as if you did expect to see this. How is that possible?"

He shook his head. "Not this, not so much change. It's just..." Balarion's forehead wrinkled. "Those scholars who visited my village, there was one among them, a big man with a bushy white beard and flowing white hair. Big eyebrows and blue eyes. He came several times and was a philosopher. He would talk about the world and our place in it, not as Alkindorans, but as people who had a duty to our king, our nation, and to the world.

He would tell parables and fables where the people were wooldron and evil people were wolves—usually dressed in wooldron's clothing."

He looked up at us. "For example, once he told a story of a wolf digging a den high on a hill, and the wolf kept telling the wooldron who lived below that they had nothing to fear from him. He just wanted to dig his den, and he would leave them in peace. Then he cut down trees on the hillside to build rafters and posts so his den wouldn't collapse. And the wooldron accepted this as only right and proper. Next, he scraped across the line of the hillside to create terraces to plant seeds—to grow food, he said, so he would not be tempted to eat the wooldron. He begged the wooldron to help him. He told them that they could have all the spare food, because he would not eat much.

"So his neighbors did his bidding. They cut down trees for his den. They cleared land for his planting. They planted where he directed, then uprooted plants and put them elsewhere at the wolf's whim. They did so because he seemed nice, and yet the occasional flash of fang reminded them what he truly was."

Balarion sighed. "And then when the rains fell, the water ran down the hill. There were no trees to hold the earth together. The unplanted fields became mud and ran with the water. A torrent, it washed over the wooldron, burying them up to their necks in mud. So they cried out to the wolf to come help them, as they had helped him—for his den had weathered the storm and he had remained high and dry. But the wolf just descended the hill and slaughtered them all, because he was a wolf and they were wooldron."

I handed Krotha the second spitted springheel. "What was the lesson you took from this?"

"No matter how reasonable one sounds, or how likable a person seems, the only way to know what they are thinking is to view things from their point of view. What makes sense for them is the truth, not how what they tell you makes sense for you."

"A wise man, this philosopher of yours." Krotha nodded sagely. "What was his name?"

"Parnaeus."

Krotha's expression slackened. "You're certain?"

"Quite." The youth blushed. "When he talked of wolves and wooldron, he would look to me for confirmation of a wolf's nature. I remember him very well. I hung on his every word. Ferranos, you had asked why I had not left my village. Parnaeus had expressed how our duty to family and nation and one another outweighed our personal desires. Were it not for him, I might well have wandered, but whenever I considered it, I recalled his wisdom."

I brought the third tiny beast to the fire. "What is it, Krotha?"

"Parnyr. The description Balarion has given could easily have described the king."

"And hundreds of other men."

"But hundreds of other men did not sign poetry they'd written with that name." Krotha shook his head. "The king, when touched by a service we had performed, would write a poem to memorialize what we had done. He would sign them 'Parnaeus,' citing his shadow self and its penchant for fancy."

I turned the first springheel over to cook the other side. "What else do you recall Parnaeus teaching you, Balarion? What were you thinking of when you mentioned you'd not expected to live to see how the world had changed?"

The youth rose and rubbed a hand over his forehead. "It was the story of an old wolf who ruled over an enormous pack, and he had three children, each of whom was very ambitious. They each wanted the whole of the pack, and he knew that would destroy them *and* the pack. So he said he was going away, to a place beyond three locked gates. He divided the pack into equal thirds and gave each of his children a key, one to the first gate and so on. He left, and they locked the gates behind him. And as he imagined, the children, each in their own way, ruined the pack and the territory they'd been given. And yet it could have been worse, but each key holder feared the power of the others, so they did not go to war. They struck a balance and prevented the complete destruction of the pack."

I stared into the fire. "And he described this sort of ruination?"

"Hinted, really, then asked each of us children how we thought they had ruined the pack. Being kids, we gave vent to our fears and strove to top the horrors others had described. I don't recall anyone talking about the dead walking the earth, but I described it as being overrun by 'bad wolves.'" He folded his arms over his chest. "He used the terror of it all to emphasize how we have a duty to one another to stop such a thing from happening."

I glanced at him. "And was there a resolution to this fable? Did everyone live happily ever after?"

Balarion nodded. "One day a young wolf won the key from each of the other wolves. He unlocked the gates and invited the old wolf back to the pack. The children were put aside, and the old wolf returned and made things once again as they had been in the past. Which, now that I say it aloud, seems to describe a mission for me. If Parnaeus *was* the king, did he foresee the conflict with his children and in this way let me know my role in his return?"

I turned to the Knight of Virtue. "Could that be so, Sir Krotha? Not the insight, but the method in which he would deliver his message to Balarion?"

"I always saw to the heart of things. The king said I always saw to the truth of things. With others, he could be subtle, as needed to suit their nature. Zyritha of Shadows always liked a degree of ambiguity." He shrugged. "Though to the other point about his children, their vying for his attention and favor, each to the exclusion of the others—a blind man could have seen their antics for what they were. And Parnyr, he could have planned for what would have eventually happened. As he prepared Balarion, he could have used a similar story to trick his other children into sending him beyond the gates."

"So Alkindor could yet exist, split among your siblings, Balarion." I turned toward the east and tried to see into the distance, or the future. "To us it falls, then, to find the keys and bring the king back to his rightful place in the world."

CHAPTER 10

Our trek took us east, into lands unknown. We passed from dry hillsides thatched with golden grasses into a tortured land of red earth, slivered grey rocks, and plants that covered themselves in finger-length needles. The plants, which grew to the height of a man and often had a half dozen arms, took note of our passing. They oriented toward us, and if we tarried, a limb would move, and the plant would swat us with one of their flat pads.

I was a recipient of the first strike, which left a handful of needles buried in my flesh and decorated the plant with dull grey threads from my cloak. I felt no real pain, though whatever toxins the needles released stiffened my muscles. A drink from the flask countered that effect, and Balarion drew the needles out carefully.

"I am less concerned about the needles than the sense that this path is maintained."

Krotha, who'd found us a clearing in which to pause, nodded. "We're being channeled downhill and then into that gully over there. That's clearly been eroded by whatever rains fall here, but this path was not."

"But what would live out here and cultivate a trail for an ambush?" I looked around. "A highwayman would starve here."

Balarion pointed toward the side of the clearing. "That looks like scat, and this might have started as a game trail and yard for something that eats these plants, perhaps?"

"That scat is dried-out and old."

"Perhaps herds migrate between seasons, Ferranos."

I nodded. "Fair enough assumption. So will the hunters be waiting for us, or will they be somewhere else, hunting something else?"

Krotha donned his helmet. "One way to find out."

"Wait, Sir Krotha." Balarion rested a hand on the man's armored shoulder. "I don't doubt your courage, but the last fire of the sort you favor was two days back. And if I die, there will only be one fire for me, and if I rise from it, it will be as smoke. It seems that if we expect the local denizens to be waiting on the north side of that gully, then walking down through it is a bit foolish."

The knight's voice echoed from within his helmet. "What would you suggest?"

Balarion pointed directly north. "If we chop through the plants here, and again over there, our fight will be on even ground, not with us conceding the heights to our attackers. We choose the battlefield—a lesson you have drilled into me."

The knight nodded, then turned and used his shield to move aside limbs enough to let him chop down at the plant's base. Greenish fluid oozed from the wounds, smelling of fresh-cut grass and the bitter scent of singed hair. The sturdy plant required a half dozen cuts before it fell, and each blow shook loose one or more of the broad, flat pads. Because the needles at the base were shorter than those farther up, the pad pointed its new end toward the ground, and tiny rootlets, white and wriggling like worms, sought the earth's warmth.

Using sticks, Balarion and I batted away pads from the path Krotha cut for us. He broke through the plant wall quickly enough, and the sparse growth of the flora elsewhere lent credence to the idea that the path we'd been on had been deliberately laid out.

Rather disturbingly, the other plants nearby began to vibrate and track us more closely. I hated to imagine that we'd just cut our way into a living forest that considered us murderers. The vibrations shook plants thirty yards away at the very least, and likely farther. Presumably, the plants intended to scare us from them, but that wasn't the only value to their signal.

Krotha pointed to the ridgeline from which we'd feared an ambush. "If there are others about, the plants having the shakes could alert them to our presence. Over to the rocks quickly!"

We moved as fast as we could, which was with more speed than prudence. Krotha bashed his way past several of the needletrees. Balarion deftly ducked and twisted away from their vengeful ripostes. I fared not as well, catching one slap on the left side of my face, half blinding me.

Unthinking, I stabbed my staff into the plant's trunk and cast a spell. The bolt of blue energy passed instantly into the needletree and exploded it, casting green pulp and ragged bits in all directions. A sticky, acrid pulp splashed over my face and body, and likely would have choked me had I actually needed to breathe.

"They've stopped moving, Ferranos. They fear your magick more than they do my sword."

I trotted to my companions. "Your cuts give them a chance to grow and spread. The magick does not. Instead of trying to frighten us away, they hope we give them no further notice."

"Mind your step here, Ferranos." Balarion had braced himself halfway up the last rise and offered me a hand. "Big steps, that's it."

"Thank you." I topped the rise and came to a flat area that someone had clearly prepared for launching an ambush down into the gulley. They'd placed large rocks on the upper edge, either to act as cover or simply to roll down on whatever ran below. A bit farther back lay piles of bleached bones and a couple of firepits ringed with blackened stones.

Except for one, toward which I headed immediately. "This is a welcome find." I inserted my right hand and kindled the spirit fire. "If we are to fight, this is a good place for it."

Balarion toed a couple of the bones. "Wooldron, or close to them, but larger. Some other things mixed in. They were butchered here to feed the hunters. They let these creatures get into the gulley, then rolled rocks down on them. Cut marks on the bones from butchery, and these bones are cracked for the marrow."

Krotha pulled off his helmet. "Bones don't look like they've been scavenged, all nice and neat in a pile."

"So we only have to worry about the things that killed them, not the things that *eat the dead*?" I forced levity into my voice, and likely looked the buffoon with the needletree's pad still stuck to my face. I wrenched it off and, with the third try, managed to throw it away, then set about plucking needles from my fingers with my teeth.

I'd made a little progress when they found us, the creatures I later learned to call Yjatka. Slender and gangling of limb, with bulbous heads and animal skins to clothe them, they came at us from the east and north. They'd covered their pasty white flesh with an earthen pigment, which hid them well during their approach, and they skittered low and fast on their final attack. I would like to suggest that I saw them first, but they had approached from my blind side and, until they let out a piercing shriek at the last second, been as silent as death.

The one who attacked me thrust a stone-tipped spear through my left thigh. He yipped triumphantly, a keening cry that rose sharply in pitch, then died as my left hand closed around his throat. I squeezed, punching the remaining needles all the way into his flesh, then twisted my wrist and ripped. Fluid, warmer, darker, and more metallic-smelling than the needletree pulp, gushed over me. The Yjatka trembled and jerked as the needletrees had, then fell loose-limbed as I cast him aside.

Krotha lashed out with his shield, battering a leaping Yjatka aside. His sword came up and around, splitting the next one from crown to breastbone. That creature sank to its knees, then flopped back as Krotha wrenched his sword free of its body. He parried the thrust of a spear, then came around with a shield strike that crushed a third attacker's skull.

Balarion, clad only in a tabard and boots, wielding a wooden cudgel, did not shy from the assailants. He twisted away from a spear thrust, then struck a backhanded blow against the Yjatka. Teeth flew and blood sprayed. Before his assailant could hit the ground, Balarion grabbed the spear in his left hand, then brought the club down in a fearsome strike that caved in the rear of his attacker's skull.

He threw the club at another attacker, then brought the spear up and around, the tip quivering. He parried a thrust wide, then stabbed his spear through the next Yjatka's belly. He pulled it free again and whipped it up and around, slashing an attacker across his pale chest.

My staff came up, and another magickal bolt flew. This one caught a Yjatka in the face, burning away everything from the bridge of his nose on up. As he died, I felt a jolt. His soul evaporated and bled into me. I caught a fleeting vision of a grey life. The Yjatka's greatest accomplishment in life had been rolling rocks onto desert roundhorns; and his most fearful moment came as my spell devoured his head.

Krotha's blade came around in a bloody arc, bisecting a Yjatka from right shoulder to left hip—severing the right arm completely in the process. The Knight of Virtue wore a smile as broad as the dead man's open wound. His eyes widened as he, too, drank in the souls of those he had slain.

A heartbeat later, the Yjatka whose throat I'd ripped out died, and his frightfully tiny life burned through my consciousness as a dying star burns through the night sky.

Balarion's spear clattered to the ground as he dropped to a knee and pressed both hands to his head. "What is this? What is this?"

Krotha crossed to the youth immediately, for he was not hampered by a spear stuck through his leg. "My lord, are you hurt?"

"No. I don't know." He looked up, eyes wide and face haunted. "These things. I saw their lives. It's like they are in me."

Krotha shot me a look. "Is that possible?"

"I don't know." I reached down and pushed the spear a bit farther through my thigh. That gave me enough of the spear to grab and snap off the head. "He's not one of us, so I don't know. My lord, can you describe it more completely? Does it hurt?"

"No, not physical pain." He closed his eyes and rubbed a hand over his forehead. "I feel their emotions, their fear and excitement. The first one has—had—a family. The other one was afraid. You melted his brother's head."

Krotha recovered his helmet. "It is for him as it is for me, but he's clearly not dead."

"I agree." I started twisting the spear haft to screw it back out of my leg. "But this could be good. You and I get stronger, more vital. And if we are killed, we would reappear here. Perhaps it will be the same for you, my lord."

Balarion shot me a sidelong glance. "As hopeful as you make that sound, I have no desire to learn if you are correct."

I frowned. "My lord, how many did you kill?"

"Two." He pointed at them.

"Krotha, I saw him slash a third. Did one get away?"

The Knight of Virtue trotted out to the north and dropped to a knee. "We have a blood trail, heading northeast."

The youth looked up. "Both of them lived in a canyon. There's a pool of water and a waterfall, a little village."

"If it supported a band of eight hunters, it's not so little." I pulled the spear free and discarded it. "Do we run, Krotha?"

"We do, my friend, but toward him. If we can overtake him before he warns the others, we make our lives safer."

I took a pull on my flask and watched the hole in my thigh close. "Then let's move. Far better to be the hunter than the hunted."

* * *

Balarion coursed ahead of us, far more the wolf than a flock warden. He ran with ease and even some joy. I would have ascribed it to the pleasure of being free after millennia of being trapped in that amber tomb, but for him, he'd slept for only a night and been released less than a week ago. No, this was how he faced every day, and his pleasure served as an antidote to the world's ruined nature.

We gained on our prey. The Yjatka fell several times. Once, he scraped past a needletree, leaving it anointed with his blood. That slowed him down. He began dragging his left foot. Finally, I saw him slip over a small hillock, scarcely fifty yards ahead of us.

Balarion reached the point where the Yjatka had disappeared, and he crouched. Krotha ran up after him, and I brought up the rear. My leg functioned fine—it wasn't the reason I slowed. Just the grim glances the two of them exchanged suggested that what lay beyond wasn't good.

The path descended steeply into a canyon. Our quarry scrambled along it, dropping past cutbacks and sliding even lower. Had we a convenient rock to roll down, I had no doubt we could have splashed him over the ochre earth, but that would have done us little good. Because up to the north, a series of huts on stilts and some caves dug into either canyon wall housed a moderate village built on wide sandy beaches beneath a cascading waterfall. Spring flooding wouldn't reach the caves, and the pool into which the water flowed held enough fish that I imagined the Yjatka farmed them.

I turned to Krotha. "No telling how many live in the caves. I would guess, given the light color of their skin, they prefer the darkness. The band we encountered likely responded to the alarm."

The Knight of Truth nodded. "Couple of side trails could have led to caves and outposts. They could have taken us for their roundhorns and got more than they bargained for."

"There's something else." Balarion pointed at the waterfall and the mist rising from where the water foamed into the pool. "There's a cave back there."

I nodded. "Bones warding the approaches on either side. Bones that would get washed away with flooding, so they're replaced and, unless I miss a guess, arranged very specifically. See, the skulls, they face toward the cave, threatening the thing inside."

Balarion smiled. "They must think it intelligent; otherwise, why would it be scared by bones? Think it's a ghost? Something worse?"

"It must be fearsome, if they have not killed it yet." Krotha pointed down toward the village, where the ambush's survivor had pulled himself from the river and was crawling across the sand. "A mystery we're not going to solve, since we lost the race. He'll raise an alarm."

"We'd best get going." Balarion stood. "And not back the way we came, I think."

I turned toward our back trail. "I think we have a problem, my friends."

Krotha had been right. The side trails led to small garrison posts. A little band of Yjatka had let us pass and trailed us. One of them—I'd like to think of him as the best hunter among the group—had launched a spear. It struck me high in the chest and punched out my back. As I suggested we had a problem, I pitched backward. The protruding spearpoint held me two feet off the ground, the shaft pointing toward the sun.

And then, for me, the world ceased to exist.

DARK SOULS

MASQUE of VINDICATION

CHAPTER 11

I found myself seated at the fire burning above the gorge where we'd been attacked. The Yjatka bodies had vanished, though bones lay scattered amid the forest of needletrees. This disturbed me because I'd reemerged at the fire almost immediately after I fell, the spear wound closing and needles still stuck in my face. The carnivorous plants had had little time to consume the bodies, but they'd done a wonderful job of it. I wondered if the needletrees could consume me such that I would never return, or would return over and over again so they could spend an eternity consuming me.

Thrusting such concerns aside, I set off down the path I'd so recently traveled. I had no trouble following the tracks of our previous passage. They'd faded not at all in the sun and light breeze. This time I spotted the side trails Krotha had mentioned. I followed them back to the outposts he had theorized existing and used my magick to sterilize them.

When I reached the spot where I'd gone down, bisected bodies and pooled blood attested to the hard battle my companions had waged. In trailing those who had struck us from behind, I guessed that there had been a half dozen Yjatka in the hunting party. The sum of the parts Krotha and Balarion had left behind added up to seven individuals. The fact that no spears remained suggested my friends had retreated in good order, though the only path left open to them would have been down into the canyon.

One look confirmed my assumption. Warrior bodies lay on the sand, with women and children straightening limbs and raising their voices in keening lamentations. A couple of wounded Yjatka warriors had been dragged to the shade of the stilted huts to have their lopped limbs bandaged. Others stood guard at the cave mouths, spears at the ready, while a knot of older warriors gathered toward the north end of the canyon, well shy of the bone barriers, their attention and spears pointed toward the cave.

Clearly my companions had fought their way to the cave. I had to hope they'd escaped with minimal injuries. I had no idea if Krotha's flask would help Balarion, but I had to hope so. If Krotha had somehow succumbed to wounds, I could expect him to be trotting up behind me soon. I cast a glance in that direction, but saw no sunlight flashing silver from his armor.

I decided in an instant that I could not afford to wait on the possibility that they'd gotten him. There was no telling how long it would take for the Yjatka to gather their courage to attack into the cave. While I might not have the sort of power needed to wipe them out in one fell stroke, the fact that, even when slain, I would return should make me almost as scary as whatever they'd trapped in the cave.

Moreover, they might have had enough of battling for the day. They'd lost a significant portion of their warriors and hunters. Perhaps they'd let me pass if I showed them I intended to do them no further harm. With this hope in mind, I began my descent into the canyon. I made no attempt to hide my approach, and walked slowly and serenely—clearly of benign intent.

I even believed I was succeeding, for the young guards at the nearest cave withdrew into its shelter when they noticed me.

Then one of the grieving females picked up a rock.

* * *

Soaked to the skin, I stepped into the recess beyond the waterfall. It began as a natural formation, with the rock worn smooth by eons of water splashing over it, but in the center, a narrow doorway had been cut into the stone.

Artisans had chiseled words above it, but in the half dark I had a hard time making out the lettering. A short corridor led into a round chamber, faintly reminiscent of the place we'd found Balarion.

A dome had been cut twenty feet high into the ceiling, and black pillars supported the mountain above. Red rock, polished until it reflected as if water, formed a round dais beneath the dome. A light shone down on the center, trapping a woman in a golden column. She knelt on one knee, her leather armor red and trimmed in black. She bore a curved sword in each hand and had them crossed over her chest. Her head had been lowered. Her long brown hair and its shadows hid her face.

Krotha noticed me first. "You took your time, Ferranos."

I gestured vaguely beyond the curtain of water. "I made each journey as quickly as I could. I found the natives...*hostile*."

"How many times did they get you?"

"Three, four. One loses count." I smiled. "One old warrior killed me twice, and then his heart exploded from fright when I returned again."

"It's good to have you back." Krotha, who had stripped himself of his armor and been polishing it, slapped me on the back. "Balarion is napping."

"Was he hurt?"

"No." The Knight of Virtue chuckled. "He may have been a flock warden, but he fights as if he were one of the Knights."

"I take that as a good sign." I turned to look at the woman. "What do we have here?"

"Phylasina, one of the Knights. Of Fidelity." He frowned. "She doesn't appear to be one of *us*. Perhaps that light has done to her what the box did for our young companion. Must have. I seem to recall her having been a bit more talkative than she is now."

Sarcasm tinged his words, but I did not ask for further elaboration. I walked around the dais, looking for an inscription, but saw nothing. "Fidelity requires something else to which to be faithful. Perhaps the key to unlocking her is something else, someone else."

"I think there's more than one key to this lock." Krotha approached the dais, but did not set foot on it. "There are blood spots on the ground. Likely from those things outside. I assume hostile attempts to enter this place result in her being freed to defend. It would explain why they set up those bones to keep Phylasina back."

"It also suggests there's something to defend here. Might just be her, but I doubt it. What did Balarion think?"

"He thought we should wait for you." Krotha returned to his armor and set to cleaning it again. "Those things might not amount to much, but he's absorbed a great deal of their vitality. I think it was overwhelming."

"Yes, I can see that. By the way, they think of themselves as the Yjatka. That much I got from them. And perhaps a recipe for a fish stew, though I have incomplete knowledge of a few ingredients."

"Good thing we don't have to eat."

"But Balarion does, and likewise your Phylasina."

"Not mine, that one. Never was."

An odd memory came to me unbidden. "For some reason, I remember her name being linked with that of Prince Dolared."

Krotha looked up from his task. "Because she is Fidelity, the court trusted her and entrusted things to her, Dolared especially."

"You did not get along with her?"

"No serious problems, but I am the Knight of Truth. I am loyal to Truth. She is loyal to people, which means our aims and purposes at times did not agree."

"Faithful to people." I ran a hand across my jaw. "I wonder…"

I crossed to where Balarion lay and gently wakened him. He smiled when he saw me, then rubbed sleepsand from his eyes. "How long have you been here?"

"Only just arrived. And I need your help."

"Anything."

I slipped the stone that had rested on his brow from my satchel. "I believe you are the person who can awaken her. As this stone kept you asleep, I think it may be instrumental in helping you rouse her."

He stood and stretched. "What do you want me to do?"

"I am not wholly certain. Perhaps because it laid upon your forehead, you should press it to hers?"

Balarion accepted the stone from me and approached the woman. He mounted the dais and circled her just outside the golden light. He glanced at the stone, then edged it into the glow. Some of the gold bled into the amber stone, and a rune appeared—a diamond shape with two legs below and a pitched roof above. He looked at me, but I just shook my head.

He continued around her and, when behind her, smiled. "Here, at the back of her neck, where her hair has fallen away, it's exposed her skin. She has a symbol tattooed there, just like the one on the stone. Do you think?"

"Try it."

As Balarion brought the stone toward her, Krotha drew his sword and edged near the dais. The youth's hand did not tremble. The rune glowed brightly as he reached out and gingerly settled the stone on her flesh. He released it, then stepped back.

The light intensified, and the edges of the cylinder bent as radiance poured into the stone. The luminescence even seemed to swirl as if water draining into a pipe. It filled the stone, and when the amber glowed like the midday sun, the light flooded into her through the rune.

Her head snapped back, and gold played through her eyes. It glowed from within her ears and nostrils. It pulsed down her neck and throat. Her arms slowly slid to her sides, the twin swords rasping sibilantly against each other.

Krotha dragged Balarion off the dais.

The woman half rose from her crouch, then shook violently, casting the stone off her neck. Her knees buckled, and she dropped down onto them, but never lost hold of her slender blades. Her chest heaved as she began breathing, and she looked around as if she'd been daydreaming for centuries and only just returned to reality.

She glared at me, then doubled that scowl when she set eyes upon Krotha. I drew back, bringing up my staff, and Krotha raised his sword into guard position. I thought certain she was going to attack one or both of us, but then her gaze landed on Balarion.

She averted her gaze and again crossed her swords over her chest. "My lord Balarion, you have come. I have waited faithfully for you."

Balarion stepped fully clear of Krotha's shadow. "How do you know me?"

"It is my nature. Krotha Truthteller will confirm it. I am Phylasina, the ever faithful. I was charged with the duty of helping you. There is nothing in this world that can prevent me from acquitting this charge."

I made my way around the dais and recovered the stone. "I am Ferranos, so we all know one another. You were charged with awaiting Balarion. Was that your only duty?"

Her brown eyes narrowed. "My duty is to him, not to one such as you."

Balarion held a hand out toward her. "Please, Ferranos and Krotha are the reasons I am here. They awakened me as I awakened you, and they have fought valiantly to see me thus far."

"But they are…"

"They have carried their duty beyond the grave, yes." Balarion smiled easily. "And I would know what Ferranos asked. Is there more to your being stationed here?"

"Yes, my lord." She extended a hand toward me. "The stone."

I handed it to her.

She withdrew from the circle of light, revealing a small round depression at the heart of the dais. She pressed the stone into it, and unsurprisingly, it fit perfectly. As she pulled her hand away, the light again filled the stone. The rune shone as if gold were inlaid, then the dais shuddered and ground. It slowly descended into the floor, with oblong bits of the edge remaining stuck to the cylinder to create a spiral staircase.

"Please, my lord."

Balarion descended. The stone's sinking opened several alcoves in the cylindrical hole's walls. One contained a mannequin adorned in ring mail washed in gold. Another had a black tabard with a red double-headed eagle in flight, a serpent wriggling in its talons, and a golden coronet above the crest. A smaller alcove yielded a sword and a shield, the latter bearing the same eagle crest.

Phylasina looked up, beaming. "Your father ordered this to be placed here for you, and I have watched over it ever since."

Balarion nodded. "The light must have sustained you."

"Were it not for my duty, my lord, I should have died."

Krotha brushed a hand over the mail suit. "This is fine work, Balarion. Ring such as this is not unknown in Alkindor, but is usually reserved to the Knights or those the king particularly favors. It will ward you well."

Balarion crossed to the weaponry and chose a stout broadsword. "Now we can be matched when we spar, Krotha."

I descended into the pit and explored beneath the stairs. "The doorway here, is this how we leave this place? Unless I am turned around, it would head us toward the east. Is that still the way we go, Balarion?"

He glanced over his shoulder at me, somewhat distracted by the treasures that had been revealed. "Yes, I think so."

"Good, then we should prepare to travel, perhaps after you eat and rest. I would imagine, Phylasina, you, too, should want food."

"If my lord wills it."

"Of course." Balarion turned away from the swords. "There are fish in the pool. I can get some."

"No need, Balarion." I mounted the steps again. "The Yjatka have dried fish and flesh stored back in their caves. I can find enough, and some bags to carry more in."

Krotha started after me. "I'll help."

"Not necessary."

"I'd prefer caution and to save you another long walk."

I nodded, leaving Balarion and Phylasina to attend to the weapons and armor. Krotha and I passed through the waterfall and emerged on the eastern edge of the canyon. "That cave up there has most of their stores."

"By the gods!"

I arched an eyebrow. "What?"

The Knight of Truth studied the landscape, strewn as it was with twisted, burned, and blasted bodies. A few still smoldered. "Did you…? Are all of them…?"

"As I said, they were *hostile*." I shrugged. "It could have been worse. On my last trip in, I almost came with an armful of needletree pads, to let them colonize this place."

Krotha shook his head. "If I ever have to kill you, I'll make certain it takes."

"I shall bear that in mind." I ran up a short path to the cave and led him into its deeper recesses. We grabbed some leather carryalls and filled them with dried fish and roundhorn flesh. I had no idea if it would taste good and had no desire to sample. And while I remembered almost nothing of who I had been, I felt certain I'd never been reduced to eating such fare.

Carrying as much as we could, and wrapping it up so it would remain dry as we transported it beyond the waterfall, we returned to the chamber and a resplendent Balarion. Clad in mail and the surcoat, he looked every bit the warrior Krotha did, and of a match with both Knights of Virtue.

"Very good, my lord." I solemnly bowed my head. "Those who oppose your father will quake when they catch sight of you."

"Thank you, Ferranos." Balarion extended his hand to me. "Down there, I found this. I think you should have it."

He handed me a gold ring with a large ebon cabochon shot with lightning-like gold veins. I took it with slender fingers, and the weight felt right in my hand. I had an instant sense that it belonged on my finger, but I could neither recall it nor recall ever having possessed so magnificent a piece of jewelry.

"No, my lord, I cannot. It is too much."

"I insist, Ferranos, for services already rendered and in anticipation of many more. I know you and Krotha serve of your own will, but this is a promise from me, that when my father renews Alkindor, you will likewise be renewed."

"Then I must humbly accept, my lord." I slipped the ring onto my finger, and it fit perfectly. "My life, or lack thereof, is yours to command."

CHAPTER 12

From the chamber, we followed the tunnel heading east for a day—or what we guessed to be a day. Then we emerged from a cliff face. A wide body of water shimmered blue. Barely visible in the distance, the dark tracery of shoreline suggested itself to the east. I believed we were on a lake, but a current flowing to the south made it possible we stood on the bank of an immensely wide river.

With a couple days' labor, we fashioned a raft of wood, poles, and oars to let us cross. Krotha and I manned the poles, and the river remained shallow enough for us to make good progress. Then, halfway to our goal, the river gained depth. We discovered, at that point, that even with all four of us paddling hard, the oars did not help us against the current. We would travel where the water wished us to go and have very little say in the matter.

Fortunately, and most unnaturally, the current did not strand us in the middle of the river. It angled us gently southwest. The distant shore grew closer and appeared to be largely grasslands with patches of forest here and there. We saw no other boats, no animals at the shore, no villages nor even smoke from some. The only movement came from breezes teasing long grasses.

We gained the far shore toward evening on the third day, and drew the raft up as high as we could on a sandbar. Spring flooding had deposited a fair amount of wood there, so we were able to build a fire. While Phylasina and Balarion used other wood to create a makeshift lean-to, I ventured east, into the grassland.

I was not certain what I would find and, therefore, was not wholly disappointed—but neither was I overjoyed. The grasses rose between waist and shoulder height on me, with a few strands going twice as high. Those grasses had already turned gold, and their stalks bent beneath the weight of grain. Not being a farmer, I wasn't certain if it was edible, so I harvested some to bring back for Balarion to identify. Still, it struck me, with the way the grain stands had clumped together, that this land had once been tilled, but it had long since returned to nature.

With that as my conviction, I searched around for any buildings, or remains thereof. My search went unrewarded. It could very well have been that whoever had worked this land had lived in a hole dug into a hillside, or in some sort of sod house that had long ago fallen to ruin. But again, to a layman, it seemed a fertile place to raise crops and tend a herd of wooldron or kuddan.

As light drained from the world, I headed back to the camp, drawn like a moth toward the fire's light. I met Krotha on the way. He'd scouted along the shoreline. "Did you find anything?"

He pointed to the north. "There's a pool up there, stones around it. Not natural and not recent. I would bet that spring floods fill it and even deposit some fish. I saw no other sign of people."

"Nor I, save what I took as fields that might once have been worked." I showed him the heads of grain I'd harvested. "I thought Balarion might be able to identify this. If it's edible, it would be a change for them."

"It is, if you're a saddle-beast." The undead knight smiled. "*Emaranta*, also known as beastgarhme. People can eat it, but it takes some soaking and boiling. If you grind it into garhme-dust, it has to be milled twice; but saddle-beasts and kuddan take it fine."

"Having it will be better than nothing."

I started back toward the camp, but Krotha caught hold of my upper arm. "We might want to look around a bit more, give them some time…"

"So I was not imagining things?"

"If there was anything left to imagine, I'd think you'd not gotten all the needles plucked from your eye."

"Show me your pool, then."

We headed off to the north, and I found things much as Krotha had reported them. I worked my way back toward the river and stubbed a toe on a post driven deep into the ground. "A piling from a jetty?"

"Possibly. If the pool has fish, the river would as well." Krotha frowned. "Good water, good land, easy means for transporting goods. There should be a town here."

"Yet no sign there ever was." I shrugged and started walking along the shore toward the distant firelight. I had no sense of uneasiness per se, since nothing even remotely resembling a threat had manifested itself. Still, I carried no love for the illogical. This place should have been full of people, and that it was not suggested something very wrong had occurred.

By the time we returned, Phylasina had put the finishing touches on the lean-to by thatching the roof and covering the floor with fresh grass. She and Balarion sat close together, laughing and smiling—displaying a full range of emotions that felt alien to me. She rested a hand lightly on his knee, then flipped brown locks over her shoulder as she laughed at his comment.

I spoke from the dark so our return would not frighten them. "We found signs of what might have been a farm a while back, but no shelter. I do have beastgarhme, and we can get sheaves more if we desire."

Phylasina shook her head. "Animal fodder for the prince? You jest."

He patted her thigh. "Would not be the first time I've eaten it. I used to quite like it in a porridge."

"No, my lord, that is peasant food." She rose and stretched. "I shall find you something proper, some game. If the grain is as plentiful as Ferranos suggests, something shall be eating it."

Krotha knelt by the fire and fed another scrap of wood into it. "We saw nothing. No track, no sign, no trail through the grasses. Could be

that herds come here later in migration, but now, unless you fish it from
the river, it's beastgarhme and what's left of the dried fish we had off the
Yjatka."

She looked at Balarion. "Say the word, my lord."

"No, Phylasina, stay. I trust their claims." He looked up at me. "Not even
a road or a path or anything?"

I shook my head. "When people were here, the river likely provided
transport. I'd suggest heading south along the shore, but the choice is not
mine. Do you still feel drawn to the east?"

"Yes, but not as strongly. It is as if being here has evaporated some of the
urgency. We are on the right track." He chuckled. "I just wish the right
path actually was a path."

"There is no reason we cannot strike east. The walking will be a bit
cumbersome, given the height of the grasses, but over the next line of hills
we could find a road." I sat across the fire from our charge. "My major concern is locating another fire that suits Krotha and myself. Were something
to happen here and now, we would reappear on the far side of the Yjatka
village."

Phylasina rested her hands on her swords. "I will protect him. We would
leave you signs of our passage so you could catch up."

"A great kindness, sister." Krotha stared at her for a moment, then shifted
his gaze to Balarion. "We are yours to lead, my lord, but I do believe we
will be safer if we travel together."

"I agree." Balarion turned to Phylasina. "That does not mean I believe it
unsafe under your care alone, my dear."

"I would die before permitting anything to hurt you."

"Yes, I know, and this I should like to avoid." Balarion stood, brushed
sand off his tabard tail, then pulled it off over his head. "So I am for sleeping now and getting an early start. You two will watch over us while we
rest."

I nodded. "As always, my lord. My sincere pleasure to do so."

* * *

Balarion and Phylasina finally woke with the sun, and shortly thereafter we began our trek inland. Though Phylasina refused to harvest grain—choosing instead to stand guard while we did so—she did consent to hauling one of the carryalls filled with beastgarhme. Balarion, similarly burdened, took point and led us. We made decent progress, though as I had predicted, having to push through long grasses did slow us down.

After several hours, we crested the line of hills to the east. I checked our back trail, but the gentle breezes rustling the grasses had fully erased any signs of our passage. Down in the valley beyond, we spotted what turned out to be a long-disused road, which encroaching grasses had well narrowed. Still, when we reached it, we made far better time than before.

The road angled toward the south and then turned east again just beyond a small forest. In the woods, we noticed the first real signs of habitation. Trees had been cleared from several lots, most of which had already begun to grow back. Likewise, the general lack of deadwood and windfalls suggested that people regularly gathered readily available timber for fuel.

To the east, the road widened, and by noon we reached a point where it descended into a broad valley. A few miles below, built near what appeared to be a wide stream, a couple dozen houses huddled together. Surrounding them lay fields where someone was cultivating beastgarhme and a handful of other crops. I felt certain I saw kuddan in some of the fields, and Balarion pointed out what he thought were wooldron, though he'd have expected them to be farther away from the village, in meadows in the hills to the south.

And people. We definitely saw people, and that presented a problem. "My lord, Krotha and I, given our state of being, might not be received well down there."

"Ferranos has a point." Phylasina drew one of her swords. "Allow me to go ahead and scout the situation. To be cautious."

Balarion's brow furrowed. "No, I think you and I both should go, show-ing them we're afraid of nothing. We can determine how they feel. We will come back for you or signal. If we do not do so immediately, head back to the forest and we will find you after night has fallen."

"That's well and good for Ferranos, but, armored as I am, no one could see I am not among the living."

"Sir Krotha, this is true, but were you asked, you would tell the truth of your situation. More important, were they to discover what they thought was deception…" Balarion shook his head. "…It would erode any trust we sought to establish."

I nodded. "Despite the risk if there is trouble, I think Balarion has the right of it, Krotha. We shall just be here to come to the rescue as needed."

"As you wish, my lord." Krotha turned toward Phylasina. "Ward him well, sister."

"As you would have, brother."

The two of them wandered down the road as if children returning from gathering wildflowers. They did not appear to have a concern in the world. I almost followed them, and I think Krotha would have aided and abetted me in that, but I thought better of it. Maintaining Balarion's trust was important, and part of training him to be a leader was for him to have confidence that his commands would be followed. If we were to see this adventure through to the end, he would have to become a great leader, and fairly fast. Thus, undercutting him would not help our cause.

I said none of this aloud, but Krotha's thoughts paralleled my own.

Or so I imagined from his solitary grunt.

A handful of people came out from the village to greet them. At my distance, I could not see great detail, but much bowing appeared to go on. After several minutes, Phylasina marched a dozen feet back up the road and waved her arm from side to side.

"It appears we will be tolerated, Ferranos."

"I think I should feel happy or trepidatious, and yet there's nothing."

I sighed and headed down the road. "And this absence of feeling is not comforting."

"Well, if they are planning to ambush us, they've had troops in hiding before they knew we'd found their village." He clanked along in my wake.

"I doubt they do."

"So we're safe."

"Any warrior who ever thinks that is on his way fast to the grave."

No ambush awaited us in the village—at least, not a martial one. The village itself was full of surprises. It looked much better from a distance. Close-up, the mud-daubed walls of the various buildings clearly had not seen paint in years, and roofs had been patched in a clumsy, haphazard way. Worse yet, the people were hollow-eyed and half-starved, and whatever they used the water in the stream for, it did not include bathing.

The grain looked perfectly normal, though it had not grown to the heights we had seen back toward the river. The kuddan were undersized, and half appeared to be blind. At least, I assumed their milky-white eyes precluded being able to see much of anything. The only remarkable thing about them was the hue of their shaggy coats, which ran to a golden blond. Likewise, the wooldron, which again appeared smaller than what I would have expected, bore long golden fur of superior softness.

We entered the village and saw among the population a few Hollows— the cast of their skin being the only difference between them and the villagers. They'd been hobbled, and served as beasts of burden, fetching water and pulling plows. Normally, kuddan would have been used for such things, but these blind, stunted beasts seemed suited for nothing more strenuous than eating.

The greatest curiosity stood in the heart of the village, atop a stone pillar ten feet high. The statue of a rotund little man perched there, with bulging grain sacks at his feet, a scepter in his right hand, and a crown on his head. His potbelly made him out to be as well-fed as these people were starving. I found him somehow, distantly, familiar.

And the statue, by all appearances, was made of solid gold. Or, if not that, gilded and kept in good repair. The sun reflected brilliantly from the surface, and a couple of villagers hauled buckets of water up a ladder so they could wash the day's dust from the figure's golden skin.

I glanced at Krotha. "What do you make of this?"

"We're standing in Kadarr." The knight nodded toward the statue. "That is Tsaleryk."

Balarion joined us. "Careful, my friends. That is *King* Tsaleryk. He is the golden king of this land. As he prospers, so does this nation." The youth lowered his voice. "And as this nation prospers, so his people starve."

CHAPTER 13

An emaciated man scurried from the largest of the buildings to Balarion's side. "My lord, a place will be cleared for you and your...companions." He hesitated, giving me a good look up and down. While they did have Hollows in the village, none of them wore anywhere near as many clothes as I did, and all of them showed signs of wear and work. Beyond that, I appeared to be healthier and more well-fed than any of the actual villagers.

Whatever his consternation, it evaporated when he caught sight of the ring on my finger. His eyes widened, and he began to tremble. He looked from the ring up to Balarion, then dropped to his knees. "Oh, my lord, you treat your servants so well, to allow one to wear your ring."

Balarion shook his head. "It is not *my* ring. I have given it to him."

"You permit him gold?" The man shivered, and other villagers within earshot gasped. "My lord is too generous."

"My companions are worth more than I can give them." Balarion reached down and pulled the man to his feet. "You have told us that we are in Kadarr, but where? What is this place?"

"We have not earned a name yet, my lord." The man shrugged. "We are just a village. The Gold Guards give us a number on their maps, a grid reference."

Phylasina rested a hand on the headman's shoulder. "What would that be?"

He shook his head.

Balarion smiled. "If you travel to the next nearest village, what do you call your village when you tell them where you come from?"

The headman again shook his head, more slowly and with more gravity this time. "We do not travel, my lord. It is not permitted."

"Then how do you take your goods to market?"

The headman blinked. "The Gold Guards do that, my lord. Surely you know that." He stared at Balarion, then his eyes narrowed for a moment. "But yes, you do know that, my lord! You are testing me!"

Balarion smiled quickly. "Yes, yes, you are correct. And I would test your knowledge further. How far is the capital? And how do you pronounce the name of the capital?"

The headman pointed east-northeast. "There, many days, many. And we pronounce it correctly, as per decree. Darrxan, my lord."

"Very good. And no one refers to it as Dares'shan?"

"No, my lord. Not since the decree."

Krotha hovered behind my left shoulder. "Dares'shan was Tsaleryk's pleasure palace, as I remember."

"Your memory is better than mine." I looked up at the statue on the pillar. "That representation of him does not look familiar. Likely I just do not remember."

"The eyes, yes, close-set as they are. Otherwise..." Krotha's armor clanked with his shrug. "I do not remember this place, but neither do I recall a place that appeared to be so poor."

"Or the people so starved amid plenty." What struck me as even more curious about the people was that while they moved with a lethargy that I ascribed to their being underfed, none of them looked unhappy. I saw no great joy on any faces—save perhaps those of the people washing Tsaleryk's statue—but no discontent, either.

The blast of a trumpet from the village's eastern edge brought me around. Four riders in golden raiment, riding saddle-beasts in golden livery, crested a hill and started down a wide path. Behind them came a large wagon pulled by six plodhooves, the driver wearing a gold tabard. The draft animals, which seemed normal if slightly undersized from what I recalled, had their tails and manes braided with golden ribbons. The driver's companion had blown the horn, and quickly hid the instrument in a box beneath his seat.

At the sound of the trumpet, everyone in the village came running. They formed a circle around the king's statue, faced it, dropped to their knees, and began singing. The lyrics had the complexity of a child's rhyme, and the melody was best suited to being performed with a whistle and bone flute. I dimly recalled the song having different lyrics and it being enjoyed by a bawdy audience, deep in their cups, late at night in a dingy tavern.

Even the village's Hollows dropped to their knees. Mercifully, however, they did not attempt singing.

Krotha, wearing armor and being a Knight of Virtue, remained standing. Balarion, his face composed solemnly, sank to one knee, and Phylasina joined him. I drew a step back and one over to be behind Balarion. I remained standing, but placed my hand over where my heart lay still in my breast. Not a gesture of respect on my part, but the most expedient way to let the sun glint from my gold ring.

The four riders made their way to the village's center. Two bore arms and clearly functioned as guards. The lead rider carried a staff with a gold pennant flying from it. The last rider, with his shaved pate, beard braided the same as the saddle-beast's tail, and an elegant golden robe, took a look down his long nose at us, then held up a hand. The procession stopped.

The headman let the song's verse end, and as his compatriots began the refrain again, he hurried to the bald rider's side and knelt at the left stirrup.

The rider dismounted, using the headman's shoulder as a stool. He brushed wrinkles out of his robe, then applauded slowly and mockingly as the song came to an end. "Be assured that even now His Illuminated Majesty's ears ring with your voices. He is comforted and pleased that you praise him."

The headman looked up. "Every day, my lord Auditor, as by decree, but with great joy in our hearts, we praise him. Him from whom all good things come."

"Yes, quite." The auditor looked past him toward the largest building and the double doors set in the north end. "Show me."

The headman stood and clapped his hands.

The people immediately rose and organized themselves into two lines, Hollows freely interspersed along each of them. The headman passed down through the lines as if a general inspecting his troops, then opened the big building's double doors. The first two people assisted him, then hauled out a heavy sack of grain. They lugged it to the foot of the statue and dropped it, then returned to the back of the line as the next two people ran forward to get another sack.

The villagers repeated this process with grain, kuddan hides, wheels of golden-yellow kuddan-cheese, and bales of golden wooldron fur. As the village's bounty piled up around the statue, a few people ran to other buildings and brought out blankets and robes woven with the fur, and bags crafted from the golden leather. In a very short time, without complaint, they organized their village for a market day, displaying material wealth well beyond what I would have ever guessed possible, given their absolute poverty.

Once they'd unloaded everything, the people gathered off to the side and knelt again, staring at the ground.

The auditor strolled forward languidly, his gait equal parts boredom and revulsion. He did not look at any of the people, just the grain and the goods. He made a show of inspecting things, for he never opened a grain sack and only plucked a hair or three from a fur bale. The woven clothing he toed, and the leatherwork he sniffed at—disdain, not an attempt to catch the rich scent.

Finally, he stopped in front of the headman. "Your village has done well for this season. You will load half the grain, half the fur, and three-quarters of the leather."

"But, my lord Auditor."

"You have heard me."

The headman spread his arms. "My lord, half?"

"You have an issue with my assessment?"

"Yes, my lord." The headman stood. "Look at our village. Look at our people. Do you not see that we love the king? Have we not made that clear, my lord?"

"Quite."

"Then you must take *more*, my lord." The headman smiled broadly. "You must take it all, my lord."

The auditor shook his head. "I cannot take one hundred percent."

"But we love the king one hundred percent, my lord. That he might go a day, an hour, a heartbeat cold for lack of fur, or hungry for lack of grain, or without shoes for lack of leather, this would cause us pain. You must take it all."

"You mistake me, Headman. I cannot take it all. By decree of His Illuminated Majesty." The functionary looked past him to address the village's entire population. "Do you think that His Majesty does not know you? Does not know your devotion? That you would go hungry hurts him. That your blankets have become threadbare hurts him. That you go barefoot hurts him. He will not let you hurt yourselves, for it will hurt him. And yet he respects your desires for his well-being. Thus, by his will, I shall take six of ten. The rest is for you."

The headman fell to the ground and kissed the auditor's feet. The rest of the village knelt and bowed deeply—not to the auditor, but to the statue. Then they rose up, organized themselves again, and began the process of loading the wagon—their efforts going beyond the six of ten proscribed.

The auditor freed himself from the headman's grasp and approached us. "Who would you be?"

Phylasina rose fluidly, barring his path. "This is Balarion, brother to your king. I am Phylasina, Knight of Virtue, and that is Krotha, my brother knight. And that is Ferranos, whom you will know by his ring."

The man studied us, lingering longer on my ring than he did on Balarion. "You are newly come to Kadarr."

Balarion rose to his feet. "We have come a long way. We have business with King Tsaleryk. We are bound for Darrxan."

"I cannot take you that far, but we are bound in that direction. You may, if you desire, travel with us."

Balarion nodded. "Thank you. How shall we call you?"

"'Auditor' will suit." The man offered a wan smile. "I have not yet earned a name."

* * *

We left the village with the Gold Guards. They did not offer us a place in the wagon, but with its load, the wagon traveled at a very gentle walking pace. We had no trouble keeping up with the wagon as it wended its way east along dusty roads that seemed to carry very little traffic. The road grew a bit broader after a couple other roads fed into it, and I found it easy to imagine they led off to other small villages like the one we'd just left. And sunlight glinting brightly in the distance suggested each village had a gilded statue at its heart.

What I found quite curious was that the road cut through fields that, like those near the broad river in the west, were full of beastgarhme ready for harvest. For the villagers, it would be a bonanza for which they did no work whatsoever. Had the headman somehow convinced the auditor to take every scrap of food they'd offered, the beastgarhme could have more than sustained them.

When we stopped to water the saddle-beasts later in the day, I asked the auditor about the beastgarhme.

He looked at me as if I were insane. "King Tsaleryk does not like beastgarhme." His tone suggested this fact should have been obvious and that the king's dislike of it rendered it valueless in Kadarr.

"I see." I frowned. "And he has no love of fish, either."

"For consumption, no." The auditor smiled. "In Darrxan, there is within the Golden Palace a vast lake filled with goldfish. They grow to be enormous, their scales flashing as they surface, reflecting sunlight and starlight, day and night."

"It sounds beautiful."

"Yes. It is my wish that I am able to visit someday." The man focused distantly and smiled. "When I have earned my name."

He turned away quickly, and I retreated to where my companions sat in the shade of a tree. "It will come as no surprise that in Kadarr, if the king approves of it, it has great value. The reverse is also true. And the reason we will be allowed to visit Darrxan is because we have names."

Balarion's eyes narrowed. "The village, and this auditor, they have not 'earned' names. I do not understand that."

"I think I do, or understand enough to make a guess at things." I crouched and lowered my voice. "I believe that at some point in the centuries, Tsaleryk grew bored with having to remember so many names, so he simply indicated he didn't want to remember them, or only wanted to remember a few. Those around him took this as a chance to solidify their power. In his name they issued a decree that to have a name, one had to earn it. A name is earned through service to the state, which means pleasing the king. If you please him well enough, he will recognize you and grant you a name. Likewise, you earn the permission to travel and to do so many other things that, you are told, are for the benefit of you and society and, through society, of benefit to the king."

Krotha grunted. "They believe that, clearly. They would have given everything to the Gold Guards had they not been stopped."

Phylasina slipped the dagger she'd been sharpening into a boot sheath. "You've all noticed how everything is gold or close. The kuddan are bred for that color, even though blindness seems to go with their breeding. And the wooldron for that color fur."

I raised a finger. "Also notice that they accept that we have names because we have told them we do. They are trained to obey their superiors, which, because we have names, they believe us to be. I would imagine that to claim a name and not to have earned it likely will cost your head here."

Balarion nodded. "And you especially benefited because Phylasina wisely pointed out your ring."

"You are too kind, my lord."

"'Tis true, my dear." Balarion gave her a smile. "But your point, Ferranos, is that we should always act superior, as if we have a right to our names."

"Yes. Not arrogant, but accustomed to privilege." I ran a hand over my jaw. "One last thing—the people clearly love the king. No matter what you think of him, no matter how odd their customs seem, to speak against him would be the same as shouting blasphemy in a high temple. Name or no, they will kill you because your words cause him pain."

"Thank you, my friend." Balarion gained his feet and smiled. "We'll save the words that hurt for when we've reached Darrxan. Words that hurt we can deliver direct."

CHAPTER 14

Toward dusk of the following day, we reached a square fortress large enough to house four of the villages we'd first encountered in Kadarr. The thick stone walls rose to thirty feet above the ground, with corner towers adding another twenty feet. A small barracks housed the garrison, and a slightly larger barracks provided shelter for the workers. A stable and a small wagon barn occupied one corner. As with the villages, a golden statue of Tsaleryk stood atop a tall pedestal and greeted all visitors.

Grand warehouses occupied the rest of the space. The wagon headed directly toward the largest of them, where the grain and cheese were off-loaded. The wool went into another and the leather into a third. The auditor distributed the blankets and woven clothes among the warehousemen, save for the best of it, which he presented to a woman I took to be his superior.

Two things seemed quite out of place. First off, the fortress was the only structure in the area. Under normal circumstances, when the kingdom permitted free travel, a tavern or two would have sprung up, as well as a livery stable, perhaps a smithy, and certainly a shrine. Even a laundry would have made sense, as well as a market street. This place had none of those things, however. While the roads leading in and out clearly made it a transit center, it might as well have been some remote end point in a far-flung wilderness.

The other thing that caught my eye involved four workers wielding clubs and brooms. They raced in and out of the food warehouse, then all around it. They chased scurrying little tsogarron. They bashed the rodents to death and collected the bodies in an old grain sack. While none of that was unusual for warehousemen, they only went after black and brown tsogarron. Other tsogarron, rather rotund and well-fed, graced with golden pelts, moved about with lethargy and apparent impunity.

Just as curiously, I saw no stinkers or ferpine—both of which could be very efficient predators to control tsogarron, but were unlikely to discriminate by pelt color.

I saw no Hollows within the fortress, nor did I notice anyone regard me or Krotha with reservation. As with the villagers and the auditor, the fortress's denizens did notice my ring, viewing it with awe more than greed. That the auditor introduced us to his superior by name seemed to reinforce the idea that we were not ordinary.

The resident auditor actually had a name: Lashalla. As she explained, she'd earned it for twenty years of service to the Crown; and with it came her appointment to manage this particular depository. A pleasant woman whose sharp eyes missed nothing, she invited us to dine with her. Balarion accepted for all of us, but Krotha and I begged off. No matter how accepting people might be, or how alluring a gold ring, dining with the undead might have killed her appetite and any sense of congeniality.

Krotha and I instead chose to take a walking tour of the area. The fortress lay in a depression amid a circle of hills that, in turn, rose above the surrounding plains. Towers on hilltops would have made the place a truly commanding presence. As it was, we could see fairly far from the hilltops. Aside from what we took to be a campfire here and there, I got no sense of any significant population nearby.

"It makes sense, Ferranos, if you wish to keep these goods as a strategic supply against famine or invasion."

"I understand the purpose, my friend, but I should think having it closer to the capital or another population center would be of greater practical utility."

"It would, but I have a feeling that practicality is not highly valued in Kadarr."

I arched an eyebrow. "You noticed the gold vermin, too."

"That and how the clothes made for the king were handed out to the warehousemen. Not that they should be naked, but…" Krotha spread his hands to encompass the depository. "Clearly no one fears that the villagers will ever come and see what has been done with their gifts for the king."

"And were that to happen, I would imagine some decree from the king would justify it all, theft thus being transformed into a virtuous action." I shook my head. "I would consider asking the king how Kadarr fell into such a state, but I am certain the answers would make no sense."

"And yet the people endure this insanity." The Knight of Virtue sighed. "Insanity, the depths of which we'll plumb when we make it to court."

* * *

The journey took us to Darrxan in eight days, when it should have required no more than four. The delay came because each day ended at a depository, where the same ritual unloading of the wagon took place. By nightfall, every scrap and grain of our cargo made its way into a warehouse. Then, the next morning, warehousemen would load the wagon back up with approximately the same load it had come in with. They would hitch rested plodhooves to pull the wagon, and we would set off. The transit auditor we brought with us would remain behind, and a new transit auditor took over to lead the group.

The primary difference on each leg was the size of the depository, each growing by a factor of two as we drew closer to the capital. On our third leg, a second wagon joined us, and our caravan doubled again for the last leg into Darrxan. Aside from size, however, I should have been hard-pressed to find any difference between depositories or their methods of operation. The larger the warehouses, the greater the tsogarron population, of course.

We caught sight of the Golden City in the distance, with the late-afternoon sun burnishing the domed roofs. The palace, with all its precincts, sat in the heart. Square walls were built around it, then another square out from that. Four sets of walls in all surrounded the city, and more buildings spilled out around the last wall. Each set of walls had two gates, which lay offset by ninety degrees of those in the next wall. With towers built along the walls, the success of any siege would hinge on starving the city, because an invading army would die between the walls.

We saw plenty of gold vermin on our way into Darrxan, and not just tsogarron. The residents clothed themselves in finely woven gold cloth, and most had blond hair to match. Not all of it natural, of course. Older men ran to the same paunch as Tsaleryk's statues did and, again, not all of that real. Given the unnatural way some stomachs moved, most all tailors set the gold standard for their clients by simulating prosperity through padding.

And as nearly as I could see, none of these golden people actually did anything.

Moving into the city, we went from squalor to opulence, progressing sharply as we passed through each gate. Immediately inside the wall lay the merchant quarter. Next came the temple district and the realm of guild-halls. Beyond that, next to the palace, the nobility took up residence. With each progression, the districts became cleaner and kept in better repair—especially the walls and facades that faced the palace. The residents dressed in greater finery, and appeared better fed and decidedly healthier—and the few Hollows must have had flasks of their own.

Many wore filigree masks of gold, delicately fashioned of slender wire, as if the webs of golden spiders. I had an aversion to such ostentation, yet I still found it mesmerizingly beautiful.

We reached the palace unopposed and stood there for a moment. Whereas the carefully wrought masks attracted me, the gaudy excess of the palace revolted me. Gold covered every surface, which would have been too much even had every surface been flat. Far from it. The palace's interior walls had been styled as if they were a thicket of golden bracken. Thorned vines might part to reveal something beyond them, but that would most likely be a statue of the king or a golden tableau of him playing out a heroic tale of the past. In one place, the artisan had actually captured Krotha's likeness from his famed battle with a dragon. In this version of the tale, however, Krotha cowered on the ground as an incredibly muscular Tsaleryk—with his paunch yet—dealt the beast a mortal blow.

The throne room, tall and wide as it was, had been crowded with treasures. Piles of coins rose halfway up the walls. Chariots and carriages, small boats and massive thrones, all made of gold or so thickly gilded one could not tell they were not, left only a narrow pathway from doorway to throne. And, at that, one had to step over dunes of gold coins here and there.

Tsaleryk's throne, fashioned after the coils of a rampant winged snake, glared down at us with topaz eyes. The structure made a dwarf of the king, who did himself no favors by lounging crosswise in it. A gold crown hung askew on his head, and a gold cloak covered him like a blanket. It only left exposed his slippers, which had been worn through at the ball of the foot.

The Minister of Protocol banged a heavy gold staff on the floor. Coins, disturbed by the vibrations, slid down to new levels. Their hissing slither caused Tsaleryk to glance up, roused from indolence by alarm. He ignored the Knights of Virtue being announced, and likewise me, but sat up when the minister pronounced Balarion's name.

He straightened his crown. "Balarion. The Golden Child."

"No longer a child, brother."

If Tsaleryk objected to the claim of kinship, he gave no sign. His eyes narrowed as he leaned forward. "It could be you, I suppose. You look more like our father than Dolared ever did. I see it around the eyes, like mine."

Balarion approached, easily avoiding the gold slides. "Our father sent me away for the sake of safety, to return when I was needed. That is now."

The king sat back in the serpent's coils. "Yes. You have come for the Key of Gold."

Krotha and I, three paces back, exchanged glances. I caught no threat in Tsaleryk's matter-of-fact comment, nor any resignation. *If anything, anticipation?*

"I believe, yes, that the task charged to me requires that key."

"Good. I have been waiting for you. For this day. It has been much too long in coming." Tsaleryk stood slowly, as if the crown and cloak sought to press him back down. "You have no idea the struggle to hang on to hope and to prepare for this day."

"Prepare for this day?" Balarion shook his head. "Have you seen...? When was the last time you ventured outside your palace?"

"I cannot leave. I am a prisoner here, fettered by my duty."

The youth pointed roughly west. "We have come through your realm. It is islands of poverty within an ocean of plenty. Had you roads, you could move many goods. Your economy would prosper. Your people would multiply and spread."

"Yes, yes, I know that." Tsaleryk raised a finger. "And they would come for it all. Dolared and Jaranessa. They have wrought ruin upon the world, and they have forced me to do the same. But I have done as our father wished. I have kept the Key of Gold for you, for this day, so you can undo their work. You will tell our father that, won't you? Tell him I was not with them."

Balarion scratched the back of his neck. "Of course, brother." He turned and glanced back at Krotha and me, which earned each of us a glare from Phylasina.

"Forgive me, sire, but as you see our purpose as vital and in service of Kadarr, perhaps it would be best for us to expedite the retrieval of the Key of Gold." To emphasize my humility as I spoke, I pressed my hand to my chest, letting him see the ring.

While he clearly noticed it, it had less effect on him than it had upon his subjects. "Yes, yes, toward that end, I agree. But..." Tsaleryk turned his attention back to Balarion. "...Brother, I would have of you a minor service, a little favor, so to speak. I scarce dare to even ask this of you, to ask you to trifle with it, but it, too, is in furtherance of our conjoined missions."

"Of course, brother." Balarion bowed his head. "How may my companions and I be of service?"

"Service, yes, of service. And I trust your Knights of Virtue will serve you better than they ever have me." Tsaleryk descended from the throne and pawed through a pile of coins to the left. He didn't find what he was searching for, so he shifted to a pile on the right. He dug down and finally came up with a single coin, which lay heavily in his palm. He studied it for a moment, then extended his hand toward Balarion.

The youth approached and reached for the coin, but the king's fingers snapped shut around it. Balarion drew his hand back, and Tsaleryk's fingers opened as if a flower blossoming. Balarion peered at the coin closely, but not overly so, lest the fingers close again. "I see a map, brother."

"Yes, I had this coin struck to commemorate…something. But here, in the north, there lies an ancient city. A ruin, really, but at its heart is the Temple of Glittering Darkness. The gods it served are long since dead, eaten by their own progeny, who, in turn, fell prey to some disaster. But there in the temple complex is a scepter, fit for the hand of a god, made of the purest gold. I would have it. I *need* it for our effort, brother. You understand that, yes? It should be a simple thing for you to fetch it for me. Then the time of our brother and our sister will begin to end. As our father wished."

"We shall do this for you, brother." Balarion stepped back carefully to avoid trampling coins underfoot. "We should rest and draw stores."

"No, I should not delay you with the trappings of polite society when your mission is so urgent." Tsaleryk snapped his fingers. "Minister, they shall have saddle-beasts and food, as they require. On my order, on their account."

I frowned. "Our account, sire?"

"For the historians, Ferranos. So they will know exactly what you did."

"Yes, of course, sire." I bowed in the king's direction. "For the historians."

* * *

Five days later—five days of hard riding and visits to three different depositories to change saddle-beasts—we reached the vicinity of the ruins. The city, or whatever it was built upon, had ages ago collapsed from the center and formed a great crater. The collapse must have happened slowly, because the city had descended into a ragged collection of concentric circles. Each circle sank twenty to thirty feet to the next, with the temple district at its heart, deposited the deepest.

Viewed from foothills a safe distance away, the source of Tsaleryk's concern would have been obvious even to a blind man. The temple itself had been built of black basalt blocks that had been mortared with gold. Odd sigils and signs had been inscribed, then inlaid with more gold. The structure still exuded power, and I had little doubt that were Tsaleryk ever to see it, he would rebuild his palace in its image.

As magnificent as the temple was, the city's outer precincts were anything but. Broken in some places, seemingly melted in others, the city appeared to have been home to a series of battles that had lasted centuries. From afar, we could not get a good look at what lived there now, but things moved in the shadows, and fearsome howls pierced the night. The warfare that razed the city likely never ended, and the city's denizens—be they Hollows or something else—were not likely to welcome new interlopers.

"A *minor* service, he called it." Phylasina crouched on a ledge halfway up a cliffside. "I see no clear path in."

Krotha towered above her. "In the daylight, perhaps, we can pick out a path."

"Sunlight, moonlight, you seek in vain." A strong voice rolled down from above us. "This place, this fell place, devours all foolish enough to trespass within."

CHAPTER 15

Balarion's sword had cleared its scabbard with a rasp before I had a chance to turn around. "Who speaks?"

Above us, on a tiny ledge, a man knelt on one knee. He wore armor similar to that of the two Knights of Virtue, but he lacked the breadth of Krotha. He clasped his battle-ax just below the head and used it to help himself stand. "I have watched for a long time and know the truth of which I speak."

Phylasina laid her hand on Balarion's forearm. "Stay your hand, my lord." She looked up at the figure above us. "Has that long time dulled your senses, Garvyne? Do you not recognize your companions?"

Garvyne closed his eyes for a short time, then looked upon us again, staring intently. "I'd scarce thought it possible I would recognize a face here. But you, Phylasina, I should know anywhere. Of your companions, I only know one. Krotha, I believe."

Krotha doffed his helmet. "It has been an age."

Garvyne looked at me. "You I do not know."

"Ferranos, in service to my lord Balarion."

"Balarion..." Garvyne's eyes tightened, then he chuckled. "There is sense in that, then."

Returning his sword to its resting place, the youth looked up. "Sense of what?"

"A once-dead prince now come to conquer this place of the dead."

Balarion shook his head. "I have no idea what you are talking about."

Krotha glanced at Garvyne and shook his head.

"True, like as not. You were very young." Garvyne slowly descended to our level. "One winter, a cold winter, the coldest Trafaram had ever known, the king charged me with the duty of seeing how you fared. The harvest had been poor that year, and wolves—*Wiervar*'s get—were about. So I ventured to your village and asked after you. Because of my inquiry, your parents discovered you were missing, and the village fell into an uproar.

"Through a blizzard I tracked you, drawing close quickly. Quickly enough to see you venture onto a small pond and fall through the ice. I went for you, but the wolves that had been hunting you decided I would be a better feast for their pack. I slew them swiftly, but by the time I dragged you from the icy water, you were as cold as death. Your heart lay still in your breast, and you did not breathe."

The dark-haired knight frowned. "I carried your lifeless body back to the village and told them you had died. But an old hedge witch cackled and told me you slept, as you would sleep again before you met your destiny. She ordered a fire built and brewed a tea. She tossed aromatics on the fire, filling her hut with thick smoke redolent of pine. She sent me out to fetch back the biggest pair of the dead wolves. She carved out their hearts and baked them, and had me skin the beasts—not as hard as doing your dragon, Krotha, but unpleasant work in the cold. The witch sewed the skins together into a blanket, having cured the pelts swiftly through means sorcerous and foul."

Balarion stroked his chin. "I had a cloak of wolf hide that always kept me warm."

"Better use than a blanket." Garvyne shrugged. "All night and all the next day I stayed with her, doing what she commanded. She spoke to you as if you lived. She sat you up by the fire, set a place for you at the table, then laid you back down again when it was time to sleep. I thought her quite mad, but then, on the morning of the third day, you awoke with a gasp. You devoured wolf-heart stew and drank her noxious brew. Back then I did not know how to see within, to see life and death, but now, after so long, life and death are mixed in you. You are the bridge between Krotha and me."

That explained, then, how Balarion, while living, could absorb the essence of the dead. The youth had known death, just not the long sort that Krotha and I had endured. What magicks it was that returned us to a semblance of life I did not know. Clearly the hedge witch's magick had chopped back whatever hold death had on Balarion. It had not rid him of its taint entirely, but life predominated. Still, that bit of death allowed him to absorb life essences as we did.

Krotha pointed toward the black-and-gold temple. "How is it you are here, Garvyne, known as the Undaunted? Phylasina we found warded by magick to preserve her life. How is it that you yet live?"

"The answer to your first question is simple: King Parnyr tasked me to scout this place and 'to strike when the time is right.' So I have done. I have scouted it many times and have prepared to strike, but then something changes. I repeat the process, but the time is never right. Never has been. But I have been true to my duty."

Garvyne peered toward the temple. "In the time I have waited and watched, gods have died in there, then their children and their demi-beast grandchildren. Their worshippers have brought sacrifices and in turn have been sacrificed by other sects, or riven by heresy and fallen upon one another. The temple devours all and, I daresay, preserves me, just waiting for the day I shall enter its dark domain."

Balarion crossed to his side. "Sir Garvyne, I am sorry I do not remember you saving me, but I remember the cloak. You should know that when that hedge witch died, I saw to it she was wrapped in that cloak so the chill of the grave would never reach her."

The knight nodded. "That is right and just."

"To you, sir, I owe my thanks. And my life." The youth rested his left hand on the hilt of his sword. "I would again put my life in your hands.

As my father charged you with a duty concerning this place, so my duty concerns it. My companions and I are sent to recover a scepter from the temple's heart and bring it back to Tsaleryk. I would ask that you accompany us. That you lend us your wisdom so we will succeed."

Phylasina approached, linking her arm through Balarion's. "Yes, brother knight, you must join us. King Parnyr sent you here for this moment. You who fear nothing are here to bolster our courage."

He who was undaunted turned, weariness slackening his expression. "I do not know that this is what the king would want. It could be that he wishes me here to convey to him word of your fate."

"But even you said you were told to strike when the time was right." She rested a hand on his shoulder. "When will there be a better time?"

"When will be the best time, Phylasina?"

I cleared my throat. "Perhaps, Sir Garvyne, we should have your counsel about the temple. We need details on what to expect in there."

The knight nodded. "You and Krotha will want to know of the fire circles. There are a few scattered about, but only around, not within. You'll find one less than halfway to that shattered gate there to the left, near that standing stone."

"Of the rest, can you draw us a map?"

"Within the temple complex are nine precincts, each a circle, each circle smaller and lower than the one above." Garvyne crouched and drew in the dirt. "They are ruins, infested by whatever creatures have survived. There are bands of people, not like you two, but like me, unaging because of the godsblood painting the streets and walls, hanging in the air. Blood fog, and the tang of it, will not leave your throat for years. But this is not the most dangerous aspect, because those rings... They revolve. They grind slowly, always, but sometimes, especially when blood flows, they move swiftly. You could enter here, then find yourself there. Passage to the center could be blocked and only opened with sacrifice."

Krotha stood tall above the map and studied it. "You have done your job well, brother. I can see plainly why the time has never been right for you, as there is always more to learn and see. I must ask, have you seen the scepter we seek? Is it in the temple?"

"I have seen it, yes, many times. And heard it. It calls to you. It calls to them all." Garvyne stood. "Many seek it. A few find it, and a scarce few have taken it from its resting place. But getting it out? No. This has never been done. It always returns to its cradle, calling more to their deaths."

I frowned. "How close have they gotten to freeing it from the complex?"

"Sometimes the eighth ring. Once the ninth."

"Thank you, Sir Garvyne." Balarion glanced at the map and then at the complex in the distance. "I tell you this, we *will* succeed in removing that scepter. I would have you with us, because while this may not be the best time, it will be the *last* time. Come with us, or your duty will be left eternally undone."

* * *

Balarion's comment turned the tide, which freed Garvyne of his concerns. He helped us pitch camp and happily shared a meal with us. He ate as one would expect of a man who had missed every meal since before Alkindor fell; and he had no complaints about the meager fare Tsaleryk had given us "on account."

The living slept peacefully while Krotha kept watch. I sat on a rock, less watching than feeling. Vibrations came through from the complex. For the most part, I had to concentrate to feel them, for they came gently and soft, as if ripples on a pond. But occasionally, they came sharp and quick, moments after a thundercrack echoed. In the distance, a tower might crumble—a result, not the cause. And then, over hours, it might reassemble itself in a process I did not witness, save to discover the tower renewed by some invisible agency.

Morning came with the sun hidden behind thick thunderheads. We broke camp, but stored our gear in a small cave that Garvyne had used in times of foul weather. Armed and armored, the Knights of Virtue led the way through a small canyon toward the temple. Bones, many scattered by scavengers, clustered here and there. A few showed signs of combat, but more seemed pristine and well-bleached by the sun.

Halfway to the city, we found the spirit fire, and I kindled the ethereal blaze. I glanced at Krotha. "It is my intention never to visit this place again."

"Save on our way back to Darrxan."

"Well, yes, of course."

Climbing down into the city, we found more signs of those who had gone before. The winds ruffled scraps of old robes clinging to skeletons. Some had clearly fallen from great heights, either thrown to the winds or willfully diving down in some act of devotion. Others showed clear signs of damage, from sheared bones to gnaw marks. Some of the latter had harder edges and traces of gold dust within the cuts.

I straightened up from my examination. "None of this is your work, Garvyne?"

"No, I maintained my watch, waiting for this moment." He bowed his head toward our leader. "My lord Balarion is correct. This *is* the time I was meant to move forward. The king, in his wisdom, charged me with such duty; and his wisdom will show itself as we accomplish our mission."

"About that, you were told to wait and then strike."

"Yes."

"Strike *what*?"

"Ah yes, that." Garvyne regarded the rest of us as we marched along. "I have never seen it, but I have felt it. Heard it. As people have battled their way to the heart of the complex, sounds of warfare have echoed. Then silence for a bit, a short bit, then horrified screams, some growing closer. Perhaps, Ferranos, those peculiar cuts are from what made them scream. Some have gotten this close. Occasionally."

The trail we followed turned sharply south, clinging to the upper edges of the crater's inside wall. The complex sank into the concave pit, mostly in shadow, but the western edges burned gold where the sun touched it. Garvyne's previous description had been as simple as his dirt-drawn diagram—wholly inadequate to describe the truth of the complex. The outermost circle, into which we now descended, had been repaired in places and fortified. Where ramps and stairs and paths provided access to the next lower level, the citizens had done the most building. We would have to pass through those strong points to eventually reach the temple itself.

Though long since laid to waste, the temple was monumental compared to the puny constructions raised in the circles above. Between the front portico and the rear, the roof had collapsed, leaving round black pillars uncapped. The triangular frieze on the front remained intact, despite listing perilously to the left. Because of the shadows, I couldn't make out the scene depicted, yet I had an unsettling sense that the figures moved of their own accord through a series of obscene interactions with each other. It seemed as if the temple had been shaped out of the bones of a demon, and within the frieze played out its blasphemous dreams.

Gold, indeed, formed the mortar for everything. It oozed from between stones, running down to the street like candle wax. Gold dust flowed through the streets as if desert sand, creating dunes here and there. Gold enough to satisfy Tsaleryk's grandest dream of avarice lay in plain view, and glinted from the arms and armor of those manning the fortifications below.

Balarion crouched on the pathway and studied the complex. "Our best plan, I think, is to scout around before attacking. We want to find more of the fire circles."

Phylasina rested her hand on his shoulder. "Some of the people may wish to parlay. They'll let us descend in return for the chance to destroy us and steal what we've taken on the way back out."

Garvyne frowned. "Would they be guileless enough to believe we would let that happen?"

"Only if they believe we are guileless enough to agree to such an offer." Balarion stood. "We will bargain in good faith and keep our word, yet be merciless if opposed and betrayed. Capture the first we encounter of any of these creatures and send them back to their people as a sign of good faith."

"I'll lead the way, shall I?" Krotha settled his helmet in place and drew his sword. "I shall share truth with them, and give them truth if they refuse to understand."

"Perfect, my friend." Balarion drew his sword. "Onward, as the king wills it."

CHAPTER 16

In retrospect, having Krotha, huge as he was and encased in metal, lead the way down might not have been the best way to encourage negotiations with those who had become residents of the temple complex. The first group we faced warded a long set of stairs leading down to the next level. The guardians were sylph-slender albino warriors and warrior-priests who bore serpentine swords and wore dark armor. Time had tattered their cloaks and surcoats, imparting a shifting and shaggy texture to our foes. It enhanced the swift fluidity of their motion.

Krotha took the lead, and Garvyne stepped up beside him as these creatures drew steel in answer to what we hoped were peaceful overtures. Krotha worried less about blocking their attacks than he did sweeping his blade through them. The thicker they came, the more damage he could do. Black blood spurted and slender limbs fell as he laid into them.

Garvyne matched him blow for blow, but applied his ax more surgically. An overhand chop would bury the broad head in a rib cage, then he'd wrench the weapon free. He crushed a jaw with the haft's steel cap, then whirled the ax around in an arc that took a leg off at the knee. He kicked that enemy out of the way, blocked a sword slash on the haft, then chopped his new foe in twain.

Phylasina matched the slender swordsmen cut for cut, dueling with an élan that appeared to impress her foes. She parried their strikes quickly. Her ripostes struck viper-fast and found the tiniest gaps in armor. A stab to the throat would send an enemy reeling, then she'd parry and thrust through another fighter's thigh. Blood geysered as she found arteries. Chest wounds bubbled, and her victims stumbled back before collapsing.

As skillful as the Knights of Virtue were, however, they lacked the solemn passion with which Balarion fought. He had learned his lessons from Krotha well. He kept his style simple, blocking and parrying, advancing and retreating, forcing his foes to tire themselves. He remained steady, then struck when they faltered. His blows might not have been as powerful as Krotha's, nor as quick as Phylasina's, but he cut a swath through the enemy that left as many bodies behind as the others did.

I, for my part, dueled sorcerously with the warrior-priests. They attacked with pale green fireballs that hissed as they shot through the air. I eluded several and attacked back with blue-white lightning. My first shot hit its intended target, wreathing the priest in corrosive ivy that clawed the flesh from his face. He crumpled and further melted before my spell spent itself.

One of their fireballs hit me on the right hip, twisting me around and knocking me down. I landed hard and tumbled back, coming to rest in the shadow of a broken wall. I didn't even bother to look down. The bubbling sensation from the joint and the grind of my femur disintegrating told me everything important. I twisted to my left—my leg choosing to remain on the ground—and pulled myself up on the rock.

I thrust my staff forward and allowed myself a smile. The warrior-priest who had hit me couldn't see where I'd fallen. She came around to her right and was in the process of climbing up on a rock herself. I cast. She turned as she reached the pinnacle, which is when my spell caught her square in the chest.

It blasted her back in a long arc that ended with a splash in the next circle down.

At that point, the essence of the first warrior-priest sizzled into me. I could not tell when his life had begun or where—if in some other land or even another dimension. His long training and devotion to serpentine gods, the sacrifices, including that of his own parents and siblings, to increase his power, flooded over me. Honor was, for the Vangion, the reason for living. At some point in time, their godling and the one to whom the temple had been dedicated had developed an undying enmity. They had traveled here to honor their god, and those who held this first staircase had been tasked with waiting for their bravest cohorts' return from the complex's heart.

The second warrior-priest's essence hit me, and I slid back off the stone. I aped the serpentine motions that defined her devotions, drawing myself closer to my abandoned leg. I dragged it over and jammed it against the stump, then drank deeply of my flask. Fire exploded in my belly and coursed down into my leg. It hurt more in the fixing than it had in the severing, but after a minute I could stand again. Shortly thereafter, I regained full use of the limb. I walked across a carpet of bloody bodies to rejoin my companions where they had secured the staircase's upper end.

Krotha, his armor dappled with black stains, drank from his flask. Garvyne removed a gauntlet and began to wrap a cut on his hand. Phylasina had doffed her helmet, her hair pasted to sweaty forehead and cheeks. The three of them appeared to be peasants taking a breather after reaping.

Balarion had sunk to a knee and had his head bowed. I crossed to him and likewise knelt. "You saw?"

He nodded very slightly. "The Vangion. Holding this place was a sacred duty for them. Their faith, their devotion, hard to describe."

"Pure." Krotha slipped his flask back into the pouch on his belt. "But that does not mean, my lord, that it is right or just or even sane. They have waited here for a very long time. Half those I slew had been born here, raised here, trained by those who others left behind. Their belief in their duty was vital because it gave them purpose."

The youth frowned. "What do you mean?"

I pointed toward the complex's lowest point. "These Vangion believed they had been ordered to stay here to secure their elite guards' line of withdrawal. But in this place, why would you divide your force? Those who ordered them to stay gave them a mission so they could salve their honor, but truly, the elite guards thought them useless, unworthy, or incapable of honorably acquitting their duty. We have freed them from a pointless mission. We have allowed them to die with honor—the honor their compatriots denied them."

"Yes. Yes, they had waited a long time." Balarion shook his head. "Our mission reveals to them the falsehood of their belief."

"But, my lord, *they* never knew that." I stood. "They fought well and with honor. When your father comes into his power again, tell him that and let him honor them."

* * *

Destroying the Vangion had one consequence we had not anticipated. They had been highly successful in keeping a variety of peoples bottled up in the complex. Unable to leave, groups had carved out their own little fiefdoms and fought battles to avoid being utterly destroyed. Not many had been there longer than the Vangion, but a number had lived in the complex for multiple generations. Some even thrived there, with one group laying claim to a domain on three different levels.

Once we smashed the Vangion fortifications and opened the stairway, people began to drift out. Most appeared fearful, and more than a few were lost. Once they reached the stairs, they scrambled up as quickly as they could. Some possessed enough sense to carry gold with them. Most of the others had dwelled in and around it for so long that it had ceased to carry any value. I would have happily wagered that those born and bred in the complex had no means to understand how coveted the gold was in Kadarr.

Balarion kicked open the door to what once had been a stable. Every stall had been stacked high with gold bars. Gold dust had gathered in corners. Incalculable wealth found shelter in a building that could easily blow down in a stiff breeze.

"If Tsaleryk had any idea of how much gold was here, he never would have trusted us to come." He bent and picked up a bright gold coin. "This level alone must have more gold in it than he does in the rest of his realm. Why hasn't he moved in force to take this place?"

Phylasina shook her head. "Tsaleryk is as blind as the people born here. He cannot see the true value of all this. For him, the blindness is willful. If he thought his accumulated treasure was insignificant, he would see himself as insignificant. That this mocks his world is something he would sooner know nothing about."

I chuckled. "That condition is not limited to your brother, my lord. Many people refuse to see those things that would force them to reevaluate their world and their purpose in life. The Vangion had to know their elites would never return. If they acknowledged that, they would have to acknowledge defeat. They would have to abandon their last mission to report back to others about how things had gone badly. For them, the illusory reality in which they dwelled was comfortable. It was a world they knew. To abandon that comfort was to embrace fear, and few people are willing to do that."

"So this is what the world has sunk to, then, in my father's absence? This is what he dreaded?" Balarion sighed. "People enslave themselves to fear. They tell themselves that their fetters keep them safe, and surrender freedom for that safety?"

Krotha grunted. "The freedom to be wrong is one few people wish to exercise."

"With my father's return, that will all change." Balarion nodded solemnly. "I will tell him about all we have seen. He will open this realm again. He will allow Alkindor to flourish again. The people will know true joy."

Our emotions buoyed by that sentiment, we pressed on. We avoided the most heavily fortified areas of the complex. At one point, we had to fight through a descent, travel a quarter turn around the circle, and then ascend a level and make another quarter turn before we could plunge deeper.

Most of the other denizens were more open to negotiation than the Vangion had been. Some, ancient and haggard, recognized the Knights of Virtue and took Krotha at his word that they would not be molested. We gained safe passage that way several times. As we descended, the groups became more fatalistic and uncaring. To their minds, if we wished to enter the temple and die, they'd scavenge our bodies, and that would be an end to it all.

The grinding of circles had broken the staircase to the lowest level. We could descend a half dozen broad, white, marble steps, then look to the right and see the lower half a good twenty meters away. Since none of us could leap that vast distance, and because we'd not brought rope, we opted to climb down through unstable ruins. Had the circles chosen to slip at that point, we'd have been buried and King Parnyr's grand plan would have collapsed with the ruins.

Our luck held, however, and we reached the temple itself. We worked our way around toward the front. There we found a dozen skeletons, or pieces thereof, with enough armor scraps and shattered weaponry to identify them as Vangion elites. They'd been bigger than their brethren, and their bones evidenced cuts stained with gold. The bones had weathered poorly and broke easily, suggesting the elites had died centuries ago.

I brushed bone dust from my hands. "One mystery solved."

Garvyne studied the bones and the area surrounding them. "See the stones, how they are arranged? They had time to create breastworks. They were not ambushed here, but pursued, I think. By whatever dwells deeper."

Balarion nodded. "Then let us see what that is."

I crept forward, staff at the ready, every sense alert. My companions worked their way up the broad black stairs with similar caution, save for Garvyne. Undaunted he was, not strolling, but moving with a deliberate rhythm and sense of destiny. I marveled at that, at how a living man approached the unknown fearlessly.

There was much to fear. The frieze above the entrance had twins over other lintels. Stone figures moved of their own accord, playing out scenes from legends or nightmares. The dark figures had fluid gold shadows and bled gold blood. I thought I recognized bits of the drama here and there. At one point, some seemed to reenact the last battle of the Vangion elite.

Shortly thereafter, we, my companions and I, appeared in a dark shadow play that I did not recognize. I hoped, given its outcome, it would in no way be prophetic.

The original sinking of the complex had broken the temple, shattering columns and crushing statuary. Bones, the ragged remnants of clothing, and mangled armor marked where a few of the most intrepid adventurers had gotten to. We wended our way through a tangle of debris and into the temple's center.

The center provided a sharp contrast to all else. The floor, though cracked in places, had been swept clean of debris. A tall statue of a youth stood in the middle atop a squat pedestal. Clean-limbed and handsome, he had on a belt that bore an inscription I recognized as old, but could not read. He appeared to be a hunter, armed with a boar-spear, and a pair of wolfishly lean ferpine flanked him, each looking up at him adoringly.

Before him, hovering in the air above the temple floor, a golden scepter floated in a bright bubble. Though I had grown bored with gold by this time, the scepter amazed me. As long as my forearm, it had a fist-sized diamond on one end, a wreath of rubies surrounding the diamond's setting, and a slender shaft, which ended in a ruby the size of my eye. The goldsmith had engraved words and designs all over the scepter, some of which I could read, all of which appeared arcane, and none of which I comprehended enough to get a true sense of the scepter's nature or purpose.

I stared at the bauble, in awe of it. As my compatriots all wore closed helms, I could not read their expressions, but none of the Knights of Virtue took a step toward it. That fell to Balarion, who shouldered his way past Krotha and Garvyne. Phylasina raised a hand to restrain our leader, but he had passed beyond her range. He marched up to the bubble, took off his left gauntlet, and reached out to take the scepter.

Clever boy. If he loses that hand, he can still fight with the other.

His hand closed on the scepter's shaft. Light flashed. The bubble burst.

He raised the scepter high in his fist, triumphant.

Which is when the statue moved.

DARK SOULS™
MASQUE OF VINDICATION

CHAPTER 17

The golden statue shimmered and wavered as if a superheated column of air had pierced the broken roof to engulf it. The edges and the finer details softened as the gold skin brightened. Sunlight poured down to infuse the statue with enough energy to convert it to fluid.

A flood of molten gold would have been more than enough to finish us, but the statue maintained its structural integrity. Instead of flowing down to the ground, new plates and angles surfaced through the gold. Armor rose to encase the youth's limbs. His spine expanded, lifting his shoulders to make room for a second set of shoulders. From them grew another pair of arms, also armored. A long, curved sword sprouted from each mighty fist.

The statue stepped off the pedestal, his footfalls shaking the stone floor, and charged at us. Balarion leaped above one cut, then blocked a second. That blow sent him tumbling through the air. The godling, Aurduwyne, slashed at Krotha and Phylasina to keep them back as he turned toward Balarion. Only Garvyne the Undaunted stood between Aurduwyne and our leader.

The godling raised the four swords as he towered over Garvyne, certain death glinting in sunlight.

The Undaunted broke and ran.

I leveled my staff at the metal deity and triggered a spell. Energy sizzled in a roiling blue ball and blasted into the back of the godling's right knee. Molten gold splashed, and the knee buckled. Aurduwyne sagged to the right, casting two swords aside and catching himself on two hands.

Phylasina dashed forward and leaped onto the small of his back. She hacked away at his armor, slashing great rents in it. Her swords came away edged with gold. The blades bit deep and fluid gold flowed, prompting her shrieked cry of triumph.

But that gold, though not hot, was not blood, either, and it splashed upon the floor wastefully. It welled in the wounds she had opened, then flowed up and away, over her feet and calves. It encased her to the knees, freezing her in place. The twin swords likewise became fluid. The gold rivulets resolved themselves into ferpine with armored hide and daggerlike fangs long enough to puncture a man from front to back. Their claws gouged black stone as the beasts gathered themselves, sprinted, and leaped.

Phylasina, trapped, could only turn her head as the beasts launched themselves.

They'd have had her, but Krotha intercepted one, splitting it from front to back with a single blow. The gold beast's front half twisted in the air. The bisected creature failed in its attempt to snap at Phylasina. It did, however, succeed in knocking its companion awry. The ferpine spun through the air, just missing its target. It bounced off Aurduwyne's broad back, then smashed into a broken pillar. The impact snapped its back, then spun it off into the shadows.

I cast another spell, sending blue lightning skittering over the godling's back. Phylasina screamed as it reached her, but the gold trapping her melted. She leaped away and regained her balance after a few steps. She turned in my direction, blades ready, and for one fascinating moment, I thought she meant to kill me.

What she had seen was that the back half of the first ferpine had melted into a half dozen smaller puddles, which resolved themselves into a small pack of ferpine. Though the size of puppies, they launched themselves at me with lethal zeal. I twisted away and splashed one with a hastily cast spell, but her blades shredded the others with blurred strokes.

With her occupying them, I dashed around the godling's right side and ran to Balarion. He'd already regained his feet and had thrown away his dented helmet. A little blood trickled down at his temple, but his eyes focused on me. "How do we kill him?"

"I do not think we can. We just have to outrun him."

Balarion slipped the scepter into his belt. "We better move quickly."

I cast another spell at Aurduwyne, this time hitting his right knee from the front. The armor crumbled, but the lightning couldn't boil its way through. The tip of Krotha's blade poked through the thigh from the back. Had the creature been mortal, that blow would have bled him to death, but it merely annoyed the godling. He reached back around and swatted Krotha away.

Aurduwyne made a grab for Balarion, but the youth leaped out of the way. The godling slipped to the side, then struggled to stand. He rocked back, straightening the ruined leg. Gold flowed, and all the damage I'd done repaired itself. Beyond him, the ferpine with the shattered spine melted into a gold puddle that drained away into cracks in the floor.

I ran around to where Balarion was helping Krotha to his feet. The Knight of Virtue took a long draught from his flask, and his left shoulder quickly rose to the height of the right. Phylasina waved us on toward the exit, ducking out a low door that we all hoped would slow Aurduwyne.

As the godling chased after us, he realized that fighting in the four-armed form conveyed no advantage. Rushing toward the doorway, the figure shimmered once more and became an amorphous torrent of fluid metal. Pouring through the doorway, he resolved himself into a titanic gold serpent. The head rose and the hood spread. The fanged mouth opened and gold streams sprayed.

They shot past us, splashing over a broken wall. Dripping down, they eroded the golden mortar. Stones shifted and rocks tumbled. The pools began to writhe, serpentine forms wriggling to the surface, surrounding us, cutting off all retreat.

Aurduwyne hissed.

Then, from above, from the pinnacle of the portico, Garvyne leaped out and down. He flew at the snake's flat, broad head, his ax pulled back. As he landed, the broadax's blade arced around and down. The steel bit deep, cracking the snake's skull. Molten gold gushed, and the snake reared back, smashing Garvyne against the lintel.

The snake's limp body melted. Garvyne splashed down in a puddle of fluid gold. Ripples sloshed over him, with one fat droplet tracing a tear down his cheek. The gold ran off his armor, and the larger puddle began to harden against his back and around his legs.

We ran to him, Krotha pulling off his helmet. "We will free you, my friend."

Garvyne coughed, and bright red blood dribbled from the corner of his mouth. "No, I am done."

Balarion crouched beside him. "You cannot be. You saved us."

"No, I saved myself." Garvyne freed his right hand from his gauntlet and reached out to caress Balarion's cheek. "I was the Undaunted because I feared letting anyone see how great a coward I was. Aurduwyne... For eons I heard the screams of those who faced him and knew he would be the end of me. That is why I waited."

My eyes narrowed. "Then why join us?"

"You were the only ones who knew who I was. If I stayed, you would know me to be a coward. I was not the Undaunted, just the Vain."

Balarion grasped his hand. "And yet you saved us. You will forever be known as the Undaunted because of that act. So yes, we knew you, and you are the person we knew you to be."

Garvyne, teeth stained red, tried to smile, but a whimper robbed the expression of its courage. "You will remember me, but soon enough I shall be as the others here, the Vangion, all the rest, memories held in no hearts, heard of in no songs. Legends of a lost time, worth nothing."

"My father shall know of your courage."

"And yet in my presence here, your father will know of my cowardice." Pain washed over his face, then his hand slipped from Balarion's grasp. "At least I die true."

I reached down and closed his eyes. "This is a fitting place for him to remain."

Balarion stood. "My father will exalt him."

"Then let us move." Krotha pointed his sword back in the direction we'd come. "We may have won, but we still can lose."

* * *

We faced a very real problem in escaping the complex. Everyone else within appeared to know that we had destroyed Aurduwyne, or at least that the godling had died. Some of the more militant groups maintained hope that they would be able to wrest the scepter from us and complete a mission they'd begun eons before. I suspected centuries had passed for some of them without conscious notice, and I wondered, if when we escaped this place, how much time would have passed outside the temple's precincts.

Night crept forward, the crater's umbra climbing slowly up the eastern wall as the sun sank. We worked our way farther around the circles, doing our best to ascend in different spots than where we had descended. Some forces had moved to possess strongholds we'd cleared out, and they now defended their new possessions against others. We skirted major battles as we worked our way up through a handful of circles. As we hit the second, however, forces from below tracked us, and forces above made it impossible for us to ascend.

We found a defensible ruin of black stones joined with gold. Krotha happily mounted a small wall and banged his sword against his shield. "I am Krotha. I am the Truth. I am a Knight of Virtue in service to the Alkindoran King Parnyr. Come, face me, if you wish to be counted among the throngs of his dead enemies."

His declaration cowed a few groups, save for one cohort of thickly built men with chartreuse flesh and long hair of a slightly lighter green shade. Their plate armor appeared metallic, if judged by the dark iron hues, but had an encrusted texture that suggested a barnacle infestation. They bore massive clubs wrapped in dark iron or flails on rusted chains, and they rushed into battle with impatience and fury.

Balarion and the others waited to engage them, but I immediately employed my magic. Energy built along my staff, then penetrated the ground. A straight line of crystals erupted from the earth, tearing a swath through the oncoming warriors. Others moved to fill the hole in their ranks, but they had not brought the force together by the time they hit our redoubt.

Krotha split the skull of the first warrior to get close, then took a heavy blow on his shield. That staggered him, and a stone shifted beneath his right foot. He fell back, and a warrior leaped up onto the wall. I spitted the man with a blue-white magick spear, pitching him off the wall and into the churning mass of his compatriots.

Balarion took Krotha's place. Though lacking his size, our leader proved he had learned his lessons well. He caught a flail blow on his shield, but kept his feet. He thrust at the warrior's throat, the tip of his blade sliding up beneath the gorget. Cerulean blood sprayed in an arc as Balarion ripped his blade free. He chopped down, severing an arm at the elbow, then crushed a warrior's skull with the edge of his shield.

Phylasina mounted the wall to Balarion's right, a handmaiden to death. Her twin blades hissed through the air. They unerringly found armor gaps, slashing through flesh as if it were paper. Blue blood became a mist drifting back down over the attackers. Dead and dying warriors flew back from the walls, crushing their compatriots and becoming wet adjuncts to the walls we defended.

A club swept Balarion's legs from beneath him, but Krotha's interposed shield caught the following blow meant to dash out our leader's brains. I cast again, my magick's crystal line reaping thickly packed bodies. Krotha regained the wall, decapitating the first warrior to get close. The head popped into the air, and Krotha swatted it with his shield.

The chartreuse warriors' eyes grew wide, and, to a man, they pointed at

Krotha, his armor dappled with blue droplets. The front ranks tumbled away, the corpses of their comrades making for horrid footing. The rearmost ranks turned and fled, and Krotha screamed imprecations at their backs.

He spun, thrusting his sword in the air. "Did you see them..." His voice trailed off.

I whirled. There, a hundred yards on, one of the gold warehouses had burst and coins had spilled out into the street. A remarkable sight, made terrifying by the addition of the coins gathering themselves into long-limbed, gangling creatures of glittering metal. The coins covered them in a scaly flesh. The fingers grew extraordinarily long and curved down into hooked claws. The creatures slowly stood erect and began to shamble around aimlessly until their gait improved. They turned toward the biggest of their number, one matching Aurduwyne in height, and it pointed a sharp claw in our direction.

"...'Ware, my lord!" Phylasina shoved Balarion aside. Golden mortar had liquefied and begun to flow around Balarion's feet to root him in place. "We have to run."

"Where?" Krotha pointed above and below with his sword. "There are more gathering themselves above and below us."

Balarion's eyes narrowed. "The cuts you found on the old bones, Ferranos, those things made them."

Phylasina stomped on the fluid gold as if a child disapproving of a mud puddle. "But Aurduwyne is dead. Garvyne slew him."

Something sparked in the back of my head. I turned to Balarion. "Give me the scepter."

"What?"

"I haven't the time to explain. If you want to live, give me the scepter."

Phylasina made to stay his hand, but Balarion plucked the golden rod from his belt and placed it in my grasp.

"Good." I smiled and clutched it to my breast. "Now, my lord, *kill me*."

CHAPTER 18

By the time my companions returned to the spirit fire I'd kindled at the start of our descent, I had recovered myself. They appeared a little worse for wear—armor dented and scratched, but their limbs intact. We'd have to find Balarion a new helmet and sew up the cut on his head, but we had escaped the ordeal largely unhurt.

As long as one did not count Garvyne's death, that was.

I had just finished piecing back together the diamond capping the scepter, flawlessly sealing it so no one could tell the difference, when they arrived. Balarion's smile signaled his relief. I could read neither Krotha's nor Phylasina's face, though when Krotha removed his helmet, he appeared to be as happy as Balarion. Phylasina's expression, when revealed, perhaps was not as joyous as the other two, but she did appear to be relieved.

I suspect that is because she did not expect me to still be at the fire.

Balarion clapped me on the shoulders. "How did you figure out what would happen?"

I shrugged. "Tell me first what happened."

Krotha laughed heartily. "The moment Balarion took your head—a mighty stroke well worthy of song—you evaporated, and the scepter with you. I will admit I didn't like the prospect of facing those gold things with only three, but they stopped coming for us. The small ones climbed one upon the other, creating a ladder for the larger one to scale the circle's rim.

Up it went, and the others flowed with it. They scattered those who had been waiting for us above, then began an assault on the last circle."

Balarion nodded. "It is as he says. They were clearly setting off after you, but before they could get beyond the complex, they flew apart. They just went to pieces and sprayed themselves all over the road. We saw them as we ascended. What did you do?"

I frowned. "One of the warriors we slew, when his essence drained into me, he had a different name for the godling. Not Aurduwyne, but Aurwyn. Aurwyn was the spirit-godling of a river, the Gold River. So named because of the gold that could be found in it. Aurduwyne was the name given to a hero from that area. The statue had been formed in his image. But it was the spirit of Aurwyn himself that had been trapped in the scepter."

I handed the golden rod back to Balarion. "Aurwyn controlled and shaped the gold. Our fighting and Garvyne's sacrifice disrupted the godling's magick. It took a while for it to regain control of nearby gold. We carried our doom with us, so I sought to carry it here. Then I shattered the diamond, and Aurwyn's prison was no more."

Phylasina's expression darkened. "You destroyed the scepter we are to trade for the Key of Gold?"

"Can you imagine what would have happened if we brought it intact to Tsaleryk?" I clasped my hands at the small of my back. "Aurwyn would have taken control of the palace and slaughtered everyone."

"But this thing is now worthless."

"I don't believe so, Phylasina." Balarion shook his head. "Tsaleryk never had a true understanding of what the scepter was. He knew it as an artifact of great power, but had he known it could control gold, he'd not have sent us for it. He would have feared we would use it to dispossess him of his realm."

She sighed. "That is likely true."

I pointed at the scepter. "The diamond has been returned to its flawless state. Moreover, there is enough residual magick in the scepter that controlling some gold is possible. I believe, when we reach the court, I should be able to use it to shape for Tsaleryk one of those things we faced toward the end. I would make it into a bodyguard for him, as incorruptible as the gold that forms it. He and his court wizards should be occupied enough with that to allow us to get the key and escape."

"Good. I like this plan." Balarion scratched his jaw. "I think it best that we agree to tell my brother that tales of gold are exaggerated. Were he to learn what is here, his nation, which functions poorly, would be turned to salvaging all the gold. Harvests would be forgotten, and the people would starve in a land paved with gold."

I nodded. "I believe you are wise in suggesting this, my lord."

"Worse, he might demand we lead the way back." Phylasina rested a hand on Balarion's shoulder. "Then would come another demand, and another. Our quest would never see an end."

Krotha shook his head. "I will not gainsay you in spinning a tale for him, but I can have no part in lying. I am the Truth."

I turned toward him. "But which truth, my friend? The truth of the riches of this place, this pit of blood-soaked metal, which is so abundant to be valueless? Or the truth that, as Balarion has said, Tsaleryk will destroy his realm and doom everyone in it, sacrificing them on an altar of his greed?"

"As you say, they are both truths."

"But which is the greater?" I opened my hands. "Of what value is truth if it destroys the innocent?"

Krotha chuckled. "You must have been a philosopher when alive, Ferranos. The truth is the truth. It is the objective fact of the world. It is the basis upon which all rationality is based."

"And you think Tsaleryk is rational?"

"The truth is, I do not." He held up a hand. "Please, I pray you, do not ask me to shoulder this burden."

Balarion nodded. "As you wish it, my friend. We would not have you discomfited."

"Thank you, my lord."

* * *

The truth of our journey back to Darrxan was that it took no longer for us to return than it had for us to travel forth. Yet the next night, the moon appeared in an earlier phase than it had when we set out. More interestingly, spring floods had eroded roads, and fallow fields showed midsummer grass growth. It was not until we reached the capital and were conducted into Tsaleryk's presence that we were given full measure of how long we had been away.

"I had given you up for dead, dead as were all the others." Tsaleryk's shoulders slumped more, and his paunch had grown. The path between piles of gold in his palace had vanished, and two layers of boardwalk raised us above the shiny metal. "Five years I have waited—faithfully, mind— never doubting that you would return. You have it?"

Balarion advanced and dropped to a knee a half dozen yards from the throne. "We have succeeded, brother. We have the scepter, the Scepter of Aurwyn."

Tsaleryk's eyes narrowed as Balarion pronounced the name. "The Scepter of Aurwyn. Yes. Yes. Of course. And you have it? Give it here."

Our lord slipped it from his belt. "You had promised the Key of Gold for it in exchange."

Tsaleryk drew back. "You doubt me?"

"No, brother, I fear you will be distracted by the wonders you can work with this scepter." Balarion extended it to me. "I would have Ferranos demonstrate."

I accepted the scepter, then bowed to Balarion and then to Tsaleryk. "My lord, this scepter was fashioned in accord with instructions whispered by Aurwyn, the god of the Gold River. It has properties that guarantee prosperity and security for the one who possesses it. Long ago, it was stolen from the people who worshipped Aurwyn and secreted away. Without access to their god's power, the people fell to invaders."

Tsaleryk hung on my every word. We'd crafted the story about the scepter on our journey, linking gold and prosperity and security to the scepter, since we knew these were the things Tsaleryk treasured. As I spoke, the pink tip of his tongue became visible, moving across his lower lip like a slug on a leaf.

I grasped the scepter in my left hand and pointed at a pile of coins to the right of the throne, halfway between Balarion and Tsaleryk. I focused my mind, and a few coins danced, ringing melodiously. Again coins bounced and popped. Soon the pile's surface roiled as if the gold were boiling.

Then the dancing coins began to take shape. Hands with long talons clawed their way past the surface. A scaled head appeared, with tall ears growing erect. The creature, slender and long-limbed, hauled itself free of the pile. One leg came clear, then the second. The creature squatted for a moment, then stood a full eight feet tall, the imprint of each coin visible in its flesh—a Vangion warrior rendered in gold.

Tsaleryk stared up at it, aghast and yet reaching for it. Then he cut a glance at me. "Is that all? A simple parlor trick?"

I went to a knee. "It is all I have yet been able to do, my lord. My mastery of magicks is meager, and yet I can shape for you this guardian. Your court sorcerers are superior to me, and they can impart to you the secrets that would allow you to raise a cohort or an army. Perhaps you could even create a dragon to course through the skies."

"A dragon I could ride."

"Yes, my lord." I returned the scepter to Balarion's hand.

The gold construct remained standing.

Balarion bowed his head. "As you can see, brother, we found and fetched for you that which you demanded of us. We have upheld our part of the bargain."

"You have, yes, you have." Tsaleryk stood abruptly, his expression shifting through so many emotions I could not decipher them. For half a moment, I wondered if I would have to command the construct to kill him, but he composed himself, and my concern drained away.

Tsaleryk pulled his sleeves back to his elbows, and for the first time, I noticed a finger-width ribbon of gold encircling his right wrist. At least, this is how I first saw it, but it reflected light oddly and moved with him. It then appeared to be a gold tattoo, a cuff of sorts, with no sigils or embellishments. The paunchy prince extended a finger and drew in the air the rough shape of a key pointing down at the floor. He opened his right hand and pressed it into the space where he'd written the symbol.

"Now you, Balarion."

Balarion stood and shucked the gauntlet from his right hand. He reached out, pressing his palm against his brother's. Their fingers closed, interlacing. The gold cuff on Tsaleryk's wrist flowed up over his hand, through his fingers and through Balarion's fingers, to then drain down into Balarion's thick wrist.

Tsaleryk reached out with his left hand. "And now the scepter."

Balarion passed it between their bellies, and as its full weight fell into Tsaleryk's hand, they broke their grip. Balarion staggered back, and Phylasina steadied him.

Tsaleryk stared down at the scepter, then looked at the construct. It gazed back at him. The prince returned to his throne and sat. The guardian squatted.

Balarion flexed his hand and smiled. "Are you satisfied, brother?"

Tsaleryk smiled. "Our bargain is done, but you still have accounts to be squared. You owe me for five years of food."

Phylasina blinked. "You did not give us five years of food."

"You were gone for five years. No one in my realm has reported feeding you, nor have they reported thefts, thus the food I gave you lasted five years. That is a debt." He held out a hand. "You must pay that debt."

I cleared my throat. "The question would be, Highness, what is just compensation? I would suggest that as a bard earns his meals recounting tales, that we repay you in that way."

Tsaleryk arched an eyebrow. "Have you five years of tales to tell, wizard?"

Balarion, who rubbed at his right wrist with his left hand, smiled. "We have a tale of an adventure that lasted five years, brother. It is a story of great hardship, sacrifice, and nobility. You see us here as we were when we left you, but another of our company has been and died. Were it not for Garvyne the Undaunted, we would truly have been lost and you would not hold the Scepter of Aurwyn."

The prince frowned, and the guardian's ears sank back. "Garvyne, of the Knights of Virtue. What of him?"

I opened my hands. "We found him outside the pit in which the scepter had been secreted. Your father had tasked him with watching and waiting until we came. He led us down into the pit, slaying demons and crushing enemies from lands far away and long ago. And when we came to the final guardian, the one that stood between us and fulfilling your wishes, it was the Undaunted who put an end to the creature."

Phylasina stepped forward. "It is as Ferranos says, Highness. We fought a horrid creature standing fourteen feet tall, with four arms and armor. It rose from a pool of mercury and shaped itself into this quicksilver devil that fought ferociously. When we cut it, even a small part of it, the mercury flowed back into the creature. But Garvyne understood what had to be done. He climbed to a height and split the creature in half with a mighty blow of his ax. He cleaved it from crown to groin. Ferranos used his magic to boil away one half while Balarion snatched the scepter from the bottom of the empty pool."

In crafting our story, we added quicksilver to it, since its ability to coat gold was well known and had to terrify Tsaleryk. The detail appeared to do the trick, for he drew back. Even the guardian hunched its shoulders and sank down into the coins a bit.

The prince's expression sharpened, then he tapped a finger against his chin. "A tale, an interesting tale. You tell it well." He looked past us to Krotha. "And you, Knight of Truth, you remain silent. What say you of this fantastic story?"

Krotha sank to a knee and hung his head. "It would pain me, my lord, to answer your question. Do not ask this of me."

"I must insist, then, Krotha. They are convincing, but you I would trust. Your recital I would trust. Why would telling the story cause you pain?"

"Because, my lord, you notice in their telling of it that I do not merit a mention." Krotha sighed heavily. "Had I done anything worthy of note, I would have been content with however humble an inclusion in the story. I wish to say nothing more than that I asked them to keep me out of the tale and not to fashion lies on my behalf. To my shame, Highness, the thing we fought swatted me as if I were but an insect, and had Garvyne not intervened, I surely would have perished."

CHAPTER 19

Tsaleryk thought on what Krotha had said for a moment, then three, then longer, to the point where I grew uncomfortably certain that he might actually analyze our tale. With the covert flick of a finger, I made the golden guardian shift, and coins slid down in a ringing cacophony around its clawed feet. The sounds and movement reminded Tsaleryk of the prize I'd conjured for him, and the promise of yet more such creatures when his wizards mastered the magicks.

Balarion immediately announced that while we would have loved to pass a fortnight in the palace to recover, we could not justify distracting Tsaleryk from important affairs of state. He said we'd be heading off to Trafaram as soon as we possibly could. Phylasina negotiated supplies with some minister or other, and Tsaleryk—distracted by his guardian because of its nature, not anything I did—agreed we would acquit our debt by another recital of tales when we returned to his realm.

Phylasina's negotiations had not included a room for the night, so we headed out on the road, angling to the southwest. We opted to travel on the roads, but made our camp away from villages. This created no great hardship for us, as what we had seen in the west of Kadarr held true for the east. Our saddle-beasts fared well, given all the forage available to them, and we did not suffer overmuch. Krotha and I remained on watch, since sleeping was something we'd already managed to compile in century-long lots. Balarion and Phylasina, being mortal yet, got all the rest they needed.

As they slept, the night dragged on slowly, and Krotha stared into the distance. "I once had a wife. Children, too. I can no longer conjure their images in my mind, but not all is lost to me. The happy laughter. Even now, I recall that fondly."

He looked to me, and I felt he wished me to share a similar memory. "I am pleased for you, my friend. I am certain she must have been quite happy with you. Your children as well."

"I hope it is as you say, but I recollect little. Once I became a Knight of Virtue, I spent more time away from her than I did with her." He picked up a pebble and tossed it beyond the circle of firelight. "The truth was— and I remember this truth clearly—she had another lover. Perhaps many. I did not gainsay her that because I knew she loved me, too, and I only wished her happiness."

"You recognized and accepted a truth that would have torn most people asunder."

"I cannot ignore the truth."

"But you do find and elevate slices of it." I smiled. "You told Tsaleryk the truth, your truth, and that allowed him to believe our lie."

Krotha chuckled. "I tell you that truth is the objective reality upon which we must all agree, but I know each person has a truth. Often is it false, and to act upon it will doom them, but they do not want to give it up. What Tsaleryk heard in my tale of shame was his own tale of shame. He could have done what we did—that is his truth—had he been brave enough to venture forth. His shame and mine matched. To question mine would be to question his, and he had no desire to do that."

My eyes narrowed. "You see the truth very well, my friend."

"Well enough, when I wish to, when it is required of me." He half smiled in my direction. "And your truth, Ferranos? No wives? No children? No hushed whispers and moans in your life?"

I opened my hands and spread them apart. "I do not recall, my friend. I believe I look now as handsome as I ever did, which would suggest others were far more attractive than I. I can also suppose that learning the discipline of magick required much time and concentration, thus I imagine I would have had little time for courting and romance. But again, I do not know."

"That is a pity—not the not-knowing, but if it never was. It says something for a person that they can love and be loved." Krotha shrugged. "And it is said that every person has his match in the world. Perhaps yours is just waiting over the next hill."

"I hope not." I sighed. "I do know I detest keeping others waiting. I should hate to think she has been so long anticipating me; and I fear the price I should pay for my inexcusable tardiness."

* * *

Our journey southeast passed quickly enough, and we paused on a hilltop overlooking the border, less to orient ourselves than to ponder the contrast between the two realms. Kadarr, right up to the border, remained a place that had been allowed to lay fallow. Golden grain, green woodlots, and overgrown villages remained constant. But there at the border, along a line drawn as straight and sharp as if a god had slashed a knife through the land to sever one nation from the other, the landscape changed.

And changed most curiously.

From our vantage point, we could see the transition where the road crossed from a wooded part of Kadarr into Trafaram. On Tsaleryk's side, the wood was a mix of trees, its borders irregularly shaped as it and the prairie struggled for dominance. But to the east, tall trees lined the road for as far as we could see. That stand of timber was perhaps fifty yards wide on either end, then beyond it lay a wasteland of stumps and unkempt underbrush. The tall trees had all been taken down, yet not all of them hauled away. We could see some small woodlots where people were clearly salvaging the smaller trees and chopping them for fuel, but plenty remained that could have formed joists and planking to build dozens of Tsaleryk's depositories.

Beyond that, patches of deep green, all square and arranged in a quilt pattern of like-sized lots, surrounded villages. Else the land lay undeveloped and even barren. Dust devils rose with the wind and danced through the tan lots. Dry streambeds appeared more serpentine than necessary, though without water coursing through them, I found it impossible to discern the forces that had created them.

We descended to the roadway and passed into the other realm. Balarion immediately smiled, and Phylasina did so right alongside him. The towering trees shaded the road. The woods looked to go back forever. Had we not seen them from Kadarr, I would have assumed they did. And the trees along the road, the wildflowers blossoming around them, and even the mushrooms growing on the darker side had been perfectly shaped. No bugs nibbled the plants, and what few small creatures revealed themselves—springheels and striped dagorron—were quite handsome examples of their species.

I understood the smiles, for within the shadowed arches that shielded the road from the sun, peace and perfection prevailed. We'd seen that this perfection was an illusion, and yet a very seductive one. There seemed no doubt that Trafaram benefited greatly, from comparison to Kadarr.

Riding down into our first village appeared to confirm that notion. Set in a grassy bowl, the buildings lined up in concentric crescents, based at the point where the road provided access. No golden statue dominated, and the people went about their work at a comfortable pace, greeting one another with waves and smiles. The people looked more robust and taller than their brethren from Kadarr.

Drawing closer, however, the anomalies became obvious. Both the houses and the clothing had been gaily colored in reds and greens and blues, with hints of brown here and there, especially in wooden structures. All of the buildings had been stuccoed and then painted, and quite recently, judging by the weathering. Everyone wore clean clothes, and things had been patched symmetrically, such that the clothes appeared stylish and pleasing whether worn by a farmhand, washerwoman, or flock warden.

The village possessed buildings of a uniform size oriented around the green. Dairy kuddan grazed there, and claw-wings roamed free. They were bigger than their golden counterparts from Kadarr and seemed far healthier. The claw-wings had grown ornamental feathers around their necks and along their spines, making them quite magnificent.

The people of the village struck me as odd, but only in that they lacked peculiarity. All clean-limbed and presentable, they looked well-groomed and quite hardworking. And yet I couldn't see a single person who did not wear some form of cosmetics, whether to even out skin tone or to enhance the eyes, brows, and lashes. They even painted their fingernails and kept them in remarkably good repair despite the physical nature of much of their labor.

That work struck me as the oddest. Many of the people busied themselves by repairing, trimming, and painting. They did this to absolutely everything. The houses, certainly, but also flowers. They cut away dead bits and applied tiny dabs of paint to make petals and leaves uniform in color. Milkmaids would milk the kuddan, but groomsmen would brush the beasts down and wash them. People gathered clothes, sorted them, sent them for repairs, then washed the lot in a communal laundry. I even got the sense that individuals didn't possess clothing as much as it was shared throughout the village.

Our arrival caused some notice, and a woman approached us. She studied us up and down, then addressed herself to Phylasina—the most striking of us as appearances went. "Welcome to the village of Fair Haven. I am Malassa-fair. How can we help you, my beauty?"

Phylasina dismounted. "I am Phylasina, and I have the pleasure of presenting to you Prince Balarion. We are travelers, bound for Aethemia, and would like lodging for the evening. Can you arrange that?"

"Of course. You, my beauty, and the handsome with you, will find a place here. Your companions, after they have been prepared, will find lodging over there." She pointed deeper into Fair Haven.

Balarion frowned. "You need not segregate them because of their condition. They are true and loyal friends."

The woman sniffed. "They have needs that you do not and shall be housed accordingly. You see, as you, Phylasina-bright, are beautiful, and your Balarion-bright is handsome, you will lodge in our welcoming precinct. Your companions will have accommodations among their own kind."

I took another look at the village and began to perceive subtle differences I hadn't noticed before. What Malassa referred to as the welcoming precinct was the area into which any visitors would naturally pass. A spur from the main road led to the village, guaranteeing guests made that particular approach. The welcoming precinct extended to the village green and the first row of buildings just to the other side of it. Beyond that point, however, the buildings shifted from residential to functional, including the cleanest ironmonger's I had ever seen, and the laundry and stables. Out farther lay farms that appeared, from a distance, to be in good repair, but the paint might have been peeling, and I saw no sign of rogrash wallowing in sties anywhere.

I also noticed how Malassa addressed herself to Phylasina preferentially. Elsewhere, men tended to defer to women and certainly answered to them at the laundry and in other business. I put that down to Trafaram being the realm given to Parnyr's daughter, Jaranessa. Of her I could remember little, save for one story where she demanded the head of an engraver who had fashioned her profile to be struck onto coins. Her nose had been made too big or too small—the details escaped recollection. The king demurred, though Jaranessa's devotees burned the man out of his house and murdered him by pouring molten gold over his face.

"Fear not, my lord, Ferranos and I shall fare well." Krotha patted Balarion on the shoulder, which raised a small cloud of road dust.

Malassa clapped her hands sharply, and two boys came running over with brushes. They swiftly dusted Balarion with quick, brisk strokes, then plied their brushes in a far gentler manner to Phylasina. A young girl then approached with a hairbrush, smiling.

Phylasina looked at us, her expression ecstatic. "I think I shall like it here. Try to stay out of trouble." She took the young girl's hand and allowed herself to be led off into the welcoming precinct.

One of the boys herded Prince Balarion in the same direction, while the other chased us deeper into the village. People took notice of us as the boy drove us toward them. They scattered as if we were the rude and ravenous undead, and I began to look for avenues of retreat. *A spell to disperse some, then Krotha can cut our way free...*

Krotha glanced in my direction, and we both were sharing the same thought.

Then a tall woman, thickly hewed, ducked through a doorway and posted her fists on her hips. With her square jaw and prominent cheekbones, she lacked the sort of feminine beauty Phylasina possessed, but the light in her eyes and her quick smile gave her a presence I found intriguing. She looked us up and down, then nodded. "So raise the dead I shall. Follow me."

As she had, Krotha ducked to enter what I came to understand later was the "Reclamation Center." I passed through without having to bow my head. Many people crowded in behind us and forced us to the middle of the room. We'd have gone farther, but two big wooden tun halves dominated that side of the room. The large woman looked at us again, then past us. "You know what to do."

People fled, then returned, bearing buckets of steaming water with which they quickly filled the tubs. A hundred hands stripped my equipment from me and then my clothes. They took everything off save for the ring, which, apparently, was beautiful enough to remain. The woman herself lifted me into the nearest tub as if I were a child, while villagers armed with brushes and lye soap attacked me. When I sought to complain, someone grabbed my ankles and pulled, smothering my complaints with bubbling water.

When I came up again, hands rubbed soap into my hair with a vengeance before dunking me again.

Once I'd been scrubbed down, they pulled me from the bath, dried me off, and applied oils and unguents to me. I had a sense that this would have been how my body had been prepared for my burial. That left me uneasy, though Krotha's booming laughter proved a cure for that. He, being bigger and broader than me, required children mounted on the shoulders of adults to dry, comb, and braid his hair.

Once I'd been oiled and scented, they sat me down on a stool, and the next cadre of workers set upon me. They covered my face with a powder that masked my dull skin tone, then applied blushes and rouges to bring me back to some semblance of life. They painted my lips red and my fingernails a much paler shade. Likewise, my toenails, which they'd cut and filed before painting. They even oiled my hair, providing it the dark sheen of a raven's wing.

Finally, they brought me clothes: a wraparound tunic of red trimmed with gold, tied with a gold sash; scarlet pants below; and garishly red leather boots that reached my knees. They fitted me with a broad-brimmed hat of dark brown that had a cockade of fanciful feathers. Then they returned my belt, which had been cleaned, oiled, and repaired, and my satchel, which had received similar treatment. They'd even cleaned my staff and shod the rough end in iron.

Krotha, whose armor had been polished to a mirrorlike sheen, nodded at me. "You look almost alive."

"Yes? And you look an actor in some imperial pageant."

The large woman grinned at the two of us. "They brought me the Razed, and I have raised you to Fair. Perhaps, for you, Krotha, even raised to Bright. *Now* you are worthy of our village, and you will do us proud. Go and let everyone see how we honor Jaranessa-Solar's edicts, and let them fear they will never be our equal."

CHAPTER 20

I had no sense of how I should feel after I had been *reclaimed*. I got the sense that the words *solar* and *bright* and *razed*, when appended to our names, implied rank based on appearance. I assumed that Solar, since it had been applied solely to Jaranessa, was the highest rank possible, which made sense. That Krotha and I had achieved the rank of *Fair* placed us in the middle.

Clearly, I should have felt honored. Definitely grateful, and yet I felt no gratitude. When I looked in the glass one of the villagers offered me, I did not see a thing of beauty. I certainly looked more lifelike than I had, but all the paint and color could not alter the fact that I was dead. They had painted a mask on me, and in their eyes, that mask *became* me. Their only criteria for judging me became their handiwork, which was akin to praising a painting for the colors, not for what it presented or represented.

Krotha did not share my apprehension. He got one look at himself, his armor all shiny, his flesh returned to a lively hue, and he roared with laughter. He did look every inch a Knight of Virtue, but as I had noted, the operatic kind. Everything was overdone, making him into a caricature of himself. In that glass, the Knight of Truth did not see truth—he saw the mask and chose to believe what it reminded him of himself.

We got paraded through the village, with much praise lavished upon us and more upon our makers. The villagers seemed to take us to be a treasure or a wonder or a community project to which all had contributed. We might as well have been a barn or a bridge or a watchtower, yet neither of us had such substance nor could be of such value to a village. And still they eyed us the way Tsaleryk did gold, with pride at our making foremost in their minds.

So much attention being paid to me was something I found unsettling. Krotha, however, reveled in it, overplaying his part. I understood, in part, that desire to return to what he had been, because being a Knight of Virtue in Alkindor meant he had risen above all but his peers and the king. To lose that, to have been judged and felled by the great leveler, Death, and then to only slowly be regaining a sense of how much he had lost, had to be disorienting at the very least. Here, he didn't have to think about why he was being praised—he merely had to luxuriate in the praise to let himself ignore the hole in his psyche.

Balarion and Phylasina had likewise been remade. Each had been bathed and groomed, shucked of their armor, and clad in bright silks. Balarion wore greens and browns, a huntsman's outfit with a hat similar to mine but lacking the fancy cockade. He seemed more at ease than he had been, and I guessed that was because these clothes felt more familiar than the armor. Just being free of its weight would have come as a welcome change.

Phylasina had been transformed into a fey creature utterly unlike her martial self. Her silks had the weight of spiderwebs and revealed more than they hid. She held her head up and walked with poise, clearly aware of all eyes being upon her and seeing that as her due. Her eyes flashed as brightly as the gemstones at her throat and in her ears. The expressions of others made it clear that they envied Balarion for his association with her. The vision of her would fuel many a fantasy.

As afternoon moved toward dusk, the village gathered itself for a celebration in the grand hall. People threw themselves into decorating. They harvested flowers, hung banners and bunting, and began preparing food. A few—it looked to me to be the most attractive—left off work early and cleaned themselves up. Those who remained working did not appear to complain or harbor animosity. It seemed as if they believed that the joy the others felt would somehow pass down to them.

In this preparation I noticed a curious thing. A dozen tables would be set, and Malassa would order three taken away. Of the eighteen arrangements of flowers, six were adjudged unworthy. The headwoman tasted soups and wines, inspected loaves of bread and roasted claw-wings, and arbitrarily rejected some portion of them. Those deemed acceptable got served at the feast, while the others were hauled away to a smaller gathering toward the back of the village and set on the rejected tables for the reclaimers to enjoy.

I watched all this from the shadows. I did not feel a part of the village, and since I did not need to eat, I saw no reason to attend the celebration. Balarion and Phylasina, as the guests of honor, were obligated to attend, and I could not blame them for enjoying themselves. This was the first time they'd had any respite from the quest. Krotha, for all the aforementioned reasons, likewise enjoyed the celebration. To his credit, at least once as I watched, he looked around for me, but he never saw me peering into the grand hall from the darkness outside.

I backed away and cloaked myself more deeply in the night's warm embrace. I wandered to the village's perimeter and beyond to the basin's ridgeline, letting music from the hall and honest laughter from the other dinner slowly fade. I sought to understand how people could countenance living in a system where cosmetic beauty conferred superior status, especially when it was their own hard work that could take someone like me, one of the Razed, and elevate me to Fair. This was not to suggest that I believed that to be beautiful immediately transformed someone into an imbecile. I believed that no more than I imagined that an obese person had to be morally weak or that a warrior without battle scars was a coward. What struck me was the idiocy of believing that cosmetic transformation somehow made me better than those who had reclaimed me.

Somewhere out farther in the darkness, something clanked. A chain against a pot, perhaps, nothing worrying. I turned in that direction and perceived movement. I approached and caught the soft lowing of a plodhoof and the creak of a wooden cart being pulled along slowly. As I drew closer, I could make out people, a dozen and a half or so, making their way through a dry riverbed below.

I headed down toward them, trying to make as little noise as I could, but this was not a simple task. Beyond the basin's rim, the land became harsher. Gravel covered it, and runoff had carved gullies here and there. Scrub vegetation had grown thick, and detritus had piled up in places where Fair Haven's villagers clearly dumped their refuse. I picked my way around all that, then entered the riverbed behind the group and quickly caught up.

"Wait, please."

It might have seemed foolish to openly approach people moving through the darkness, but I did not fear them. To a man or woman—so swaddled in cloth were they that I could scarce tell them apart—they gave no sign of menace. I didn't see weapons on but a few of them, and those I marked for elimination if I had to fight. They were all on foot, with their baggage in the cart, and the cart had one wheel that wobbled fiercely.

They stopped, and when they saw me, they dropped to their knees, each mumbling something like "Avert your eyes, my lord. We wish to give no offense." And I must amend my description, for not all dropped to their knees: Those who walked with crutches cast them aside and fell heavily to the ground, at which point they rolled onto their bellies and joined their fellows in the ritual chanting.

"Hold. Wait. Stop." I dropped to a knee myself. "I am no lord, but a visitor for whom your ways are a curiosity. I would know why you are out here, why you have passed Fair Haven. Why do you travel at night and not on the roads, which would make your passage much easier?"

Even as I asked the questions, the answers came to me. The swaddling. The crutches. At least one person lacked half a leg, and that one over there had a twisted back and a hump on one shoulder. These were the people who could not be elevated. The halt. The lame. Those to whom life had been cruel, rendering them so hideous that their nation saw them as worthless.

They kept their gazes averted and continued their chanting.

"Please, I travel with Prince Balarion. I must know the ways of Trafaram so I can tell him the truth of this nation."

One of them looked up. "Balarion? King Parnyr's get?"

"Yes, him. He's there in Fair Haven. We are bound for Aethemia to see Jaranessa." At the mere mention of her name, the travelers writhed, as if in the hope that they could dig themselves more deeply into the sand. Some even tossed dirt over their backs in a bid to disappear.

The speaker rose to her feet. She stood tall enough to look me in the eye, and she bore a wickedly curved sword. Her black clothes revealed only her dark eyes. She had both arms and legs, and had risen to her feet with no difficulty. She turned to her traveling companions and motioned for them to rise.

"Thank you, my friends. He is here because I am here. My trek is ending, and for you, the journey to Vataria yet remains incomplete." She moved to assist some, and I helped others, not wholly understanding what was happening. Those I touched stiffened and resisted me, at least initially, then allowed me to help them. Even so, they never met my gaze and took great pains to conceal themselves within their robes.

The travelers resumed their journey. The speaker remained at my side. She stared after them wistfully, but did not raise a hand to wave. Then again, none of them looked back, but continued slowly to the southwest.

I turned to my companion. "What is this? Am I wrong in thinking those people were all from among the Razed? You, certainly, and others did not seem to share my condition."

"All these people are well beneath the Razed. No amount of paint will return a leg or arm or nose; it will not straighten a spine or heal a badly broken bone." She pointed at the departing people. "They travel the Road of Exiles. It is a dangerous road, and many die along the way."

"Does Jaranessa know about this?" I frowned. "She must."

"Jaranessa-Solar does not bother herself with the lives of monsters. Should a flood sweep their ugliness away, or bandits ravage them, it is merely to cleanse Trafaram of their imperfection. So they will not give offense to tender eyes, the Exiles travel hidden and at night."

"Of course." It finally made sense. The thing that had struck me as odd about Fair Haven was that I'd seen no one who was broken or even wrinkled with age. Cosmetics might have hidden a myriad of imperfections, but no one had lost a finger or bore pox scars. As with refuse piled in middens, the broken people were discarded.

"Can it be that in Trafaram a family would exile the patriarch for crow's-feet or a missing tooth? Is baldness a cause to drive someone away, or does a wig forgive that sin?"

My companion chuckled as she began to unwrap the ragged cloth concealing her face. "You claim you do not know this place, but you understand it. The Road of Exiles winds around villages like this so the travelers will not alarm the fairer in Trafaram."

The cloth came fully away, and I beheld the most beautiful woman I could ever recall having seen. Phylasina was breathtaking, but this woman's beauty could still the moon in its orbit and the stars in their perturbations. Long, wavy black hair, shining in the starlight, flowed down over her shoulders. Her dark eyes, now unshaded, displayed amber facets amid the darker umber. Her dusky skin, her strong, sharp features, and the ease of her smile made me wish that I had indeed once enjoyed love and that somehow my love had been reborn in this woman.

Even the scar on her forehead, starting near her hairline on the left and running down to almost her eyebrow on the right, added to her allure. A tiny scar, really, thin and straight, it hinted at exotic adventures. It emphasized her otherwise flawless complexion and made me wish I had healing magicks that could make the scar vanish.

She stared at me, her voice sinking to a whisper. "Who are you?"

"I am…"

She silenced me with a finger pressed to my lips and continued to stare at me. *And through me.* I feared her gaze might pierce the paint and she'd see me as I was, simply because I did not want to see her face twisted by horror.

"I see who you are." Her finger fell away. "I am Ceresia, a Knight of Virtue in service to the throne of Alkindor."

I swept off my hat and bowed. "You are the Knight of Beauty. I am Ferranos, companion to Prince Balarion. I travel with Krotha and Phylasina. Krotha is like me, dead. She, however, and even Garvyne, whom we also encountered, have defied death for all these eons. How is it that you, too, are alive?"

"Duty to my king precludes allowing me the luxury of death. King Parnyr charged me with seeking the beauty within his nation and discerning its true nature. Balarion was part of that so many years ago; but from his mother, that should come as no surprise. So I have gone everywhere, seen everything."

"How is it that you come to be in the company of Exiles?"

"Do not think, Ferranos, that they lack beauty. They have as much as you do, and that is my gift. I can see that beauty, and I aid them to preserve it."

I nodded. "Then this Vataria must be a place of incredible beauty."

"I should think so."

I frowned. "You've not seen it?"

"I take them only so far, then I seek more." She canted her head. "It is my vanity, you see. If I visit Vataria, I shall have fulfilled my duty completely. Then I could chance to become like you. Or worse. And now I know I made the right decision, because Balarion has come, and there are things he must know if he is to fully blossom into the beauty that is his destiny."

CHAPTER 21

"Then, please, join me." I headed back toward Fair Haven. "There is a celebration in Balarion's honor, and I think you will be a most welcome guest in that company."

I led Ceresia back by a route that was not entirely direct. I told myself it was the easiest path, the one least likely to cause us injury. I also knew I lied. There was something about being in her company that I found seductive. She intrigued me, for she clearly took delight in all manner of things, yet had the maturity and intellect to hold the world's wonders in context. As we walked, I studied her—covertly, I hoped, but I felt certain she noticed.

And I found it good that she did not object.

We arrived late to the celebration in the village longhouse, so most of the people had finished a cup or three of wine. Krotha remained unaffected, *if* he had drunk at all; and Balarion had relaxed, smiling broadly and roaring loudly at jokes. Phylasina likewise had indulged and often leaned toward Balarion, whispering in his ear and trailing a finger along his arm or cheek.

Our arrival elicited little notice until Ceresia strode into the room and dropped to a knee before Balarion. The Trafarami recognized her clothes. Their faces closed and their gaiety died. As she bowed her head, her luxurious hair hid her face, doubtless convincing our hosts that she had to be hideous, since no other defect made itself known. Then, as she tipped her head back to look up into Balarion's eyes, the Trafarami gasped at her perfection, much as I had.

"It is my honor to be of service to you, Prince Balarion. I am known as Ceresia."

Balarion stared at her, then nodded as a smile grew. "I remember you. You traveled with us for a short while as we went to the pyramid where I slept. You are the Knight of Beauty."

"You are kind to remember, my lord."

Phylasina straightened herself in her chair. "What a pleasure to see you again, sister."

"And you, sister. I see you have not changed." Ceresia turned and smiled at Krotha. "You, my brother, my incorruptible brother, I have sorely missed."

"Likewise, Ceresia, though I am no longer unspoiled, as you can see."

"Beauty does not confine itself to the living, Krotha, and great beauty dwells within you yet." Ceresia stood, opened her arms, and slowly turned to display herself to the Trafarami present. Our hosts, once they saw her beauty, became at ease. Slowly, they resumed their chatter, though it was hushed. After someone brought the Knight of Beauty a goblet of wine, the festivities recovered their momentum and volume.

I remained drawn back, immune and aloof. I recognized the apprehension among the villagers when Ceresia first arrived, and their relief at her attractiveness. Yet the clothing she wore, the rags of the Exiles, must have reminded them of loved ones they sent out on that lonely trek. Or was Trafaram a place where the people remained willfully blind to reality and mesmerized by the ephemeral? Were they like the village, presenting its best face to the outside with the least-beautiful parts hidden, or did their deception become their reality, with all else forgotten?

I had no doubt that, as with Kadarr, the society's orientation began in the capital. That such an unrealistic way of life held sway even so far out in the countryside suggested dire consequences for deviation from court dictates. That those who became Exiles could, in essence, cease to exist suggested anyone could be declared ugly and discarded, with no one caring or reacting.

The celebration continued until the wee hours. Many of the celebrants took great joy in each other's beauty, grouping up and pairing off to enjoy the pleasures of their companions' company. They wandered off into the night. Phylasina and Balarion remained, engrossed in deep conversation filled with wonderment and laughter. Those among the villagers who had neither the will nor inclination to find a partner sat and drank alone, staring off into nothingness. I dimly recalled having seen people in such a state before and lamented that people had not progressed beyond that behavior in all the time I'd spent in the grave.

Never having acquired a taste for voyeurism for its own sake, I walked into the night and stared up at the stars. I found it odd that the constellations had changed so and yet people had not. Alkindor had once been a vibrant nation where gold and beauty and strength abounded. In the centuries since I last walked its roads, the nation's virtues had fallen to a parody of itself. Society mocked what it had grown from. I wondered how Parnyr would take that, and could easily imagine his fury cleansing the land. He would trim away deadwood as a gardener might and wait for everything to grow back strong.

"There is a cold beauty in the stars, is there not, Ferranos?" Ceresia's voice came soft and soothing, warm and familiar. "They have shifted over the years, but that aspect of them has never changed."

"All that has changed is the observer, not the observation." I turned to face her and smiled. "When we found Balarion, you figured in his dreams."

"Good dreams, I hope."

"Why would they be anything but?"

She frowned, which in no way diminished her radiance. "His final trip was not the first time we met, though his recall of that meeting would have been extraordinary. You see, I attended his birth. I was there when his mother died, and when he almost died as well."

I cocked an eyebrow. "Of this I did not know."

"The king sent me on my first survey of Alkindor to locate beauty, and I found Mysanthe, a woman of uncommon beauty. There was something about her, something I could not identify." She raised her face to the stars and stared into the past. "Foolishly, perhaps, I brought her to court. Parnyr took to her immediately, setting aside his wives, who were none too pleased, and she besotted him. She recited poetry, and it entranced the king. She wove wildflowers into bracelets and garlands, which he wore in place of his crown and other gold ornaments. And he took her to bed, remaining in his chambers for days on end, and finally he got her with child."

I tapped a finger against my chin. "I do not know this story. I doubt Balarion does, either."

"He does not, nor should he." She sighed. "Parnyr's wives knew that were her child to be born, the king would set him above their children, and this they could not tolerate. So they plotted to rid the kingdom of her. To destroy her and her child, leaving their children to inherit."

Ceresia turned toward me. "There was a beauty, a terribly beauty, to the court. The king had his Knights of Virtue, shining champions to uphold his law and promote the welfare of the nation. But to balance that, he had an agent, a darkened soul, a fiend summoned from perdition, some said; others called him the Knight of Deceit. Some even thought the king had a legion of these murderous agents, who collectively became described as the Scorpion. The wives somehow attracted the Scorpion's attention and set for him the task of destroying Mysanthe.

"The Scorpion, for reasons, told Parnyr of the threat to Mysanthe, so it was given to me to move her to safety. I did my best, and as she grew heavy with child, we eluded the Scorpion. Then, when she was in labor, the assassin caught up with her. He used poison—the prick of a needle stained with some foul venom—and Mysanthe died, the child yet in her womb, dying from that same venom."

She shivered, and pain washed over her face for a moment. I reached out to her, to steady her. "What did you do?"

"I had failed to save the woman. I watched her beauty expire, so I cut the child from her body, and I managed over many days to bring the infant back to life and keep the boy alive. I bore him to the village where he grew up, and only after knowing he would thrive did I tell Parnyr."

"Which is why so many Knights and scholars visited his home to educate him." I stroked a hand over my chin. "And this explains another thing."

"Yes?"

"Krotha and I, when we slay something, anything, we draw into ourselves its essence. We see memories, its life, and we grow stronger. Balarion, he, too, likewise absorbs essences. Garvyne had related a story of Balarion descending into death, but because he is not like Krotha or me, I was never wholly convinced of that explanation. But were Balarion born dead and then brought back to life..."

Ceresia nodded solemnly. "His resurrection would have happened well before whatever enabled you and Krotha to return to life. Perhaps the circumstances of his birth even sparked the circumstances that have resulted in that change you have undergone. It might also explain *why* the world changed so swiftly after we laid him in his sanctuary. While awake, his mind may have held off the catastrophe, but as he entered stasis, it expanded unchecked."

I studied her face. "How quickly did things change?"

She glanced down at the ground. "Reckoning the time in generations of men, very swiftly and in waves, often wearing a different face. A plague here would wipe out a people. An invasion, a genocide, then earthquakes and titanic storms doomed others. A river shifts in its bed, and a port city withers, becoming forgotten. A century of drought kills the heart of an empire, and all of its provinces dissolve into barbaric strife."

She became quiet for a moment, staring off into space. "For me, the beauty of Alkindor faded in an eyeblink, but perhaps a nation where a queen could plot the death of an infant was not that beautiful to begin with."

My eyes narrowed. "Balarion is on a mission to release his father and restore Alkindor. Can you condone that if you question its beauty?"

"Do you imagine, Ferranos, that Alkindor will return to what it once was, warts and all, or that in its remaking it might know perfection?" She pressed her palm to her heart. "To see the beauty of Alkindor truly realized is what I wish for."

"A goal worth fighting for." I bowed toward her. "I welcome you to Prince Balarion's company. This morning I believed we had the strength to accomplish this end. Now I believe we have the heart to carry us all the way through."

* * *

By midday, we headed out again, our pack-beasts laden with gifts to be brought to court from Fair Haven. The road to Aethemia lay straight and true and, when not flanked by strips of forest, lay in a small depression with wildflowers sowed to either side. If we mounted the banks and looked beyond the road, we found a more desolate place, but within the cocoon of the road, Trafaram retained its beauty.

We *did* leave the main road to visit villages and, as we drew closer to the capital, towns. All presented well from the road. In the larger towns, we never got past what Krotha deemed the *theater district*. Each new location worked us over, undoing what the last town had done, and turned us out in the latest fashions, up to the current standard of beauty. I often felt I was a piece of furniture being refinished every time we stopped.

But across the board, they left Ceresia untouched.

Fetes continued, gifts abounded, and though I knew the truth of the Road of Exiles, I found it easy to accept the fantasy that most people embraced. While Ceresia saw beauty across a spectrum that went beyond physical attractiveness, for everyone else beauty ended there. The people desperately sought to be more than they were, and winning favor merely meant resorting to flattery. People preened when even I, an undead thing, praised them.

A few people possessed the wit to see past what so captivated others, and yet only shared their observations with those who were not easily beguiled. One man told me of an old Trafarami saying—"Nothing is so corrosive as a lingering glance"—warning me off looking too closely at anything. Insecurity about losing one's looks, or being caught at a disadvantage, or even just aging, inspired haunted glances. It seemed to me as if one day the entire population would wake up to the realization that they lived in a world of illusion, and that their knowledge would collapse everything in on itself.

Finally, we reached Aethemia, cresting a hill to be given perfect view of a magnificent city. It appeared less built than grown, with very few straight lines and many elaborate curves and curls and filigree. Towers reminded me of seashells, spirals grown up to stab into the sky. The walls flowed and the roads slithered, gently curving through neighborhoods with round windows and bright paint. Murals depicted nothing realistic because a true representation could be done poorly. Instead, splashes of color bled into ribbonlike loops and lines that playfully teased the eye, beckoning on farther and deeper into the city. Even the cobblestones, each perfect and level, had curls worked into the surface.

Gate guards sought to stop us, but Ceresia bared her face and charmed them. Four riders mounted up and paraded us through the streets. As we moved from the outer precincts to the inner, guards of higher rank, from companies with more ornate livery, took over in the relay. The citizens on the street likewise became more beautified and their finery more brilliant. By the time we reached the palace—a castle that looked as if it had been cast from molten mother-of-pearl—the people swathed themselves in so many silken layers that they could scarcely manage a stride that advanced them a foot per step.

Ministers wearing tall hats and stacked shoes greeted us with painted faces and lace veils. They presented each of us with what appeared to be a black blindfold, save that it had been fashioned of lace and did little to blind us. We followed them into Jaranessa's palace, shortening our strides to match theirs. We traveled down a lengthy, tall corridor along a plush red carpet. Statues of beautiful women, all bearing the same face, stood in alcoves between wall panels covered in paintings, again with the same woman depicted. They showed her in all manner of dress and undress, in congress with men and women of legend—all of whom appeared to be quite entranced with her beauty.

This, then, I assumed, was Jaranessa, and these paintings immortalized her life as similar portrayals had exalted Tsaleryk in his palace. The ministers passed along, raising their right or left hands to block their view of the artwork. I wondered at that. As beautiful as Jaranessa was depicted of being, I couldn't imagine them finding her embarrassingly erotic, or that having seen the images time after time didn't somehow lessen their impact. Regardless, in keeping with their practice, I turned a blind eye to the art.

They conducted us into the throne room, which I found curiously close. Panels of ivory, carved into a fine filigree, hemmed us into the center of the room. Six pillars ran from the door to the end, with the carpeting continuing to a panel that lay across it. Beyond that panel stood an opalescent throne with red velvet cushions. The throne's back spread out in a lotus pattern, but asymmetrically, as if a mighty wind twisted leaves and petals toward the right.

To the left, deeper, past the ivory screens, a figure stirred. Gaunt and impossibly tall, it moved slowly, each step eating up but inches. It wore a scarlet robe trimmed with gold ribbons. Its headdress, also in scarlet, rose to the height of four feet and sparkled with a constellation of small diamonds. A finely wrought golden mask covered the figure's face and so perfectly matched the statues outside that there could be no mistaking her identity.

Servants, each a magnificent specimen wearing nothing more than a scarlet silk loincloth and a scarlet blindfold, hurried forward to aid the ministers as they sank to their knees. The centermost minister, his hat a handspan taller than the other two, turned toward Jaranessa as she torpidly made her way to the throne. "Light of the world, Jaranessa-Solar, we have come to present to you a man calling himself Balarion…"

Jaranessa's hand came up. Her sleeve slipped back, revealing long fingers and longer nails. "I know who this is." The expression on the mask—or what I had taken to be a mask—sharpened. "He claims to be my brother, but truly he shall be my death."

CHAPTER 22

I watched her hand, her fingers. So very like a spider, the fingers moving slowly, bedecked with rings, and nails painted in stripes and stippled, the colors matching those of her rings. It appeared as if her hands crawled along an unseen web, drawing her forward toward her throne.

Then I noticed her gaze remained devoted to her prime minister, effectively ignoring us. This made little sense, because so bold an accusation had to accompany a shift of attention. One would only say that to provoke a reaction that might reveal our true intent. Yet she stared toward her minister, though not exactly *at* him, as if she did not actually see him and had oriented herself toward the sound of his voice.

The prime minister bowed low three times, his forehead touching the floor. The metal band on his headdress rang with each impact. His fellows likewise bowed, with the blindfolded servant helping them become upright again. The prime minister set his shoulders. "Then we shall remove the ugliness that is this Balarion."

I raised my voice. "I would think, Jaranessa-Solar, light of all that is worthy of your beneficence smiling upon it, that this is hardly a beautiful solution to a situation that has not yet fully blossomed."

The metal mask's expression eased. "And you would be?"

"One unworthy of your notice, Most High." I glanced over at Krotha. "I would have our companion Krotha, Knight of Truth, speak to Balarion's character and intention. To proceed otherwise would be to despoil your time with distasteful obfuscation."

"A Knight of Virtue. Krotha, I recall you. You once told me that the world would never know beauty greater than mine. Did you speak the truth then?"

Krotha clanked down to a knee, shooting me a hooded glance as he did so. "Jaranessa-Solar, if it was not the truth, it was only false in that I had underestimated your beauty."

The prime minister glanced back over his shoulder at the knight. "Most Radiant, this from the mouth of one whom death has rejected."

Jaranessa had begun to smile when Krotha spoke, then her brow creased in response to her minister's words.

Krotha managed a chuckle. "Your minister tells the truth, Most Radiant. I succumbed to death because I had seen the beauty of the world; and I resisted the grave, in the hopes of seeing you again. The mere sight of you makes me wish I were yet alive, like my lord Balarion."

The minister sniffed. "The boy he mentions cannot be your brother, Mistress Scintillation, for he is plain in presence and affect."

Krotha's rich voice filled the room. "He is humble, Most Radiant, and awestruck."

"He is dumbstruck, Jaranessa-Solar. He has the cast of a flock warden and the dull eyes of one no smarter than his charges."

Krotha's eyes narrowed. "The minister, then, does not realize that flock wardens seldom wear armor or wield a sword; nor do they have as companions three Knights of Virtue who are sworn to his service and have followed him from Kadarr to your court in pursuit of his mission."

The minister would have replied, but Jaranessa's hand came up again and silenced him. "More, Knights. Proclaim yourselves to me."

Phylasina stepped forward. "I am the Knight of Fidelity, Most Radiant. I serve Balarion as I served your father."

"Always faithful, yes, of course. And you, the other knight?"

"Ceresia, Light of All."

"Ah, the Knight of Beauty. How is it that you have not visited me over these long years? Have you been in the grave as has poor Krotha?"

"My mission has been to seek beauty, Jaranessa-Solar, not to inflict my ugliness upon your court. It was not until I was in the company of Balarion that I believed his radiance would please you enough that you would not notice me."

Jaranessa spread her arms, both hands now visible, two spiders plying that invisible web. "But I recall you so well, Ceresia, your beauty darker than mine but in no way diminished. My father would tell me to watch you, the way you moved, the way you spoke. He said your unconscious beauty would never fade."

"Your father was most kind."

"And who was it who spoke first, the unworthy one?"

"Ferranos, Most Radiant. A dust mote in a stellar array, basking in the light of your being."

She looked in my direction, and I realized she was not blind at all, but somehow did not notice us if we were displeasing to her eyes. She could force herself to take notice, but a castle's drawbridge would more quickly come up than we would appear in her sight. Rising to her notice would be a goal for her people and yet would invite her to view them in all they were. That would result in judgment, and I feared the result of that judgment would be more harmful than passing beneath notice.

She stared at Balarion. "And you, brother, would you speak for yourself, or be content in lessers speaking for you?"

"I thought to remain quiet, Most Radiant. In your presence I find myself unable to express myself properly. I want my words to please you, but I am not elegant. I am a flock warden, a warrior, and a man fulfilling a duty to your father."

"Softly spoken, yet direct, without aimless flattery." She cocked her head, and I feared the weight of the headdress might snap her neck. "Simple elegance can be so much more pleasing than complicated formalities, which ensnare the innocent and reward those who think far too much of themselves. Simple elegance is a strength."

As Jaranessa spoke, her voice went from loud to soft, with a hint of gaiety flowing into it. Her hand gestures became smoother, as if she stroked the fur of a beloved pet instead of plucked at the strands of a web. Her expression eased, and a girlish hint of innocence teased a smile across her lips.

Her embracing simplicity and elegance struck an emotional earthquake in her court. Across the board, her servants froze for a moment, then shoulders shifted and gaits loosened. Even torches in wall sconces guttered languidly, and the ministerial robes revealed wrinkles here and there as the officials changed their posture. And yet, while rigidity drained from their spines, they watched their queen intently, reading her for even the most minute clue as to how she would react going forward.

"Speaking directly is all I know how to do, Jaranessa-Solar. Your father wishes me to gather the three keys. From Tsaleryk I have already won the Key of Gold. From you I seek the Key of Beauty."

Her chin came up, as did her right hand. An opalescent band ran round her throat, in her flesh, as if a living tattoo. The colors in it flowed and eddied, swirled and darkened, diving deep before rising in new hues of red and yellow and blue. Even half-obscured by the ivory screen, the ever-shifting patterns mesmerized me.

"He told me that one day you would come. Perhaps not *you*, but one claiming to be his agent. He gave me the freedom to set you a task to complete before I transferred the key to you. The task was to be anything, but sufficient to prove you were truly worthy of the responsibility and not just a mountebank hoping for quick riches."

Balarion bowed his head. "I am your servant in this matter, Jaranessa-Solar."

The queen of Trafaram seated herself upon her throne, her headdress rising higher than the chair's back. "You do not call me sister."

"I would be making a claim upon you I have no right to make." Balarion kept his head down and his gaze toward the floor. "During my life, I believed my mother had died when I was barely born, and I never knew who my father was. Since Krotha and Ferranos awakened me, I have learned that we share a father. But you do not know me. You never even knew of me. I would be foolish and rude to think you would feel toward me what you feel to the brothers you grew up with."

"You have seen Kadarr and Tsaleryk, and doubtless intend to visit Scilliric and Dolared. You should count yourself lucky that I do *not* think of you as I do of them."

"You are kind to think of me at all, Jaranessa-Solar."

"Think of you I shall, and of the key." She pointed at her prime minister. "You will house them in the Dawn Wing and prepare them. We shall dine this evening in the Stellar Vault. By then, or by morning, I shall have an answer concerning the Key of Beauty."

"Yes, Most Radiant." The prime minister bowed, his forehead pounding the floor five times, and then made it to his feet with help. Likewise, his companions gained their feet, then the three of them backed blindly through our company. I half expected Krotha to knock one off-balance just to enjoy the resulting panic, but he resisted the temptation. Once they had removed themselves, we also backed out of the throne room, leaving Jaranessa on her throne, as still and beautiful as the statues filling the palace.

Servants conducted us to the Dawn Wing, and I noticed one peculiar fact. All of the statues and all of the portraits depicted Jaranessa as just a bit younger and more innocent, reflecting the new expression on her mask. I'd not sensed magick being worked to make all those changes, and it would have taken a legion of painters and sculptors to make the changes before we passed. It occurred to me that magick simply had to be involved, but it wasn't so strong that it actually altered the statues and walls. Instead, it manipulated the way we perceived them, which meant that everything in the palace, and perhaps even in Trafaram, was a massive illusion that let the beholder see what would please them.

And please Jaranessa.

Reaching our quarters required us to ascend two broad sets of stairs that turned back on themselves, giving each of the lower floors twenty-foot-tall ceilings. Eight cavalry warriors could have ridden abreast up the stairs, and twice their number along the corridor. Tall bronze double doors opened to a common room with four apartments off it. Master crafters had created the furnishings from a variety of woods and fabrics. The chairs served best those who wished to lounge, and my tomb had been tighter for space than the bed upon which I would have slept *if* I slept. The servants also led us farther east along the corridor to the room that capped that wing: the baths, which had a wall of windows looking out toward sunrise.

By the time we returned from that side trip, other servants had set the table in the common room with kuddan-cheeses, grapes, nuts, fruits I could not recognize, and pitchers of wine and mead. Though Krotha did not require nourishment, he smiled in anticipation of drinking the mead and then frowned when the taste did not match his memory.

Balarion took a goblet of wine from Phylasina. "What did you think would happen to us, Ferranos, when you stepped in?"

"The prime minister would have had us destroyed. Maybe not killed, but certainly made into Exiles." I looked at Ceresia. "Am I interpreting correctly what was likely?"

"There are, among the Exiles, those who have been maimed. Mostly by accident, but occasionally as punishment. Mostly on the village level, though. I cannot recall disfigurement being a staple of discipline here. Given how beauty is prized, to mar someone intentionally precludes their ever being rehabilitated."

Krotha shook his head. "I do not get the sense that Jaranessa is terribly forgiving."

"No, she is not." Ceresia hugged her arms around herself. "More troubling is what we saw at the end, I think. Jaranessa-Solar may just have been speaking her mind, not even giving those thoughts any weight, but her people took those idle musings as if they had the weight of an imperial decree."

Krotha set the mead back on the table. "I fail to understand the screens and the blindfolds on the servants, and Jaranessa swathed in layers of cloth to hide her beauty."

The Knight of Beauty shifted her shoulders. "The screens, the blindfolds, the clothes, none of that was to hide her beauty. That was to protect us. Jaranessa-Solar is so beautiful that, were we to look upon her openly and then be removed from her presence, we would literally despair at our loss and kill ourselves."

Phylasina frowned. "She cannot believe that."

"It matters not what *she* believes, sister—it is what her people believe." Ceresia walked over to a window looking out into the city. "The people living nearest the palace, they dress to please their lady. Look. Since she said simplicity suffices, word has gone out."

I joined her at the window. People had cast off half their clothing, stripping off layers. Citizens walked with full strides past the palace for the first time in ages. Servants scurried about gathering discarded clothing—which, to be fair, had been neatly folded and piled by color and texture in places where a tiny splash of that particular color was appropriate. Curiously enough, the people thus revealed still appeared to be perfect—no Exile had been wandering the city in disguise.

Krotha grunted. "So if tomorrow she were to comment that rings should only be worn on one finger of one hand, every jeweler in this city should be ruined."

"Likely, my friend, or…" I allowed myself a smile. "Tomorrow a minister would clarify, noting that different rings should be worn on different days. Perhaps we'll see a decree indicating that now that people are not wearing layers, they should change for meals, or have morning clothes, afternoon clothes, and evening clothes. Perhaps even a sleeping costume. And something formal for celebrations."

"Several somethings, for many occasions." Balarion shook his head. "It's silliness compounded."

"But it is not, my lord." I turned again to the window. "It is order. People comply because it gives them an advantage over others and provides them something tiny to worry about. Thus, they have no time to consider larger issues. If you are concerned about where to find a red hat, or a ring with a stone to match, you do not think about the injustice of an accident reducing a prince to an Exile. And it has the advantage of keeping your economy flowing, as new products replace those that are not yet worn-out. What appears to be ridiculous actually boosts the economy and stabilizes the nation."

Ceresia laid a hand on my shoulder. "Save for the Exiles, whose lives are ruined."

I nodded. "I did not say it was a good system, merely an effective one in keeping people distracted and compliant."

Balarion drained his cup. "We cannot afford to be distracted. We will work within Jaranessa's system as long as it serves our mission. Let us hope things do not turn ugly."

CHAPTER 23

As the sun set, servants came and helped us prepare for dinner with Jaranessa. Krotha and I had our paints reapplied, albeit in somewhat thicker coats. My clothing arrived in darker blues and greens. Not at all unpleasing, and in fewer layers than we'd seen on the street before. Neither of us received headdresses, and those of our companions were modest and covered by a flowing, grey silk sheet, which hid them almost entirely. As they walked along, it appeared as if their heads shouldered and leaked smoke.

Our companions' raiments differed in that Balarion stood dressed in a red silk tabard embroidered with the old imperial crest on the front and back. His pants and the shirt beneath the tunic matched in color, and his knee-length boots had been made from red leather, the crest embroidered at ankle and toes. His headdress matched, and he had no scarf obscuring it. He was also granted a small scabbard, in which rode a golden knife of no practical combat application.

The Knights of Virtue had been similarly attired, all in a dark green, with Phylasina and Ceresia receiving flowing gowns. The many skirts would make movement difficult. Krotha's tunic had the Knights of Virtue crest—a sword impaling a rising sun—on the breast. That crest appeared on the left shoulder and right thigh of the gowns. The grey veils hid the nature of the headdresses they'd been given, but they only rose to a handspan and were no bigger around than a very small sweet cake.

What impressed me was that the clothing fitted exactly, and could not have been prepared in advance. This was especially true of the embroidery. For what reason would Jaranessa have people randomly embroidering the crest of the Knights of Virtue on swaths of silk? She must have had a legion of skilled seamsters and tailoresses prepared to produce clothing in the blink of an eye. Given that the society recalibrated its standard of beauty at her whim, this made perfect sense, and yet the impracticality astounded me.

Phylasina, as she had in Fair Haven, looked stunning. Even though her clothes did not match Balarion's, they clearly belonged together. She appeared quite happy, and the light in her eyes when she peered at Balarion made her yet more beautiful.

That said, she could not hold a candle to Ceresia. On her, facial cosmetics *hinted* and *suggested*—they did not define. She seemed uneasy to be out of her dark clothing, so she shyly embraced her new garments. Her wonderment at them, at how they felt when she moved, enlivened her. A love of life flashed in her eyes, and color rose to her cheeks when she noticed me admiring her.

"I am sorry, Ferranos."

"For?"

"Appearing thus and distracting you."

I pressed a hand to my breastbone. "Had I a heart that beat within my chest, your beauty would arrest it."

"You are most kind." She glanced away, but the barest trace of a smile suggested she enjoyed how I perceived her.

Unlike Balarion, none of the Knights had been granted even a ceremonial weapon, and I left my staff in my room. Servants arrived and led us at a slow pace along the corridor to the stairs, where we ascended again. The setting sun lengthened shadows and applied a ghostly quality to the trailing veils, which I, being last in line, could appreciate. We were ghosts from a past long dead come to visit the living.

We emerged onto the roof and beneath a portico that rose to a height of thirty feet. The dome above us contained a mural of stars and planets in the alignments from the days when I lived. The vault's background was blue, with stars in gold leaf and planets splashed with color that matched their astrological symbolism, not any observable hue. Servants had set a long table with seating for thirty, which extended east beyond the portico's boundary.

Directly beneath the vault, a labyrinth of ivory-and-ebon filigree screens surrounded a small round table with a single grand chair. The chair had been angled such that it did not face directly down the longer table, but off to the side. None seated outside the screens would see aught but Jaranessa's profile.

A variety of guests had already been seated, with gaps left for our party. Krotha and I found our places farthest from the round table. Balarion sat closest to it, in the place that would afford him the greatest chance to see Jaranessa's face. Ministers, now wearing headdresses of modest proportions and fewer robes, sat near him, with other guests seated in diminishing levels of importance until they reached us. While the guests at our end of the table were not difficult to look at, and acted perfectly gracious and charming, they mostly listened and limited their conversation to gentle flattery.

After five minutes, in which I'd grown bored with my dinner companions, a servant arrived and announced, "Her Radiance, Jaranessa, is imminent." He rang gentle bells to warn of her approach. Then more servants appeared behind us—one per guest—and settled a dark lace blindfold over our eyes. Given that the full moon and stars were the only light sources on the roof, the blindfold only made it marginally more difficult to see.

Jaranessa appeared from the stairway and walked toward her ivory cage. Servants bore panels of diaphanous grey silk for her to walk behind. She still appeared artificially tall, but she moved more easily, since she wore fewer robes. She had to be positively skeletal beneath it all. Her headdress had likewise shrunk, but still made her the tallest person in Trafaram. Her robes, in the same scarlet that Balarion had been given to wear, had stars and planets embroidered in gold all over them. The broad fan of her golden headdress represented the dawning sun, and indeed reflected some moonlight at us.

She herself was the radiance to bring light to our world, and her presence illuminated the feast.

She settled herself into her chair, then nodded vaguely in Balarion's direction. "Thank you, Balarion, for coming to our realm. We wish you to know it for what it truly is. We hold this banquet so you may see and understand and consume the beauty that is Trafaram."

An unseen servant clapped once, and our servants filed in, each bearing a plate ensconced beneath a big silver turtle. They set the plates before us, and when hands clapped again, they removed the turtles in unison and with a flourish.

My dinner companions gasped.

And not without reason. This first course consisted of various vegetables of appropriate colors cut into stars and crescents and planets, each arranged around a golden fruit slice centered on the plate. The chefs had arranged each item with great precision, yet every plate appeared to be different. For the Knights, the arrangement marked the position of planets in the sky on the day they had been made a Knight of Virtue. For others, I gathered the display marked their birth.

I could attach no significance to the display on my plate, save that it marked a date in the distant past or predicted one in the near future.

At this point I noticed something odd. Neither Krotha nor I had utensils at our places, which I ascribed to the fact that, being dead, we weren't expected to eat. Or perhaps we were expected to eat with our hands. The other diners had a veritable phalanx of cutlery at their disposal, yet no one reached for anything. They sat there, hands in laps, and discussed their plates.

Then the servants returned and bore the plates away.

For course after course, plates arrived, were unveiled, and then taken off without a single morsel making it into a mouth, much less being disturbed in any way. The soup, a thick, creamy white, formed an ocean upon which bobbed a fleet of tiny ships crafted, as nearly as I could tell, of bread. The raw red flesh of fish shaped into dragons chased each other roundabout over a bed of saffron rice. A herd of slashhorns carved from beetroot stampeded over a green prairie of basil puree, and golden honey oozed from a pastry volcano to finish the meal.

Jaranessa had invited us to "consume the beauty" that was her realm. Beautiful indeed were the plates offered. The artistry with which the food had been prepared exceeded everything in my memory and in the memories of those souls I'd ingested since my return to life. In all that, this meal had no equivalent, nor anything close.

And truly, the touch of a knife or a fork or a spoon would have destroyed the plated perfection. Yet as pleasing to the eye as the food was, the purpose of food was greater than pleasing the eye. More meals like this one, and we would simply starve to death.

While being able to marvel at the beauty killing us.

Thus it was with Trafaram. By raising cosmetic beauty to the defining goal of the nation, Jaranessa had shifted the focus of life from necessity to luxury. A blacksmith does not lose his skill when, by accident, he loses a toe or a finger or an ear. A painter who loses the use of her legs doesn't require exile—she requires a lower easel. And regardless of beauty, an able teacher can pass along knowledge that benefits all, and can make the society progress, whereas beauty cannot be communicated, and the standard thereof, as we'd seen that afternoon, can change capriciously.

When the last dish had been carted off, Jaranessa spoke again. "We thank you all for having joined us. You were beautiful companions. We would have you leave now, save for my brother and his friends, but we would have you return when they do, to celebrate their success."

The diners rose and quietly filed out, led by their servants.

"We trust, brother, that you enjoyed the meal?"

"Never have I sat for so beautiful a meal, Jaranessa-Solar."

"This pleases us." Her right hand emerged from the sleeve of her robe. Her nails had shrunk, and all had been repainted to resemble the flowing colors within the Key of Beauty. "We have considered your request for the Key of Beauty. We would not consider it, save that your mission comes from our father, whom we did love the best. To honor our father, we shall give you the Key of Beauty, which is so wonderful a thing as to have no parallel nor superior, provided you and your companions perform a service for us."

"You have but to ask."

"In our realm, there is a wound. It festers. It poisons us, the poison a black venom that courses through Trafaram on nights like this, beneath this beauteous moon, mocking it. Mocking us. Mocking Trafaram. It denies all we are."

Balarion sat forward, his forearm on the table. "Tell us, Jaranessa-Solar, and we shall deal with it."

"Oh, would that sharp steel and fire be enough. Were that so, we would summon our legions, ranks upon ranks of men and women arrayed in martial splendor. They would march forth and root out this evil. We should give that command, save that we are generous and kind and beneficent."

Krotha and I exchanged a glance. Unless we had missed something, Jaranessa had no legions. A company or two of guards around the city, yes, and perhaps battalions scattered in fortresses upon her borders, but hers was not a mighty nation. While troops on parade, with their armor polished and pennants flying high, might be beautiful, war was a machine that consumed beauty. She would no more field an army than Tsaleryk would part with a gold flake.

She turned her head ever so slightly in Balarion's direction. "To the south is a city known as Vataria. It was once a place of great beauty, unparalleled beauty, but as it aged, it changed. Do you remember it? Do you know of it?"

"Only from rumor, Jaranessa-Solar." Balarion glanced at Ceresia. "I hear it is the place where Exiles go."

"Yes. We allow them that refuge. Why, you ask?" She grinned indulgently. "Can we know it is day if we do not have night? Can we know what is wet if we do not know dry? Is it possible to know beauty without acknowledging that ugliness threatens it every moment?"

"No, Jaranessa-Solar."

"Thus, for the benefit of Trafaram, as distasteful as it is, we have allowed Vataria to exist and those who take themselves there to live in peace." Her fingers curled in toward her palm, in the closest approximation to a fist her nails allowed her to create. "There is a rumor that has reached our ears, of a child who has been born in Vataria. This child, she is said to be more beautiful than anyone there and, some say, the most beautiful in all of Trafaram."

"But not as beautiful as you, Jaranessa-Solar."

"So perceptive of you, brother. And doubtless true." Her index finger rose to make a point. "And we would not have such a radiant creature grow within that horrid place. We would bring her here. We will make her a Daughter of Aethemia and keep her safe with her beautiful sisters. We will show the Trafarami that ascension is possible, if not for them, then for their children; we will prove that our nation has a future, a beautiful future. Thus, my task for you is simple. Travel to Vataria. Find this child. Fetch her here. When you bring her, you shall have the Key of Beauty."

"As you wish, Jaranessa-Solar. It shall be done."

"We have every confidence in you." Jaranessa stood and exited her cage. As she descended the stairs, a thin cloud drifted across the moon, sinking the roof into complete darkness.

Krotha pulled off his mask. "It would seem she asks a simple thing. How long a journey, Ceresia?"

"A fortnight, were we to travel with Exiles." She untied the knot on her blindfold and removed it. "We would not be limited to traveling at night, so could be much swifter. I would ask that we do not do that, however."

Phylasina shook her head. "Obtaining the Key of Beauty is not a task with calls for us to tarry, Ceresia."

Balarion held up a hand. "Hold on. Why would you want us to travel as Exiles?"

"My lord, the Road of Exiles is a dangerous path. I have spent centuries, I suppose, helping Exiles reach Vataria. I would, with your help, bring more there."

Phylasina frowned. "We do not have the time."

I chuckled. "I would remind you, Knight of Fidelity, that our task for Tsaleryk took us five years."

"I agree with Ceresia." Krotha tapped a finger on the table. "While I've seen no legions, I should hate that anything I do or say or report back would lead Jaranessa to field an army to destroy a city. Could one convince her that such a war would be beautiful? In the blink of an eye, she would become an avatar of slaughter and this nation a land of knives and poison."

Phylasina chewed on her lower lip for a moment, then nodded. "Your wisdom, brother, is unassailable."

Balarion smiled. "Good. Then we gather supplies tomorrow—enough for ourselves and others. This time tomorrow, we begin to make our way to Vataria. Jaranessa's will shall be done, but only in a way with which we can live."

CHAPTER 24

Curiously enough, the most difficult part of preparing for our journey to Vataria was finding a pair of plodhooves to draw our wagon. Jaranessa opened her stables to us, and her stable master set about finding us the best draft animals; but they defaulted to the most handsome beasts instead of those best suited to drawing a heavy wagon over a rough road. Moreover, the stable master wanted to give us a matched pair of plodhooves, which presented a whole other set of issues.

Finally, Balarion was able to explain that since we were going on the Road of Exiles, a matched pair of beautiful plodhooves was exactly the last thing we wanted. He persuaded Jaranessa's people to give us the most utilitarian beasts by convincing them that with the draft animals that could pull the best, we'd pass the journey most swiftly. The stable master understood the reluctance to be on the Road of Exiles for a heartbeat more than necessary and only then acquiesced to our desires.

Obtaining clothes and bulk supplies created less of a problem than the desire of porters to pack the wagon in a way that made the load pleasing to the eye. Phylasina undertook the battle to make sure efficiency of the load took precedence over the proper matching of colors, but she surrendered quickly enough to their protestations and decided we'd just repack things on the road.

Ceresia, once again in her Exile clothes, led us out of the city come dusk.

We traveled a good ten miles east before we cut across a track that angled south. It ran through forest for a quarter of a mile, then broke into an area that had been clear-cut beyond the wooden curtain. We traveled into a land marked by tree stumps and half-eroded hillsides. The road writhed over whatever flat ground it could find, occasionally running through streams, then cutting up along old logging roads.

It didn't take us too long to come across Exiles on the road to Vataria. Not all of them had been maimed or disfigured. One twelve-year-old girl carried her eighteen-month-old brother. He'd been bitten by a bug and his left eye had clouded over. Her parents had taken him to the place near their village closest to the Road of Exiles and abandoned him. She didn't know if they expected someone to carry him to Vataria or for him to die in the wilderness, but she ran away to care for him.

"What will you do when you deliver him to Vataria?"

She shrugged. "If someone will have him, will take care of him, I will come home. Or I won't. Not sure beauty lives in that house anymore."

I nodded. "Would you stay in Vataria to care for him?"

"If he needed me, yes." She bared her forearm. "I can burn myself here, or cut myself. Something that will scar. Then they'd have to take me."

I lifted her and her brother onto the back of the wagon. "I hope it won't come to that."

"Not my brother's fault his eye is bad. And he's not ugly. Just some people, they don't see it that way."

I left her to care for her brother—a toddler who smiled a great deal and laughed easily—and fell back to walk beside Ceresia. "How many have you seen like her, down through the years, willing to sacrifice her life for another this society has discarded?"

"A few, but seldom so young." She bared her face and sighed. "Most often it is an adult helping an aged parent make it to Vataria. Not a big sacrifice, since many would be discarded soon, too. Still, the love they show for another has its own beauty. Those who recognize that, who act upon it, are rare. It is easier to believe that your day of exile will never arrive than it is to reject a society that forces exile on people for trivial reasons."

"Did you never think to go to Jaranessa and explain to her what was wrong with her nation?"

Ceresia regarded me with a stare that stripped me naked. "She is a woman who looks only for beauty, but cannot truly see it. With the boy, she would only see his blind eye, not his smile. She could not hear his laughter. Her world has but one dimension, one color, and she remains willfully invisible to aught else unless, on a whim, she fixates on something new. So I could have gone. I could have spoken to her, but she would have remained immune to anything I said because defying her is an ugly act in her eyes."

I thought for a moment. "She does not see the beauty of reason."

"No, she sees reason as a blade that cuts an arbitrary line." The Knight of Beauty touched her forehead. "And she would see this scar and, by it, judge herself my superior."

"Even when I first saw you, road-weary and in half light, I thought you more beautiful than the best of the statues in her palace." I frowned. "Why would so tiny a scar make you less than she?"

Ceresia stared off into the darkness and remained silent for a while. Finally, she shifted her shoulders and lowered her voice. "In the days of King Parnyr's court, I was named Knight of Beauty. This made Jaranessa's mother jealous. She complained to the king and asked him to send me away. He refused—not because my beauty attracted him, but because he would not have her ordering him about. Jaranessa found her mother frustrated and in tears. The child was eight, perhaps, likely younger, and asked her mother why she was crying. Her mother explained, so the little girl ran off to her father. She asked him who was the most beautiful woman at court. The king said I was. And the girl said to him, 'Why would you permit anyone to be more beautiful than your daughter?'"

"Parnyr did that to you to please a child?"

Ceresia shook her head. "He had me do it to myself to prove my loyalty to him."

I rubbed a hand over my forehead. "But she took it as a sign that no one was more beautiful at court than she was; and if that was true at court, it had to be true for all Alkindor."

"And so it has been." Ceresia shook her head. "At least until the birth of this fabled child in Vataria. If the child *is* more beautiful, I fear Jaranessa's reaction."

* * *

As the night wore on, we gathered a dozen Exiles to us. With dawn approaching, we got off the road and to a campsite that others had used before. It had good water, and others had gathered branches and deadwood to create rough shelters. We built a fire at the heart of the camp, and I kindled another spirit fire elsewhere, then the living bedded down to sleep through the day. Krotha and I tended to the plodhooves and stood watch.

The raiders came when the sun reached its zenith. They had clearly hit this camp before, because they approached from behind some low hills. A dozen men with eight saddle-beasts between them. Clearly not from Trafaram, since their armor had seen better days, their boots had long since worn through here and there, and their tabards hadn't been laundered in months. The tabards all bore different crests, but each had a unifying mark: a scorpion crowning the crest.

I recalled Ceresia's story about Balarion's birth. *Is it possible the Scorpion has survived and his agents seek to complete his work by murdering Balarion?* I would have thought it unlikely, but then nothing much made sense in the world I'd returned to.

"Krotha, wake Balarion and the others." I took up my staff, then bent myself forward, as if an ancient man who could not walk without the assistance of a stick. I crested the nearest hill and peered down at the raiders in the gully. "You there, you're welcome in our camp. We will share what we have."

My appearance clearly surprised the raiders, and I do not refer to my being dead as part of that. They'd obviously planned to descend upon us, kill those who offered resistance, and take the rest of us captive. The only thing of value the Exiles carried with them was their muscle, so we'd be rounded up, and those of us who survived the march east to Scilliric would be sold into slavery.

A moment after they got over their initial shock at the sound of my voice, they smiled easily. A couple slid swords from scabbards. The largest man, whose leather vest defied being buttoned over his belly, chuckled. "We'll take what we want, and we don't want your kind."

His men laughed as he started up the hill toward me. I straightened, no longer old and broken, but taller and, while still dead, more threatening. His companions called out to him, though not in warning. "Wolf in wooldron's clothing, that one. Watch out!" He cursed at them, and at the hillside, which, because of the erosion, had the effrontery to shift beneath his heavy tread, dropping him to a knee.

Which proved to be most unfortunate for him. As he came up at me, I cast a spell that I intended to take his head off at the neck. Because he slipped, he dropped down, and the azure ball of lightning struck him in the forehead. It took his skull off at the level of his eyebrows. What was left of his brain boiled over and spilled down past his ears. He stared at me, as dead as I was, then flopped over onto his back and slid down to the gully.

Even as his fellows charged along the gully and up over the hill toward the camp, the man's essence flowed into me. It tingled, the hurtful bit being his sense of betrayal as I killed him. It found parallels in his life with his wife cheating on him, and his father heading off to market day without ever coming back. The rest of his life became a spiral of violence, which culminated in his becoming a slave raider, feeding the poorest of his Trafarami neighbors into the nihilistic machine that was Scilliric.

None of his companions wanted to deal with me and instead pressed their attack on our camp. Their logic escaped me, for they'd have to deal with me eventually, even if they raided and killed those I traveled with. Perhaps they thought a hostage or two might get me to leave them alone.

Hard to understand their reasoning, even on that point, for none of them would have cared a whit about the fate of a comrade who'd fallen into enemy hands; but then these were slavers, and they'd not descended to that lot in life through careful calculation and good life choices.

What they learned as they charged the camp was that I was the least of their worries. Balarion, clad only in silken breeches, scythed his blade through one man's flank, spun, parried a sword cut, then gutted that second attacker. Phylasina, her twin blades ringing, sprayed blood in red arcs. Krotha's great sword flashed in a grand arc, splitting a man from crown to groin, then it came up to impale a second.

Those three were fearsome and implacable, but Ceresia was lethal beauty. She did not duel—she danced. Nimble, she darted forward, whirled, ducked, and brought her blade up in so keen and gentle an arc that her victim didn't know he'd been cut until blood pulsed from his armpit. A return cut drew a delicate red line across his throat. He stumbled past her for two steps, then crumpled.

Of the last of them, two showed the good sense to run away from my companions' bloody steel. It fell to me to see that they did not get far. My spells lacked the elegance of Ceresia's swordplay, but they proved just as effective. Burning a man's spine to ash put an end to his hopes of escape. Likewise did melting the shocked expression off his companion's face.

The commotion of the battle awakened the Exiles, who, once they understood what had happened and stopped thinking about what might have happened, reverted to what humans have done for eons after a battle. They gathered the bodies, stripped them of anything useful, then dumped the corpses in another gully downwind of the camp. Some of them gathered the raiders' saddle-beasts and shifted their burdens to those creatures.

Over the rest of the journey, we had only one more confrontation with raiders, which went as badly for them as the first had. Because that second raid came while we were on the trail, I couldn't be certain that some raiders hadn't escaped, so it was possible we traveled the rest of the way unmolested because the survivors warned other bands. More likely, however, was the fact that we'd grown in number as we traveled, and any band that had drawn that close to Vataria had long since learned how to deal with raiders. Smaller bands simply made for easier pickings.

As the nature of our group changed, so did the people in it. The half-blind boy and his sister found a young pair, themselves brother and sister, to care for them. Exiles grouped themselves into small families, and former strangers helped each other. This made sense, as they traveled together, but more than that united them. They shared the common experience of having been cast aside by everyone else, including those who should have loved and supported them. Their new bonds became all that much stronger because they were made by choice, not just circumstance.

The change in Balarion impressed me the most. He'd always been personable and valiant, but in our company, he had no cause to show kindness. Yet within the caravan, he treated everyone as an equal and did not hold himself above others. He pitched in, helping as he could. He arranged defenses and hauled water, doing more than his share of the work.

The people respected him for that and began to look to him for guidance. He blossomed in that role, accepting the responsibility and authority they'd entrusted to him. Even when weather reduced our road to mud and the wagon became mired, he didn't curse. He saw to the welfare of the Exiles, then worked to shift the wagon and keep us moving forward. The people began calling him "my lord" even before Phylasina let slip the secret of his blood.

Krotha stood beside me, watching Balarion tell children a story as we waited for the sun to set. "He is not the boy we released from that casket, is he?"

"No, but perhaps he has become every inch a prince." I rubbed a hand over my chin. "He believes his father will remake Alkindor, restore it to its glory. I wonder, though, if that task would be better suited to him.

Balarion has an understanding of what this world has become, and thus a better idea of what it needs."

The Knight of Truth looked at me. "You think Balarion would set himself in opposition to his father?"

"When he realizes that none of this would be as it is save for his father's complicity in Alkindor's collapse, perhaps." My eyes tightened. "And if he does choose to rebel, I think, my friend, he will have my support."

DARK SOULS
MASQUE OF VINDICATION

CHAPTER 25

Having, until recently, spent the majority of my time in a tomb buried beneath tons of sand, and having journeyed across the face of a land I did not recognize, I had not been certain of what Vataria would look like. The idea that it attracted the broken and disfigured suggested it would be a broken place itself. The walls would have been shattered ages ago in a war, and the people would live in little more than pathetic hovels, poorly built, that provided meager shelter against the elements. Corpses would lie in open sewers, and feral animals would wander, scrapping for whatever tidbits could be found. Chances were, we'd smell the place before we ever saw it.

Because we approached it before dawn, the first clue I had to its nature was of stars being eclipsed by multiple towers. As we drew closer, and the first hints of false dawn lit the sky, a white city emerged with seven tall towers and a ribbon-wall surrounding the town. We traveled over a grassland that gave way to cultivated fields. The sun's growing light added green to the plants, save where red and orange, green and yellow marked out the fruit.

The road brought us to a large gate in the whitewashed wall. Four guardsmen, albeit older, stood at their posts, though their spears rested against the wall behind them. Instead of viewing us with suspicion or contempt, they approached, welcoming us. For them, we were not strangers, but the lost who had found their new home.

Balarion passed the wagon's reins to Phylasina and climbed down. "I am Balarion. We've come a long way and brought many Exiles with us. We need to speak with your leader."

The eldest of the guards pulled off a battered steel cap and scratched his head. "I guess that would be the Council, but they aren't meeting today. Probably not this week."

"It is urgent. We have come from the court of Jaranessa, in Aethemia."

The man's face closed up. "I will send word to the Council. Until then, come in."

Above us, high on the wall, a bell pealed loudly. At first, I thought this was a summons for the Council, but in the loud ringing I could sense no pattern or code. Perhaps the fact that it rang a dozen times had significance, but were that true, I could not determine it.

Our party passed through the gate and into a large open space that surrounded a fountain fashioned of white marble. On a pillar at its heart stood the figure of a woman, naked, narrow of hips, arms flung wide, head drawn back, and face to the sun. Water shot in a jet from her mouth, splashing down over her body and draining into the fountain. Droplets glittered in the sunlight, and a rainbow spanned the fountain's width.

Not surprisingly for so early in the morning, the courtyard around the fountain had been all but devoid of people when we entered. But quickly enough—obviously now summoned by the bell—people bled into the space and formed a cordon at the far side. Their expressions betrayed no hostile intent. Instead, I read curiosity as they studied us, and even joy, especially on the faces of the children peering out from between adults.

More important, despite many of the people missing limbs or having bodies that had been burned or ravaged by disease, each had an innate beauty. I felt as if I were seeing the world through Ceresia's eyes, for the contentment on the faces communicated an inner peace I could not remember ever having seen before. These people knew something I did not, and the secret knowledge they held gave them a confidence and generosity of spirit I could not help but find alluring.

A woman on crutches, missing the lower half of her left leg, approached us. "Welcome to Vataria. You are home. To remain, to become one with us, you are invited to take the waters of the Fountain of Fascination."

Our Exiles held back, likely confused by the open acceptance of strangers following the rejection of all those they had known before. Then the girl, bearing her brother in her arms, advanced. She never hesitated, and the woman on crutches smiled. Together they reached the fountain, the woman sitting on the rim. They stripped the clothing off the boy, then the woman raised him for all to see.

The people in the courtyard lifted their arms and grasped the hands of those next to them, linking them all. They bowed their heads and began to mumble a rhythmic chant, the words of which I could not discern. It resembled neither the hissing of a snake nor the crisply punctuated bark of a cur, more the soft whisper of a lover.

Seating herself on the fountain's edge, the woman dunked the child in the water, fully immersing him, and brought him up again quickly. The boy looked surprised, both eyes wide, then burst out laughing. She dunked him again, and then a third time, before lifting him high. As water dripped from his naked body, the crowd's chanting rose to a warm crescendo, then dissolved as hands fell and applause began.

The most curious thing then happened. The rainbow descended and wrapped around the child. For a heartbeat, it colored his dark skin, then passed into him. It swirled through his milky eye, then burst forth again to spread itself in the arch. The child fairly glowed in the wake of its departure, and that dead eye had cleared.

The child's laughter echoed from the walls.

The woman returned the child to his sister. "Your brother is one of us. You are free to remain and care for him, or to leave as is your will."

"I will stay." The girl made to hand the child back to the woman, and kicked off her sandals. She clearly meant to take the waters herself, but the woman shook her head. "The waters are only for those who need them. What you have done for your brother shows you do not." The woman regained her crutches and stood, nodding to a couple of people in the crowd. "You are both now Vatarian. Come, I shall introduce you to your new family."

Another of our Exiles hobbled forward, and a new host emerged from the crowd. He helped the woman disrobe and eased her into the fountain. In her case, a broken leg had healed poorly, deforming the limb. As the crowd chanted and the water splashed, the woman submerged herself three times. When she came up the on third, the rainbow surrounded her and sank through her. She threw back her head, much as the statue above depicted, and laughed gloriously. The rainbow drifted out of her throat and reset itself as the woman climbed out of the fountain.

Phylasina pointed. "But her leg is not healed."

The woman, a placidity in her expression and demeanor settling over her, shook her head and sprayed water everywhere. "What crippled me was not the bone, but the fear and shame of not being pleasing or perfect. How wasted is a life decided by the judgment of others?" She stared at the Knight of Fidelity for a moment, perhaps hoping to read understanding on Phylasina's face, then gathered her clothes in her arms and let her host lead her off to meet her new family.

One by one or in small family groups, our Exiles approached the fountain. They each underwent the ritual, guided by a host. The rainbow accepted them all. In some cases, it healed them—never of baldness or old age, mind—but in all cases they emerged with that sense of peace engendered by the chant. Outside, because of their imperfections, they had been despised and hunted. On the road, they had banded together out of necessity. Here, in becoming Vatarians, they knew the true acceptance that had marked their lives up until the point when they ran afoul of Jaranessa's arbitrary laws of beauty.

The crowd drifted away, taking with them our traveling companions. The Exiles had abandoned those meager possessions they'd brought with them. I wondered at that for a moment, then realized such things were simply detritus of their old lives—lives with which they had no connection to, nor any use for. The people they became as Vatarians needed nothing from their previous lives.

A dozen Vatarians remained behind as the crowd dispersed. An older woman, legless, pulled herself forward on a small, wheeled cart. "We are the Council. I am its Speaker. We are told you bear a message from the queen of Trafaram."

Balarion advanced, then dropped into a cross-legged posture before her, so as to look her in the eye. "I am Balarion, son of Parnyr. I have been given a mission by my father to gather the keys that will open his prison and allow me to free him so he can restore the world to what it was before."

The Speaker smiled indulgently, as one would when dealing with a child or an idiot. "If this is truly your belief, then perhaps you should take the waters, Balarion."

"I know the tale is fantastical, and I would share all of it with you, but it is also the truth."

She held up her hands. "Do not be offended, Balarion. I dwell in Vataria. I see miracles each day. I believe you have survived eons, as have your Knights of Virtue."

Balarion blinked. "You recognize them?"

"Vataria is an ancient city. Murals celebrating their glories have survived." The Speaker's blue eyes narrowed. "The part of your story I question is your belief that your father will restore the world to what it was before. Why would he do such a thing when, clearly, from that foundation we now have this world? It would be as foolish as expecting that a rosebush cut back to the earth would grow to produce anything but thorns and roses."

The prince nodded slowly. "There is logic to your words. However, starting from the same foundation does not mean we must end up here, does it? Once he knows how things turned out, might he not make changes to avoid the world becoming this way again?"

"I hope your belief in your father is justified." The Speaker rested her hands in her lap. "What would Jaranessa have of Vataria?"

"She has heard a rumor that in Vataria a child, a girl, has been born. A child who is simply the most beautiful ever. She wishes us to bring that child to her court. She wishes to raise that child as her heir." Balarion's expression darkened as he spoke, as he realized the true import of his words. When Jaranessa had given us our charge, we imagined Vataria to be a hellhole from which any child, beautiful or not, deserved to be freed. We were being sent to rescue a child and bring them to a life they deserved. *Deserved, according to the dictates of Jaranessa's society.* But now we were asking the Vatarians to give up a piece of themselves. In accepting this mission, we had accepted Jaranessa's judgment of the Exiles and their value. Standing here, it became clear that by accepting her charge, we'd welcomed her view of reality and had become the sort of monsters the Exiles fled.

Instead of recoiling in horror at the request, the Speaker raised her hands above her head and clapped. "Bring the children born of Vataria here, those born in the last five years."

The other members of the Council withdrew to carry out her command. Within a handful of minutes, people led children to the fountain courtyard. Some were still babes and had to be carried. Others dutifully held their parent's hand or, if a twin, clung to their sibling. More than one carried a somewhat ragged and clearly well-loved doll.

Ceresia sank to a knee. "Impossible."

"What?"

She pointed out one child, and then another and another. "Look at them. Each is more gorgeous than the next."

I could not deny that each of the children was beautiful. Well-formed, clean-limbed, and with plump cheeks and bright eyes, each waited in eager anticipation, as if we were going to give them a prize of some sort. Their parents, too, appeared happy, even though the Council member must have told them we had come at Jaranessa's behest. None of them made any attempt to hide their children or shield them from our gaze.

Balarion's mouth gaped open. "So many beautiful children."

The Speaker nodded. "And each more beautiful than Jaranessa. They are the fruit of those she has discarded. Please choose any of them."

Our leader turned toward Ceresia. "Knight of Beauty, the choice is yours."

Sweat hung in a crystal droplet from her nose. "Please, my lord, do not ask this of me."

"Yours is the keenest eye and sharpest judgment in such things."

Ceresia regained her feet and walked toward the line of children. She first headed to the right, then, after a step, turned left. She hesitated and wiped sweat from her brow. She reached out and stroked a small girl's flaxen hair. Ceresia brought her hand away and stared at it.

She turned toward me. "Ferranos, please." Her eyes rolled up into her head, then she wavered and collapsed.

I darted forward and turned her onto her back. Her body shook and her eyelids flickered, revealing only the whites. Froth appeared at the corners of her mouth as her body quaked uncontrollably. Her spine arched, locking her rigid for a moment, then she gasped and went limp. Her chest yet rose and fell, and though she uttered sounds, none of them made sense.

The Speaker's shadow fell across Ceresia's face as the woman wheeled herself over. "We know of this one. She has led so many here—including me, ages ago—but she always withdrew before the sun kissed our towers."

"What has Vataria done to her?"

"Broken her reality." The Speaker looked me in the eyes. "The Knight of Beauty, think on it: By what yardstick did she measure beauty?"

I wiped spittle from the corner of Ceresia's mouth. "Her own beauty."

"Just so. Her vanity defined her world. Here she learned there is beauty beyond her comprehension." The Speaker laid a bony hand on Ceresia's brow. "The truth has broken her mind."

I looked toward the fountain. "Let her take the waters."

"The waters only heal that which others have inflicted upon us. They will do nothing for her." The Speaker sighed. "But Vataria will care for her.

Not because we are in her debt for bringing so many here, but because we understand that acquiescence to reality is the most difficult battle any of us will ever face."

I reached down and gave Ceresia's hand a squeeze, then stood. "The choice, I believe, my lord Balarion, now falls back to you."

The prince stood, then paced back and forth before the line. He looked at the children, then at their parents. One by one, he thanked the parents, then dismissed them and their children. Finally, he selected a raven-haired girl of four with light eyes and a ready smile.

He dropped to a knee in front of her. "I am Balarion. I have been commanded to bring to Aethemia the most beautiful child in Vataria. Will you help me?"

The little girl nodded.

"What is your name?"

"Syra."

Balarion extended a hand toward her. "And this, your doll, your friend. What is her name?"

"She is Allosi."

"You love Allosi very much, don't you?"

Syra nodded solemnly.

"Then I would ask you, Syra, to let me take Allosi back to Aethemia and present her to Jaranessa as the most beautiful child in Vataria."

Syra took the doll in both hands and held her out to the prince. "Allosi, you be good."

The doll, with its embroidered smile and single button eye, accepted the order without comment.

Phylasina gained Balarion's side as the girl placed the doll in his hands. "My lord, this will not fool Jaranessa."

"Allosi is well-loved, very well-loved. Better loved, I am certain, than any of my father's children." Balarion stood. "Something worthy of so much love simply must be the most beautiful thing here. So it is in Syra's eyes, and now is in mine."

CHAPTER 26

Our company remained somber on the return journey. Changes in the landscape suggested we had lost time while in Vataria—not as severely as when we'd returned to Tsaleryk, but a good six months. It seemed longer to me, for in the absence of Ceresia's company, time dragged like a sharp thorn across the flesh.

Not even running across and slaughtering a handful of slaver bands could raise our spirits. We were particularly merciless in destroying them because my companions recognized that had we taken Syra, instead of her doll, we would have been every inch as evil as the slavers were. I did my best to kill them swiftly—though according to the souls I absorbed, my definition of *swift* and theirs, informed by pain, differed a great deal.

Krotha and I sat on a rock in the wake of an ambush—we ambushed them, not the other way around—and drank from our flasks to repair what little damage they'd inflicted. He grinned at me as I stuffed the last bit of intestines back into my belly before the crosscut closed. "You have taken better to combat, as our journey continues, my friend. I think, however, you've missed the key that every warrior knows. 'Tis better to hit than be hit."

"I understand that, Knight of Truth. I've drunk enough warrior souls to have heard them all lament that they failed on that count. Most also consider me a less than honorable combatant, as my magicks can't be parried, and few outmaneuvered." I shrugged. "I find the warriors' great delight in poking me with sharp things most disagreeable."

He nodded. "As I inherit souls, and inherit the power of those souls, combat grows easier. When I was alive, even when we first met, the idea that four of us might ambush a dozen and a half would have been synonymous with suicide. Now, we prevail, and in the next fight we shall prevail more easily."

"True." We'd run across a number of different bands, and a few wore Scorpion crests. They'd been tougher than the others, but we overcame them handily regardless. "The next fight is likely to be in Aethemia, at the palace."

"You do not think Jaranessa will accept the doll, do you?"

I slipped my flask back into the belt pouch. "You do?"

Balarion wiped someone else's blood off his face and joined us. "She will accept the child."

Krotha frowned. "How can you say that with such certainty, my lord? I agree with your decision that we cannot take a child away from her family for Jaranessa's amusement, but she would have to be blind not to realize the deception."

"She will not recognize the deception because she does not believe she can be deceived." Balarion pointed north and west. "Tsaleryk has created a whole nation that values gold above all things. Golden wooldron, golden fur, golden grain, and golden vermin, they all thrive because of their symbolic value. The tsogarron make his nation poorer, yet are treasured because of their color. And he, surrounded by gold, seeing only gold, believes they are treasures. He will not let himself see the truth."

I smiled. "So it is with your sister."

"It's worse with her, Ferranos. Tsaleryk shaped his kingdom through neglect. He never issued an edict to protect vermin, but he certainly caused the fur of golden wooldron to be valued. People came to associate that color with value, so anything gold took on extraordinary worth. I gave you a gold ring, but in their eyes, it might as well have been a crown. Without intention, Tsaleryk ruined Kadarr.

"Jaranessa makes mention of something she finds pleasing, and her ministers immediately let her wishes be known. There they take conscious control of her whims, and they become law. Perhaps she has no idea of the effect on her nation, but I doubt it. She exists in that world behind screens, screens that cage her, but that cannot blind her to the nature of things. If she were to leave the palace and travel the streets of Aethemia, she would see the truth."

Krotha grunted. "What *is* the truth in Trafaram?"

"Truth is whatever Jaranessa believes is beautiful." Phylasina slid both of her blades home at her waist. "How do we convince her that Allosi is beautiful?"

I shook my head. "We do not convince her that Allosi is beautiful. We convince her that Allosi is *more beautiful* than she is."

The Knight of Fidelity gave me a withering glance. "That's even more difficult a task."

"No, Phylasina, Ferranos has it right." Balarion's eyes widened. "It appeals to a fear she's known all her life. She hides behind her screens, hides her face behind a mask, has us wear blindfolds so that we are not hurt by her beauty. Really, it is so none of us can see her clearly and realize she is not the most beautiful person ever. She dreads the day someone who exceeds her beauty will appear."

A shiver ran down my spine. "Ceresia told me how she got the scar on her forehead. Parnyr forced her to cut herself so Jaranessa's beauty would be unrivaled."

"Yes, Ferranos, you prove what I have been saying." Balarion sighed. "That fear that dwells deep in her heart, we will awaken it. She will believe that we have succeeded. She will give us the key, and we can leave this place."

"But, my lord, how will we convince her?" Phylasina took Balarion's right hand in hers. "She may be insane, but she is not a fool."

"Fear makes fools of us all." Balarion turned and kissed Phylasina on the forehead. "Allosi will become all that Jaranessa fears, and we will use the rules of Trafaram's society to do the convincing."

Being drawn by only one plodhoof—a plodhoof that had been blindfolded—our wagon came to a stop a quarter mile from the main gate to Aethemia. Balarion, also wearing a blindfold, walked ahead of us and spoke to the guards. He handed each of them a thick blindfold like his, torn from tabards we'd taken from dead slavers.

Though I could not hear what he said, he apparently spoke it well enough to scare the guards. Not only did they put on the blindfolds, but one of them started ringing a bell while a second sent a black flag up a pole above the gate. Other bells sounded in the city, spreading like fire from our gate throughout. More flags waved from poles, and a squad of guardsmen bearing black banners and handbells assembled on either side of the roadway.

Each of those men wore a blindfold.

Krotha started the wagon forward again. We picked up Balarion halfway to the gate and continued on. The prince smiled and kept his voice low. "Telling them that one of our horses had seen the child and died on the spot was enough."

Phylasina rode in the back of the wagon next to a basket shrouded in black. "What are the bells about?"

"An old system. If Jaranessa wanted to walk through the streets, the bells and black banners warn people to stay inside or wear blindfolds so her beauty does them no harm."

I laughed. "It is as you predicted, my lord."

"It was obvious, Ferranos, from her entrance at the banquet."

Krotha chuckled. "This may well work."

The guardsmen, with their banners and bells, guided us through the city. Shutters slammed closed as we passed. Some people on the street fainted. Parents hustled small children indoors. The people, who had been so happy and beautiful when we first arrived in Aethemia six months ago, now let fear and blindfolds turn them ugly. We knew not if they had been told of our mission, but the story Balarion had fed the guards spread through the city well ahead of our procession.

The Trafarami knew that our return, and the child we brought with us, could fundamentally change their society. Were the child dark-haired and light-eyed, this could become the new standard of beauty by which all others would be measured. In the blink of an eye, those who enjoyed elevated status because of their hair color or eye color could be thrown down. The most high would become Exiles; and those who had been beneath them would rise to replace them.

We arrived at the palace in due course. The prime minister and his two deputies waited for us at the top of the stairs. Guardsmen took the plodhoof and wagon away. Citizens filed into the courtyard behind us, murmuring. I should have liked to turn and look at them, save that doing so would have given away the game. Still, the sight of a nation of people who willfully blindfolded themselves because of a rumor was so rare. The vision should have been treasured.

The prime minister reached out to peel the shroud from the basket, but Krotha caught his wrist. "Would you have the sun die for its shining down upon this child?" He said it loud enough that the crowd moaned. The prime minister staggered back when released, then led us again to the throne room. We progressed along the carpet and found Jaranessa seated on her throne, awaiting us.

Balarion advanced toward the ivory screen and set the basket on a little wooden table a dozen feet from his sister. "As you asked of us, Jaranessa-Solar, we have journeyed to Vataria. We confirmed the rumor of a beautiful child, and we have brought that child to you."

"There, in that basket? Is the child asleep? It makes no sound."

As we had rehearsed on the road, I stepped forward to play my part. "Most Radiant, this child knows the absolute beauty of silence. She is doubtless awed by your beauty, for never has she seen anyone as beautiful as you."

The mask that was Jaranessa's face became impassive. "You are lacking one of your number. Ceresia. She I could trust to assess the child's beauty."

Krotha replied to that, since only he could be believed. "In Vataria, Most Radiant, Ceresia saw such beauty that she could not understand it. It shattered her mind. It was beauty she had not seen before."

Not a lie, not a word of it, and delivered well by the Knight of Truth. Jaranessa regarded him, then her eyes half closed. "Tell me of this place. How did you get the child away?"

Phylasina advanced to Balarion's side. "As you would imagine, Most Radiant, the city of Exiles is a dark place. As you said, a festering wound. A pit of poison. We found our way there—slaying many Scillirician slavers as we went—and announced ourselves. At the mere mention of your name, the twisted, malformed creatures that call themselves Vatarians, they shrank away as if shadows before sunlight. Ceresia ventured forth, and she found the child. She brought her to us. Her name is Allosi. She brought the child in this basket, beneath this shroud, and warned us not to look, but to blindfold ourselves. And then, as the Knight of Truth relates, our sister fell, stricken, frothing at the mouth. Having seen Allosi, her mind broke. She became a creature of Vataria, doomed to dwell there forever."

Jaranessa's serenity slipped but for a heartbeat. Her lips rose in a sneer, which vanished almost immediately. For her, the idea that Ceresia would remain in Vataria, could only live in Vataria, seemed perfectly fitting.

"Minister Valadine, this child shall be made a Daughter of Aethemia. Gather all the ministers. Gather the dukes and duchesses. Have them here in an hour. Go."

The prime minister, his expression grim, led the other two ministers from the room. Jaranessa, resplendent in her green-and-blue silk robe, paced as if a tigress staring at a morsel from within her ivory cage. The features on her mask sharpened, making her appear more feline, and though her pace remained stately and slow, the fluidity of her movement had an undeniable predatory aspect to it.

Balarion opened his arms. "Sister, I appreciate that you shall present this child to your people at court, but there is the matter of the Key of Beauty to deal with."

Her hand rose to her throat. "I had not forgotten. You have earned your reward." She stepped back, and with an echoing click, one of the ivory panels separated from the next just wide enough for Balarion to squeeze through. "Come, brother of mine."

The way they moved, their stature, was a study in contrasts. She, over-tall and slender, elegance personified. Balarion, youthful and well-muscled, with a smile that came too easily. He slipped into her enclosure, and the panel slid shut again. Phylasina took a half step forward, as if concerned for his safety, then caught herself and tended to the basket containing the child.

Jaranessa approached him wordlessly. She reached out with her right hand, stroking his left cheek. A gentle gesture, only undercut by the bony thinness of her fingers. Then, striking quickly, she sank her fingers into his hair, cupping the back of his head, and pulled him to her. She tugged, forcing his chin up and his head back, then lowered her face to his, her mouth to his, and kissed him. Kissed him deeply and completely.

Magick pulsed from them. Though the ivory cage offered limited visibility, the opalescent band slid up her throat, then disappeared beneath her mask. How long it remained out of my sight I could not honestly say, but then it appeared just beneath his jawline. As they continued to kiss, it crawled down his neck and eventually nestled itself on his shoulders and collarbone.

Jaranessa broke the kiss and hissed something at Balarion. He staggered back a step, then dropped to a knee and bowed his head. She reached out and stroked his hair, then laughed lightly. One more caress, then she lifted her hand from him and turned away—much as a cat does when interest in prey has evaporated.

She looked at Phylasina over her shoulder. "Once again, he is yours."

Balarion remained down and seemed listless, until a hand strayed to his throat and he touched the key. The key on his wrist joined the one around his neck in glowing, albeit faintly. That same light appeared in his eyes, then he blinked and stood without any indication of weakness.

The ivory panels again parted, and Balarion returned to us. Phylasina hugged him tightly. He whispered something into her ear, and she smiled. The two of them then returned to the basket containing Allosi, smoothing invisible wrinkles in the cloth, which hid the interior.

The prime minister returned with his fellows, all wearing predominantly blue robes with green trim. Following them, nobles entered wearing green robes with blue decoration. Some of them had been at the dinner we had enjoyed before our trek, though if memory served me well, only a few remained with the partners from that evening.

The prime minister produced a slender, sharp dagger, the blade barely the width of my narrowest finger. "The most luminous and brilliant Jaranessa has, in her glowing wisdom, decided that this child shall be made a Daughter of Aethemia. You, her loyal ministers and beloved nobles, have your part in this. Yours is to perform what Jaranessa wills be performed."

Clutching the dagger's hilt in both hands, the prime minister thrust it blindly down through the cover and into Allosi. Shock blossomed on his face. No cry greeted his strike, and there could be no mistaking the difference between a live child and a stuffed doll as a knife skewers it. His eyes grew wide.

In a heartbeat, of which I had none, I slid past Phylasina and wrapped my hands over the prime minister's. I stared into his eyes. "Such a perfect child. So beautiful. She does not even bleed."

A shudder ran through him. "She does not even bleed."

I retained my grip on the dagger as I shouldered him aside. I glanced at the next minister. "Come, do as your radiant mistress demands." With the blade held in both our hands, I made certain the thrust had emphasis. Each of the ministers and then the nobles uttered that false epitaph—"She does not even bleed"—joining the others in the deception. Some did so with tears in their eyes, others with guile, and most with fear of being discovered. But as more and more of them joined the conspiracy, the lie came more easily to their lips. Each realized that the exposure of one was the exposure of all.

Krotha sealed it by taking his turn. "I, Krotha, Knight of Truth, do swear this Allosi does not even bleed."

Balarion, a bit ashen-faced, turned to his sister. "Where is it that she can join her sisters as a Daughter of Aethemia?"

Jaranessa's mask again hid all emotion. "The prime minister will convey her."

"I began her journey." Balarion hefted the basket and clutched it to his breast. "I would see it safely completed."

"So noble." Jaranessa dismissed him with the casual wave of a hand. "As you wish."

We followed the prime minister in a solemn procession that carried us as far below the earth as we had been above it when in Jaranessa's presence. The stairs became rougher and narrower as we descended. We used lanterns and torches to complete the journey into depths that had never been touched by natural light. We passed through the foundation and wound down into a cavern that had formed over eons but men had worked into its present shape.

All over the floor, which had multiple levels and little side chambers, biers formed neat rows. In the torchlight, a dozen became easily visible, and more hid in shadows. How many more I could not even hazard a guess. The largest could accommodate an adult, but the prime minister steered us away from them. He led us to an area with smaller stones, ones that would suit Allosi very well.

And she would rest amid so many children who would have loved to play with her.

Balarion set down the basket on an empty stone, then looked at the prime minister. "How many?"

The man hesitated, then hung his head. "Too many. A beautiful child is consigned here as Allosi was, but the beautiful are not alone. Were a mother to bear an ugly child, the loss of status would be devastating. So a rumor begins about how stunning this child is. And that child joins the Daughters of Aethemia, saving her family through her sacrifice."

Krotha frowned. "And you condone that?"

The man looked up, weary. "To free a child of what she would have to endure in this place, yes." He pointed off into the darkness. "My daughter, at three, caught the Snow Pox. She survived, but the scars... She now knows no pain, no humiliation."

The idea of a society where ugly children are claimed to be beautiful so they will die, and where some beautiful children are declared ugly so they can live in Vataria, puckered my flesh. I glanced at Balarion. "The sooner we are away from here..."

"Yes, you all should leave. This place is not meant for you." The prime minister shook his head. "But you are bound for Scilliric. Much death abides there, too, in the ugliest forms you can imagine. Survive a day there, and you will wish you were here."

DARK SOULS
MASQUE OF VINDICATION

CHAPTER 27

We opted to leave Aethemia before dawn. Krotha joked it was because we knew none of the capital's residents would be awake that early. Fact was, however, that neither Balarion nor Phylasina slept at all well, given Allosi's fate. I wasn't certain that we would be able to get away with the deception, but I packed up my material and headed out with the rest of them. The guards were not in the least diligent, and we made good headway before the sun was up.

Transportation was a matter of concern, since we'd returned to Aethemia with a wagon and a plodhoof, and those had long since been led away. We elected to steal saddle-beasts for our trek, and in keeping with Trafarami cultural safe practices, we stole only ugly mounts from Jaranessa's stable. Balarion did leave her a very polite thank-you note, mentioning that none of us felt worthy of being in her presence and that we were bound for Scilliric to fight the slavers who had been besetting her people.

We followed the Road of Exiles, heading east-northeast. It wasn't a direct route to the capital of Hyeracia. Were Jaranessa going to send troops in pursuit, we decided they'd take the most direct route toward the capital. By heading on a more eastern track, we could avoid pursuit, or delay it at the very least. Having learned from our visits to Kadarr and Trafaram, a bit of time to become accustomed to Scilliric seemed like a good idea.

It took us nearly a week to clear the border between Trafaram and

Scilliric. It turned out that while we'd come away from Aethemia with little more than the mounts, our gear, and some simple provisions, we'd carried with us something even more valuable than gold in Kadarr. We had *gossip* from the capital about the latest in fashions, and people paid well for that sort of information. We traded stories for good provisions and better mounts.

The interaction worked well for my company, in that social interaction forced us to be polite and even effusive, though our experience had inspired little by way of sociability. As we traveled between villages, we barely spoke other than to point out water or places where I could kindle a spirit fire. The artificial beauty of Jaranessa's regime reminded us of Allosi and all the other people who lay buried with her in the underworld beneath Jaranessa's opulence.

Crossing into Scilliric broke a dam inside us, and not because this land rivaled Trafaram for beauty. Far from it. Harshly bright and bitterly cold, the nation had winds that whipped razored snowflakes and stinging sand across the landscape. Scilliric appeared to be emerging from a long winter where snows had crushed golden grasses. Here and there, new green shoots appeared, and the howling wind tortured the delicate leaves. The snow crunched beneath hooves, and even when we gave the saddle-beasts their leave to graze, they found little to their liking.

Balarion pulled a blanket around himself as if it were a cloak. "As much as I hate this place, I prefer it to Aethemia. This land is ugly and makes no attempt to hide it."

Phylasina gazed back west. "I hope it is possessed of even a fraction of the sanity that the Trafarami have surrendered. What if we had actually brought a child. They would not have hesitated, not even for a heartbeat, to destroy that child."

"You are right, and this is why my father prepared me to free him." Balarion shook his head. "I would have killed to save a child. I would have slaughtered all of them."

Krotha grunted. "They did not hesitate because they had killed so many before them. In their minds, the murder of children became a virtue—they were dutiful parents sparing their offspring from the pain of growing up in that insanity."

I spread my hands. "They spared the children, yet did nothing to change the system. Were one of them to stand up, others would tear them apart. And none of them would strike at her because they had grown up with her being unto a goddess. Who would dare strike down a god?"

"It is more than that, Ferranos, and the very reason I should have struck her down." Balarion glanced back at me over his left shoulder. "When she kissed me to transfer the Key of Beauty to me, it created a connection. It opened a door. My mind was wide open. She could have understood everything, for I could have hidden nothing from her. Our deception could have been discovered, and I was powerless to prevent it. I wouldn't have been able to warn you of the danger."

Phylasina spun and clung to his side. "You would have found a way, my lord."

"No. As much as I would have desired it, I could not have." He glanced down. "She would have known everything through that connection, but she did not use it to interrogate me. Instead, she projected her vision of herself into me. She is beautiful, of this she is certain, and most wonderful. Her people love her, as have her many lovers, though none of them have been truly worthy of her."

He took Phylasina's hands in his. "She intimated that you were beneath me and that, were I to join with her, we could destroy her brothers and rule as gods ourselves."

My eyes narrowed. "She would have destroyed you."

"She would have *consumed* me, and then, when I was a spent husk, she would have discarded me. Were I lucky, I'd have escaped to Vataria. If not, I would lie in the same darkness as Allosi." His expression soured, but fire blazed in his eyes. "She and her attitude, her obliviousness to reality and her contentment to live in a paradise that extends only as far as she can see from within her cage, this is why she is one whom my father will have to destroy. She is part of the reason I am here—*we* are here. The faster we can get to Dolared, and I to the Key of Might, the better for all that we know."

The conviction in Balarion's voice steeled our spines and poured molten desire into our hearts. Even our mounts became infected, champing at their bits for us to move along. The snow-striped landscape offered little shelter, so we pressed on until we cut across wagon ruts beneath the snow. Hooves crushed the snowy crust. The ruts headed north, as did we.

The landscape changed gradually enough that I missed the difference initially. Here and there along the road, green grasses and wildflowers poked up through the snow or on the edges of its retreat. As we rode along, the green became more easily visible, but it wasn't until we rode into a narrow valley where green predominated that the dirty snow began to fade. Farther north along a modest stream, cultivated fields had garhme and wilak crops, which brushed my boot soles as we rode. Even though the stalks had not attained full height, some of them looked ready to harvest, as did the peas, beans, and gourds in their garden plots.

Central to the valley stood a small walled town. The huts and long-houses featured wattle-and-daub construction and thatched roofs. The same construction formed walls around the village, with the sticks rising out of the wall, having been sharpened at the top. The villagers had dug a trench around the base of the wall, adding height and using the dirt to reinforce the barrier, but a stiff wind in a pouring rain would have blown apart the whole affair.

But the villagers did not have a storm to fear. Instead, a company of Hollows, most wearing rusted armor and half-rotted tabards, launched themselves at the village. They slammed themselves against the walls, cracking the dried mud and pulling at the exposed sticks. Some climbed up, only to be flung off the wall by villagers using pitchforks and mattocks. One Hollow managed to impale herself on the sticks at the top, flailing wildly and hissing furiously at the defenders.

Balarion drew his sword, and my companions followed suit. They set spurs into the saddle-beasts' flanks and charged toward the company of undead. I reined my mount toward the left, veering off in my approach. "Stay clear of the trench!" I hoped they heard me over the thunder of hoofbeats.

The three of them in formation stabbed deep into the Hollows' company. The saddle-beasts blasted withered soldiers up and back. Krotha, on the left flank and closest to the wall, swept his sword down and around, cleaving one Hollow from crown to hip. Phylasina's twin blades shredded Hollows, and Balarion's sword work sent Hollows spinning away, their disparate parts flying in all directions.

I leaped from the saddle as my mount reached the trench. I jumped down into it and smiled. The trench ran straight north to the point of assault, and none of the Hollows I had flanked noticed my presence. I leveled my staff and began casting in earnest.

The fireballs zipped down the trench and burned their way through one Hollow, then they ate into another. I leaned left, aimed carefully, and sent another sizzling right along the wall, bisecting a Hollow and leaving a scorch mark on the whitewash. By then, the Hollows realized the danger I represented. A half dozen of them broke off the attack on the wall and shambled in my direction.

The trench packed them in tightly, and my magicks burned through the lot of them. Greasy black smoke rose from the corpses, obscuring the battlefield. I scrambled up and out of the trench, wreathed two more Hollows in flame, and walked north to escape the sickly sweet stench of burning flesh.

Phylasina remained in the saddle, ranging east to cut down Hollows who had the presence of mind to flee. Her blades flashed in the sunlight as she took the Hollows to pieces. One head tumbled through the air in an arc high enough to eclipse the midday sun, then bounced to a stop next to an orange gourd roughly twice its size.

Krotha and Balarion had dismounted and fought shoulder to shoulder.

They were a metal-clad rock upon which the tide of Hollows shattered. The reach of their blades described a circle within which only they could live. Hollows, and parts thereof, thumped to the ground all around them. Those in the fore of the Hollow formation died as others in the back pressed them forward; and the few with shreds of intelligence remaining fled, only for Phylasina to find them.

As the Hollows I'd destroyed ceased to exist, bits and pieces of their essences flowed into me. These had once been warriors of Scilliric, highly trained and banded together into companies bound by honor and tradition. All of them gave me sharp, prideful flashes of a drillmaster or beloved teacher handing them a tabard with a gaudy crest emblazoned on the breast. For many, this memory proved to be the crowning moment of their lives. For others, it was just one of many instances of such honors. Though they could not remember who they had been or how long ago they had been consigned to the grave, these honors defined them even beyond the ends of their lives.

The din of battle ceased. I found my mount and led it toward the gate. Phylasina gathered the others' mounts and did likewise. Balarion had dropped to a knee, sweat pouring off his face. Krotha, ever alert, stood above him, facing the village gates as they opened. Balarion looked up and smiled at the expectant faces of the people within.

Of my companions, the people took little notice—save for their presence creating a bit of a roadblock. The villagers poured forth, baskets in hand or hung on their backs, and raced into the gardens. They began harvesting everything they could, making faster work of the produce than my companions and I had of the Hollows. And curiously, when I looked toward the orange gourd I'd noticed earlier, I could have sworn it had swelled considerably since I'd last looked at it.

As villagers bustled in and out of the gate, hauling loaded baskets and returning with empty ones, an older man bearing a staff of office marched from the village. Two youths followed him, one of each gender. The girl carried a book and thumbed it open as the old man stopped before

Balarion. Her companion carried a banner, bearing a crest that depicted a crossed flail and scythe on a field of green.

The old man straightened up as best he could. "We owe you thanks. To which company do you belong?"

The girl behind him had a quill poised to write.

Balarion stood. "I am Balarion. These are my companions. Krotha is the Knight of Truth. Phylasina is the Knight of Fidelity. And this is Ferranos, a valued member of our group."

The man nodded. "To which company do you belong?"

The repetition of the question, this time in decidedly formal tones, narrowed Balarion's eyes. "We are not of a company, sir, but companions on a mission for my father."

The old man shook his head. "You must be of a company. You fought here. You clearly have lost your banner. But I must know your company. If I do not know your company, how can I send an accounting to your masters? Now, to which company do you belong?"

Balarion cleaned his sword on a threadbare piece of tunic. "We are of no company."

Blood drained from the girl's face as she scribbled a note.

The villagers, as they continued on their way, gave us a much wider berth.

I stepped forward. "Forgive me, but we are travelers from afar. The only Scilliricians we have met did not fight under banners. They were slavers in Trafaram. I can see our answer to your question proves unsatisfactory, but without context, we cannot know how to answer."

The old man shrugged. "It is out of my hands now. You have fought without sanction. I will send a rider to the district headquarters, and they will come to take you into custody. May the gods have mercy on your souls."

CHAPTER 28

Balarion raised his hands. "We will comply with your request, but would ask two things of you. First, what is the name of this place?"

The old man looked at the banner the boy carried. "There."

Our leader scratched the back of his neck. "I see no words."

"It is obvious: Best Southwest Grain Valley." The old man shook his head. "You Trafarami know nothing."

As he spoke, I sidled around and caught a glimpse of the book the young woman was keeping. The pages had no words, but instead were inscribed with symbols. Most were abstractions, but many recognizable. A series of gravestones were one of the most recent additions, which I took to indicate the Hollows who had attacked. Four swords and a fireball represented us, along with saddles for our mounts.

I glanced at the old man. "She writes in symbols, as they did long, long ago. Have you lost words here?"

"Words went with Alkindor, and Alkindor went because of words. So Prince Dolared has proclaimed. He returned to the old ways, the *pure* ways. The symbols tell what needs to be told." The old man looked back to Balarion. "You wished something else from us?"

"We saved your village, so I would ask food, water, and shelter for us and our beasts. That seems fair."

"I shall grant you two baskets. Gather what you need." He pointed off across the gardens toward the stream. "Other side of that, by the big rock, there's a firepit. You can camp there."

Phylasina frowned. "Your people have gone through the gardens as if locust. There is nothing left for us."

"You know less than nothing." The old man snorted. "Get the baskets, and you'll see." He turned on his heel and stalked back into the village, shouting an order. His charges followed him, and two children bearing modest baskets ran out and left them with us.

Phylasina kicked the baskets, scattering them. "What does he expect us to do with these?"

Krotha laid a heavy hand on her shoulder. "Look before you judge."

"What?"

I walked halfway to the nearest garden plot. "This is curious."

Balarion scooped up a basket. "What are you seeing, Ferranos?"

"Something so remarkable I am sorry I did not see it before this." I spread my arms. "I should like to think I would have noticed, had the Hollows not distracted me. How exactly is this place different from the road we traveled upon to find it, and the countryside we made our way through?"

"It's much greener." Balarion's expression brightened as he thought. "And warmer, which it should not be. No snow."

I nodded, crossing to the nearest plant. I dropped to a knee and held up a squash no bigger than my thumb. "Unless I have been inattentive, this was not here when the baskets arrived for us, and it is growing against my palm."

Balarion approached, and the green squash grew heavier in my hand. "How is that possible?"

"I don't know, Majesty, but I believe this land responds to our presence. The green we saw on the road had grown there because of the proximity of our passage. Perhaps the presence of this village provides warmth or light or vitality that the plants draw upon to grow?"

Phylasina shook her head. "And the people eat the plants to create the vitality, which in turn grows more plants? It would seem an impossible system, allowing for no growth in population. There must be something else. Something in the air or the soil that contributes to the cycle."

"A mystery that will not feed you." Krotha crouched and studied the plants as if they were enemy troops. "My arms master once told me that harvesting men meant I'd never have to harvest vegetables."

Phylasina laughed. "And he's gone now."

"Is he?" Balarion started picking peas. "He might well be as Ferranos or Krotha are."

"We can only hope. He and Dolared spent much time with each other." I glanced at my dead companion. "You knew Dolared?"

"As well as Phylasina. We were Knights of Virtue together." Krotha laughed. "This is to say I did not know him well. He was the Knight of Victory; and Truth and Victory seldom see things the same way. Victory *imagines* more than it remembers."

Phylasina started harvesting beans. "I remember he danced well, at banquets."

"I do not recall being invited to many of those." Krotha stood again. "But then, I was often off winning the victories that allowed him to dance in celebration."

A saddle-beast and rider heading off at a gallop out of the village cut off any further discussion. We took the fruits and vegetables we'd gathered to the site the village's headman had specified and made camp. I kindled the spirit fire while Balarion built a real one. Krotha and Phylasina took care of the saddle-beasts, which fed well on the grasses lining the stream.

It truly did seem as if our presence accelerated plant growth, though I noticed that things slowed down as the sun sank lower in the sky. This led me to believe that growth occurred most quickly around noon, when the sun provided the most light. I wondered how things fared when clouds hid the sun and imagined I'd be able to puzzle out the answer to that question before our adventure in Scilliric came to an end.

An hour or two past dawn, the village's rider returned, and in his wake came a troop of six soldiers—four men and two women—all wearing tabards emblazoned with what I took to be Scilliric's national crest: crossed swords, hilts low, on a field of red. They also wore red sashes looped around their waists, right above their sword belts. They had been worked with other crests and symbols, and embroidered with great precision. The eldest of them had the most, with the two youngest having one or two.

The soldiers consulted with the headman, then rode over to our camp. Their leader dismounted, tossing her reins to her lieutenant. "I am Captain Vevanya. I have authority in Southwest Military District Seven. I place you under arrest. You will accompany me to Southwest Military District Seven Headquarters to be tried for imposture. Defy me, and this thirsty land will drink deeply."

Balarion nodded. "Will you require our weapons, or will you accept our word that we will accompany you willingly?"

"You ask as if there is a reason I should know you and, thus, trust your word."

"I am Balarion, brother to Prince Dolared. These are my companions. We are killers of Hollows."

If his claim of kinship meant anything to Vevanya, she gave no sign, but his short declaration of our occupation struck a chord. "I will accept your word."

We gathered our saddle-beasts and prepared to ride. The presence of the six warriors did seem to speed growth of the grasses beside the stream, which I found interesting, but none of them appeared to notice. Vevanya chose to ride at the rear of our formation, with her two new soldiers in front. Krotha and I rode side by side, trailing Balarion and Phylasina. Balarion had made a show of binding his sword's scabbard to his saddle, making it marginally more difficult for him to draw it, which Vevanya noticed with a nod.

Because the village's rider had gone out the previous afternoon and come back in the morning, I anticipated a long journey. In truth, we rode for only four hours, and not at a hard pace, either. The headquarters lay due east of Best Southwest Grain Valley, but the roads took us past a number of other villages. Many of them had the crossed flails and scythes, but on different-colored fields and of varying sizes. All of that doubtless had significance and nuance to the residents, but the villages seemed substantially identical to my eye.

Some of the larger settlements—towns, I would guess, which is why their banner had a small symbol of an affiliated banner on it—had a separate compound built on the outskirts. They looked like little fortresses themselves, but the crests on their walls didn't match those Captain Vevanya and her troops wore. While they were martially oriented, a circle surrounded the swords or spears or bows at the heart of their crests. Shouts and the ringing of sword-on-sword combat—to which our escorts paid no attention—suggested these were martial training academies. Next to foodstuff, warriors seemed to be Scilliric's cash crop.

Southwest Military District Seven's headquarters appeared to be a large fortress, with eight of what I took to be academy barracks surrounding it. I recognized crests on two of them from village academies we'd ridden past. All eight had banners atop the fortress's walls, and there were a number more without associated academies. I assumed they represented the schools that taught the soldiers stationed at that fortress.

The fortress itself had been properly built of massive stone blocks. The oval described by the walls could have contained several of the villages we'd passed and, at the southern end, had a small quarter that was home to farmers and other laborers who kept the fortress running. This included slaves, who I assumed had been taken from the Road of Exiles. At the fortress's heart, four barracks and two stables surrounded a courtyard. A curving ramp led down to the main gate. Any force that shattered the gates would have serious trouble fighting their way up that incline, since warriors on the walls and in the courtyard could rain arrows and stones down to crush them.

A large keep dominated the northern end, and it was toward this that Captain Vevanya led us. Slaves took charge of our mounts, and we followed her into the main hall. Because forests had been few, far between, and little more than wooded lots, the abundance of thick timbers supporting the room's vaulted ceiling surprised me. The wood, which likewise covered the walls and floors, had been finished to a glowing honey color. Banner after banner hung on the walls about two and a half yards above the floor. Those closest to the door appeared the newest, with those on the far narrow wall seeming ancient.

A white-haired man sat at a massive table at that end of the hall. He looked up at our entry, then waved us all forward. Captain Vevanya preceded us, and two yards from the table she dropped to a knee. "General, it was as reported. These four fought against Hollows in Best Southwest Grain Valley. They have no banner and they claim no school. They wear no crests."

Her superior officer looked us up and down. "Is Captain Vevanya's report correct?"

Balarion stepped up to Vevanya's side and also dropped to a knee. "It is."

"Very good. I will pronounce sentence now."

"What?" Balarion stood. "Wait, we haven't offered a defense. You haven't let us explain."

"There is no defense, nor explanation. You admitted you fought without sanction."

"We slew Hollows."

"You stole honor!" The general pounded a fist against the table. "Men and women of Scilliric train all their lives to perfect the art of war. Look at Captain Vevanya's sash. Each of those crests is a school she has mastered, through training or through defeating a champion of that school. And those white squares, each of them represents a Hollow. The squares that have black dots at their heart represent a hundred Hollows. When a handful more Hollows fall beneath her blade, she will be promoted to major and given a small outpost of her own. You have robbed her of her chance to advance."

"My apologies, Captain, but I would point out, General, that neither Captain Vevanya nor her troops were anywhere near the village when we

MICHAEL A. STACKPOLE   227

destroyed the Hollows." Balarion looked back at me over his shoulder. "How many did we destroy, Ferranos?"

"There were so many pieces, Majesty." I shrugged. "At least two dozen."

"Impossible!"

A rumbling laugh issued from Krotha's throat. "General, I am Krotha, the Knight of Truth. Ferranos has told you what we did. I laid nine to rest myself."

The general waved away our statements. "I shall hear no more. You fought without sanction. You will be burned at the stake tomorrow at noon."

Krotha advanced, stepping heavily. "Has Scilliric abandoned all civilization?"

"That is the prince's law. There must be discipline."

The Knight of Truth snorted. "Discipline, yes. Law, yes, but I speak of tradition. Cannot a capital sentence be appealed? Can we not demand a trial by combat?"

The officer groaned, rubbing a hand over his forehead. "Trial by combat is only allowed for those who fight under a crest. You have no crest, thus you are denied."

Balarion pointed to the back wall. "I have a crest. It's that one."

Phylasina gasped.

He pointed to a red tower on a black field. A gold crown formed the top of the tower, the crenellations being the spikes on the crown. "That is my crest, mine by right of birth."

The general turned and shook his head. "You compound your crimes. Do you know what crest you claim?"

"The crest of the Royal House of Alkindor." Balarion smiled. "I am half brother to Prince Dolared, as your captain Vevanya has been informed. I shall fight beneath that banner."

The officer stared at his subordinate. "You knew?"

"I gave his claim no credit. Nor should you."

The general came around from behind his desk and looked at Balarion. "You are ignorant of our ways, thus I shall give you a chance to reconsider."

"And you will lift our sentence of death?"

"I cannot do that."

"Then I shall fight beneath my birthright."

"Understand this: When you fight beneath a banner, you represent all who fight beneath that banner. Had you chosen one from a school or some tiny unit, you would have faced their champion here for your trial by combat. Because Scillirician warriors are the world's best, you would die, but the agony would be over swiftly. But since you claim the royal banner, every champion of every school and unit and House here has the right to oppose you. By my count, in this garrison, that is two dozen warriors you will face. You cannot prevail."

Balarion chuckled. "I will do better against them than I would fire."

"Your friends will share your fate. As you fare, so shall they." The officer returned to his side of the table. "This is your last chance. What say you?"

"I say, get an extra-long pole." Balarion nodded solemnly. "Tomorrow, I wish all my foes to have a good view of the banner beneath which they will die."

CHAPTER 29

Captain Vevanya made accommodations for us in District Seven's stockade. She granted each of us our own cells, but the doors stood open, and she even placed keys in the locks. I wasn't certain what would motivate her to do that. We were under a death sentence, so we had ample incentive to escape. Perhaps it was a continuation of her willingness to take us at our word previously, or some newfound admiration at the audacity of Balarion's claim and his sticking with his decision despite the consequences.

The stockade's barred windows did afford us a clear view of the courtyard. Combatants made preparations throughout the night. Each faction erected a tent for its champion, quickly ringing the courtyard with gayly colored pavilions. Most had broad stripes, often picking up the red or green or blue of the crests in vertical striping. They all had peaked roofs, and each had a small pennant with their crest flying atop their center post. Their actual standard stood in a posthole beside the entrance.

Vevanya did not give Balarion his extra-long pole for his chosen banner, but she did hang it from the stockade's eaves, which made it hang higher than any of the others.

Krotha and I watched the preparations while Phylasina sat with Balarion in his cell. The undead Knight of Truth grunted. "The warriors are earnest in their exercises. Do you think they will cheat?"

I frowned. "This is all tied up in honor, so cheating would seem an anathema to all that. Whoever defeats him will gain from the victory. I cannot imagine they would want to have it blighted. I have noticed something curious, however."

"Yes."

"This fort, the barracks, how large a garrison could this place hold? How many troops should a general have under his command?"

Krotha turned toward me and leaned against the windowsill. "Eight barracks with bunk beds, forty warriors per—double that if they share bunks with those who are on watch—including officers, as much as five hundred in the garrison. But we have seen perhaps a hundred—which means Balarion will face a quarter of the garrison?"

"Yes. And recall the general said that Vevanya, when promoted to major, would be given a small fortress of her own. Fifty people in her command, maybe?"

"Ah, perhaps I see where you are going with this: Scilliric appears to be a very martially oriented society, yet has very few troops under arms. That ought not to be so, should it?"

"I should think not, unless they are so highly skilled that few are needed to defend the land."

Krotha smiled. "From what? Trafaram has no army, nor does Kadarr."

I arched an eyebrow. "Internal struggles? Have warlords divided Scilliric and have civil conflicts drained the military?"

Phylasina, scowling, emerged from the cells. "What does that matter? Balarion will die, and you are doing nothing about it. Have you a plan?"

Krotha shook his head. "No. I trust him to win."

"Against two dozen?" Her eyes flashed at me. "Prove yourself useful. Find magick to help him."

"M'lady, doing such would doubtless violate rules of the battle and forfeit it in favor of the state." I pointed toward the window. "You may think our conversation useless, but the more we understand how this place functions, the better our chances of winning."

MICHAEL A. STACKPOLE 231

She snorted. "That will be cold comfort in the grave, magician."

"As one who has spent much time there, I can assure you *nothing* is a comfort in the grave."

"Please, enough." Balarion stood in the cell. He did not look at us, but beyond us, his eyes focused on something distant that we could never see and likely not comprehend. "I will win tomorrow. I must. It is my father's will. And I shall win because to lose means you will die, too. You have my word that I will not consign you to the grave."

Krotha bowed his head. "I have never harbored a doubt of that, Majesty."

"Nor I." I turned back to the window.

"Forgive me, Balarion." Phylasina's voice sank into a soft whisper. "It is just that I do not want to lose you. My fear is born of not wanting to be without you, not of doubt for your abilities."

"I know." He reached out and caressed her cheek.

She caught his hand and kissed his palm. "You will prevail."

I stared out the window and watched the faction champions continue their practice by torchlight. They carried different weapons and all worked through a set routine of highly choreographed strikes and blocks. A giant of a man wielding a war hammer took prodigious swings with the weapon. His body glistened with sweat at the exertion. A smaller woman wielded a longsword and a lengthy knife, using speed and agility to fend off and defeat a half dozen invisible foes. So it was with the others. Each was a master of a particular form, and even to my uneducated eye, it seemed obvious that some had been developed to specifically oppose others. Likewise, a few suited the powerful, while others gave the advantage to the lithe.

As I watched, something itched at the back of my mind. "Krotha, watch them. There's something there I don't see, but I should. What do your eyes show you?"

The warrior turned back to the window and stared silently for a minute or three. His head bobbed ever so slightly as he followed one champion's movements, then another's. He straightened up, stepped back, and swayed to and fro, as if dancing with an invisible partner. He'd nod, then shift his gaze to another champion before altering his rhythm and motion. At some point with each, he'd break the pattern, grunt, and move on.

Finally, he stopped and turned to me. "I saw it."

Balarion arched an eyebrow. "What did you see?"

"What he saw, Majesty," I smiled, "is exactly what will win you the day tomorrow."

* * *

At midmorning, Captain Vevanya came for Balarion. "You should know that if you best all the others, you will face me last."

Balarion smiled. "The more of your people I defeat, the even greater honor of defeating me, no?"

"It is a pity so clever a man must die in this place."

"You'll want to limber up now, Captain." Balarion pointed toward the center of the courtyard. "None of them will be embroidering my crest on their sash."

Balarion slid his sword into its scabbard as he walked to where the general stood in the center of the courtyard. The older man unfurled a slender scroll covered with the Scillirician sigils and began to read aloud. "As directed by royal decree 103, this man, Balarion, has been tried and convicted of fighting without sanction. He has appealed his conviction on behalf of himself and his companions, claiming for himself the crest of the Royal House of Alkindor. You, by your efforts, shall adjudge him. As his is a capital offense, you battle to the death for the honor of your House, your academy, and your nation. Let us begin."

The general then approached the courtyard's far side and produced a black velvet bag. He worked his way down the line of champions. Each one deposited a round chit into the bag, apparently marked with the crest beneath which they fought. Once he had a chit from each of them, he shook the bag and drew one. He held it high for all to see. "Cytharan, to you falls this honor."

A tall and very slender man bearing a long-bladed spear stepped out of line, bowed to the general, then advanced toward Balarion. He bowed, then announced himself. "I am Cytharan, of House Tsah and Academy Beicor. I have slain a hundred Hollows. I have won seventy-seven duels and endured defeat a dozen times. I fight for Justice and the Rule of Law."

He dropped into a fighting stance, left leg forward, the spear's point angled down. The scarlet tassel, fastened to where point met shaft, dangled to a hairbreadth above the ground.

Balarion drew his sword fluidly. "You appear more suited to digging turnips with that thing than fighting."

The other fighters gasped or tittered. Cytharan's eyes opened wide in shock, then the spear flicked forward faster than a serpent's tongue. Balarion stepped wide of the thrust, then arced his foot up and over the tip as the spearman tried to slash Balarion's leg. Cytharan jerked the spear sideways for another cut, but Balarion batted it aside and leaped back a step.

Cytharan moved to the right around the courtyard, the spear flicking now and again in response to feints Balarion made. In return, the spearman would dart forward, the point still low, then angle up to stab at Balarion's groin or stomach. The prince parried those thrusts aside and grunted. He moved toward his left, toward the direction of Cytharan's advance, and the Scillirician danced away to the left.

Balarion stepped back and let his guard fall. "This is a battle to the death, Cytharan, but I assure you I shall not die of old age. Do something."

The other man's eyes slitted. He probed again with low thrusts, then darted forward a full pace. He thrust at Balarion's heart. Balarion's sword came up to parry, so the spearman looped his blade low through a short, sharp thrust aimed straight at Balarion's thigh.

Balarion twisted, drawing his right leg back. The thrust narrowly missed scoring flesh and drawing blood. Then, before Cytharan could recover from the thrust, Balarion closed his hand around the spear's shaft, just inches beneath the head, and yanked. Cytharan loosened his grip enough to let the spear slide forward, but he tightened his hands before he lost possession of the weapon.

Balarion's sword came down in a shining arc and cleaved through the spear. He tossed the other end aside and rushed forward. Cytharan tried to withdraw, but Balarion crossed the space between them too quickly. The prince smashed his right shoulder into the taller man's chin, snapping his head back. The spearman pitched over backward, his head smacking hard onto the courtyard's stones. Had he not been unconscious from Balarion's blow, the impact with the stone would have knocked him out.

Balarion bent and quickly unknotted the sash around the man's waist, then drew it off. He wiped sweat from his face with it, then tossed it over into the shadow of the stockade. He turned toward the general. "It seems I am without opposition. Who is next?"

The general drew another chit from the bag and held it high. "Brathnia, to you falls this honor."

A woman who, save for her long red hair, could have been Phylasina's twin bowed to the general. Bearing two curved swords, she advanced toward Balarion. She bowed to him, then kicked the bottom half of the broken spear out of the courtyard. Turning back, she smiled easily, though her eyes remained narrowly wary. "I am Brathnia, of House Dekanna and Academy Xilong. I have slain eighty-three Hollows. I have won an equal number of duels and endured defeat seven times. I fight for Justice and the Rule of Law." She slashed the air before her with the blades, then set herself with one blade low and one high.

Balarion bent to scoop up the business end of Cytharan's spear, then set himself and raised the spear high, mocking her stance. "Come, daughter of House Dekanna."

She came at him furiously and fast. Her blades blurred as she slashed. Balarion ducked beneath some cuts, sidestepped others, and blocked the rest with either sword or spear. He jabbed with both weapons, never reaching her flesh, but only because she leaped away in a heartbeat, then bounced back immediately to attack.

Balarion shifted his stance, advancing the spear as if it were a sword. He blocked and parried with it alone, still jabbing as opportunities presented themselves. He pressed her backward, forcing her to yield ground, which she surrendered reluctantly, constantly glancing at his sword, wondering when he would bring it to play.

Her frustration grew, so she shifted the focus of her attack and trained her swords on the spear itself. With three lightning-fast cuts, she amputated the head from the haft, halving the spear and leaving Balarion with nothing more deadly than a stick.

Snarling, Balarion threw the stick down at her feet.

Brathnia's upper lip curled contemptuously, and she leaped above the spear's haft as easily as a child might skip rope. Only at the apex of her leap did she realize her mistake, and a moment later realized she could do nothing to save herself. As she had leaped, her hands had naturally come down toward her hips to help maintain balance. This left her open as Balarion's sword came up.

Had Balarion lunged, he would have spitted her cleanly, but he didn't. Instead, he raised the tip of his blade and, twisting his wrist, whipped it forward. The flat of the blade caught her square in the face, crushing her nose and smacking her forehead. Balarion shifted his grip, bringing his sword hand up so the pommel caught her beneath the chin, snapping her mouth shut. She arced back through the air, hitting hard on her shoulders. Her swords clattered as they bounced away, and in a heartbeat, Balarion had a knee on her chest, a foot on her right wrist, and the edge of his blade pressed to her throat.

"Yield to me, Brathnia. There is no reason you should die because I killed Hollows to save a village."

The woman nodded once, then unknotted the sash from around her waist. Balarion drew it from her as he stood, then tossed it with the first one. "If you please, General, another."

Krotha and I exchanged smiles. What I had noticed the previous night was that the sashes the champions wore told stories of great victories, but their bodies did *not*. Their exposed flesh had far too few scars for them to be the veterans of all the battles their sashes claimed for them. I did not doubt the accounting, but realized that the duels had to be largely ceremonial—to first blood or adjudicated by some other standard—to preserve the lives of the soldiers. Scilliric possessed far fewer soldiers than they should have, which meant they fought without killing—except in the cases of Hollows. And since the Hollows we fought had been soldiers, coupled with the fact that I saw no cemetery near the fort, this suggested that those who died in combat had a higher-than-normal chance of coming back as undead, which was a prospect no one wanted to face.

In short, when opposing the living, they did not fight to kill. Against the living, they did not truly know how to kill.

Krotha, with a warrior's eye, had noticed that and more. Each of the champions had mastered a style of fighting that was perfectly suited to the weapon they wielded. Thus, the focus of their training, the substance of their dueling, concerned itself with their weapons. Take away their weapon, as Balarion had done with Cytharan, or use unconventional weapons or use them in an unconventional way, and these warriors lacked the skill to adapt quickly enough to succeed. Hollows would be unorthodox to be sure, but chopping kindling with an ax required more martial skill than hewing down Hollows.

Those things, plus the added strength Balarion had won off everything he had killed, made him fast enough and strong enough to beat every one of the garrison champions. Whether he shattered their weapons, used an elbow or knee or kick to end a fight, or simply let a warrior exhaust himself, Balarion bested each and every one of them. He harvested their sashes for his pile and then invited the next to step forward.

The general turned the bag inside out to show he had no more chits.

Balarion bowed to Captain Vevanya. "So it is now down to us."

The woman shook her head and removed her sash. She extended it toward him. "It will be my pleasure to lead you to Prince Dolared."

Balarion nodded. "We will leave at dawn, then, or sooner—whenever your seamster can prepare me a sash that records all of *my* victories."

DARK SOULS
MASQUE of VINDICATION

CHAPTER 30

We set out the next morning, several hours after dawn. We did not travel alone. After Captain Vevanya offered to be Balarion's guide, he bid her put her sash back on. Then, one by one, he offered those he had defeated their sashes back. They all accepted—the unconscious by proxy. So the next morning, we formed nearly a *company* with a diverse array of banners. In fact, I was the only person who did not have one, since the locals kindly ginned up a couple for the Knights of Virtue.

Because I served Balarion, his banner covered me.

Despite the formality and quick judgment to which we'd been subject, the warriors dealt with us in a most agreeable manner. They regarded Balarion with pure awe in their expressions and voices. Captain Vevanya kept her appreciation mostly under wraps, but arranged to ride beside our leader and discuss the reality of her nation with him. That should have put off Phylasina, but she paired up with Brathnia. They happily chatted away about the finer points of wielding two sabers and rode as our vanguard.

I traveled on Balarion's other side and asked a question of Captain Vevanya. "Based on far too little data, it seems to me that Scilliric's Hollows are almost exclusively warriors. Is this true, and do you know why?"

Her expression made it plain that she'd not expected so thoughtful a question from me. "You are not incorrect, Ferranos. On rare occasions does anyone rise who is not a warrior, and none of them return to us with the presence of mind you and Krotha exhibit. As for why, this is a question philosophers and theologians would argue back and forth, had we any appreciable population of either. It is said that many centuries ago Prince Dolared had raised a vast army with which he intended to reunite the three kingdoms into the heart of Alkindor, and then reestablish his father's empire. He had gathered and trained soldiers, assembled ample crops, and set his troops marching. Neither Jaranessa nor Tsaleryk could have stopped him, but a great blizzard blew out of the west, freezing everything and burying it in snow. Troops died of exposure, and many others of gangrene from frostbite and a host of diseases that followed.

"In his anger at being frustrated, the prince dedicated his nation to the god of war—not Farthune, whom we all worship, but an older god."

Balarion sat up straighter in his saddle. "*Wiervar.*"

I glanced at him. "How do you know that name?"

"All flock wardens do. We curse it. He is the god of wolves." He shook his head. "When winter comes early or leaves late, and wolves hunger, it is *Wiervar*'s doing. He is a savage and bestial god."

"Here he is known as the Lord of Scorpions, my lord." Captain Vevanya scanned the fields on either side of the road. "The magicks that seize the land honor the warrior. It feeds us quickly so we can grow strong, but is thirsty for our blood. With its coming, brutal battles raged over Scilliric. Men were as beasts, ravaging hordes, lacking discipline or cause, sowing destruction. It would have annihilated us."

Balarion's eyes brightened. "Chaos reigned until the academies began to teach discipline. Small units, exquisitely trained and evenly matched. Dueling for honor, not blood, so as not to slake the land's thirst."

The Scillirician officer nodded. "The old madness seems to swell when we gather in large groups. When we do fight, when a warlord wishes to wage war, elite troops in small bands go to battle, with victory conditions set and reparations or tribute negotiated before swords cross."

My eyes tightened. "Then our crime of fighting without sanction could have ignited a wider, wilder conflict because we have no discipline?"

"Exactly."

Balarion sighed. "And my brother has done nothing to reverse what he did?"

"That question is beyond my answering, my lord. None of us have ever seen the prince, much less spoken to him about such things." She gave Balarion a faint smile. "Perhaps you will have answers where the rest of us can only have guesses and fears."

* * *

The journey to the capital took a fortnight. We could have made it faster, but to do so would have dishonored Balarion and those who followed him. As we wended our way north, we came to larger towns and small cities. Where academies that were rivals to those that produced members of our company stood, we faced challenges. Each academy would send out their best warrior, and we would offer their rival. The two warriors would stand well away from each other and go through a set routine of strikes and counterstrikes: blocks, parries, and ripostes. Each combatant moved fluidly and quickly, with such discipline and skill that determining who would have prevailed had they actually struck at each other was all but impossible.

The home champion was always adjudged the winner, but graciously allowed the defeated the hospitality of the city or town until the next dawn. In most cases, we didn't linger that long in hostile locations, but instead passed through and on to the next place. A couple academies did send out students to watch us leave, but I took that more as a scouting exercise for them than any true threat to us.

We stopped in towns where we had one or more academies that had trained our warriors. The first day out, in fact, we camped at Southwest Wool Vale Nine, which was home to Academy Xilong. Brathnia and Phylasina preceded us to the academy, and by the time we reached the twin-towered compound, the grand master of Xilong had come out with bread and water to greet us. Balarion partook of both by way of greetings, then the student body turned out to take care of our mounts and show us to our accommodations. That is to say that they led us to their rooms, gave us their bunks, and slept the night on the floor at the foot of the beds.

That night, the grand master gathered us all into the school's torchlit courtyard. The students had swept it of sand and set up tables on the main building's porch. Aside from those serving us dinner, the students ringed the courtyard. They varied in age from six years old on up through their thirties. Each wore a red sash, though only half the width of anyone who had graduated from the school and a quarter of the width of that which the grand master wore. Little symbols decorated the student sashes, corresponding, I assumed, to achievements in their studies.

They offered meager fare, but in keeping with the nature of Scilliric, all of it had been freshly harvested. The food for Krotha and me came in tiny teacup portions, since we'd not eat it, whereas the others got as much as they could possibly consume. Balarion ate not a single spoonful more than the grand master or Captain Vevanya, a courtesy both of the others noted.

In between courses, students of Academy Xilong took to the courtyard in displays of martial splendor. Though they dueled for demonstration purposes only, they fought with live steel, and very sharp steel at that. They all worked through identical routines as a prelude, with the complexity and speed increasing with each age group. Once they'd demonstrated their basic proficiency, they leaped into different routines that displayed incredible agility and precision. They made it very clear that the key to Balarion's victory had been his willingness to play outside their rules, which they would never do. To lack discipline would destroy Scilliric, and that would have been the height of dishonorable conduct.

The final act of their entertainment marked a departure from the previous. Brathnia stepped into the court bearing her twin swords and bowed to the grand master. She wore an unadorned tabard with an ivory silk panel tacked on over the back and a black leather mask covering the lower half of her face—indicating that she was not playing herself in the coming drama. Red ribbons hung from her tabard's seams and hems.

Her opponent wore a full wooden mask of blank affect, painted black save for a gold scorpion adorning the center. The tail extended down along the bridge of the nose, and the claws spread wide over the forehead. The black silken robe had the Scillirician royal crest embroidered on the back, with a gold scorpion positioned above it. That scorpion image repeated on each breast and again on the sleeves, and gold ribbons decorated the robe's seams and hem.

I found it hauntingly familiar, but understanding lingered just beyond my conscious comprehension. "Krotha, do you know...?"

"Legend." The Knight of Truth's expression tightened grimly. "Her foe is meant to be the Scorpion, but he was a creature of the king. What the Knights did by virtue, he did by the opposite. And I say 'he,' but I do not know that the Scorpion was male, or was but one person."

"Tell me everything. Ceresia hinted..."

"I will, my friend." Krotha held up a hand. "After this..."

The grand master clapped, and the two combatants launched into a swirling, skirling battle. Blades whistled through the air. Sparks flew. Metal hissed as blades slid against each other. Silk snapped and ribbons danced. As razor edges slashed, bits of ribbons flew into the air and lazily drifted to the ground, in sharp contrast with the lightning-fast fighters.

Brathnia flowed through moves as fluidly as smoke and with the precision of a cobra's strike. Gold scraps whirled in her wake. She ducked from some cuts and leaped above others—but never repeated the mistake that had cost her the fight against Balarion. She and her foe proved evenly matched—at least as judged by the gold and red flotsam littering the courtyard. And at least twice she could have opened his belly or cost him a hand when all she did was harvest a ribbon.

Then the Scorpion spun, pairing his blades high to the right. He brought them down in a cross-body slash. Brathnia caught the double-strike on crossed swords, but the force of the blow drove her to a knee. Again, the Scorpion attacked on that line, and she repeated her block, this time going to her other knee. The third strike came as a twinned overhand blow, which she blocked for a second, then allowed her blades to part. His swords slowed and spread, touching her shoulders ever so gently as she let her blades clatter to the courtyard stones.

The Scorpion straightened and crossed his blades over his own chest. Then he extended one to her. With bowed head, she accepted the blade in her upraised hands. She came up to one knee and turned so the Scorpion could strip away the ivory panel. It came off easily, revealing the Xilong crest emblazoned proudly on her back. She completed the circle and handed the Scorpion one of her swords, concluding a stylized pledge of fealty.

And thus, Academy Xilong proves the legitimacy of its founding at the hand of the Scorpion—agent of the god who had sowed so much havoc. The beatific smiles on the students' faces confirmed my guess. The Scorpion, as an agent for the crown, had tested the academy's founder and decided his skill was such that the academy would be sanctioned.

I leaned toward Krotha. "Clearly Academy Xilong traces its origin to the Scorpion."

"An ill omen if what I recall is true." Krotha nodded, his eyes focusing distantly. "In one of the last acts I performed for him, King Parnyr sent me to a bandit fortress to the north. It would have been beyond the borders now claimed by Kadarr. He said the bandits there had become an annoyance to the locals, and he wished me to assess the truth of the matter. I set out alone, but never truly felt alone. I saw no one and nothing, and there were vast swaths of desert and plain where naught could have hidden from me. I found the fortress as night fell and torchlight began dancing through windows and along walls from bonfires. I could have pressed on, but I decided to rest and get a better look in daylight.

"The next morning came, and I set out. Five hundred meters from where I had made my camp, I found four of the bandits, each dead, but none of them having more than a stab wound—and not a deep one, none of them—to account for his condition."

I arched an eyebrow. "Poison?"

"So I assumed." Krotha shrugged. "On to the fortress I went, and found the portcullis up but a sally port open. I heard nothing from within but the howls of dogs. Overhead, vultures circled. I ventured in. I found the bandits dead, *all* of them. Many died as the scouts had, with minimal wounds, but a few had put up a fight. It had not gone well for them. And the wounds, the thrusts, when shallow, were plain as can be, but when they went deep, one side showed horrific damage. Likewise with heavy slashes. The attacker used a double-edged sword with serrations on the lower third. Ripping it out of a body sawed through flesh and sinew, scored bone."

"You think the Scorpion did that?"

"I do not know, but the bandit chieftain lay in a pool of blood and her entrails. On the floor, she'd written 'Thus the Truth.' I found it close to what Parnyr had charged me with, and yet I found it mocking me. I felt certain someone had traveled with me from the court. I thought then that it must have been the Scorpion."

I shook my head. "Why would Parnyr send you to verify what he had tasked the Scorpion to do?"

"Perhaps he doubted the Scorpion's loyalty. He *did* test us, all of us, from time to time." Again Krotha shrugged. "But that is less a mystery to be solved than learning how the Scorpion is tied up with Scilliric's early years."

"A valid point."

While Krotha and I had been discussing the Scorpion, Balarion had risen and stepped to the floor. He greeted and thanked both Brathnia and the Scorpion. I wondered for a moment if he would challenge the Scorpion to a duel, but instead he asked the both of them to walk with him. Then he worked his way around the courtyard, greeting each of the students, asking their names, praising their performance, and asking what this symbol or that on their sash represented. He bid them farewell by name and moved on down the line to the next student.

The grand master looked pleased, and the students radiant. We had come into Academy Xilong at best an unknown entity and at worse an enemy who had unfairly defeated one of their own. By the end of his circuit, Balarion owned Academy Xilong.

During the rest of our journey, we stayed at four other academies, all of which put on similar displays, including the Scorpion sanction drama. They made one thing clear: The Scorpion must have been a fighter of prodigious skill, for he bested each of the academy leaders fighting in their style. They all pledged fealty to him and, through him, to the crown, and each of the academies had a level of legitimacy they shared with all the others.

The depiction of the Scorpion in the martial ballets seemed at odds with Krotha's tale of the fortress and Ceresia's portrayal. So overt a duel with skilled foes seemed to be out of character for the Scorpion. If he was the antithesis of the Knights of Virtue, fighting someone without deception would have been highly unlikely. And would so shadowy a figure be so openly linked to the crown?

None of it seemed right. But then, when we reached Hyeracia and saw the capital for the first time, I understood why the warrior academies of Scilliric accepted it as true.

CHAPTER 31

Hyeracia sprawled at the heart of a broad, flat, red-earth valley. A wide, muddy river bisected valley and city alike, with a broad oxbow projecting from the southern shore toward the northeast. The prince's palace stood in the oxbow, dominating the landscape, for it rose to twice the height of any other building in the city. Red rocks, quarried from the mountains to the north, had been shaped into a massive fortress that served Prince Dolared as his home.

As impressive as that looked, it seemed insignificant next to the monumental decoration atop the palace. Gilded, and therefore shining brightly, a scorpion statue topped the palace. Its body and tail ran the length of the structure, with the claws outstretched over the east and west wings. The tail curved up, and the stinger glinted and glistened as if a droplet of venom wet it.

I raised an eyebrow. "There, Krotha, is your scorpion."

The knight nodded. "The god of war to whom Dolared dedicated this land…"

"*Wiervar…*"

"Yes. In Trafaram, we always thought of him as a wolf, but here, if dim memory serves, his adherents saw him as a scorpion." Krotha sighed. "On those occasions when Dolared was moved to do something, he never did it by halves."

The river, known locally as the Hyeric, took its color from the red mud and moved with the speed of clotting blood. Ferries abounded to carry traffic back and forth, with the only bridge being a massive arching construction connecting the walled fortress in the north to the other half of the city. Lower walls divided the city into precincts, each of which had a smaller fortress in it, and unless I misread the banners flying above them, academies staffed and maintained those lesser fortresses.

We rode into the city through a gate controlled by Captain Vevanya's academy—Rykaranji—and quickly picked up an honor guard to lead us deeper into the city. The interior walls required us to wend a crooked path to the palace, as if we were lost in a child's labyrinth, but invading armies would face the same difficulty, so we could not complain. Of course, given the threat level from Kadarr and Trafaram, the precautions seemed excessive.

When we reached the palace gate, Balarion dismounted and Captain Vevanya with him. Phylasina and Krotha joined them, while I hung back with the others. Balarion stepped forward, allowing the guards to gaze upon his crest. "I am Balarion, of the Royal House of Alkindor. I have come to speak with my brother Prince Dolared." Vevanya, Krotha, and Phylasina likewise announced themselves. In keeping with the style of Scilliric, all three of them listed victories and honors, which the gate sergeant accepted and, apparently without benefit of taking notes, set off to convey to whomever stood over him in the chain of command.

I expected us to be kept waiting for some time, and perhaps even to be sent away to come back at first light, but within ten minutes, a breathless minister appeared. She wore a white robe with a black sash decorated with embroidered scrolls and quills. Fortunately for us, she felt no compunction to list her accomplishments—as stunning a triumph as it might be to complete a budget or audit state warehouses. She conducted us immediately onto palace grounds.

We passed through a tunnel in the fortress wall that narrowed in the middle and had portcullises at either end. Murder holes dotted the arched ceiling. The tunnel ran thirty meters and a thousand men could have filled it, being trapped and slain as burning oil or arrows rained down from above.

The scorpion iconography was not confined to the statue, in whose shadow we now walked. Artisans carved it into door lintels and into monuments. It appeared to me as if it had been added later to the older parts of the palace, but incorporated more fully into newer construction. On tapestries with the royal crest, a scorpion had been added to the crown, as if it were part of the metalwork.

It is impossible to overstate the massive scale of the palace's construction. Each of the blocks used measured twice my length for its height and depth, and four times for width. Opening the titanic bronze doors required counterweights and a legion of slaves while teams of plodhooves worked the gates. The vaulted arches within may well have been painted with fantastic artwork, but they simply couldn't be seen from below, and acres of carpeting covered stone floors.

And yet, as epic as the palace's scale was, spare was the decoration and sharply stark the architecture. The red stone and black carpeting hinted at warmth, but nothing else did. Tsaleryk and Jaranessa had surrounded themselves with finery, insulating themselves from the true nature of their realms by creating an artificial world around them. Dolared, it seemed, embraced the harsh reality of his realm in the place he chose for his home.

After trekking down endless halls and through forgettably identical rooms, we finally reached his throne room in the older precincts. Smaller than the other chambers, with a lower ceiling and screened galleries, this room also had more furnishings. Nothing opulent, however, more the practical camp furnishings one might find in a general's campaign tent. After the excessive ostentation of Kadarr and Trafaram, this was a welcome contrast, but still seemed inappropriate in a place of such power.

Dolared stood bare-chested, well-muscled, and gleaming with oil in front of a taller camp chair atop a small dais. As with that of his subjects, his flesh had too few scars to confirm the victories depicted on the double-width red sash about his waist. Clean-shaven and not unhandsome after a fashion, he wore his black hair at middle length and slicked back from his face. He had donned a red kilt and brown boots that met at knee height. Though he was unarmed, the rack beside his chair bore three blades. A dagger took the lowest position. Above it hung a saber akin to that which Phylasina favored. Topmost and largest was a double-edged broadsword, the forte of which had been serrated. Krotha and I noticed that at the same time, and we exchanged glances.

I also noticed that around his left wrist was what appeared to be a steel band with tiny rivets. It lay flush with his flesh, so I took this to be the Key of Might.

Dolared smiled and opened his arms. "Krotha Truthteller, Phylasina Fidelity, I had long supposed you had passed into legend—even *greater* legend. It pleases me to see my comrades yet live."

Krotha bowed to him, and Phylasina nodded. She then stepped to Balarion's side. "Highness, it is a pleasure and duty to present to you Balarion, your half brother."

Dolared's joyous expression slackened. "My half brother. Indeed." Then his smile returned. "If he travels with you, my fellow Knights of Virtue, he is more than the full brother I have in far Kadarr. Balarion, welcome."

"Thank you, brother." Balarion bowed his head for a respectful moment, then turned toward Captain Vevanya. "This is Captain Vevanya, from Southwest Military District Seven, of House Chaian and Academy Rykaranji. She has seen us to your palace."

She threw Dolared a salute, which he returned crisply. "Thank you for your service, Captain."

Balarion then turned and called forward each member of our company, mentioning their House and academy. He impressed me having recalled them because, to the best of my knowledge, he had only heard their full titles when he faced them in battle. In Dolared, I sensed boredom, but pure adoration lit the faces of our companions. And not for their prince, but for Balarion and his courtesy at introducing them correctly. Each saluted and was praised in turn, then turned away and resumed their place in the company of their fellows.

Finally, Balarion indicated me with the wave of a hand. "And this is Ferranos, who, along with Krotha Truthteller, has been most faithful and helpful to me."

I bowed deeply and respectfully, holding the bow for a count of five, before slowly straightening.

Dolared regarded me with a trace of puzzlement on his face, then gave me a nod. "I thank you for all you have done, Ferranos." He turned and seated himself, lounging a bit casually. "Now, brother mine, tell me why you are here."

"I have come for the Key of Might." Balarion pointed toward Dolared's wrist. "Our father charged me with the duty of collecting the keys and opening his prison."

The prince's eyes tightened. "I dimly recall something being said on that order when my father burdened me with this key. He said I could ask of you a favor, set for you a task. If you accomplish it, I am to give you the key."

"Yes. Your brother asked me to fetch a scepter for him. Your sister wanted the most beautiful child in Vataria." Balarion clasped his hands at the small of his back. "We, my companions and I, have accomplished both of those tasks. Now it falls to us to satisfy you. What would you have us do?"

"There are so many things that need doing, the variety is endless." Dolared lifted his left hand and studied the design encircling his wrist. "The Key of Might cannot be given up so easily, for it is the key to everything. Without it, you have nothing. Without it, you cannot reunite the three realms. You cannot build Alkindor anew."

"You mistake my purpose, brother. I do not seek to rebuild Alkindor. I wish merely to fulfill our father's intention for us. I am a conduit for his will, nothing more."

"And yet that is something spectacular, and thus what you shall do for

me shall be spectacular." Dolared leaned forward in his camp chair and
pointed off to the north. "There, in the mountains whose flesh surrounds
us in this palace, there is a place. A province given to banditry and rebel-
lion. Pergathae, a perennial thorn in my side and a pebble in my father's
boot before the kingdom collapsed. A woman named Argatti leads the Pergathaenes. They acknowledge no rule of law, respect no sanctions, barely
train their warriors, and rely on their mountain fastness to protect them.
They claim they wish to live in peace, but make their living through raid-
ing and theft. I would have you steal into the heart of Pergathae and bring
me Argatti's head. That done, you will be decidedly worthy of the Key of
Might."

Balarion nodded. "I will do this for you, brother, though I shall require
your aid in providing maps and guides. And I should like to take my company with me."

"Of course, of course." Dolared licked his lips. "All the knowledge I have of
Pergathae shall be at your disposal. And your company, yes, of course, it shall
be with you. I shall make all of them captains, and you, Vevanya, a colonel.
Each of you shall go to your academies and draw a company of your own for
this expedition. Your service to the state shall live in song and history forever."

Balarion smiled. "You are very generous, brother."

"You will do me a great service, brother." The elder prince stood and
stretched. "You will be setting out within the week, perhaps three days
hence. For surprise, you understand. Argatti will never suspect a thing."

"Yes, brother."

"But tonight, there shall be feasting, in honor of my knight brethren.
Go, all of you, to your academies and then to the rooms I shall have prepared for you here." Dolared crossed his arms over his chest. "You are the
pride of Scilliric."

Balarion bowed deeply to him, as did I. The others saluted. We all began
to withdraw when the prince held up a finger. "Brother, if I might borrow
your Ferranos for a moment."

Balarion looked at me, and I shrugged.

"Of course, brother."

"Most kind, brother."

I stood in silence as the rest of them departed. Once we were alone, I turned toward the prince. "What would you have of me, Highness?"

Dolared seated himself and stared at me for a moment. "Krotha and Phylasina, I know them well. They are Knights of Virtue, and their helping Balarion is a duty long ago charged to them by my father. Colonel Vevanya and the others would die for Balarion. I doubt you can read their sashes, but he defeated them and then returned their sashes to them. No greater honor could he have shown them, and no greater bond could he have created with them. It is incorruptible.

"But you, what are you? Why are you here?"

I caught hints of menace in his question, and a stronger current of suspicion. "I am but a dead man, Highness. My knowledge of myself is incomplete. From the first I felt compelled to seek out Balarion, but what compels me, I do not know. If it was your father, I found no clue to support that suggestion in my tomb. Who else, I cannot imagine. Your brother has been kind to me, and I take pleasure in my service to him."

"I can be kind as well, Ferranos. You would know great rewards were you to serve me."

"Do you seek to tempt me, Highness, to see if I will betray your brother? Do you hunt for deceit in my heart so you may protect him?"

Dolared grunted and stroked his jaw. "You know enough of my realm to know that his presence is chaotic, and that is the antithesis of the discipline we maintain so our nation does not descend into the bloody anarchy of old. I sense Balarion is honorable and true and means well. For his plans to go awry because one of his closest companions betrays him would put my realm at risk. I cannot permit that to happen."

"I can conceive of nothing, Highness, that would inspire me to betray your brother or threaten your realm."

"Then the gods be praised that they have limited your imagination." Dolared chuckled to himself. "Do you think Balarion can destroy Argatti?"

"I have yet to see him fail at any task set before him."

"Good, very good. Thank you, Ferranos."

"I live to serve, Highness."

"Splendid. I have delayed you far too long. Go, join your companions." The prince gently waved me away. "But, Ferranos, if you have any doubts, any doubts at all, please do not hesitate to bring them to my attention. You shall find me most grateful in that regard."

CHAPTER 32

A functionary led me deeper into the palace, still within the precincts of the original building. I took some comfort in that at first, given that I saw it as a sign of Dolared's wishing to keep his brother and companions close to him. Then I recalled that such proximity favored a dagger in the dark.

The servant led me to a modest room just off the suite Krotha occupied. The furnishings maintained the campaign aesthetic. My room did have shelves, but the only books upon them were military histories and collections of maxims by generals and warlords I had never heard of before. My library ran to a dozen volumes, and as closely as I could tell, most had never had their spines cracked.

Krotha filled the adjoining doorway to his suite. "I think neither Dolared nor his visitors are much given to reading."

"Nor any other serious creature comforts. Is that consistent with the Dolared you remember?"

Krotha shrugged. "I never paid much attention to him in those days. He was designated the Knight of Victory. To be practical, the Knights needed a liaison with the king, and Dolared proved useful asking his father for things. If we required something, the Knights would discuss it, then Phylasina would relay our thoughts to Dolared. He would speak to his father, and things would be done."

"I can see the value in that."

"So, my friend, why did he want to speak with you in private?"

I frowned. "He was concerned whether or not his brother would be a destabilizing influence in Scilliric. He stressed discipline and order and hoped Balarion would not disturb the latter. Truth be told, however, I think he wanted to sound me out on my willingness to be his eyes and ears within our company. He came at it from an oblique angle, and I chose to ignore his hints. *If* they were hints. I do not think him a creature of much subtlety."

"As indicated by the gaudy scorpion perched above the palace?" Krotha chuckled. "You saw the sword, yes?"

"It struck me as very like the one you described the Scorpion as wielding." My eyes narrowed. "Could *he* have been the Scorpion? Could he have been that much of a creature of his father to serve in that role and hide it from all of you?"

"I do not know." The Knight of Truth sighed. "I would not have thought it beyond Parnyr's doing, to have his most trusted agent planted within the Knights, watching us. Then, when out from beneath his father's shadow, Dolared embraces that identity, thinking it could preserve his realm as he thought it preserved his father's?"

"Possible, I suppose, but he hinted at great rewards were I to become his creature. In the Scorpion, I'd have expected more understanding of the fact that you and I, being dead, might desire different rewards."

"Is it a true thought, Ferranos?" The knight, having shed his metal carapace, dropped into a chair in my room. "I spent my life in service to the Crown, simply for the pleasure of being of service to the Crown. Now, despite being dead, I do the same thing and take joy in it. What could he offer me?"

"Nothing, it would seem."

"And what could he offer you?"

I shook my head. "Nothing that I can see. My memory of myself is incomplete, so I do not even know if what I do now is something of which I would have approved of back then. Curiously enough, in giving me this golden ring, Balarion has showed me gratitude. I do not measure that gratitude in the value of this ring, but just in his sincerity in giving it, if that makes any sense."

"I feel that, too, which makes my service even sweeter." Krotha sat forward. "I think you would find Dolared incapable of such sincerity."

"Which is why he bears watching." I drew up a chair opposite the knight. "While you, Phylasina, and Balarion look over maps and organize our coming campaign against Pergathae, I will keep my eye on Dolared and his agents. After all, there is nothing but his honor to bind him to giving the Key of Might over to Balarion. I do not expect betrayal, but the Scorpion does have a reputation."

The knight's expression darkened. "Be careful, my friend. You play at a dangerous game. Balarion will believe the best of his brother because he still believes in honor and the justice of his mission. Were you to accuse Dolared of deceit, and Dolared to level the same as a countercharge, blood might decide the matter regardless of fact."

"Your caution is wise, Krotha. I begin to believe it is a pity you did not spend more time at court."

"I am the Knight of Truth. So many lies thrived at court that spending time there was as welcome as being boiled in oil." Krotha stood. "Remember that, my friend. Dolared might not be the man his father was, but he is still a creature of the court, and decidedly lethal because of it."

* * *

Over the next four days, I learned much about Scilliric and its king, all of which remained consistent with what Vevanya had explained on the road and the other things Krotha and I had surmised to be true. Everyone believed that, were discipline abandoned, the world would return to anarchy and slaughter. While Dolared had been the one to dedicate Scilliric to *Wiervar*, he had also been the architect of the order that had subsequently brought peace to the land. This latter point was stressed and the former forgiven if not forgotten. Dolared had cemented himself in the minds of his people as being their savior, and they all owed ultimate allegiance to him.

My interactions with the king came primarily during the feasting, which capped each day. The feasts were curious affairs in and of themselves. His people did not stint on providing food, and massive quantities of it, but no one partook in a way that even hinted at gluttony. Wine and other spirits appeared in abundance, but again, people controlled their consumption. In addition, servants watered the alcohol, so even if someone was to drink to excess, they would suffer no ill effects from it.

As I explored the palace and nearby precincts, I began to discern differences in things from before and after the imposition of order. The older portion of the palace, for example, had more in the way of decorative stonework murals, which had long since faded. Outside, the older streets had larger stones, which had been fitted together by artisans. The newer roads featured quite regular cobblestones, set in simple patterns—and each stone could be replaced by another in a matter of minutes.

In the time before order, Scilliric had welcomed creativity.

In the time since, fear of disorder had dulled the Scillirician mind and encouraged obedience to the dictates of the state above all.

When not occupied with my explorations, I attended the planning sessions for the campaign. While heading directly north would be the shortest route to Pergathae, and take us along the best roads, the bandits would have spies out and know of our advance long before we ever saw the mountains. Instead, the army would march east for two days, then turn north. We'd travel along two parallel roads, allowing us to move quickly. We could assemble on the plains in the foothills and challenge the bandits to face us in open combat.

That plan appealed to Dolared, who appeared at the meetings on an irregular basis. Because of his approval, we enjoyed unstinting support, which was why Balarion felt a bit bad in keeping a secret from him. The secret was that while the army would make this direct approach, Balarion, Colonel Vevanya, a select company of elite warriors, the Knights of Virtue, and I would all travel west and then northeast as fast as we could. While the Pergathaenes took alarm at the army's arrival and prepared defenses or, foolishly, decided to take the field against us, we would slip into the mountains, kill Argatti, and bring her head back for the king.

It was a plan born more of Balarion's belief in his companions than practicality, but as we had seen as we studied the maps and intelligence about Pergathae, *no* plan to oppose them could be considered practical. To root them out, we'd require a vast army the likes of which hadn't been assembled since before the coming of *Wiervar*, and by legend, such a host would plunge Scilliric into anarchy and death.

A few times, the king caught me alone, and seldom did such meetings take place by chance. He always inquired after my welfare and asked for my opinion on how preparations for the Pergathaene campaign were going. He remained courteous and listened to what I had to say, but always completed these meetings with an invitation to seek him out in case I had anything I thought should be called to his attention.

The day we were to depart for Pergathae dawned grey, with the sky fully overcast and showers intermittent. The weather did not dull our troops' enthusiasm. They mustered beneath their banners, armored and armed. Teamsters had assembled wagons laden with supplies, and hostlers had wrangled together whole herds of saddle-beasts so we would not want for fresh mounts. Though I thought we had too few troops to successfully invade the bandit province, our troops were confident they could have conquered the world by nightfall, and that after having paused for a leisurely lunch.

The only true difficulty came in that Phylasina had fallen ill. It had begun the day before with coughing and a runny nose, but had grown to include a fever the morning of our departure. "I will not be a burden, Balarion. You must let me come."

Balarion, standing there in a blue tabard with the double-headed eagle of Alkindor in red on a field of white, with a crown above, took her hand in his. "This would be brutal enough were you hale, my love."

Balarion alerted Dolared, who summoned the best healers in Hyeracia. As we waited for them to show up, Balarion issued orders for the army to begin the march east. Dolared applauded the decision even as Phylasina protested it—though ill, she had presence enough of mind to preserve our deception before the king.

The healers arrived within an hour of being summoned and conducted a thorough examination of the patient. While they differed on what exactly she'd contracted, they agreed that a week of bed rest coupled with consumption of noxious elixirs would have her back on her feet as quickly as possible—and that within a week beyond that, she would be her old self again. Phylasina did not take well to a reminder of how old she truly was, and tried to rise from her sickbed, but Balarion pushed her back.

In her weakness she could not resist.

The king rested a hand on his brother's shoulder. "Fear not, Balarion. I shall see to it that she is well cared for and that she returns to you hale and hardy."

Balarion smiled. "And you will send her to me once she is whole?"

"Immediately."

The brothers hugged, then all of us save Balarion followed the king from Phylasina's sick room. The king saluted Vevanya and hugged Krotha. "I know my brother is in good company. I can trust you to follow orders and see to it that no harm comes to him."

Krotha nodded. "Of this no doubt should linger in your mind."

"None does, brother knight." The king turned to me. "And you, Ferranos. Not a soldier, but so faithful in service."

"It is who I am, Highness."

He took my hand in his and raised my ring to his lips. "My brother is as precious to me as this ring is to you. Do not forget that."

"Never, sire."

Balarion joined us in the hallway and again embraced his brother. "I know you will keep her safe and well. Do not let her go until she is wholly fit."

"Of this you have my promise." Dolared nodded solemnly. "Now, history awaits you. May the gods speed you and favor you."

Leaving Dolared to oversee Phylasina's care, I led Balarion, Krotha, and Vevanya through the twists and turns of the palace. During my explorations, I'd located a side entrance to the older part of the palace that serviced an underground tunnel. Long ago, King Parnyr—and possibly Prince Dolared—had used it as an unseen passage for conducting confidants and paramours in and out of the palace unnoticed. We entered and headed west, passing beneath the palace walls. We emerged up through a steep stairwell that opened into a stable. The elite warriors destined to accompany us on the fast strike at Pergathae waited for us there—our saddle-beasts laden with kit and ready to go.

Balarion surveyed the company and smiled. "You've done well, Ferranos. Dolared, I am certain, never suspected a thing. And if we fooled him, we have fooled any spies the Pergathaenes might have in Hyeracia."

"I fervently hope so, Highness." I fiddled with the stone in my ring, and it clicked. The stone rotated to the side, revealing a flat, golden surface. I showed the symbol incised on it to Vevanya. "You understand what this means, Colonel?"

She nodded.

I pointed toward Balarion. "Good. Seize him, bind him, and put a hood over his head. And Krotha, lest you betray the truth you hold so dear."

Balarion stared at me, wide-eyed. "How could you?"

I sighed at the hurt in his voice and showed him the ring. The stone had revealed the image of a scorpion inscribed on the previously hidden surface. "You trusted Dolared, Balarion. You should never have trusted the Scorpion. Dolared has so much to offer, the seduction was accomplished almost before it began."

CHAPTER 33

We returned deep within the palace's older precincts without raising any alarms. I led the assembled company through darkened corridors and to a space a floor below Dolared's private quarters. I tugged the hood off Balarion's head and held up a finger. "Absolute silence. The least little sound will get us all killed."

Balarion mulled over the caution and appeared ready to shout, but Krotha reached out and squeezed his shoulder. "Do not, my lord."

"Have you turned against me, too, Krotha? Is that the truth?"

"I am yet on your side."

"Then kill Ferranos and free me."

The Knight of Virtue shook his head. "I trust Ferranos has his reasons. And if they are not good enough, I will do as you ask."

"If my reasons prove false, Krotha, I shall let you kill me." I gave the Knight of Truth a quick smile. "I would have told you of my plan, but you cannot lie. Making you unique among our company."

I pressed the ring against a dark depression in the wall, and something clicked. Muffled gears ground, and a portion of the wall drew back and to the side. It opened onto a slender chamber with a steep set of stairs ascending to the right and another descending to the left. I pointed upward. "Colonel, go up to the second landing and wait there in silence. Take Balarion and Krotha. The rest of you, follow them."

Once the entire group had mounted the stairs, I closed the door again, then squeezed past the soldiery to the second landing. A third set of stairs headed up, and I climbed the first two before turning back to Balarion. "The issue with the truth, Balarion, is that there are times we do not want to believe it. For example, your brother sought me out multiple times and made it quite clear that if I became his creature, he would reward me. I resisted for a while, since he would not respect me if I capitulated immediately. And yet, were I to completely refuse him, he would have me killed to remove me from supporting you. Thus, when the time was right, I agreed to work for him."

Balarion stared at me. "You're lying." He said this with conviction, yet still kept his voice to a whisper.

"Which is why this exercise is necessary." I ascended another couple of steps, then turned. "In my explorations of the palace, I discovered these passages and these stairs. They allowed me to uncover much more."

The others followed in silence as we climbed to a narrow corridor with wooden lattice panels on the interior wall. Light bled through them, though not much. A second set of more ornate panels covered these, but by moving over and twisting my head just so, I looked down upon Dolared's private chambers. Thick pillows covered the center of the floor, with a giant bed opposite the doors and a few daybeds against the walls. The only furnishings that were not soft or silken were two armor racks, and the armor and weaponry hung on them.

Phylasina, having staged a remarkable recovery from her illness, lounged on a mound of pillows close to the stand with her armor. She held up a golden goblet for Dolared to pour her dark wine. He, being ever so clever, drank straight from the pitcher. Wine splashed down over his bare chest. She, laughing, raised her hands to shield herself from splatter, then licked the spray from her fingers.

He sank his fingers into her hair and pulled her head back, stretching her throat. "I have waited so long to share your company again."

"As have I, beloved." Phylasina laughed. "I have always been faithful to you, my lord."

Dolared raised an eyebrow. "It did not appear so when you were in my brother's company."

"To be faithful to you, I had to deceive him." She smiled. "And I know, through the ages, you have not remained faithful to me, but that matters not. You are who you are and have your needs, which I have never opposed. It was for this day, the day of our victory, that we labored. And it all shall be worth it, my prince."

"Good. I am counting on it." Dolared perched himself on the foot of the bed and drank deeply again. "Kadarr and Trafaram, they cannot oppose us?"

"Kadarr's troops are few, poorly armed and untrained. Your brother is too penurious to have created a viable fighting force. Of course, he has so mismanaged his realm that anyone could conquer it, but no one would want it." She sipped her wine. "Unless, of course, they had a mind to dine on plump vermin served on golden platters."

"I'll take Tsaleryk's head on such a platter." Dolared wiped his mouth with the back of his hand. "And my sister's realm?"

"Worse. She has troops, but only for looking good on parade." Phylasina shivered. "Hers is a perverted realm, built on lies. She is so stupid, she accepted that a doll was a living child, and so cruel as to invite her people to murder it. Promise me, lover, that when she dies, it will be at my hand."

"Done." The prince stood and began to pace. "Do you think Balarion will bring me the bandit queen's head?"

"He has proved astute at accomplishing the impossible when trying to further his mission. Then you will slay him, and the other two keys will be yours."

"I will have to obtain the keys, *then* kill him. When the bearer dies, they return to the previous owner—or have when others of my father's get have collected them." Dolared shrugged. "They failed on missions no less dire, so my desires have been frustrated."

"Balarion will not disappoint."

"Good. Once I obtain the keys, I shall free my father, slay him, and fully claim what should have been mine all along. It has been enough time coming." Dolared shook his head. "There were times I stopped believing any more of my father's agents even existed. Then Balarion comes, and he brings you with him. And the other one. Krotha. I have never liked him, so righteous, so believing in himself and the truth."

Phylasina stretched. "It would please me to rid you of him, beloved."

"And you shall have that privilege, Phylasina." Dolared spread his arms wide, wine sloshing in the pitcher. "For the longest time I feared him, Krotha Truthteller. And then I learned an important...truth. The truth is what you make it. What begins as a lie can become a rumor and then a legend and then common wisdom, which itself becomes the truth. People think I dedicated this land to *Wiervar* because we had lost so many troops. We lost those troops because I sacrificed them to *Wiervar*. That act consummated my becoming the Scorpion. The warriors trusted me, and I betrayed them because that is what a scorpion does. To strike is in his nature. And then I created the academies and circumscribed combat outside sanction so no one could gather enough forces to oppose me—save for the Pergathaenes, whom I permitted to exist so those who hated me could have a place to flee to. Until Argatti, they were never organized enough to be a bother."

"You are very wise, Dolared."

"Yes, yes I am." He grinned. "So I get my enemy to do my work for me, then I shall destroy Balarion and his troops upon their return. Then you and I shall eliminate my father and rule Alkindor as gods."

They both dissolved into laughter, much too pleased with their wickedness.

Balarion and Colonel Vevanya stared at me.

I nodded and kept my voice to a whisper. "Colonel, you and your people thought you were acting on the Scorpion's orders, but now you know he is unworthy of your loyalty. Your trust was better placed in Balarion. I hope you will forgive me for the deception."

Vevanya nodded, then released Balarion's bindings.

"And you, Balarion, I hope you can forgive me." I looked back over my shoulder at the lattice. "Had I told you that your brother wished you dead and that Phylasina had been his creature for millennia, you would not have believed me."

The youth glanced down. "How did you know?"

"My memory is yet incomplete, but I have been in Hyeracia before, in this palace before. When I saw them together, something sparked. Then..."

"You're right. I would not have believed you." Balarion scrubbed his hands over his face. "I accepted she was the Knight of Fidelity and thought she was faithful to me."

Krotha grunted. "The truth of it is that she was only ever absolutely faithful to herself."

Balarion sighed. "What do I do now?"

I tapped a finger against his breastbone. "You come to realize a great truth: The Key of Might will never be freely given; it resides with the strongest."

I turned and walked on a dozen feet to where another stairway led down. I descended, paused at the base, then pressed my ring against a locking mechanism in the wall. It ground and squeaked, then a hidden door slid open. Balarion burst through, his sword springing into his hand, and Krotha followed.

Dolared, shock on his face, rolled to his feet. One hand came up, imploring his brother to stop, while the other pointed at Phylasina. "She is a witch, brother. She seduced me into betraying you as she did."

Phylasina rose, contempt twisting her features. "How curious that your father gave the Key of Might to the weakest of his children." She walked over to the armor racks and flung Dolared's scabbarded sword at him. "Defend yourself, if you can."

Dolared, his eyes yet wide, plucked the blade from the floor. "But he has mail, and I am unarmored. At least offer me a fair fight, brother."

My eyes narrowed. "'Ware, Balarion. The Scorpion can never be trusted."

Krotha snorted. "Don't you worry about his armor, Dolared. I trained him. You won't be touching it, much less be getting through it."

Dolared dropped back a step. "I see it now, how you all were in it. She seduces me so you can catch me unawares. Ferranos poses as my ally to lure me into what appears to be treachery, but is simply me safeguarding my realm. I've known you were each in it all along. I had to move against you, to save Scilliric. Colonel Vevanya, I command you. Do your duty for your nation. Kill them."

Vevanya folded her arms over her chest. "Balarion has earned our loyalty. You always assumed it should be yours. You no longer serve our nation."

Eyes wide with panic, Dolared turned toward the doors. "Guards! Guards! Murder!"

At Dolared's shout, voices rose from outside the room. Men started pounding on the door. Vevanya and her soldiers spread out to address the issue of guards from outside, while Balarion advanced on Dolared. He stalked forward, fury tightening his features, and pointed his sword straight at his brother's heart. "I am Balarion, son of Parnyr. I have slain dozens of Hollows and bandits and warriors bold. I fight for Justice and the Key of Might."

Without preface or ceremony, Dolared lunged. Balarion's blade clanged against his as he batted the lunge aside. He could have riposted, and he would have spitted Dolared cleanly, but he didn't press his advantage. He let Dolared jump away, and didn't pursue even when the prince landed on a pillow and slid back. Instead, Balarion straightened and waved Dolared forward with his free hand.

Phylasina slid both her blades from their scabbards and crossed them over her chest—much as she had stood when we first met her. She looked up at Krotha. "Did you always know it would come down to this? To me killing you?"

"Your truth is not my Truth, Phylasina." Krotha drew his sword and grasped the hilt in both hands. "I would give you time to don your armor."

"So kind, but I would not have an abomination's blood stain it." She glanced at me. "After him, you."

She leaped forward, her dark hair flying and her blades blurred. They slashed in parallel from high left to low right. She spun and squatted, cutting one blade at ankle height. It rang off Krotha's greaves while the other sword blocked his overhand blow. She leaped away to her left, landed, then lunged back with her twin blades, plunging their tips into Krotha's armpit.

Krotha grunted. Had he been alive, her blades would have severed an artery. Bright red blood should have sprayed. But for an undead warrior, her strike severed no muscles nor nerves. They scored ribs and might have even punctured a lung, but Krotha hadn't drawn breath in centuries.

He brought his sword across and down, knocking her blades free of his body. His blade trapped them against the floor, forcing Phylasina to bend forward. Then Krotha twisted, smashing his left elbow into Phylasina's face. She reeled back, swords lost, hands rising to her shattered nose. Implacable, Krotha pounced. He plunged his sword through her belly, just below her navel, and drove her against a tall bedpost. The sword pierced the wood, and the cross guard pinned her against the post.

The chamber doors burst open, but before Dolared's loyalists could enter, Colonel Vevanya and her people charged into the corridor beyond. More guards ran up the hallway, engaging Balarion's allies. Blood splashed and men screamed.

Determination possessed Dolared's expression. He advanced, his blade probing, striking, trying to provoke a response. Balarion ignored the feints and the ill-timed attacks. He batted away anything threatening to strike him, and did so with ease. He closed with his brother, more intent on cutting the man off from escape through the door than killing him.

It wasn't that he toyed with Dolared out of contempt; he dominated him out of need to demonstrate which of them was better.

Dolared launched a lightning-fast attack, spinning his blade through attacks high and low. Balarion sidestepped the first few, withdrew from two more, then parried the last and bound their swords together. Face-to-face over crossed steel, they glared at each other. Spittle flecked Dolared's lips. Then Balarion shoved his brother back with ease.

Another pillow slid from beneath Dolared's feet. He faltered, cracking a knee on the stone floor. The prince cried out. His sword's tip dipped to the floor. He looked up imploringly at Balarion and sagged to a hip.

Balarion, his expression softening, lunged forward, extending a hand to help Dolared.

The prince's blade came up, thrusting at Balarion's belly. The point hit. But before the blade could pierce the mail, Balarion twisted to the side, and the blade skittered wide. A cut in Balarion's tabard provided the only evidence of the blow.

Dolared shook his head. "Bastard."

"But still your better…"

With one clean stroke, Balarion separated the prince's head from his neck.

"Fools. All of you fools." Phylasina's hands rested on the hilt of Krotha's sword. Bloody spittle dappled her lips as she spoke. "You are all—*we* are all—creatures of Parnyr. He created us for his amusement. You could never see that truth, Krotha, because you choose never to look beyond the truth that makes you happy. You were a puppet seeing reality on a tiny stage, not seeing the puppeteer's world and its reality."

Krotha frowned. "And you did?"

"Yes, because I was faithful. To myself." She coughed, then spat. "And now you think you have won. The puppeteer remains, and the drama is not over."

"Alas, for you, it is." I slashed her throat with my dagger and stepped away from the spray.

Pain and confusion warred on Balarion's face.

I shook my head. "She would have spent her last breath distracting you from what must be done, my lord. Her petty revenge would be your undoing. Yours is the Key of Might."

Balarion turned and raised his sword. With one quick, sharp stroke, he severed Dolared's forearm. He shucked off his own left gauntlet and picked up the limb. He raised it over his head, unmindful of the blood slowly draining from it. The fingers, as if making a last grasp at life, curled inward.

The steel band circling the wrist began to shimmer. A light built in it, flashing white, then dulling into a red glow. Flesh sizzled, and a sickly sweet scent filled the room. The band flowed down toward the arm's ragged end. Balarion hissed as the band touched his fingers, and his arm began to tremble. The red light poured slowly down his arm, as if wax dripping from a candle. As it reached the middle of his hand, he dropped Dolared's forearm. Balarion clawed the air, then the band settled around his wrist and cooled to the steel grey it had been before.

Bent over, Balarion stared first at his left wrist, then his right. He raised fingers to touch the band circling his throat. "It's done, isn't it, Ferranos?"

"Very close, my lord, so very close."

Balarion smiled.

Which is when the city's alarm bells began to toll.

CHAPTER 34

The urgent peeling of the alarm bells stopped the fight in the corridor. Krotha yanked his sword free of Phylasina's guts and dashed toward the door. Balarion, casting only a quick glance at her sagging corpse, followed in Krotha's wake. I trailed last, stepping over dead and dying guardsmen as we worked our way toward the front of the palace.

More guards found us before we'd gotten very far, and they steeled themselves for a fight. The general commanding them saw blood dripping from our weapons. "Where is Prince Dolared?"

"Dead. Assassins." I slipped to the fore. "They struck so fast, from a hidden passage. We slew some. You must have seen the others. Where are they, man?"

"We saw nothing."

"You must have. You raised the alarm."

The general caught himself. "No, not them. That is for the invasion."

Krotha stepped forward. "What invasion?"

"From Kadarr." The general spun on his heel. "Come."

We followed him back along the corridor and down two flights of stairs. He led us into a small room where a woman lay half-naked on a bloody table. The same healers who had tended to Phylasina worked on her. She had a nasty slash over her ribs, which they struggled to close. The arrow through her thigh had golden feathers for fletching.

When we entered, she tried to sit up, but Colonel Vevanya pressed a hand to her shoulder and forced her down. "What happened, soldier?"

"An attack, Colonel, from Kadarr. King Tsaleryk leads it. He's riding a dragon of gold, Colonel. I saw it with my own eyes. And he has a bodyguard of gold guardians—made of gold, with gold claws. But the bulk of his force, Colonel, they fight under the Pergathaene banner."

The general looked at Balarion. "Can it be that Kadarr has fielded a force? How could they have gained Pergathae's trust?"

"They bought it." Balarion shook his head and turned toward Krotha and me. "Did Tsaleryk venture to the sunken city and use that gold to buy the Pergathaenes?"

Krotha shook his head. "It took us five years to go there and back, so he could not have come this fast from there."

I frowned. "Unless the breaking of the Temple of Glittering Darkness shattered the magick that slowed time there."

"Regardless, we showed him that gold was his army, and he created the dragon he desired. Somewhere in that process he must have realized that with his gold he could buy trouble for Dolared." Krotha looked at the wounded soldier. "Where are they?"

"I was stationed at Northwest Regional Defense Headquarters Nine. They hit us there and are bound southeast toward the capital. They are a day out, maybe three." Pain washed over her face. "I stopped where I could, sent riders. We were under orders to assemble all troops here."

Vevanya patted her shoulder. "You did well, soldier." She looked over at Balarion. "Orders, Highness?"

Balarion blinked, then turned to Krotha. "You trained me to fight, but not to wage war. What do we do?"

Krotha smiled. "General, you will organize Hyeracia to withstand a siege. You will be in charge of the city until the siege is lifted. Do you understand?"

"Yes." The general hesitated. "How will you lift the siege?"

The Knight of Truth pointed east. "We sent an army east this morning.

I shall ride to it and take command. We will turn north after a day, and after another, we will angle to the northwest. We will cut across their line of march, scatter reinforcements, then hit them from behind. Hyeracia will be the anvil, and we shall be the hammer."

Balarion nodded. "Will Colonel Vevanya come with us, or remain here to oppose the siege?"

"The colonel will be coming with me, to be sure." The undead warrior smiled. "I'd sooner surrender than have it any other way."

"Of course." The youth frowned. "Then what of me? What will you have me do?"

I laid a hand on Balarion's shoulder. "To you falls the most dangerous task of all. Rest assured, Balarion, that the general here and Krotha will prevent the city from falling, but in the process many, many Hollows shall be born. Legions of them. Just as the living enrich this land with life, so the Hollows shall poison it. They will emerge from Scilliric and sweep over the world, destroying all life. There will be no stopping them."

"But how can I prevent that, Ferranos?"

"Do what you have been meant to do since your inception, Balarion." I spread my arms. "You have accomplished the task your father set for you. You have brought the three keys together: Gold, Beauty, and Might. You must go to Shadow Mountain. You must free Parnyr, for only he can put an end to this nihilistic spiral. It is what you were born to do."

Krotha nodded. "You are the only one who can do it. I would attend you, but I have other duties. Ferranos will see you there."

"Me?" I shook my head. "I am much better suited to go with you, Krotha. Tsaleryk has his wizards and his gold guards. I may well be the only person outside of his company who knows how the gold magick works. I may be the only one who can undo it."

"You have forgotten, Ferranos, that more important than the gold magick is the magick that awakened Balarion and Phylasina. Had you not been there to solve those puzzles, we would never have gotten this far." Krotha clapped hands on my shoulders. "Without you, Parnyr may never be free."

I looked at Balarion. "If you think it is for the best that I accompany you, my lord, I shall."

The youth smiled. "Having you at my side is the only positive note in this whole affair, my friend." Balarion then drew my poniard and used it to cut the scorpion from his tabard's crest. "We will prevail because we must."

"Yes, my lord." I accepted the knife back, then turned to Krotha. "It has been a long and odd journey, my friend. I hope this is not the end."

Krotha shrugged. "We both know what it is to be dead, so the worst turn of events will be no surprise. But yes, we can bore each other with stories of our exploits when sitting around a spirit fire."

"It will be a pleasure."

The warrior offered Balarion his hand. "I have taught many people to fight through the ages, but you alone became a true warrior. It has been an honor."

"Thank you, Sir Krotha, for everything." Balarion clasped Krotha's hand in both of his. "If I... *When* I return, my survival will be due to you."

"Then may the gods speed you on your way." Krotha threw him a wink. "Ferranos and I will let you join us at the fire to spin stories."

Balarion led the way from the infirmary, and we returned to the secret exit. We made it to the stable quickly and appropriated a string of saddle-beasts for each of us. We rode hard for the western gate and never looked back as we headed to the Valley of the Dead and Shadow Mountain at its heart.

Even had we ridden our mounts to death, our journey would have taken four days—which was approximately how long I believed it would take for Tsaleryk and his army to reach the capital. Of course, that would have been for a disciplined force under a stable genius of a commander, which was untrue of the invaders.

Unlike our foes, we did take a disciplined approach to our line of attack. The Valley of the Dead lay in the mountains to the west—a point that lay central to all three of the successor kingdoms. It had once been the mystical heart of Alkindor. The mountains appeared as dim, dark bumps on the horizon, and grew taller with each passing hour. At night, the peaks occulted stars, and lightning played through the clouds gathered below the heights. At once breathtaking and foreboding, the mountains inspired awe and terror in amounts that shifted toward the latter the closer we drew.

Late in the first night, we made camp near the main road, at a place where I found and was able to kindle a spirit fire. Balarion made a real fire out of the wood I gathered. We cared for the saddle-beasts, and he lay down to sleep. I wished I could sleep, but that night I was certain sleep would have been as elusive for me as it proved to be for Balarion. The excitement of our adventure infected us both.

Balarion threw off his blankets and sat with his knees pulled up to his chest. "Do you know what was utmost in Dolared's mind when he died?"

"No, my lord."

"Even as I struck, he expected to escape death, escape the fate he had earned." Balarion stared off into the darkness. "He could not believe that he, the Scorpion, could be defeated. He had served his father for so long and, in his mind, so faithfully that there was no way he would be denied his inheritance. Even when he felt the bite of the blade, he still believed he would win. How can that be, Ferranos?"

"I think, my lord, that he suffered as your siblings did."

"What do you mean?"

I wished the spirit fire conveyed real warmth. "Each of them defined their own reality. For Tsaleryk, it was wealth. The more he accumulated, the greater he became, and yet his fear of losing it crippled him. Not until we gave him a new way of seeing gold, did he act."

Balarion nodded. "And my sister, her world was ruled by beauty; and fear of being ugly also limited her world. For Dolared, it was physical might, and in fear of being overpowered by his own people, he crippled them and his nation's potential."

"That is how it appears to me, my lord."

"Yes, I see it. I find that disturbing, of course, but something else disturbs me even more."

I frowned. "What do I not see?"

Balarion bared his wrists. "Tsaleryk had the Key of Gold, and gold became his standard. It was not his choice, but the choice my father made for him. Likewise, my sister and my other brother. In giving them the keys he did, Parnyr cast their fate for them."

"Did he, or did he just give them the keys to which they were best suited?"

The youth frowned heavily and sat in silence for a bit. Then he chewed his lower lip. "I should like to believe the latter, Ferranos, but fear the former is true. What is this mission upon which I have been sent but his casting a fate for me? I have seen my siblings. I have seen the destruction they caused. That should make me feel I am right in bringing my father back to restore the world."

"Why would you not feel that way, my lord?"

He grunted. "At the last, Phylasina said it. She said we were all my father's creations. She said he was the puppeteer and that the drama continued."

I shook my head. "You cannot take her at her word, Highness. Recall, she was only ever faithful to herself—not to you, nor Dolared, nor your father. She was dying, and she knew it. Her revenge would be to poison your mind."

Balarion glanced at me. "Is that what you got of her essence when you killed her?"

"What I got, my lord, was a sense of sadness and insecurity. The fact that she was always supposed to be faithful to someone else meant that no one saw her as primary or worthy—her worth always derived from the person or group to which she was faithful. This is why she remained faithful only to herself, because only she believed that she was more than just an adjunct. When disappointed and frustrated, she lashed out."

"Did I make her feel that way?"

I knew the question he was truly asking and chose to answer it. "For you she had true affection. Who you are inspired in her true fidelity, something so strong and pure it frightened her, because compared to you, she *was* unworthy. She remained with you and fought for you and believed in you, yet always, in the back of her mind, the doubts gnawed at her resolve."

"Had I known…"

"It would have made no difference, Balarion. Your kindness would have made her feel even less worthy of your company." I shook my head. "I believe, coming to Scilliric, seeing so many people devoted to their academies and units and Dolared—the illusion of it all—the hypocrisy created a crisis. She knew the Scorpion would betray you, and old passions were a drug. They dulled the pain of her having to acknowledge her failings."

"But if she had told me…"

"She was not ready to risk you treating her as everyone else eventually did. Better, in her mind, that you die and she could preserve your pristine image of her than have you live and disappoint her." I opened my hands. "It may not make any sense to you, her feelings may not be the truth Krotha seeks, but it was her truth."

"It was her fate." Balarion sighed. "And my father chose her because she would be faithful to me, even if only up to a point. Krotha would stay with me because, however my father imparted to him the need to protect me, it became Krotha's truth."

"That seems logical, my lord."

"But Krotha doesn't see that this means my father trapped him. My father may have caused him to become undead. Garvyne spent thousands of years in one place at my father's order. Ceresia spent centuries hunting, again at my father's whim. And me, I am awakened from a slumber through the destruction of the world, all to serve my father." He shook his head. "And what did you do, Ferranos, to earn my father's attention? His ire?"

"I should have to think on that, my lord, for no clear answer comes to me." I glanced at the ring on my right hand. "What I do know is that you, by giving me this ring, have shaped my fate since my return. You have my gratitude."

The youth smiled, then lay back on his bedroll. "Wake me at false dawn. I do not wish us to delay seeing my father longer than we must."

CHAPTER 35

Four days of hard riding brought us to the Valley of the Dead. Sometime in the past—well before Alkindor faded—a titanic force fractured the world. It splintered the land. Tall, jagged, razor-edged obsidian thorns sprouted from the ground. Molten rock glowed red in deep fissures. Sulfurous mists choked all plant life, save for curiously spiked clumps of yellow-green weeds.

In contrast to the stone, bleached skeletons dotted the landscape. The way some of them lay, I assumed they had died gently in their sleep, the heavy mists having smothered them while they dreamed. Others showed obvious signs of violence. Limbs came to ragged ends, and staved rib cages lay beneath perforated skulls. The latter disturbed me the most because I couldn't determine if they had been pierced from without, or if something from within had chewed its way free.

Balarion and I paused at the entrance, at a line drawn as sharply as if an ax had chopped a boundary between the valley and the rest of the world. He leaned forward and patted his horse on its neck. "This is it, then, Ferranos? In there, I will find my father?"

"Yes, Highness."

He smiled. "I would not ask you to come with me, my friend. Your task was to get me here, but this place... I would ask no one to venture in."

"I will join you."

"Why?"

I rested my hands on the saddle's pommel. "You recall asking me why your father would have made me part of all this?"

He nodded.

"I think it was for this moment. He set everything into motion. He could anticipate what your siblings might do—he couldn't be completely certain, but he could make very educated guesses. Likewise for Krotha and Phylasina. They would take care of you, but, as we saw with Phylasina, they might also care for themselves."

"Not Krotha."

"I think you would change your mind if you could see him leading the army against the forces from Kadarr. Combat is Krotha's truth, and he is reveling in it even now."

Balarion grinned. "I see your point."

"As for me, well, your father needed to make certain you would complete the journey. The only way he could do that was to give you someone to care for. He chose me to be the proxy for everyone who has been hurt because of how the world has become."

"Then you have served your purpose superbly, Ferranos."

I bowed my head. "I have served *his* purpose, Balarion, not *my* purpose."

"And what do you see your purpose to be?"

"I am to serve my master as best I can." I smiled at him. "If that pleases, Highness."

"It does, Ferranos. Very much so." Balarion waved his hand forward. "My father awaits."

We entered the Valley of the Dead, and the temperature dropped. Balarion's breath appeared as white vapor, and his mount shivered. We rode between the glassy stone spikes, reining our saddle-beasts to the entrance of the path. The way sunlight glinted from the edges suggested that the slightest scratch would be enough to lay flesh open, and I felt certain my flask would avail me little in closing such wounds.

Only a mile or two in, the path curved around a hill and ran straight on toward the base of the mountains to the north. There sat Shadow Mountain, the congealed essence of darkness on a moonless night. It defied the sun, the edges reflecting no light, but the ebon outcropping glowed with its own cold intensity. As a stone in a boot worries the flesh, the very sight of it worried my soul.

Countless artisans had carved a colossal edifice from the rock. Two towering figures flanked an arched doorway tall enough to admit either of them without the least bit of discomfort. Chiseled from obsidian, their flesh glowed with a blackish-purple light visible only at certain angles. The figure on the right represented a tall, clean-limbed youth in ring mail, a tattered tabard with the crowned, double-eagle crest broad across the breast. He bore a sword, and as we drew closer, what had been a smooth, featureless face slowly resolved itself to mirror Balarion's visage.

The other figure, hooded and cloaked, had a stick and poniard held crossed over his breastbone. The figure did not look like me, as it was skeletal and the face a death's-head. *Which, actually, is me.*

Balarion stopped his mount and drank from his canteen. "Does this mean he knows we are coming?"

"He's likely known from the moment I woke, or at least the moment you did."

The youth stoppered the canteen and let it hang from the saddle. Saying nothing, he touched his heels to the saddle-beast's flanks, and the creature started forward again.

I fully expected, as we approached, that the doors would open before us. Obsidian, like everything else, they had been carved with panels depicting history. At the very top, nameless gods fought even older gods to wrest the world away from those who had created it. Descending, various legendary heroes fought abominations and monsters. Quickly, though, a tall and well-muscled figure, with a high crown and a thick beard, appeared. As with the friezes on Aurwyn's temple, Parnyr moved and fought in his panels. Creatures died, then grateful princesses threw themselves at him. He bedded them in displays as graphic as his slaying of the monsters, moving across the panels from right to left and back again in an endless cycle of victories—the victories that created Alkindor and conquered the lands around it.

Beneath that, a triptych of panels, one devoted to each of the acknowledged children, chronicled their exploits. Tsaleryk, Jaranessa, and Dolared all appeared as puppets—caricatures of themselves involved in farcical adventures. In contrast with the panels above, all three children seemed the antithesis of their father.

The next panel down showed Balarion and, as with Parnyr, wove him through his many adventures. Much was made of his mother's death, his troubled birth, and his winter resurrection under Garvyne's supervision. His battle with the wolves far outshone anything his siblings had done, and his campaign to reach this point rivaled the heroism of Parnyr himself. In fact, as the panel reflected our ride through the Valley of the Dead, even Parnyr's figure above paused to watch and smile as Balarion drew closer.

Balarion chuckled. "I wish I had seen it before this."

"What, Highness?"

"The panels. The contrasts. As with the story Parnyr told when visiting my village, he *chose* to let his children destroy Alkindor. He knew they would do it. He knew the world would fall to horrible ruin." He looked at me. "Why would he do that, Ferranos?"

I could only shake my head. "The answer to that question will lie within."

"And I shall have that answer."

We rode on, and as we reached a point five hundred yards or so from the doors, I nodded. "Now would be the time for them to open for us."

"But they won't, Ferranos." Balarion's eyes tightened. "Those doors were never intended to grant us entrance. They shall only open for his grand return to the world."

I shivered. "And you have learned to see the truth with Krotha's skill."

Another hundred yards on, a smaller door, lurking at the skeleton's heel, clicked open. We had to dismount to enter, and chose to free our saddle-beasts. We stripped them of saddles and tack, then urged them to leave. No fools they, the beasts galloped as fast as they could along the path back to the real world, leaving us alone in the Valley of the Dead.

Which, we both acknowledged with curt nods, was likely to be a place we would never escape alive.

The tiny door admitted us to a vast chamber, in which our footsteps and the rustle of Balarion's mail echoed. The door closed behind us, and off to our right, a strip of flooring wide enough to accommodate ten cavalry riders abreast began to glow the color of warm blood. It extended from the big obsidian doors into the distance, stabbing deep into the mountain.

We walked along it, me two steps behind and one to the right of Balarion, as befit his station and mine. He kept his head up, his shoulders broad. He may never have been acknowledged as a prince in his lifetime, but he strode along that path every inch a prince—grander than his siblings and even grander than he was depicted on the doors behind us.

The light brightened ever so slightly, and suddenly we realized we were not alone. Rank upon rank of soldiers stood in the darkness, facing the doors. They stood tall, with curved swords sheathed at their waists and black armor trimmed in gold. They looked vaguely familiar, but I could not place them until Balarion spoke.

"Vangion. Not the ones we fought, but their greater brethren. The ones Aurwyn killed before you shattered the diamond." He frowned. "I had the sense, from the ones I killed, that they were not from Alkindor."

"I thought the same, Highness." I studied one more closely. "Perhaps they were from an adventure your father has not shared."

He shook his head. "Look again, Ferranos. They are fashioned of the same stone as this place. Our adventures have shaped them, much as the statues took our faces. As you made one of gold for Tsaleryk, so my father has fashioned a shadow legion for me. This is a promise of glory, to keep me coming."

I tried a spell and got enough sense back to tell me Balarion had guessed correctly. "I can tell you now, Highness, that I could release them to you.

Making them work perfectly will take time, but this army is yours if you decide it."

"Thank you, my friend, but even this army would not undo the mischief Dolared caused." He smiled. "You should also know that these troops had another purpose. Had Tsaleryk ever come this far, he would have been content with them. Their look, their power, the gold, all meant to attract him."

I nodded, and we pressed on. We walked for a mile or more before we reached a central cylinder. I could not even begin to guess at its diameter. The red road brought us to a door six feet wide and twice that tall, fashioned of pure gold. It had no lock nor latch, just a black handprint at the center.

Balarion approached it and extended his right hand. He splayed out his fingers, then pressed his flesh to the metal. His skin sizzled, not at the point of contact, but at his wrist. The gold band shimmered, then crawled forward. It bled up over his hand, then poured into the door. The black handprint vanished, and a heartbeat later, the gold door slowly evaporated.

Balarion clutched his blistered hand to his breast, but laughed regardless of whatever pain he felt. "Can you imagine it, Ferranos? Can you imagine Tsaleryk's horror as that much gold simply vanished? It would have been a wonder had he not died on the spot."

The red road continued deeper into Shadow Mountain. We walked through a second cylindrical chamber, the ceiling and wings lost in darkness. More soldiers awaited us, but these were not infantry. They sat astride fantastic beasts. Some rode winged serpents. Shadows above hinted at those on giant bat-winged creatures with talons like sabers and triangular heads that ended in sharp crow's beaks. Farther along stood racks of giant pachyderms, each carrying a small wooden tower on its back, filled with a dozen or more archers.

As great and terrible as they were, I noticed two things. The first I pointed out to Balarion. "You see there, my lord, on the shields and on the elephant's armor? That symbol?"

"Yes, Ferranos, there is a similar one on the belt buckles worn by the infantry. What of it?"

"A memory, Highness. That sigil shows they are consecrated to a goddess, Dianche. In legend, she opposed—she literally hunted down—and exiled *Wiervar*. These troops, like the others, you can control, and I believe their connection with her would break *Wiervar's* hold on Scilliric. Were we to activate them now and lead them from here, we could help Krotha relieve the siege and destroy the curse of *Wiervar*."

"But you forget, Ferranos, that same curse is what allows the people to thrive here. With that power broken, the people would starve, for they could not raise a crop for months yet."

"But Kadarr has warehouses bursting with food. You could feed the people."

"And how many would die defending those warehouses?" Balarion shook his head. "Besides, you must see it. These troops were not meant for me."

I nodded, for he had seen the second thing I'd noticed. Every warrior, every beast, no matter how large or terrifying, had been shaped to perfection. Symmetrical in every proportion, with glass-smooth skin unblemished by time or a slip of the artisan's chisel, each mounted statue appeared more beautiful than the previous, yet not quite as gorgeous as the next. And yet they were not simply copies shaped from one mold, but each unique and idealized. To stare at them for too long was to get lost in a dream of beauty.

"Your sister, these were to be hers."

"To lead or to gaze upon in despair."

I followed him along the red road, and again we came to a stone cylinder with a door in it. This one had a mirrored surface, yet it did not reflect precisely what looked at it. I do not mean there was any defect in the looking glass. No, it presented back to us our perfect selves. Balarion stood taller, a bit broader. His hair shined, and his eyes glittered. As beautiful as the soldiers had been, he was more so.

And for me, the reflection returned me to life. I became who I had once been, with softly pale skin and fair hair that fell to my shoulders. I carried myself with a touch of elegance. I certainly looked better than anyone who had been in Jaranessa's court, and I would have been a match for Ceresia. We would have made a most handsome couple, and our children would have been…

…beautiful enough that Jaranessa would have seen them slaughtered.

Balarion approached the mirror and kissed his own reflection. The necklace his sister's kiss had transferred to him glowed and slowly tracked up his neck and over his head. Its brightness erased the reflection of his face, half blinding me. Then Balarion staggered back, and I caught him.

"Oh, my lord."

"I know, Ferranos. I expected this."

Clumps of his hair fluttered to the floor as if he'd been afflicted with the mange. The skin of his face had become leathery, with deep crow's-feet at the corners of his eyes. His cheeks had hollowed, and one of his eyelids drooped. And even as he grabbed my arm, his grip did not possess the strength it had but moments before.

"As bad as it is, Ferranos, it doesn't matter to me. Remember, I am a flock warden. To my flock, I always had too little fleece, and lines on my face would not matter to them at all." He straightened and shifted his shoulders. "But imagine what that would have done to Jaranessa?"

"It would have destroyed her."

"Yes. Had she gotten the Key of Gold from Tsaleryk, had she gotten this far, she would have gone no farther." He half grinned. "But farther we must go."

We set our feet to the red road again, this time with me walking closer to Balarion, prepared to steady him if he faltered. He did not, and appeared to recover from his weakness rapidly, even if the cosmetic changes remained. He marched on straight, again raising his head proudly, likely unaware he had lost an inch or two in height and that his mail hung slightly looser on his body.

"Oh yes, here is Dolared's dream."

We wandered through a storehouse of titanic machines. Siege towers, battering rams, catapults, and onagers greeted us first, but then we moved into more esoteric items. A wagon armored with dragon scales had a huge nozzle at the fore, which would spray liquid fire on targets. And war chariots capable of hauling a dozen archers, yet built on a scale three times the size suited to men, came into view.

Something appeared that I can only describe as a landship, with ballistae mounted in the prow and along the wales, propelled by wheels running on a rotating track. It had no sails, but an ethereal azure glow from below-decks suggested some mystical engine would drive it into battle.

Balarion smiled. "With that thing, you could kill dragons!"

"With that thing, you could kill *gods*."

"I wonder, then, if those sigils worked on the wales, are they to consecrate the ship, or do they mark the gods it has slain?"

I shook my head, but I thought the latter choice the most likely.

We pressed on, and, as appropriate, we came to a steel portcullis warding the way into another, smaller cylinder. "I see no handprint, my lord."

"It is the door unlocked by the Key of Might, Ferranos. There is only one thing for it. Stay close and move quickly."

"My lord?"

Balarion did not reply. Instead, he moved to the steel lattice, through which we could see nothing. He reached down and grabbed the lowest horizontal bar in his left hand. The Key of Might glowed, the sizzle echoed, and Balarion screamed. He set his feet, and there, inch by inch, the portcullis slowly rose. He pulled it up to knee height, then shifted and dragged it up farther. Bending over, he altered his grip and, using only that one hand, heaved. He got his shoulder under the crossbar, then pushed with his legs again. The portcullis rose farther, and I darted beneath it. "Come, my lord, you can make it."

"Not yet, Ferranos." Balarion laughed, low and breathless. "The Key of Might cannot be given; it must be earned. So it is with this door."

His teeth bared in a grimace, the muscles standing out in his neck,

Balarion pushed again. He began to straighten his arm. As he did so, the Key of Might flowed molten through his flesh. It poured into the portcullis. The steel likewise began to glow. Balarion gave it one final push, straightening his arm, locking his elbow, defeating the door.

The metal evaporated.

Balarion fell to the ground.

I grabbed him under his arms and pulled him away from where the portcullis had been. Yes, it had vanished, but I feared it might return and crush him. I knelt beside him, determined to shield him with my own body, for however long it took for him to recover.

He patted me on the shoulder weakly, far more weakly than he had after the Key of Beauty had done its work. "I will be fine, Ferranos."

"My lord, I fear for you." I pointed back along the red road. "Your father knew the effects each door would have. Dolared would have been trapped back there, with the gate on his shoulder. He would not have dared to make that last push, for fear he could not do it, that it would crush him."

"But here I am, Ferranos. I am not Dolared, nor am I dead. Help me to my feet."

He clung to me, and I was able to get him up. He remained in my grasp for a minute more until his legs stopped trembling. And he managed a smile. "Are you not going to tell me again, Ferranos, that we could take those machines, too, and that just seeing them would inspire everyone from Kadarr to surrender without a single arrow flying?"

I laughed. "I wanted to tell you that any of those machines could drag a plow, and that soldiers armed with scythes could harvest all the wild grain in Kadarr so no one would starve and no one would need die in any battle."

"This is why I am glad you are my companion, Ferranos. You think beyond the immediate problem. I will need that." He straightened his back, groaning as he did so. "Come, my friend, my father waits…"

CHAPTER 36

We passed through a curtain of unnatural darkness and into a round chamber with no ceiling. Above us lay the night sky. The constellations of old hung there. I wondered how that could be and then realized that inside this chamber, time passed so slowly that within these walls, my body had not yet begun to rot in my tomb. The sky might have appeared normal, but nothing else here was.

Across from us, perhaps twenty yards on, centered on a dais, sat a massive throne with a high back, carved of wood in the likeness of Death in a hooded cloak. Two skeletal beasts functioned as arms for the chair. A wolf to the right, only bigger than any I'd ever seen, and, on the left, something of the weasel family, all coiled and ready to spring.

Curiously enough, the man surrounded by those dire images seemed benign. Broadly built, with iron-grey hair and a neatly trimmed beard, he would have been quite handsome had utter and complete boredom not seized him. He wore leather armor of the style Phylasina had favored, and a slender gold coronet circled his brow. A broadsword lay across his thighs.

He looked up only when we'd crossed half the distance to him. His voice came rich and resonant, yet afflicted with a note of ennui. "Which one would you be, then?"

I frowned. "Highness?"

"Not you. Him." The man sat forward and stared intently at Balarion.

"A Trafaramite from the look of you. Thus, you must be... Wait, it's on the tip of my tongue... Baloron. That's you, yes?"

The youth straightened. "I am *Balarion*, and I believe you would be my father."

"Balarion... Balarion... Oh, the flock warden boy." The man I took to be Parnyr—primarily because of his location, though he did bear a passing resemblance to the face on the coin—clapped his hands. "Of course, Balarion. Well, the second one of that name."

"I am your son. The son you set to assemble the keys to open this prison and free you. I have done so. Now you must undo all that my half-siblings have done to destroy Alkindor." Balarion opened his arms. "That *is* why I am here, yes? Why I have done all I have?"

"From your point of view, yes, of course. You are a child of destiny. Your destiny was, you know, as you said, to gather the keys, et cetera." Parnyr sat back in the throne. "But truly, knowing what was at stake, did you think I would entrust the future of Alkindor to you? To a peasant who really had no hope of ever truly getting this far? That would be hopelessly reckless of me, wouldn't you think?"

Balarion rubbed his burned hand over his forehead. "What are you saying?"

"I'm saying, son, that you were not the only child of mine I hid out there, buried out there, to come and find me." Parnyr rose to his feet and stretched. "Now, I will say, you are the one who succeeded. A few, they've refused the calling. Others have died in one misadventure or another. Dolared has killed a number—or rather, had them killed, as he seldom does things himself if he can avoid it. I take it you slew him to get the Key of Might?"

"I did."

"Oh, very good." Parnyr descended from the throne. "The fact that you've made it this far means the time is perfect for my return. You've seen much of the world, then, as it will be?"

Balarion frowned. "I have seen it as it *is*."

"Outside this room, it is as it is, but in here, in this room, you have seen a future that does not exist." Parnyr smiled. "You see, this was the purpose of the whole undertaking. I sealed myself in here, in a place where all the time that has passed since those doors were sealed is but an hour or two, at best a day."

"What? Why would you do that?"

"Balarion, credit me with one thing: wisdom." Parnyr unlimbered the sword and took a couple of cuts through the air. "I realized that Alkindor, the realm I had made, was doomed. Entropy, enemies from without, jealous godlings, and capricious demons—even my own children—would destroy it. I fought for a long time to prevent its destruction, then realized I was fighting a losing effort. What I needed to do was not stem the decay, but to remake the whole of the world."

Balarion smiled. "Yes, yes, that is why I came to free you, so you can remake the world. I have seen what is wrong. I can help you fix everything."

"Yes, Baloron, you will." A smile slowly spread over Parnyr's face. "Just one little thing to attend to first…"

Parnyr leaped forward, slashing at Balarion's head. The youth ducked, and the blade trimmed golden locks. As Parnyr landed, Balarion kicked out, catching his father on the thigh. The blow knocked the king flying. He landed and bounced once before sliding on his belly to the wall.

White teeth flashed in Parnyr's grin. "Krotha taught you well, as I desired him to do." The king leaped up and launched himself into the attack. His blade came up and around in overhand cuts, then down and across in slashes meant to separate Balarion up from down. The blade whistled as it flew, yet for all its speed, it often missed, and what it did hit was only steel.

Balarion fought magnificently. He ducked and dodged, reading Parnyr's intent and anticipating him flawlessly. He parried blows to the side and shoved his father back. He blocked heavy overhand blows that might have driven another man to his knees, but Balarion withstood them.

That ability puzzled Parnyr, and I realized that neither Ceresia nor Garvyne had shared their tales of Balarion's brushes with death. Perhaps Parnyr, locked away in his time bubble, never knew about Hollows, or how the dead like me could absorb the essence and power of those we slew. The moment I realized that, I knew Parnyr could never slay Balarion.

Balarion locked up Parnyr's sword, then jacked an elbow into his father's face. Parnyr stumbled away, and Balarion kicked the sword to the wall in the opposite direction. "Do not make me kill you."

Parnyr dropped to a knee and laughed. Blood dribbled down his chin from mashed lips. "You *cannot* kill me, Balarion. None of you could. I saw to that. You can only do what I have prepared you to do."

"No!" Balarion bared his teeth. "You think you made me. Phylasina called you a puppeteer and said we were all your creatures. I reject that. I am *not* your creature."

"Perhaps you are not, Balarion." Parnyr wiped blood away with the back of his hand. "Alas, *he* is. Kill him, Ferranos."

Balarion turned toward me, shock widening his eyes and opening his mouth. He went to speak, but before words could emerge, my spell lanced cleanly through his chest. Blue-white lightning incinerated his heart and boiled his lungs. He looked down, down at the ruin of his tabard and mail and fire-blackened ribs, then sat abruptly and flopped back to stare sightlessly at the sky he had known when tending his flock.

Balarion's life essence poured into me, strong and cold and deep and sharp. It ripped into me, filling me with jagged memories. All his childhood dreams whirled through me: the innocent gaiety of a child laughing at simple things, the hopefulness of an adolescent courting his first love, the anguish at the death of a friend, and the steely resolve to face down terror. And then the more recent memories, of Krotha and Phylasina, of his siblings, and, most painful, of me. He had taken me for who I was: Ferranos, magician of wise counsel and courage.

How the puppet master had shaped me to be. How I wished to truly be—how I thought myself to be—until my master had issued an order and I executed it without thought.

Executing the only person who ever cared about what happened to me.

I gasped and fell to my knees. "Oh, Balarion..."

"Sentiment from you?" Parnyr rose unsteadily to his feet. "If I thought, my Scorpion, my true and faithful Scorpion, that betraying him bothered you, I would tell you that I was the one who betrayed him. He was my son, my creation, and I am the one who destroyed him, as was my right. You merely happened to be the convenient tool with which I could do the job."

"My lord is too kind."

"And you are ever faithful—as I ensured you would be." He bent and picked up Balarion's sword. He tested its balance and nodded. "He really did learn Krotha's lessons well. Can you imagine if he had actually killed me? Him, a flock warden, here with all the power needed to remake the world? His creation would have been, oh so pedestrian, so uninteresting."

"So you knew, then, that he would harvest the essences of those he slew?"

"As I intended. I needed him to harvest the power I need." Parnyr smiled. "I could have slain him. Would have slain him. But you were so conveniently placed to do it for me."

I twisted the gold ring on my finger. "Will you use that power to make the world a better place?"

"Better for whom, Ferranos? According to whom, Ferranos?" Parnyr raised the sword in both hands. "This is *my* world. It shall be as I desire it."

"And this process is to be repeated an age from now?"

"And an age after that, if I will it. How is it you dare question me? You never would have before." Parnyr frowned. "And in my new world, I shall make sure you never do again. Now hold still. I will make this quick."

The blade arced down at my neck. A clean cut would have taken off my head easily. Everything that I was, everything I had absorbed, would have flowed into Parnyr. His will would have been done.

I caught the blade in my left hand. With a casual flip of my wrist, I ripped the sword from his grasp.

Parnyr stared at the bloody ruin of his palms and the patch of flesh that flopped to the floor from the blade's hilt. "This is not possible."

I flicked my right hand at him, as if shooing away an insect. Ribs cracked, and he flew across the room. Parnyr smashed into the wall. His crown sprang free and rolled along the floor. Parnyr stared at it as he slid slowly to his knees, a bloody smear marking his descent. "You cannot do this. You cannot strike against me."

"*I* can, my lord. Ferranos *can*, my lord." I drove Balarion's sword to half its length into the stone floor. "When you chose me, when you made me your faithful Scorpion, you forbade me from ever spilling your blood. But I am not your Scorpion."

He stared at me, disbelieving.

In absorbing Balarion's essence, I gained a sense of Dolared's—his life, his desires, and his fears. "Dolared feared that you liked me more than you did him."

"I did."

"Yet you betrayed me to him. Once I had done your bidding, once I had seen to Balarion's imprisonment, you let Dolared welcome me back to the palace, congratulate me, offer me a cup of wine, and poison me."

"I actually didn't think on it that much." Parnyr shrugged. "Truth be told, I expected you to kill him."

"I could not, my lord. At that time, I could not spill *your blood.*"

"Oh, so he actually was mine?" Parnyr extended a bloody hand toward me. "Not that this changes anything."

"Yet it changes absolutely everything. You buried your good and faithful Scorpion long ago and far away." I stood and smiled. "'Tis Ferranos who awoke in my tomb. 'Tis Ferranos who found Balarion. 'Tis Ferranos who slaughtered Hollows and horrors to help him to this place. 'Tis Ferranos who slew Aurwyn in his golden prison and here, now, slew Balarion to save him from your betrayal of all he thought himself to be."

Parnyr raised his chin. "And 'tis now Ferranos who would slay me and all that Alkindor could ever become?"

I chuckled and touched the end of my staff to his brow. "You've forgotten: I have seen the future you have created. It dies here with you and your deceptions. But a new future, its promise looms."

ACKNOWLEDGMENTS

The author would like to thank Mr. Hitoshi Yasuda and Michiko Yashiroda for their aid in bringing this project together; Howard Morhaim for tirelessly pursuing all the business-related aspects of it; and Chantelle Osman, Paul Garabedian, and Kassie Klaybourne, who put up with me while I wrote it.

HAVE YOU BEEN TURNED ON TO LIGHT NOVELS YET?

86—EIGHTY-SIX, VOL. 1-10

In truth, there is no such thing as a bloodless war. Beyond the fortified walls protecting the eighty-five Republic Sectors lies the "nonexistent" Eighty-Sixth Sector. The young men and women of this forsaken land are branded the Eighty-Six and, stripped of their humanity, pilot "unmanned" weapons into battle...

Manga adaptation available now!

WOLF & PARCHMENT, VOL. 1-6

The young man Col dreams of one day joining the holy clergy and departs on a journey from the bathhouse, Spice and Wolf. Winfiel Kingdom's prince has invited him to help correct the sins of the Church. But as his travels begin, Col discovers in his luggage a young girl with a wolf's ears and tail named Myuri who stowed away for the ride!

Manga adaptation available now!

SOLO LEVELING, VOL. 1-5

E-rank hunter Jinwoo Sung has no money, no talent, and no prospects to speak of—and apparently, no luck, either! When he enters a hidden double dungeon one fateful day, he's abandoned by his party and left to die at the hands of some of the most horrific monsters he's ever encountered.

Comic adaptation available now!